Deep Dish

ALSO BY MARY KAY ANDREWS

Blue Christmas

Savannah Breeze

Hissy Fit

Little Bitty Lies

Savannah Blues

Deep Dish

Mary Kay Andrews

HARPER LUXE

An Imprint of HarperCollinsPublishers

DEEP DISH. Copyright © 2008 by Whodunnit, Inc. All rights reserved. Printed in the United States of America. No part of this book may be used or reproduced in any manner whatsoever without written permission except in the case of brief quotations embodied in critical articles and reviews. For information address HarperCollins Publishers, 10 East 53rd Street, New York, NY 10022.

HarperCollins books may be purchased for educational, business, or sales promotional use. For information please write: Special Markets Department, HarperCollins Publishers, 10 East 53rd Street, New York, NY 10022.

FIRST HARPERLUXE EDITION

HarperLuxe™ is a trademark of HarperCollins Publishers

Library of Congress Cataloging-in-Publication Data is available upon request.

ISBN: 978-0-06-146882-7

08 09 10 11 12 ID/RRD 10 9 8 7 6 5 4 3 2 1

This book is dedicated with love to the posse: Susie Deiters, Jeanie Payne, Sharon Stokes, and Ellen Tressler, with thanks for all those Saturday mornings spent in the pursuit of excellence in junking.
Happy trails, y'all!

Acknowledgments

As always, I'm indebted to dozens of people who helped this particular *Dish* become a reality. Martha Giddens Nesbit and Brandon Branch enabled me to watch the fabulous Paula Deen in action. Thanks again, Paula! John "Crawfish" Crawford of the Skidaway Institute of Oceanography gave me priceless information on the wild edibles of coastal barrier islands. The Scribblers of Raleigh, Margaret Maron, Sarah Shaber, and Brenda Witchger gave essential advice, brainstorming sessions, and support when I needed it most. Pat and Patti Callahan Henry opened their beautiful home on Daufuskie Island for research and retreat, and Ron and Leuveda Garner and Diane Kaufman of Mermaid Cottages gave me cozy nests on Tybee.

I'm the luckiest writer on earth to have Carolyn Marino of HarperCollins and Stuart Krichevsky of SKLA in my corner. Their unwavering support and tough love always pulls me through the roughest patches and darkest days.

And for my family, Tom, Andy, Katie, and Mark, no words are enough to express my thanks and love.

Chapter 1

One more week. Gina repeated the words to herself as she stood on the set, her makeup already starting to melt under the hot lights trained on her.

Five more days, two shows a day. Ten shows. And the season would be over. She would have two weeks to rest. Two weeks with no makeup. No heels. No cameras. She would let her jaw muscles relax. Not smile for fourteen days. No cooking either, she vowed, knowing immediately that was one promise she couldn't keep. Right now she might be sick of smiling, sick of staring into a camera, sick of explaining why you had to let a roast rest before carving it, sick of chopping, dicing, slicing, and sautéing. But that would pass, she told herself. Just ten more shows.

"Ready?" Jess asked, from just off camera.

Gina took a deep breath and smiled up at the camera trained on her. "Ready."

Her brow wrinkled in intense concentration as she carefully whisked the Parmesan cheese into the bubbling pot of grits on the front burner of the cooktop.

"Turn the pot toward the camera so we can see the label," Jess said quietly from the table where she usually sat beside Scott, watching through the monitor on the laptop. Where was Scott, Gina wondered? Jessica DeRosa, his assistant producer, was only twenty-four, just a couple years out of film school, and she was probably quite capable of directing a show on her own, but Scott was such a control freak, he rarely let her.

Without warning, the gas flame under the pot flared up, and then just as suddenly died. Gina stared down at it, grimacing in disbelief.

"You're frowning," Jess commented. "Come on, Gina, don't make it look so hard. Remember what Scott says. These recipes should look so easy, a trained chimp could fix 'em blindfolded."

The cameraman snickered, and Gina looked up to give Eddie a stare of disapproval.

"Not funny," she said. But it wasn't Eddie, the overweight, balding veteran of three seasons' worth of her shows, behind the camera. This cameraman was a kid, with a frizzy shock of blond hair sticking out from under a red bandanna worn piratelike, around his forehead.

Where was Eddie? she wondered. Were he and Scott in some kind of meeting elsewhere—maybe over at the Georgia Public Broadcasting offices?

"I'm not frowning because the recipe won't work," Gina said. "The darned stove is on the fritz again. The flame keeps flickering out. I thought Scott said we were gonna get a new stove before the season was over."

Jess shrugged. "I guess we're just gonna make do with this one for the last week. Does it make any difference?"

"Only if we want viewers to believe I know better than to try to cook grits on a cold stove."

"Keep stirring," Jess advised. "And smiling."

Perky, that's what Scott always insisted on. Nobody really cared how your food tasted, as long as you looked perky and happy while you were fixing it. And sexy. Which was why she was wearing a scoop-neck tank top that showed off her tanned shoulders and shapely arms, instead of the bib apron with "Gina Foxton" embroidered on it in flowing script that she'd worn the previous season, before Scott took over the show. And her career.

"Now add the cheese," Jess called. "And tell us why you need to keep stirring."

Gina made a show of turning down the burner, even though in reality, the burner was stone cold and now seemingly inoperative.

"Once your grits reach the boiling point, you want to turn the heat way down, to keep them from burning," she said. "Now whisk in your cheese, which you've already grated, and if it looks too thick, you can add some more of the cream to make sure you've got the right consistency."

She reached for the bowl of Parmesan and dumped it into the hot grits, stirring rapidly. But now, despite Jess's directions to the contrary, she was frowning again.

She sniffed as her nose, always hypersensitive, alerted her that something was amiss.

What was that smell? She sniffed again and realized, with horror, that the aroma wafting from the pot was not the honest corn smell of her stone-ground grits, nor the smell of homemade chicken stock, nor the fresh scent of cooking cream.

No. This . . . this smell . . . resembled nothing more than the stink of melting polymer.

"Gina," Jess said, a warning in her voice. "You're frowning again."

"Gawd, y'all," Gina exclaimed, shoving the offending pot away, toward the back burner. "This stuff reeks." As sometimes happened, usually when she was overexcited or totally aggravated, her carefully moderated accent-eradication coaching fell away in an instant. "Jee-zus H. You-know-what," Gina said. "What is this stuff?"

The kid behind the camera guffawed.

Jess blinked innocently. "What?"

Gina reached over to the tray of ingredients her prep cook had placed on the countertop, and grabbed the plastic tub of grated cheese. Without her reading glasses, she had to hold the tub right up to her face to read the label.

"Cheez-Ease? Is this what we've come to? Y'all have sold my soul for a tub of dollar-ninety-eight artificial cheese made out of recycled dry-cleaning bags?"

"Please, Gina," Jess said quietly. "Can we just finish this segment?"

Gina dipped a spoon into the pot of grits and tasted. "I knew it," she said. "And that's not cream, either. Since when do we substitute canned condensed milk for cream?"

Jess stared down at her notes, then looked up, a pained expression on her face. "We're having budget issues. Scott told the girls they should substitute cheaper ingredients wherever necessary."

"He didn't say anything about it to me," Gina said, walking off the set and toward the table where Jess sat.

She hated to make a scene, hated to come across as a prima donna or a food snob. But you couldn't have a show about healthy southern cooking, a show called *Fresh Start*, for heaven's sake, if you started to compromise on ingredients.

"Jess," Gina said calmly. "What's going on around here?"

Jessica's pale, usually cheerful face reddened. "Let's take a break," she said. "Everybody back in ten minutes."

Chapter 2

The crew scattered. Watching their retreat, Gina noticed for the first time that the cameraman wasn't the only new face on the set. Jackson Thomas, her sound man, had been replaced with a chubby-cheeked black girl with a headful of dreadlocks, and Andrew Payne, the lighting engineer—sweet, serious Andrew, who approached lighting as an artist approached a canvas—had been replaced with two pimply-cheeked youths whose bumbling around reminded her of Dumb and Dumber.

"Jess," Gina said, sliding into the empty seat beside the assistant producer, "where's Scott? And Jackson?"

Jess picked up the thick production notebook that was her bible and leafed through the pages detailing the upcoming segment.

"Jess?" Gina gently took the notebook from her.

"God, Gina," Jess said with a sigh. "You need to talk to Scott. Really."

"I will," Gina said. "Where is he?"

"I don't know," the younger woman admitted. "He left me a voice mail this morning, telling me he had a meeting, and he'd be in later. That's all I know. Honest."

"What about the crew? Why all the changes? And why wasn't I told anything about budget problems?"

"Scott said—" Jess bit her lip. "At the production meeting Friday he just said there were some issues with the sponsors. We have to tighten our belts to get through the rest of the season. He asked Eddie and Jackson and Andrew to stay after the meeting to talk to him. And when I got here this morning, the new guys showed up and said Scott told them to report to me." Tears glistened in Jess's eyes. "I'm sorry. That's all I know."

"It's okay," Gina said. "But no more surprises. What's going on with the next segment? The herb-crusted salmon. You're not going to tell me I'm supposed to take Chicken-of-the-Sea and make it look like salmon steaks, right?"

Jess looked off at the set, where the prep cooks were setting up the ingredients for the next shot. "Actually, you're using mackerel."

"Mackerel!" Gina shot out of the chair. "I'll kill Scott when I find him."

Although *Fresh Start with Regina Foxton* aired on Georgia Public Television, the show operated not out of GPTV's handsome headquarters in the shadow of downtown Atlanta but out of leased production and office space at Morningstar Studios, which was a bland complex of single-story concrete-block buildings located in a light industrial area five miles away in Midtown.

Two years ago, when she'd signed on to host her own show, Gina had thought the *Fresh Start* set the most beautiful thing she'd ever seen. That was when everything about television was new and wonderful. Face it, she'd had stars in her eyes, big-time.

But what could you expect from a girl from small-town South Georgia? Odum, her hometown, wasn't exactly Hollywood. Not even Hollywood, Georgia, let alone Hollywood, California.

She'd majored in home economics at the University of Georgia, gotten interested in writing there, and after a series of reporting stints at small-town weeklies, she'd ended up with what she considered her dream job—food editor for the *Atlanta Journal-Constitution*. At twenty-six years old, she'd been the youngest woman ever to hold that position. Back home in Odum, her mama and daddy were beside themselves with pride for their oldest girl.

"Do you realize who else used to be food editor at the Atlanta newspaper?" Birdelle, her mama, had demanded. "Mrs. Henrietta Dull, that's who. Mrs. S. R. Dull herself. My mama kept Mrs. Dull's cookbook right beside her King James Bible and her Eugenia Price novels."

Two years ago, Gina was doing a cooking demonstration: no-fuss holiday desserts, it was, on *Atlanta Alive!*, the noontime television talk show on the local NBC affiliate, and Scott Zaleski was the producer.

She'd been asked back to do three more segments after that, and after the fourth segment, and a lot of flirting and provocative e-mails, Scott had asked her out to dinner.

He was blond and athletic, well dressed, and wildly ambitious—for both of them.

Six months after they'd started dating, he'd sold GPTV on her concept for a new kind of southern cooking—flavorful but healthy, with an emphasis on fresh, locally produced foods prepared with an updated twist on regional traditions. It was called *Fresh Start with Regina Foxton*.

Their set was the same one she'd used for the *Atlanta Alive!* shows. But it was starting to grate on her nerves.

The cupboard doors, whose rich dark wood looked so expensive on camera, were actually just stained plywood, and they were warped so badly they had to be closed with gaffer's tape. The countertops were a cheap imitation granite laminate, and the cooktop, donated by a long-ago sponsor, was, as far as Gina was concerned, ready for the scrap heap.

Their offices weren't much either. Hers was actually the former janitor's closet. So much for the glamour of big-time show business. At least she could use the mop sink to wash her face.

She steamed toward Scott's office. How could he leave her out of the loop on so many critical changes for the show? If there were issues with the sponsor, and with the budget, shouldn't she have been the first to know?

The door was closed. She knocked, waited. "Scott?"

She opened the door and stuck her head inside. Empty.

His office was tidy as always, desktop cleared, books and tapes stacked neatly on their shelves. She plopped down in his swivel chair, determined to confront him as soon as he showed up.

Her irritation melted a little when she caught sight of the screen saver on his computer. It was a color photo of the two of them, standing on the beach last summer at sunset, his arms wrapped around her waist. Scott's blond hair glowed in the golden light, and her own face seemed to glimmer with happiness.

How sweet! And surprising. Scott was the least sentimental man she'd ever known. She had no idea the photo had meant so much to him. She reached out to touch the screen and bumped the mouse. Suddenly, the photo disappeared, and a document materialized on the computer screen.

Squinting at the print, she felt a passing twinge of guilt. The small print ran together in an incomprehensible blur. She fumbled in the pockets of her slacks and brought out the reading glasses, which also made her feel guilty.

Scott was always pestering her to get fitted for contacts, but she'd tried them once, and hated the sensation of having a foreign object in her eye. Her readers were fine, she'd protested, but he'd banned her from wearing them on camera. No glasses, no aprons, nothing, he'd proclaimed, that might give off even a whiff of Betty Crocker. Regina Foxton was young, hot, and gorgeous. No granny glasses!

Glasses perched on the end of her nose, she started to read.

The document was Scott's résumé. Laid out in neat rows of black and white, it made him out a young television phenom. Bachelor's degree in comparative lit, cum laude, University of Virginia. Master's in film and television, Florida State University. Internships at CBS and ESPN. Before the *Atlanta Alive!* job, he'd produced a Sunday-morning political debate show for a public television station in Jackson, Mississippi, and before that, he'd been a production assistant at CNN.

She read on. E. Scott Zaleski was thirty-two years old, unmarried, with professional affiliations that included board memberships for the Association of Georgia Broadcasters and the High Museum's Young Associates as well as the Nature Conservancy.

He was currently employed as producer and creator of the Georgia Emmy-winning *Fresh Start with Regina Foxton* show.

Creator? Gina said it aloud. Of *her* show? *Fresh Start?*

The office door swung open, and Scott rushed inside. He was dressed in a dark pin-striped suit, wearing the silk Armani tie Gina had bought him at Barney's in New York. He stopped in his tracks when he saw Gina sitting at his desk.

"Hey!" he said. He glanced at his watch. "Shouldn't you be taping?"

"I don't know," Gina said, crossing her arms over her chest. "I was just going to ask you the same question. We started taping two hours ago. Where were you?"

Scott set his briefcase down beside the battered wooden kitchen chair facing the desk and sat down with deliberate caution. "I was in a business meeting. But Jess is perfectly capable of directing a segment on her own."

Gina looked him up and down, from his impeccably cut and groomed hair to his polished hand-stitched English oxfords. "You look very nice."

"Thank you," Scott said, fingering the tie. "So do you. Look, Gina, let's cut the drawing-room comedy, please. What's going on? Why are you skulking around in my office?"

She lifted an eyebrow. "I wouldn't call waiting for you in your office skulking. The door wasn't locked. Why, do you have something to hide?"

He sighed. "You've been reading my memos."

"Nuh-uh," Gina said. "Just the résumé. Although that in itself was quite a revelation. I never realized you were the *creator* of *Fresh Start*."

He waved his hand in dismissal. "That's just résumé-building. Nobody takes that stuff seriously."

"I do," she said. "And I didn't realize I should have been building my own instead of concentrating on my piddly little job here."

He stood up and closed the office door, then sat back down.

"I was going to talk to you. Today. After I got back from my meeting. I'm sorry you had to find out about it this way."

"Find out what?" She felt like screaming. But she'd never been much of a screamer. "What's going on with the show, Scott?"

"God," Scott said. He crossed and recrossed his legs, then leaned forward and took Gina's hands in his.

"I've been in a meeting with the Tastee-Town people all morning. It's not good news, Geen. Wiley wants to pull the plug on the show."

Tastee-Town Foods was the sponsor of *Fresh Start with Regina Foxton*. What had started as a mom-and-pop grocery store in Hahira, Georgia, in the early 1960s had evolved into a multistate publicly traded supermarket chain with outlets all over the Southeast. Wiley Bickerstaff III was the grandson of the founder of Tastee-Town. And the current CEO.

Gina was stunned. "But . . . Wiley loves me. He loves the show. He had me cater his fiftieth birthday party last spring. He's been selling the cookbook in all the stores in Georgia. I was the guest speaker at his Rotary Club meeting last month. He invited me to lunch at the Piedmont Driving Club two weeks ago. He never said a word."

She rolled her chair around to within inches of Scott's. "Wiley Bickerstaff loves me! This must be a misunderstanding."

"Yeah," Scott said bitterly. "He's nuts for you. He just doesn't love the show anymore. Talk about passive-aggressive behavior. Wiley always wants to be everybody's buddy. He left it up to me to be the bearer of bad news."

Gina stood up abruptly. "Scott, when were you going to tell me? After you'd already fired every single functional member of the crew and hired on a bunch of teenagers? Or were you going to tell me after you had me substituting Spam for pork tenderloin?"

"Hey!" Scott said sharply. "I was trying to protect you. I still thought until this morning that there might be some way to salvage the show. That's why I slashed the personnel and grocery budget. To try to show Wiley we could still produce a viable product for a reasonable amount of money."

"And?" Gina said.

Scott's shoulders slumped. "No go. Tastee-Town's new marketing director is under the mistaken impression that their advertising dollars could be better spent elsewhere. They're putting all their money on NASCAR racing."

"So that's it? We'll be off the air?"

Scott sat back in his own chair. "Looks like it. I'm really sorry, Geen. I've been putting out feelers, hoping we'd line up a new sponsor, but right now, I'm not optimistic."

"I guess not," she said. "Since you're obviously hunting for a new job."

"That's not fair," he said, looking hurt. "And before you go off half-cocked, accusing me of abandoning you, you should know that since Wiley started making noises about dumping the show, I've pitched you all over the country. Sent *Fresh Start* tapes every place I could think of. I didn't tell you anything because I didn't want to distract you from making the best show possible."

"Oh." Now she felt like a heel. First for spying on him, and second, for coming this close to accusing him of disloyalty, when all he'd been doing was looking out for her best interests.

"Scotty," she whispered, coming over and sitting down on his lap, wrapping her arms around his neck. "I'm so sorry. I had no idea. I had no right—"

He buried his head in her hair, kissed her forehead. "It's all right, baby," he murmured. "We'll think of something. You're the best in the business. Wiley Bickerstaff is a moron. Tastee-Town's gonna live to regret getting rid of us. It's you and me against the world, babe."

She fought back sudden tears. God. She'd been so mad at him for keeping secrets from her, she hadn't thought about losing the show. Her job! She'd worked since she was fourteen years old. Made straight As in school, never failed at anything in her life. And now, staring thirty in the face, she was out of work. Fired, essentially. And if she was out of a job, so was Scott.

She felt a chill of fear run up her spine.

The previous spring, after years of renting and scrimping and saving, right after Tastee-Town signed on for another year's worth of shows, she'd bought the two-bedroom town house in Buckhead, the first home she'd ever owned. What hadn't gone into the down payment, she'd spent on furnishing it. Her five-year-old Honda Accord was paid for, but the transmission had been making weird sounds for the past month.

Now what?

"I'm almost thirty," she said aloud. "Now what?"

"Now you get back to the set and finish the show," Scott said, kneading her shoulder muscles.

"Okay. But no more secrets."

"Deal," he said.

Gina managed a small smile. "That's my girl," he said, kissing the tip of her nose. Gently, he dislodged her from his lap and stood up. "We've got ten shows left under contract. Let's make 'em the best damned shows you've ever done. And in the meantime, I've still got some irons in the fire. I'll figure it out."

She pulled a tissue from the box on his bookshelf and blew her nose. "Okay," she said, her voice unsteady. "I'll do my best. I just have one question."

"What's that?" he asked.

"What's the E stand for?"

"Huh?"

"E. Scott Zaleski. You know, your résumé. I never knew Scott wasn't your first name."

He rolled his eyes.

"No more secrets, remember?"

"Eugene," he said. "Now you know the worst."

Chapter 3

Somehow, she managed to get through the rest of the day. After the lunch break, Scott was back in his usual seat, guiding the new crew patiently through the process of filming a fairly technically complicated cooking show.

They filmed through the dinner hour, and once the last segment was in the can, Scott congratulated everybody on a good day's work, and sent them home.

"I'll call you later," he whispered to Gina as he was packing up his laptop for the day.

She smiled. Officially, their romance was a secret. But she was fairly certain Jess and the others knew that she and Scott were an item.

After Scott and the crew had gone, she walked around the kitchen, letting her fingertips trail across the scarred countertop. Spotting a grease spatter on the stainless steel cooktop, she buffed it out with the edge of a paper towel. It might be a crummy kitchen, but it was, for four more days, her crummy kitchen.

Feeling weirdly melancholy, she decided to hit the break room for a Diet Coke before she headed home for the night.

"Oh!" she said, spotting a tall man with his back toward her. He turned. It was Andrew Payne, her lighting engineer. He was tacking a note to the bulletin board.

"For Sale," it said, listing a Fender guitar and amps, a Seadoo Set Ski, and lastly a 2006 Harley-Davidson Fat Boy. "Awesome condition. Sacrifice at $18,000." All his toys.

"Oh, Andrew," she said softly, squeezing his arm. "You're selling the Fat Boy?"

"Got to," he said, his jaw clenched. "Heather's pregnant."

"I'm so sorry," Gina said. "I only found out about the show today."

He shrugged. "Heather hated that bike."

"But you loved it. It was your baby."

"Got a real baby on the way now. And no job."

He turned away and headed for the door.

"Andrew," she called.

He turned around, his face unexpectedly sullen. "Yeah, I know. You're sorry. Scott's sorry. Everybody's sorry. And me and Eddie and Jackson are the sorriest of all. Cuz we're out of work. You have a nice life now, Gina. Okay?"

She felt stung by his simmering anger. "Andrew, I really am sorry. I could kill Wiley Bickerstaff. You know what they're doing, right? Pulling our show because they think NASCAR racing is the next best thing to sliced bread. Can you believe it? The women who shop at Tastee-Towns don't care about NASCAR. They want to know how to fix simple, delicious meals for their families." She shook her head. "I don't get it. Not at all."

Andrew's smile was bitter. "That what Scott told you? The guy's got balls of solid brass, I'll give him that."

"What do you mean?" Gina said, feeling a familiar chill run down her spine. "Tastee-Town has a new marketing guru. He somehow persuaded Wiley that car racing makes more sense than cooking."

"Man," Andrew said. "Zaleski's really got you snowed, doesn't he?"

"I don't know what you're talking about," Gina said, her voice chilly. "I'm sorry the show's been canceled. Even sorrier that you and the others lost your jobs. I'm out of work too, now, you know. But it's business. You can't blame that on Scott."

"Business?" Andrew hooted. "Monkey business maybe."

"You'd better go," Gina said, turning her back on him. "Before I forget how much I like you."

"Don't worry," he said, turning. "I'm outta here."

She heard the heels of his cowboy boots clomp across the linoleum floor, and then heard the break-room door swing shut. More footsteps echoed in the empty corridor.

"Wait," she called, running after him. He was at the rear entry door when she caught up with him.

"Now what?" he asked, his voice nasty.

"What don't I know?" she asked, afraid to hear it, afraid not to.

"You really want to know? All of it? The truth?"

She lifted her chin and met his belligerent stare with her own. "The truth."

He hesitated. "Aw, hell, Gina. Jess said we should all just suck it up and keep our mouths shut. But the hell with that. You got a right to know who you're dealing with."

"Just tell me," Gina said.

He scratched his chin. "I don't know anything about the NASCAR thing. That's a new one on me. Maybe that's the story Wiley put out to save face. What I do know is that ain't the reason Wiley Bickerstaff canceled your show."

"And the real reason is?"

"Crap." He said it under his breath.

"Just tell me," she urged. "I'm a big girl. I can take it."

Andrew took a deep breath. "Last week, when you were down in Odum, visiting your folks? Scott was visiting the Bickerstaffs. Only Wiley wasn't home at the time. In fact, Scott wasn't visiting at the Bickerstaff house at all. The way I heard it, he and Danitra Bickerstaff were checked in at the Ritz-Carlton in Buckhead."

"What are you saying?" Gina whispered.

"Mr. Bickerstaff got to wondering how come Danitra had book club every Thursday night, but she never had any books around the house," Andrew said. "Dumb bitch. Book club! Have you ever met Danitra? The only book she's interested in is Wiley's checkbook. I heard he hired a private investigator. Had her followed. And last Thursday, the detective followed her to the Ritz, where she checked into a suite. Not five minutes later, Scott Zaleski showed up at the front desk, introduced himself as Mr. Bickerstaff, and asked for the key to the suite. You believe that? The bitch checked in under her own name. And with Wiley's American Express platinum card!"

"That's a lie," Gina said heatedly. "Scott wouldn't do that."

"You wouldn't think so," Andrew agreed. "No matter what else you think about the guy, you can't say he's stupid. Still, he did screw the boss's wife and manage to get all of us fired in the process."

"How . . . how do you happen to know all of this?" Gina asked, her voice breaking. "It's probably just vicious gossip."

"Nope, not gossip," Andrew said. "I'm sorry, Gina. But if I'm lyin', I'm dyin'. Jessica went to Paideia School with Meredith Bickerstaff, Wiley's daughter by the first Mrs. Bickerstaff, and Danitra's stepdaughter, who happens to be a year older than Danitra. Meredith told Jess the whole story last week, right after it happened. Half of Buckhead's heard it by now."

"Not the half I live in," Gina said.

Chapter 4

She was a zombie. Driving aimlessly around Interstate 285, circling the city, mesmerized, as usual, by the sight of the downtown Atlanta skyline illuminated in the orange-and-blue glow of an early summer sunset. At some point, she tu rned off the Honda's struggling air conditioner and rolled down the windows, wanting the feel of the hot, moist air on her face, wanting the burn of exhaust fumes in her nostrils, the smell of hot asphalt, to remind her that she was, despite all indications to the contrary, alive.

When the transmission began its ominous knocking sounds, the numbness began to wear off, and she allowed herself to recognize feelings and emotions. Tears streamed down her face. She pounded the dashboard and swore a blue streak. Damn Scott Zaleski.

And Danitra Bickerstaff. And for that matter, damn Mrs. Teasley, her fifth-grade teacher, with her frizzy home permanent and pursed-lip disapproval of Regina Foxton's big ideas about growing up to become a famous writer in New York City.

"Little girls who can't diagram compound sentences don't grow up to become writers," Mrs. Teasley had told her, after she'd stood before the blackboard, flummoxed by gerunds and participles and all the rest.

Damn Iona Teasley, Gina thought. Her caustic predictions of a dead-end future had filled a fifth-grade Regina Foxton with a steely determination to succeed no matter what. To prove Mrs. Teasley wrong. Middle school, high school, college, the years were a blur. Back in Odum, Birdelle had turned her old bedroom into a shrine of plaques, trophies, and framed certificates, all of them attesting to Gina's superlative abilities.

Mama. Oh, Lord, what would Mama and everybody else back home think when they found out their hometown star was a dud—a has-been at thirty. Maybe that's where she would end up—back home in Odum, after her condo was repossessed and the Honda gave out.

It was only when she parked the car in front of the renovated brick midrise in Virginia Highlands that she had a clear idea of her destination for the evening.

Normally, a visitor had to call up and be buzzed into the slate-floored lobby. But Gina knew the key code, and she punched the four numbers in with a fury that surprised her.

She didn't wait for the elevator, which was slow anyway. She climbed the three flights of stairs, and wasn't even winded by the time she was ringing the doorbell at Unit 3C.

She didn't actually ring it, as much as lean on it.

Scott opened the door. Music boomed from the ceiling-mounted stereo speakers. His theme song: "Eye of the Tiger" from one of the Rocky movies. He was bare-chested, wearing only a pair of loose nylon shorts and sparkling white athletic shoes. He was glistening with sweat, and clutched a plastic water bottle in his right, gloved hand.

"Hey," he said.

"Hello, Eugene," she said, sailing uninvited into the condo.

His rowing machine was set up in the middle of the wood-floored living room. His racing bike hung from hooks on the wall, and his T-shirt was draped across his treadmill. Aside from the weight bench, set up in front of a wall of mirrors, the only other furniture in the room consisted of a tan leather sofa, a glass-and-chrome coffee table, and a huge, wall-mounted, sixty-inch flat-screen television.

"Don't call me that," he said. He picked up the remote control and shut off the stereo.

"Why not? It's your name."

"Now what?"

"You slept with Danitra Bickerstaff. And that, dear *Eugene*, is why Wiley shut down my show."

His face was suddenly alive with emotion. "Who told you that?"

"Doesn't matter," Gina said. "And don't bother to deny it, because I know it's true."

"Christ," he muttered, picking up a towel and mopping his chest with it. He pulled the T-shirt over his head and took a drink of water from his bottle. "What do you want me to say? You've already got everything worked out in your head. But it's not all black-and-white like you want it to be."

"It seems pretty black-and-white to me," Gina retorted, perching on the back of the sofa. "First you screwed me. Then you screwed Wiley Bickerstaff's wife. Wiley found out. He canceled my show. Seems to me I got screwed twice. But I didn't enjoy it nearly as much this last time, *Eugene*."

"Yeah, this is all about you, Gina," Scott said, suddenly animated. "Your show got canceled. You're out of a job. You got screwed. You, you, you. How about me? Did you ever think about good old Scotty? Hell, I've got two years of my life invested in this show.

When I met you, you were just a wannabe foodie. No sense of style, no talent. You were a fuckin' joke! With your goofy-ass glasses and home-ec lady turtleneck sweater. I'm the only reason you ever got on television," he said, poking her in the chest with his index finger.

"Don't do that," she said, her voice low.

"*I* saw something in you," he continued, poking her in the chest again.

"Don't—"

"*I* packaged you, *I* pitched you to Tastee-Town, and *I* won us two regional Emmys. When Wiley started making noises about cutting back the ad dollars, *I* went to Danitra, because she was such a big fan of the show, to see if she could talk Wiley into renewing our contract. So yeah, maybe I got a little too chummy with her, maybe I made a mistake. But don't fool yourself into thinking this is all my fault, Gina."

His face was pink with anger. He jabbed her again.

"Scott, stop!" she said.

But he was wound tight as a tick.

"*I* went—"

poke

"—to the wall—"

poke

"—for you—

"And this is the thanks I get," he raged, poking her so hard she had to take a step backward to get away from him. She stumbled, and when she regained her footing, he was inches from her face.

"A bunch of jealous bullshit!" he screamed.

She ducked instinctively, but nothing happened.

"Christ!" he said, dropping his hands to his sides. He was winded, panting. "I'm sorry," he said finally. "You know I'd never intentionally hurt you, Gina."

She shook her head, wanting to clear the image of his towering over her, fists clenched.

"Gina . . ."

"I shouldn't have come here tonight," she said. She took a last look around the room, and then she walked out.

Chapter 5

Driving home, Gina tried to make her mind tackle practical matters. She still had four more days of shows to tape. With Scott. The memory of his face, twisted with anger, was still too fresh. No matter. She was a professional. She would get through this.

But then what? A new job. Where? Her old job at the *Constitution* had been filled long ago, and anyway, her heart wasn't in newspapers anymore, even if there were any job openings. Television? What was it that Scott had called her? A wannabe foodie? Home-ec lady?

She pulled into the parking space in front of her town house, but left the Honda's motor running. She found herself smiling at the thought of her home. She thought about the paint colors she'd agonized over, the window treatments her mother had sewn for the bedrooms, the thrift-store sideboard she'd stripped and refinished for the dining area. She couldn't bear to think of those rooms, stripped, her furniture and belongings loaded in a moving van. A SOLD sign tucked in the front window.

Speaking of that window . . . the living room lights were on. She groaned. Lisa. With all the trauma of the past day, she'd forgotten about her little sister. She did not have the strength to deal with telling her about the day's events. Not tonight.

Gina turned the key in the lock of her front door and with her last ounce of strength pushed it open with her hip and staggered inside. Dropping her pocketbook and laptop on the floor, she flopped down on the oversize down-filled sofa and kicked the shoes from her swollen feet.

"I want my mama," she said, groaning.

The skinny blonde sprawled on the carpet in front of the television with a headset and Xbox controls looked away from the screen, where she'd just aced another killer in her seventeenth game of Halo that evening.

"What?" she asked, removing the headset and scooting over to where her big sister appeared to be in a near coma state. "What'd you say?"

"Mama," Gina repeated. "I wish Mama were here. She'd rub my feet and fix me some supper and bring it to me on a tray in bed, and brush my hair till I fell asleep."

"I thought that's why you were sleeping with Scott Zaleski," Lisa quipped.

"Lisa!" Gina said, horrified. "Who says I'm sleeping with my producer?"

"Not you," Lisa said. "You never let anything slip about your sex life. But you are, aren't you?"

"No comment," Gina said.

"But you totally *are* screwing him," Lisa persisted. "I know you're on the patch. I see the box in your medicine cabinet. How is he, anyway? He seems kind of distant when he's around me. My guess is, he's an animal in bed. My friend Amber says those Nordic types are usually hung like a horse."

"Scott and I are over," Gina said dully. "Anyway, we are *not* talking about this."

"Over? Did you two have a fight?" Lisa said eagerly.

"I refuse to discuss my private life with you," Gina said wearily.

"Oh, give up the prissy-sissy act," Lisa said. "We both know you're no virgin. And neither am I. All these late hours you keep when you're supposedly working? My ass! I bet the two of you were screwing like bunnies. So let's stop this two-maiden-sisters charade."

"No," Gina said, sitting up with an effort. "Mama made me promise to keep an eye on you while you're in Atlanta. You're only nineteen. When I was your age—"

"You and Mike Newton went all the way at the Wayfarer Motel on Jekyll Island after you split a bottle of Southern Comfort. It was spring break, and you told Mama and Daddy you were going to the beach with your sorority sisters."

Gina's eyes goggled. "How did you know that? I never—"

"I found your old diary in a shoebox in the bottom of your closet," Lisa said, swigging from the bottle of Natty Lite she'd left on the coffee table. "Everybody at home thinks you were a model citizen. Miss Teen Vidalia Onion. Only I know the real truth. You were a bad little girl, Regina Foxton," she said, wagging the beer bottle at her.

"Give me that," Gina said, taking a swipe at the beer bottle and missing when Lisa jerked it out of her range.

"First off, I was only runner-up Miss Vidalia Onion. Ashley Johnson won the pageant that year, because her daddy sent her to Jacksonville for a nose job her junior year of high school. And if you ever tell a single soul in Atlanta that I was once entered in beauty pageants, I will personally snatch you bald. After I kick you out of this condo and slap your tiny hiney on a Trailways bus all the way home to Odum."

"You wouldn't," Lisa said confidently. "You don't want me ending up like Mama. Forty pounds over-weight, sitting on the sofa all day watching Dr. Phil and calling up her Sunday school friends on the prayer chain."

"Watch your mouth," Gina said severely. "I'm not kidding now, Lisa. Mama and Daddy have made a lot of sacrifices for both of us. It's not easy for her being home now, with both of us grown and living on our own in Atlanta. Her blood pressure's way too high, and she can't teach anymore—"

"Yada, yada, yada," Lisa said mockingly. "I'm just messin' with you, Gina. I love Mama. I really do. You know that."

"You don't show it," Gina said. "When was the last time you called her? Or went home for a weekend?"

"I've got class," Lisa replied. "And work."

"Speaking of which," Gina said, "what are you doing home tonight? I thought you have a computer lab on Monday nights."

"It's after ten," Lisa said, yawning theatrically. "Lab got out an hour ago."

"You cut class," Gina said. "Didn't you? I tried to call earlier and the line was busy for an hour straight.

You weren't at computer lab, Lisa. You were sitting right here playing that idiotic video game."

Lisa shrugged, not bothering to deny it. "The teacher's assistant who runs the lab is the world's biggest doofus. I gave my password to one of my friends, and he logs me on to the computer. This guy will never notice I'm not there."

"Lisa!" Gina said. "You have got to quit cutting. You're only carrying two classes as it is. If you flunk this class, your grade point average drops below three-point-oh, and you lose the Hope Scholarship. With Mama taking early retirement, they can't afford to pay tuition and housing and everything else."

"I'm not gonna flunk," Lisa said, tossing her long blond hair over her shoulder.

"You flunked out of Georgia Southern last year," Gina reminded her. "A whole year's tuition down the tubes. Do you have any idea how upset Daddy was?"

Lisa bit her lip. "I *said* I was sorry. I got a job waitressing at Hi-Beams and paid back every dime, didn't I? And I'm here, going to Georgia State, living right here under your thumb to save money, aren't I?"

"Do not mention Hi-Beams to me," Gina snapped. "If anybody in Odum ever saw you skipping around that juke joint in those booty shorts and that hot-pink tube-top uniform, our parents would never be able to show their faces in town again. You looked like a ho in that getup."

"I made eighty bucks a night in tips," Lisa said defiantly. "A hundred sixty a night during football season. Paid off the note on my car, and bought Mama a Kitchen-Aid mixer for her birthday. It was the best damn job I've ever had. And I'd still be doing it if you hadn't stuck your nose in where it doesn't belong."

"Enough!" Gina said, sinking wearily back into the sofa cushions. "I've had the worst day of my life. All I want tonight is a glass of wine and a hot bath."

"About the wine . . ."

"Oh, Lisa," Gina said, shaking her head. "Is there any more of that nasty Natty Lite of yours?"

"One," Lisa said. "I'll get it. Are you hungry? How 'bout a Hot Pocket?"

"I'd rather be hungry," Gina said. "Is there any yogurt?"

In answer, Lisa handed her a carton of plain nonfat yogurt, a clean teaspoon, and a freshly opened bottle of Natty Lite beer.

"Thanks," Gina said, taking a sip of beer. She scooped up a spoonful of yogurt and ate it, quickly finishing off the whole carton in eight neat bites.

"I don't get it," Lisa said, sitting down in the club chair opposite her big sister. "You're around food all day. Why don't you just eat on the set?"

"No time today," Gina said, not wanting to elaborate. "We shot two shows back to back. I was gonna have a piece of apple pie from the second show, but the crew kids devoured the pies as soon as we'd shot that segment. Just as well. They were loaded with sugar. I don't need the extra calories."

"Ha!" Lisa guffawed. "You are the skinniest now that you've ever been in your whole life. I never see you eating anything except yogurt, or maybe an occasional piece of fruit. Hey. You don't have an eating disorder, do you?"

"No. I have a perfectly normal appetite," Gina said primly. "I just have to really watch everything I put in my mouth. I've got the Sewell women's curse—small bones, big butt. And you know the camera adds twenty pounds."

"I bet you don't even wear a size eight," Lisa said. "I tried on your Juicy Couture tracksuit, and it looked like it had been spray-painted on me."

"Good. Stay away from my velour tracksuit," her sister ordered. "You have a bad habit of staining and tearing other people's clothes."

"Bitch." Lisa mouthed it—but slowly, so her sister could tell just what she was not saying. "You're home later than usual tonight," she said, changing the subject. "What's up with that?"

Gina felt her right eye twitch. "It's the last week of taping for the season," she said finally. "We're running out of money and time. Trying to cram two weeks' worth of work into one. I'm going to bed now. Turn out the lights and lock up, okay?"

But Lisa had the headset on again, locked and loaded for her next video battle.

Gina trudged into her bedroom and shut the door behind her. In the bathroom, she dropped her clothes on the floor and stood under a scalding shower so long she looked like a boiled lobster when she finally emerged from the water. She knew she should slather eye cream on her face to combat the dark circles that were already emerging. She should blow her hair dry and lay out her wardrobe for the next day's shoot. But she was too tired. And anyway, what did it matter?

She pulled back the coverlet on her bed and folded it neatly at the foot, as she always did. Got under the sheets and reached out a hand to turn off the lamp. Sitting in the middle of her bedside table, she saw her answering-machine light blinking. Call waiting.

Let it be Scott, she thought. Let him be calling to apologize. To tell her it was all a horrible practical joke. Let everything go back to the way it was before today. Her hand hesitated, but finally, she punched the play button.

"Hello? This is Mrs. Birdelle Foxton calling for Regina . . ." Her mother's voice, sweet, slow, and southern as sorghum syrup, dripped concern. "Honey, your daddy's cousin Flossie called here today, because she'd picked up your cookbook at a yard sale over in Bessemer. Flossie said she'd used your applesauce cake recipe, but it didn't come out too good. I had her read me the recipe, and sure enough, it only called for two eggs. Gina, you know I always use three eggs and an extra stick of oleo, and my cake never comes out too dry. I think you should call up those publisher folks and have them change that . . ."

Not tonight, Mama, Regina thought wearily, punching the machine's stop button. She cut off the light and lay back on the pillows, willing herself to sleep. Her stomach growled loudly.

No! she thought. Absolutely not. She rolled onto her stomach. Five minutes later, it growled again. She turned on her right side, and then her left. She tried to clear her mind, tried to meditate. It was no good. Her brain wouldn't shut up.

Growwwl. There it was again.

With a sigh, she got out of bed and padded over to the dresser. She opened the top drawer and rooted around among the neatly folded garments until her fingertips felt the crackle of cellophane. She snatched the bag from its hiding place, avoiding looking at herself in the mirror.

Tucked back under the covers, she ripped open the cellophane bag and shoved a handful of fried pork rinds into her mouth. She closed her eyes and let the pure piggy pleasure, the sandy, salty crunch, work its magic.

There, she told her rumbling tummy. There now. Shut the heck up.

Chapter 6

The morning sun shone brightly off the burnished aluminum skin of the travel trailer set up at the farthest edge of the asphalt parking lot abutting the Morningstar Studios complex. A bright blue awning stretched from the back end of the trailer, bringing blessed shade for the woman who sat under it in a plastic lawn chair. Only nine o'clock in the morning and it was already ninety degrees.

Valerie Foster put down her third cigarette of the day, sipped her second cup of coffee, and sighed loudly. She thumbed her BlackBerry, ignoring the thirty-seven unread e-mails and checking, as she did every morning, the temperature in Maine. Sixty degrees. Val didn't actually know anybody in Maine, had never actually even been to Maine, despite the fact that she'd spent two years as a floor director at the actual Fox news affiliate in Boston. Still, it gave her comfort to know that somebody, somewhere, wasn't already stewing in their own juices as she was in this beastly Atlanta weather.

She sighed again, loudly, for the talent's benefit.

But her talent didn't hear her. Or if he did, Tate Moody, the host of *Vittles*, an outdoor cooking/lifestyles show on the Southern Outdoors Network, was ignoring her, as usual.

He stood a few yards away, tossing a bright yellow disc up into the air, again and again, as he did every morning. And this morning, like every other morning, Tate's English setter tore off after the disc, feathery tail flying, nimbly catching the Frisbee in midair.

"Good boy!" Tate called encouragingly. The dog dashed to the far edge of the parking lot with the Frisbee, then circled back briskly, coming to stand six feet from Tate.

"Good, Moonpie," Tate said. Then, sharply, "Bring!"

The dog crouched down, the Frisbee clamped between his teeth, and looked at Tate, his head cocked sideways, as though taunting his owner, Valerie thought. She could almost see one of those little cartoon bubbles above the dog's grinning face.

"As if," the bubble would say.

"Moonpie! Bring!" Tate called.

"Tate, come," Valerie said.

The dog inched closer, but Tate ignored her.

"Goood," Tate said cautiously, holding out his hand for the Frisbee.

The dog wagged its tail furiously, stood up, and trotted away toward the line of scrubby pines that grew up at the edge of the parking lot. Once there, the dog plunked himself down and began happily gnawing the edge of the Frisbee.

"Tate," Val pleaded. "Enough with the dog. He's too stupid to fetch. He's like a dog version of a bimbo. Gorgeous, but dumb as a damn rock. Come on now. Let's get to work. The crew will be here any minute, and you know Barry Adelman is coming today."

Tate Moody crossed his arms over his chest, ignoring his producer's entreaties.

"Moonpie is not dumb. His daddy was a two-time grand master at the national field trials. He's hardheaded, yeah, but he's only ten months old. He's still just a puppy. That's why I've gotta work with him every day. So he'll be ready for the quail-hunting show we're gonna shoot down in Tallahassee come fall."

"That's months away," Val pointed out. "Right now we've got today's show to worry about. Adelman and his guys are supposed to get in sometime this afternoon. They'll want to see the footage we shot out at the lake yesterday, and then watch you as we shoot. Luckily, the film from the lake is spectacular."

Tate's deeply tanned face broke into a wide smile. "Wasn't that the prettiest mess of shellcrackers you ever saw?"

"Terrific. But you know all those fish look the same to me. I can't tell a shellcracker from a salmon."

Tate laughed. "Remind me again why I hired you to produce this show?"

She took a deep drag from her ultra-slim filtered cigarette. "Because I'm the best in the business, and you know it."

"And?"

She narrowed her eyes as the smoke plumed upward. "And because I'm the one who's going to get you off this piece-of-crap Southern Outdoors Network and into the big time. The Cooking Channel, Tate, that's where we're headed. New York, baby."

"You can go to New York," Tate said affably. "I'm staying put."

Val shook her head. Tate had seemed excited when she'd given him the news that The Cooking Channel was interested in *Vittles*, but he had been quite clear that he had no intention of ever living anywhere outside the South.

He reached into the pocket of his baggy green cargo shorts and pulled out one of the liver treats the trainer had suggested he use when working with the dog.

He turned away from Val and held the treat out so the dog could see and smell it.

"C'mere, Moonpie," he called. "Come, boy."

At the sight of the delicacy, Moonpie dropped the Frisbee, pricked up his ears, and came trotting obligingly over to his putative master.

"Sit," Tate commanded, holding the treat just above the dog's head.

Moonpie sat, his tail thumping the ground in anticipation.

"Sit pretty," Tate said.

The English setter sat regally erect, head up, brown eyes shining, perfectly still.

"Tell me this is not the most beautiful dog you ever saw in your life," Tate said softly, scratching the dog's chin.

"Oh, he's beautiful, all right," Val agreed. "And your viewers are going to go crazy for him when this new season starts to air. I mean, a dog sidekick. It's brilliant television."

"And so original, too," Tate said dryly.

"It hasn't been done on a cooking show before, so as far as I'm concerned, it *is* original," Val insisted. "Anyway, you know, your demographics skew amazingly female for Southern Outdoors. Something like forty-five percent. And thirty percent of those are women under thirty-five. That's one reason TCC is so hot to take a look at our show. They know you not only deliver the NASCAR guys their other shows don't draw, but the women too. And that's golden."

"The NASCAR guys I understand. Every man who lives in the South likes to think he's some kind of rugged outdoorsman, even if his idea of roughing it is a night without a remote control in his hand," Tate said. "It's the women part I don't get. I mean, what's that all about? Why are all these chicks under thirty watching a show about hunting, fishing, and cooking? And on the Southern Outdoor Network, of all places? You know, I was at Bargain Mart this morning, buying a spool of monofilament line, and when I looked up, there were half a dozen girls—none of 'em could have been drinking age—following me to the cash register. Honest to God, Val, one of 'em asked me to autograph her tattoo. And it wasn't on her arm, either."

He bent over and wrapped his arms around Moonpie, who responded by lavishly licking his hero's chin. "It's crazy, isn't it, little buddy?"

Valerie took another deep drag on her cigarette, admiring, as she did always, the view of her star's backside.

"Oh, I don't know," she said. "It all depends on how you look at things."

Chapter 7

Her cell phone started to chirp at six o'clock. After a night of much angst but little sleep, Gina was already mostly awake. She looked at the caller ID screen on the phone. Scott.

"Pig," she muttered, burying her head in the pillow.

Five minutes later he called again, this time on her house phone. And five minutes after that he tried her cell. The chirping and ringing kept up, intermittently, all morning. When she emerged from the shower, dripping wet, she saw that he'd left three messages on the answering machine. She erased them all without listening, grinning sadistically as she stabbed the machine's delete button over and over again.

Let him call, she thought as she blew her hair dry. He could rationalize, apologize, strategize. He could cry, he could grovel. She and Scott were over. But somehow, she had to get through these last shows as best she could, head held high. Dignity intact.

"I will survive," she vowed, remembering the single girl's disco anthem. She might be jobless, washed up at thirty. She might end up living in a double-wide in the Piney Grove trailer court back home, but she would survive. And she would do it without Scott Zaleski. The pig.

At seven o'clock, Regina stumbled into the studio's makeup room, a coffee mug clutched in one hand and her shooting script in the other.

"Uh-oh," said the six-foot-seven man with skin the color of cinnamon. He got up from the makeup chair and put down the issue of *Allure* he'd been reading. His head, which had been shaven clean, gleamed in the bright overhead light, and his immaculate starched white dress shirt and tight white jeans gave him the appearance of an African-American Mr. Clean, an effect he was not unaware of.

"Did we have a bad night last night?" he asked, gingerly touching her face. "Girl, the size of the circles under your eyes, we gonna need some industrial-strength concealer today!"

"Just do what you have to do," Gina said, settling into the chair with a sigh. She managed one more gulp of coffee before he took the mug from her hands, frowning.

"Caffeine? Have we not discussed that caffeine is not your friend?"

Regina reached for the mug, but he held it behind his back.

"Don't start," she warned. "Caffeine is my best friend. My *only* friend. I swear, D'John, I'll take my vitamin E, I'll drink five gallons of water a day. I'll use SPF 200 sunblock. Just don't ask me to give up coffee. It's my absolute last vice. I need my coffee. Especially today."

"Fine," he said, returning the mug and then fastening a plastic cape around her neck. "Drink your coffee. But don't blame me when you wake up one day and realize your pores are the size of manhole covers."

"I won't," Gina said, taking another sip of coffee. She picked up the magazine he'd just put down. "Anyway, I don't believe caffeine hurts your skin."

"Whatever," D'John said. He took a bottle of water and began to spritz her hair with it. "Two years of esthetician school. Two years working with the top, and I mean, the *top* dermatologist in Miami, six years doing makeup and hair for every print or television shoot of any importance done in South Beach. Not to mention my own six years on the runway in Paris, New

York, and Milan. But no, don't take D'John's word for it that caffeine is ruinous to your skin."

"Um-hmm," Gina said, closing her eyes and pretending not to hear.

"Scott's been in here twice looking for you this morning," he said.

"Um-hmm," she said, playing not interested.

"Something up with you two?" he asked.

She shrugged.

He waved his comb in front of her face. "Hello? Miss Foxton? Am I supposed to pretend I don't know the real deal? 'Cuz DJ can act if he has to. Poor baby," he said, massaging her shoulders.

Her eyes met his in the mirror. "So you know the whole story? About why we got canceled?"

"Mmm-hmm," he said. "Danitra Bickerstaff! That heifer! She ain't nothin' but a hank of overprocessed hair held together with Botox and silicon. You know, I thought Scott had better taste than that."

"Not to mention better judgment," Gina said.

D'John held up a strand of her hair and examined it. "And speaking of hair? Scott thinks we need to take you blonder. And I have to concur."

"Why? So I'll look like a hottie in the unemployment line?"

"Hello?" D'John said, arching one eyebrow. "The ash blond you're at now is fine for regional television."

He reached for the rack of hot rollers near the mirror. "But if you're going to go national, you need to look more polished." He began wrapping her shoulder-length hair in the jumbo rollers.

"What are you talking about?" Gina asked, swiveling the chair around so that they were face to face. "What have you been hearing?"

"Sweetie," D'John said. "Cut the act. That don't play with DJ. I know all about these boys from TCC. I mean, how often does a black stretch limo pull up to Morningstar Studios? And we are all thrilled to pieces for you."

"What boys from TCC?" Gina asked. "What are you talking about?"

D'John put both hands on his hips. "Are you telling me you didn't know Barry Adelman, Mr. Big Shot from The Cooking Channel, and his cute little-boy assistant flew down here from New York this morning to check you out?"

"D'John," Gina said. "I am dead serious. I have no idea what you are talking about. Why would this Adelman guy be here in Atlanta, at Morningstar Studios?"

"Maybe because he helps run a network devoted to cooking—and you happen to have a television cooking show?" D'John said, raising one eyebrow.

"My hand on my mama's bible," Gina said. "I'm completely in the dark. As usual."

"Well," D'John said, "all I know is, I saw them huddled on the set with Scottie when I came in this morning. And then this Adelman guy asked Jess to send out for espresso for him. And she came running in here, about to hyperventilate because the man handed her a hundred-dollar bill. For espresso!"

Gina pulled her cell phone out of her pocketbook and stared at the call log. A total of six missed calls from Scott. She scrolled down to the last message, which had been left less than half an hour earlier, and pressed the play button.

"Gina," Scott said, his voice near a whisper. "Stop screwing around and get in here. Barry Adelman, the vice president of programming at The Cooking Channel, is here. And I mean right here, at Morningstar Studios. I sent him your tapes last week. He's in town today to take a look at another cooking show, and he decided to come by and check us out. The show, I mean. Dammit, Gina, pick up the phone. Talk to me."

Slowly, Gina put the phone down on the counter. "You're right," she told D'John. "I thought Scott was calling to apologize. But he was trying to tell me about The Cooking Channel guys."

"And?" D'John coaxed.

"Scott sent them tapes of the show, without telling me. He never said a word! Now these guys are in town to see somebody else, and they came by to see us. Me, I mean. That is, the show."

"See?"

"I'm screwed," Gina said glumly. "You said it yourself. I look like crap. My face is all splotchy, my eyes are swollen from crying—"

"Don't worry," D'John said, patting her shoulder. "You'll be fine. Better than fine. You'll kill. Just put yourself in D'John's hands now. We don't have time for your color this morning. I've got somebody coming in as soon as I'm done with you. But tonight, when you're through shooting, I want you to come over to my place. I'll mix up your new color, and we'll send out for Chinese and play beauty parlor."

"Nothing too radical, right?" Gina said. "You know how my fans are. They never want me to change anything. I got two dozen e-mails after last season's first show, just because I got my ears pierced."

"Screw the viewers," D'John said airily. "You were born to be a blonde. And I'm the man who's going to take you there. Think Jean Harlow. Carole Lombard. Think bombshell, baby!"

"You're making me nervous," Gina told him, smoothing moisturizer over her face.

"Scott says we have to take your whole presentation up a notch if you're going national," D'John said. He bent down and looked at her face, clucking in disapproval. "And you have got to start getting more sleep. There's only so much concealer can do, you know."

"I'll try," Gina agreed. She closed her eyes and tried to relax as D'John began applying her makeup.

He hummed as he worked, and the featherlike strokes of sponge, brush, and powder puff made her sleepy. She had nearly dozed off when she heard the door of the room open.

"Oh," a male voice said. "Sorry."

Regina opened her eyes. The intruder was tall, but not as tall as D'John. Maybe a shade over six feet. His brown hair was wavy and needed combing. He was deeply tanned, with a nose that was too big for his face, and starting to peel. Intense blue eyes under bushy eyebrows a shade darker than his hair. He wore faded blue jeans, a short-sleeved turquoise golf shirt, and scuffed-up boat shoes with no socks.

"Uh," he said, looking from Regina to D'John. "Sorry. I didn't know anybody else was in here. I'll come back."

"Wait!" D'John said sharply. "Who were you looking for?"

"Uh, D'John?"

"You found him," D'John said crisply. "And you are?"

"Tate Moody. My producer, Val Foster, said you'd be expecting me."

"Oh yes," D'John said. "You're the fisher boy, right?"

Moody laughed. "Sorta."

D'John waved toward the other seat in the makeup room.

"Never mind. Sit. I'll be with you as soon as I'm done here."

"You sure?" the visitor asked, squirming in the chair and glancing down at his watch. "I've gotta be on set pretty soon. Some dudes from New York are coming in, and Val said—"

A few notes of banjo music filled the air. He glanced down at his lap, rolled to one side, and took a cell phone from his right hip pocket.

"Hey," he said abruptly.

Gina glanced at D'John and raised one eyebrow. D'John shook his head.

Her own cell phone rang. She glanced at the screen and saw that it was Scott calling again. Quickly, she shut the phone off.

D'John busied himself with her hair, removing the hot rollers, fluffing, teasing, spraying. They both worked hard at pretending not to listen to Tate Moody's telephone conversation.

"So what's the word?" Moody demanded. "I thought you were gonna call yesterday. You said we'd hear something by five o'clock, no later."

He listened but didn't like what he was hearing. He frowned and rubbed his forehead.

"No. No! That's impossible. I don't have that kind of money. I thought you understood that."

He listened, then interrupted. "Wait, dammit! No, you listen. There is no way. Okay? That's not even close to what I can afford. Anyway, I happen to know another parcel, just down the road, sold six weeks ago, for fifty thousand less than they're asking. And that piece has deep-water access. Yeah. That's right. I am watching all the local transactions. You tell them that. This ain't some dumb hillbilly they're dealing with."

He shook his head violently. "No. I'm through. I mean it. Tell them I'm walking away from the deal. Yeah. Well, you tell 'em what you want. I'm done."

Tate Moody snapped his phone shut. He inhaled deeply. "Shit."

Glancing over at D'John, his mood seemed to worsen. "Look, man, I gotta go."

"Wait," the stylist said. He gave Regina's hair a final touch. "We're done."

He stepped over to Tate Moody's chair and whisked another plastic cape out of the drawer in the makeup table.

When Regina made no attempt to leave, D'John gave her a questioning look.

She held up the magazine she'd been pretending to read. "Don't worry about me. I just want to finish this article about sunscreens. Go ahead with him." She turned and smiled sweetly at Tate Moody, who gave her a sour look. "You don't mind, do you?"

"How long's this gonna take?" Tate asked, turning toward the stylist.

Instead of answering, D'John spun Tate around in the chair. He bent low at the waist and peered into his subject's face. He lightly touched Moody's face, lifted a lock of his hair, sighed, clucked his tongue in disapproval.

"Hmmm," D'John said. "Yes. Your producer is absolutely right. You do need me."

Tate's face flushed. "Now, uh, listen. I don't really want—"

"What *have* you been doing to this skin of yours?" D'John asked.

"My skin?" Tate leaned in toward the mirror. "Nothing. I mean, I wash it. And I shaved this morning—"

"With what?" D'John asked. "A dull butter knife?"

"A razor, of course," Tate said. "Shaving cream. Barbasol. Like that."

D'John turned to Regina. "Will you listen to that? Barbasol? Who knew they still made that mess?"

"What's wrong with Barbasol?" Tate demanded.

"What's wrong with Barbasol?" D'John's voice was mocking. "Why not just wipe a piece of sandpaper across your jaw? Why not throw rubbing alcohol on your face while you're at it?"

"Huh?" Tate rubbed his hand across his chin.

Regina stifled a laugh. "I think maybe what D'John is trying to say is that he doesn't think Barbasol is an appropriate product for you to use."

"Appropriate?" D'John cried. He grabbed Tate's hand and dragged it across his own smooth brown cheek.

"Do you feel that?" D'John asked. "That's what a well-groomed man's face should feel like. Moist. Firm. Healthy."

"Healthy?" Tate seemed unconvinced.

"Now. Feel that skin of yours," D'John ordered.

Tate shrugged and did as he was told.

"And?" D'John asked, crossing his arms over his chest.

"Feels fine to me."

"Fine?" D'John shrieked. "You think it's fine that your face has the same texture as some nasty old work boot that's been left out in the sun for about ninety years? You think it's fine that a man with your looks has never properly cared for his own skin?"

"Hey, man," Tate said, his face darkening. He started up from the chair. "I thought I was just coming in here to get my sideburns evened out a little. Val never said anything about—"

"Stop!" D'John said dramatically. He pushed Tate back into the chair. "Tell me," he said, pausing for effect. "About your skin-care regimen."

"Regimen?" He glanced over at Regina, who'd given up on the magazine, and was now openly laughing.

"Your routine," she prompted. "How do you take care of your face?"

"Ah, hell," Tate said. "I shower. I shave. I use soap, if that's what you're asking. Life Buoy. What else is there to a 'regimen'?"

"Life Buoy," D'John wailed. "Kill me now."

Tate stood again and headed for the door. "Okay. Fun time's over. See you folks later."

"Go then!" D'John replied.

"I'm going," Tate said. He got to the door, stopped, and turned around, then walked back to Gina.

"Excuse me," he said, extending his hand to her. "I don't think I caught your name."

"I'm Regina," she said, dimpling sweetly. "Regina Foxton."

"And what exactly do you do, Regina Foxton?" His southern drawl was suddenly pronounced.

"Oh, I have a little show. It's nothing much. Just regional television," she said, being deliberately evasive.

"But she's probably going to be moving over to the networks," D'John blurted out.

"D'John, hush!" Gina said sharply. She turned back to Tate Moody with a shrug. "Wishful thinking. D'John thinks I'm cut out for Hollywood."

"Ya never know," Tate said, unfastening the plastic makeup cape and dropping it on the counter. "Anything can happen in television."

"Exactly," she said, giving him a little finger wave. "Bye now."

Chapter 8

J erk," Regina said quietly, as the door closed.

"Hmm," D'John said. "Cute, though. If you like the rustic look."

"Tate Moody," she said thoughtfully. "What do we know about him? And why are The Cooking Channel execs in town to see him? I thought you called him a fisher boy?"

"You know as much about him as I do," D'John said. "They usually shoot on location or over at Ajax Studios downtown, but Ajax is being torn down, so they've moved here temporarily. His producer, one of those ballsy New York–gal types, came by last week and said her talent needed some sharpening up because he was being considered for a network television slot. She said he spends a lot of time hunting and fishing for his show." He opened a drawer in the counter and dug around among the hairbrushes and combs until he came up with a business card, which he handed to Regina. "Here."

"Valerie Foster," she read. "Executive Producer, co-creator, *Vittles*, a Southern Outdoors Network production."

"*Vittles?*" they both repeated it at the same time.

"What kind of show is named *Vittles?*" D"John asked.

"Well, it must be a cooking show if The Cooking Channel is interested in him," Gina pointed out. "According to the message Scott left on my cell, he's the real reason this Barry Adelman is in town. I'm just an afterthought."

"Never," D'John said loyally. "He doesn't have a prayer." D'John gave a dismissive sniff. "He's a goober. And that skin! He has the complexion of an eighty-year-old."

"And the buns of an eighteen-year-old," Gina said. "And don't pretend you didn't notice, D'John Maynard. I saw you watching when he walked out of here."

"Oh, buns," D'John said dismissively. "We're talking about a cooking show, right? It's all about the food, right? And despite your problem complexion and caffeine addiction, nobody's food is better than yours."

"Scott says it's not about the food at all," Gina said quietly. "That's why he told you he wants to sharpen up my look. Make me blonder. Cuter. It's why I can't wear my glasses on camera, and I had to buy a whole new wardrobe for the new season. Low-cut tops, brighter colors. And obviously, Tate Moody's producer is just as concerned about his looks, or she wouldn't have sent him to see you."

"I could help him," D'John said, his face taking on a dreamy quality. "Give him a decent haircut, add some texture, some layers, maybe some chunky color around the face. And of course, the skin needs a lot of work. The clothes, too. I'd put him in earth tones—"

"D'John!" Gina said, punching him in the arm. "Whose side are you on here?"

"Beauty doesn't take sides," he said primly.

"Well, you'd better," she said. "Or don't bother to come slinking around my set looking to be fed any-more."

"Bitch," D'John said, giving her an air kiss so as not to muss her makeup.

"Pissy old queen," she said fondly, air-kissing him back. "What time do you want me to come over tonight?"

"Make it eight," he said. "You want Jade Palace or China Doll?"

"Jade Palace," she said quickly. "But no moo shu pork for me. And no rice. Just some egg-drop soup and some steamed ginger shrimp."

"B-o-r-ing," D'John sang. "See you at eight, then."

Chapter 9

Scott was standing on the *Fresh Start* set, deep in conversation with two black-clad men who pretty much had to be the visiting executives from The Cooking Channel.

"Here's my girl," he called, catching sight of her. He trotted over to her side. "What took you so long?" he whispered, his lips brushing her cheek, a proprietary arm flung casually across her shoulder. "I've been calling you all morning. Didn't you get my messages?"

"Don't push your luck," she warned, wriggling out of his embrace. "I got your last messages, about the Cooking Channel people. That's the only reason I'm here. Because I'm a pro. But I am not your girl." She looked him straight in the eye. "Are we clear on that?"

Stung, he took a quick step backward. "Clear," he muttered. "As long as we're being professionals here, remember it's your career on the line here today, not just mine. The Cooking Channel wants a southern cooking show in their new fall lineup. They're looking at you, and one other guy. This is our big break, Gina. For real. I know you're pissed at me, but don't blow this, okay?"

"Pissed?" She gave a humorless little laugh. "Oh, Scott. You are so clueless."

"Barry," Scott said, to the shorter, older of the two men. "This is—"

"Regina Foxton. Of course," Barry Adelman said, clasping Regina's hand between both of his own. "Younger and much sexier even than you look on camera." His accent was not what she'd expected. Not Brooklyn, or Queens, not even all that northern—midwestern maybe.

He was mid-forties, she thought. Quite short, with a head that looked too big for his compact body; tiny, elfin ears pressed close to his head; and gray hair, thinning on top, but in the back sweeping to the neckline of his collarless black silk T-shirt. He was dressed entirely in black, of course. Expensive black. Soft shirt, soft black trousers, and sockless feet in complicated-looking Italian leather sandals.

"You're too sweet," Regina murmured. "I'm so glad to meet you. I'm a huge TCC fan—"

"No," Adelman corrected her. "We're the big fans. Of you. And *Fresh Start*. Those tapes Scott sent. I gotta tell you, it takes a lot to get me excited. But I am very excited about you. And your show."

"Barry's wife was the one who got him to call me," Scott started to say.

"My wife!" Adelman exclaimed. "Christ! She watched the tapes while I was out of town, and ever since, she's been driving me crazy, insisting that I take a look. But I gotta say, she was right."

"Wendy is very astute about food," the other visitor put in. Gina decided he must be the assistant. Young, maybe twenty-four, with milky white skin, pale blue eyes, and short-cropped blond hair, he was dressed in an inexpensive version of his boss's wardrobe, right down to the black sandals.

"Astute!" Adelman said, with a short laugh. "You could say that. She's got every cookbook ever published, went to cooking school in Italy . . ." He snapped his fingers and looked at the assistant.

"Alicia LaRocco's school. In Tuscany," the assistant said.

"And Paris . . ." Adelman said, turning again to the assistant.

"Pierre Bouget," he said. "In Provence. He only takes three students every summer. Pierre adores Wendy."

"Not that she ever really cooks," Adelman said, laughing in a way that made Gina think he didn't find that so very funny.

"Barry and Wendy travel extensively," the assistant explained. "And Wendy is a senior account executive at Storman-Davis. So you know how crazy her schedule can get."

"Oh," Regina said, secretly wondering what Storman-Davis was.

"Crazy," Scott agreed, nodding agreement. "We'll have to send your wife Gina's cookbook." He glanced around the set until he spied the person he was looking for.

"Jess!" he called loudly.

Jessica was standing at the editing table, scribbling something in her ever-present yellow legal pad. She looked up and scurried over.

"Jessie," Scott said, "I need you to send a copy of Regina's latest cookbook to Mr. Adelman's wife."

"I can do that," Jess said, scribbling a note to herself.

"Overnight," Scott said. "Can you overnight it?"

"Of course," Jess said. "Address?"

"Mr. Adelman's assistant will give you the address," Scott said. He looked expectantly at the assistant.

"Hi," the young man said, holding out his hand to Scott's assistant. "I'm Zeke Evans."

"We're about ready to start," Jess told Scott, after she'd written down Wendy Adelman's address.

"Great," Scott said. He looked at Gina. "Ready, gorgeous?"

She felt herself flush. "Absolutely."

"Scott says you're doing seafood today?" Barry said.

She nodded. "Southerners are really fortunate that in most places, fresh fish is pretty accessible and affordable. But too many people are intimidated by cooking fish. They don't want to fry it, the way their grandmother did, but they're worried about a lot of fancy or expensive ingredients."

"Right," Adelman said. "I like what you're telling me."

"I'm doing a shrimp-stuffed flounder fillet," Regina said. "And shrimp remoulade and a crab casserole. Of course, I'll encourage people to look for fresh, wild shrimp, like the ones we get here in Atlanta that are trucked up from the Georgia coast. But even if they use frozen bagged shrimp from a discount grocer, they can get a really wonderful taste."

"Good!" Adelman said. "Accessible. Our focus groups tell us viewers like it when we show the kind of upscale recipes they get in a good restaurant, or read about in *Gourmet* or *Bon Appetit,* but they're turned off when they see ingredient lists with herbs or flavored vinegars or crap like that they never heard of and can't get in Mudflap, Oklahoma."

"Gina's all about accessibility," Scott volunteered. "For every recipe she does on the show, she refers to the Web site, where we tell viewers how they can source everything shown on the show."

"And we list prices," Regina added.

"Geen?" one of the cameramen called from the set. "Can we get some light levels on you before we start?"

"Go ahead," Barry urged. "Pretend we're not even here."

As if, Regina thought, as she stood motionless in front of her stove, while Scott and the others set up lights and worked out camera angles. Today, the set looked cheesier to her than it ever had before. Small-time, it seemed to shout. Her stomach churned, and she could feel beads of sweat pooling in the small of her back as she looked over at the small knot of people staring into the computer monitors set up on Scott's editing table. Scott and Jess were there, of course, along with Adelman and Zeke, the assistant. But there were three or four other visitors she didn't recognize, standing in back of the table. A woman wearing dark glasses seemed very interested in the whole process. And yes, damn it—Tate Moody stood there too, with that smug look of secret amusement on his face.

"Can we roll?" Jess asked loudly.

"One moment." Suddenly D'John darted to her side with a powder puff and a comb, patting her nose dry and rearranging a strand of hair that had somehow gotten out of place. "You're a goddess," he whispered in her ear. "The camera loves you. I love you. Now just smile pretty and knock their fucking socks off."

"They're not wearing socks," Gina whispered back.

"That's fine, D'John," Scott called.

The makeup man gave her a barely perceptible pat on her butt and flitted off the set.

"Ready, Gina?" Scott asked.

She took a deep breath and nodded yes.

"All right," Scott called. "Let's boogie!"

"Hey, y'all," she said brightly, looking directly into the camera. "I'm Regina Foxton. This is *Fresh Start*, and today, we're gonna cook up seafood, so fresh and simple, so delicious, that you'll wonder why you don't serve seafood to your friends and family more often. I call this segment 'Fishing for Compliments,' and in just a moment, you all will be fishing for a pen and pencil, or clicking onto our Web site, to make sure you have every detail of these wonderful recipes written down to use at home."

Later on, when they broke for lunch and she sucked down two ice-cold Diet Cokes in her dressing room while D'John repaired the makeup she'd sweated off, she realized her back ached and her feet were throbbing. She'd been so nervous, stood so rigid, smiled so hard, she felt like she'd just run a marathon.

"How do you think it's going?" she asked, as D'John held a curling iron to her bangs.

"Fabulous," he said. "Like always."

"Liar," she said. "My hands were shaking so bad I couldn't even mince the onion for the stuffing. And when the flounder fillets stuck to the pan while I was trying to flip 'em over, I thought I'd pee my pants. Darn that cheapskate Scott for using frozen fish. I've told him a million times—"

"Nobody noticed a thing," D'John said soothingly. "And the men in black are loving you. They're out there right now, scarfing up your shrimp like a couple of condemned men."

"The shrimp!" Regina cried, sitting up straight in her chair. "Did we get the beauty shots done before they ate 'em all up?"

"Relax," D'John said. "I heard Jess tell the prep-kitchen girls to fix triples of everything today, because we had guests on the set. In fact," he said, picking up a napkin-covered plate he'd snuck into the room, "I even brought a plate for you."

He whisked the napkin off the plate with a flourish, but Regina pushed it away with a shudder.

"Oh no. Nuh-uh. I can't eat. Not when I've been wrangling flounder and shrimp and crab all morning."

D'John frowned. "I never see you eat anymore. All you do is swill those horrible sodas. How many Diet Cokes do you drink in one day?"

She shrugged. "Not that many. One when I get up, while the coffee's brewing. Another couple while we're going over notes before shooting starts. And I have one with lunch."

"You have one instead of lunch," D'John said. "And it's not healthy. All that caffeine."

"I'll get a salad after we finish today. I promise." She looked at her watch. "We start again in fifteen minutes. I think I'm just gonna shut my eyes for a few minutes and take a little catnap."

"Good plan," D'John said. "Don't put your head down, and don't smear your mascara."

"Promise," she said, holding up three fingers as a pledge.

"Guess I'll go eat me some of this shrimp," D'John said.

Chapter 10

Valerie Foster waited until the *Fresh Start* crew was preoccupied with sucking up to the black-suited men from New York. When the moment came, she seized it, as she always did.

Grabbing one of the paper plates from a stack on the counter of the *Fresh Start* set, she scooped up a huge mound of the shrimp remoulade. Setting another plate atop the shrimp, she heaped it with Regina Foxton's Granny Smith apple and mint slaw. A third plate held a thick slab of buttery lemon pound cake with oozing layers of lemon curd.

Whisking a piece of aluminum foil from the pocket of her slacks, she neatly covered the whole pile, and within a minute was hurrying away from the set, with Tate lagging a few feet behind.

"Jesus, Val," he said sharply.

"What?" She turned and gazed over the tops of her dark glasses at him. "You have a problem?"

"You just looted that set," Tate said, moving up beside her. "What if somebody saw you? What if Adelman and his lackey saw you?"

"Nobody saw me," she said, although she picked up her pace just in case. "Anyway, so what if they did? This is research."

"It's poaching," Tate said. "You don't know that they don't need that food for the rest of their shoot."

"Too bad if they do," Val said breezily.

She moved through the darkened concrete block hallway at a near gallop. Not because she actually feared being found out. Valerie Foster feared little, and anyway, she did everything at the same speed, Tate thought. Flat out, full tilt.

When they'd reached the doorway to the makeshift *Vittles* set in the parking lot of Morningstar Studios, she stepped aside, her hands full of the filched food, to allow Tate to open the door.

"Hey, Tate," yelled BoBo, one of the cameramen, "I think Moonpie's looking for you. He was barking and whining and scratching at the door of your camper. I let him out on his leash a little while ago, and he peed, but he still hadn't settled down."

"Thanks, BoBo," Tate called. "But it's not a camper. It's a travel trailer." He hurried toward the Vagabond, and while he was still a dozen yards away he could hear the dog's whimpers.

"Hey, buddy," he said, standing outside the Vagabond's screened door. "Settle down. I'm coming."

As soon as he opened the door, the dog jumped down and sprang up and planted his paws on Tate's chest.

"Hey, now," Tate said, ruffling the dog's ears. "I'm back. What's all the fuss about?"

Tate sank down into a lawn chair under the awning, and the dog hopped up into his lap.

"Cute," Val said, ducking under the awning. She set the plates of food down on the top of a folding aluminum table and pulled up another chair alongside it.

"Mmm," she said, after her first taste.

In an instant, Moonpie was off Tate's lap and crouching down at Val's feet.

"Don't even think about it," Val said, poking the dog with the pointed toe of her shoe. "Bad Moonpie."

The dog whined softly. Val licked her fingers and held the plate out to Tate.

Reluctantly, he picked up a shrimp, dipped it in the remoulade, and chewed thoughtfully. Wiping his hands on the napkin that had covered the plate, he took another shrimp, hoping that the first had been a fluke.

It wasn't. In fact, the second taste revealed yet another subtle layer of flavors. He tossed a shrimp to Moonpie, who caught it in midair.

"So much for her piddly little regional television show," Tate said ruefully.

"What's that?" Val asked, between bites.

"Regina Foxton," he said. "I met her in the makeup room this morning. She obviously knew who I was, that I was the competition. When I asked her what she did, she just said she had some little sorry-ass regional show."

"She's right. It is sorry-ass," Val said. "Did you see that set? It's held together with duct tape and chewing gum."

"Doesn't matter," Tate said glumly. He pointed to his plate. "This is what matters. We're screwed."

Val kept chewing. The pile of discarded shrimp tails grew on her pilfered plate. She picked up one of the thin slices of lemon that was tossed in with the peppery pink shrimp, and sucked on it.

"So we don't do shrimp for today's show," she said finally. "What's plan B?"

"You tell me," Tate said, using his fingertips to dip into the apple slaw. "I can't fry shellcrackers for these guys. Not after they've seen that and tasted that incredible flounder of hers."

He licked his lips, and then his fingertips, then scooped up another mouthful of the slaw.

"Damn," he said, when he'd finished chewing. "Sour cream instead of mayonnaise for the slaw dressing. With apple cider vinegar. And slivers of fresh mint. Damn."

"Too precious," Val said dismissively. "Can you imagine what your fans would say if you suggested they use something besides good old cabbage for cole slaw?"

Finishing up the last of the shrimp, Valerie moved on to the pound cake with her usual efficiency.

Tate reached over and pinched off a corner of the cake, tossing it into his mouth, savoring the immediate lemon rush.

"Amazing," he said finally. "My granny made lemon pound cake, and I thought hers was the best I'd ever tasted. Until just now."

"So go back to Possum Trot and smack your granny," Val said.

"She's dead," Tate said.

"Whatever."

"And I'm from Pahokee, not Possum Trot."

"Tell me something new," Val said, yawning. "Like what we're going to do about today's show."

"Not fish, that's for damned sure."

"Fish is exactly what you are going to do," Val said. "It's too late to change the show now. We don't have time to shop and rewrite, and anyway, the crew's been working on prepping everything all morning. Not to mention the fact that I don't intend to waste that gorgeous footage we shot of you yesterday."

Tate shook his head. "We'll look like rubes next to that show Regina just shot."

"Not at all," Valerie insisted. She leaned closer to Tate and took his hands in hers. "Look at me," she said, squeezing tightly.

"I am. You've got a little green thing on your tooth. I think it's maybe a piece of mint."

"Funny," she said, running her tongue across her teeth.

"It's gone now," he said.

"Seriously," she said. "I want you to look at me and listen closely. No more funny business. Do you remember what you told me the night we met in that bar down in Costa Rica?"

"That I would have won the fishing tournament if the damned airline hadn't lost my tackle box with all my good-luck rigs," Tate said promptly. "And that wasn't a lie. You can't win a billfish tournament using borrowed equipment, I don't care how good you are."

"What else did you tell me?"

He thought about it. "That you were the most beautiful woman I'd ever met, and my roommate was passed out drunk back at the dock, and that you'd never made love until you'd done it in a hammock?"

"Speaking of semi-true," she said dryly. "But that's not what I'm talking about. I'm talking about what you said you wanted out of life."

"Oh. That."

She dropped his hands and pushed her chair away. "You remember?"

"I'd been hittin' the *cerveza* pretty heavy. I remember that part. And I remember you turning down my offer of the hammock."

"You're starting to piss me off," she warned, looking at her watch. "And we don't have a lot of time to waste right now."

"Okay," he said with a sigh. "I told you the only thing I really wanted out of life was a life—a real life, spent outdoors, doing things I was passionate about. Fishing, hunting, a good dog, a good woman. Like that."

"And I told you?"

"You told me I could have it all, if I hired you to produce my show." Tate said. "And if I wanted it bad enough."

"And do you?"

He reached down and ruffled the soft white fur on Moonpie's head. "Yeah. I do."

"Good," she said, standing up. "Then let's go get what we both want. Barry Adelman is down here because he's seen all your shows. He approached us, not the other way around. He sees something he likes in you, Tate. Just like all those girls in the Bargain Mart. And those horny housewives sitting in their Barcaloungers in Birmingham. Not to mention the NASCAR guys. You let me worry about little Suzy Homemaker and her kitchen tricks. You just do what you've been doing. Right?"

"I guess," Tate said. He crumpled up the empty plate and tossed it in the trash barrel by the Vagabond's door. He coaxed the dog inside by tossing him the last bit of fried fish.

"Sorry, buddy," Tate said, fastening the screen. "Time to get back to work."

"Just a minute," Val said. She leaned in close and wiped a trace of sour cream from his upper lip, then unbuttoned the top two buttons on his work shirt. "There," she said, satisfied.

He blushed.

"One more thing," she said, stopping him with a hand on his arm. "No more stalling. Tomorrow you go see D'John, and let him work his magic."

Chapter 11

Tate felt himself relax as soon as he heard the
Vittles theme music piped through the studio. He
ignored Barry Adelman and his unnamed assistant and
gazed steadily into the camera, doing the same thing
he'd done that first time Valerie Foster aimed her hand-
held camcorder at him on that beach in Costa Rica.

He grinned easily—as easily, Val said, as if he were
talking to his mama and daddy, down in Pahokee,
Florida.

In fact, that's how she'd instructed him to start the
show. "Don't think about talking to an audience," she'd
suggested. "Just think about talking to your folks."

"Hi, Mama, hi, Daddy," he'd always say at the start
of every show, flashing his dimples, as if to say, "Look
at your boy now."

His viewers loved that kind of cornpone stuff, according to Val. And the smiling and the dimpling came easy to him, just as most things in his life did.

"Today," he said, once the theme music faded, "I'm going to take you with me, out to a little lake just outside—"

"No," Val called.

The cameraman glanced over at her.

"Today, Moonpie 'n' me are gonna take y'all to a little bitty ol' lake," Val coached, laying on her version of a phony southern accent that set his teeth on edge.

Tate's grin disappeared. "I'm not illiterate," he said evenly.

"I'd never suggest you were," Val agreed. "You're just folksy, okay?"

He shook his head and frowned. But Val winked and gave an almost imperceptible nod in the direction of Adelman, who was seated right beside her at the editing table.

"Folksy," Tate said finally.

"Just pick it up with the lake bit," Val said. "And while you're at it, go ahead and walk over to the fridge while you're talking, and get out the dish with the fish fillets."

"The fillets are right here on the counter," Tate said, pointing to them.

"Well, I want them in the fridge. It's too static and boring having you just stand there like that. Could you do that for me, please?"

"There's a dish of fillets already in the fridge," offered Darryl, the prep chef. "Do you want them already soaking in the buttermilk? Or, we could have him add the milk on camera?"

"Let's have him mix up the buttermilk and . . . what goes in it?" she asked, looking down at her notes.

"Hot sauce," Darryl said, holding up a bottle of Texas Pete.

"Right," Val said. "Yes. Let's have him do all of that on camera. We're cutting the shrimp segment we'd planned, so we can afford to have him stretch out the fish fry a little bit."

"No shrimp?" Darryl's thin face darkened. "When was that decided?"

"Just now," Val said firmly, letting him know the subject was closed. "Tate, just take all the steps slowly. You know, pour the buttermilk, add the hot sauce, like that."

"All right," Tate said.

"You can blather on about the stone-ground cornmeal, and what to substitute if you don't have cornmeal or buttermilk—"

"If you don't have the buttermilk or cornmeal, you oughta just forget the whole thing, and go to Captain D's," Tate said.

"But if we're going to eat fast food, we don't need *Vittles*, now, do we, sweetie?"

"Right," Tate said. He leaned against the counter and watched as Darryl poured vegetable oil into the deep-fat fryer.

"How long do I have before that thing starts sputterin' and smokin'?" he asked.

"Five or six minutes," Darryl said. "And don't forget to check the temperature gauge before you submerge the basket with the battered fillets," Darryl said. "According to the manufacturer, you want it right at 425 degrees."

"Good point," Val said. "Make sure you tell what the oil temperature should be when frying fish, even if you're just using whatever pan you have at home."

"Like a cast-iron skillet," Tate said.

"Perfect." Val beamed. "In fact, say something like that. You know, like, 'Mama, this new fryer's great, but it'll never beat your old cast-iron skillet at home.' "

"My mother never fries anything," Tate said. "I don't think she even owns a cast-iron skillet."

"Keep that to yourself," Val advised. "The point you want to make is that kitchen safety is right up there with God and country at Tate Moody's house."

"Trailer," Tate said.

"Whatever," she said. "Let's get this show moving."

Chapter 12

That's it, everybody," Scott said, after they'd finally finished with the setup shots for the next day's show. It was close to six, and the crew had been working steadily since eight. Adelman and his assistant had slipped away much earlier in the afternoon, but Regina felt as if she'd completed a triathlon.

She slipped out of her shoes and reached down to massage her aching calves. At the start of the new season, Scott had insisted that she wear heels for the show because he said it made her look sexier.

"The viewers at home can't see my legs," she'd pointed out.

"No, but the heels make you two inches taller, and they make your boobs look bigger," Scott said.

She'd looked down at her chest, her feelings hurt.

"You know what I mean," Scott said quickly. "The heels accentuate what you've already got. And that's a good thing."

Gina watched now as Scott, standing behind the editing table, chatted with Deborah Chen, the station's publicist. His blond hair contrasted sharply with her shining, blue-black, shoulder-length hair. She laughed at something he said and pretended to slap his face. Scott looked away and caught Regina watching.

Gina looked indifferent. Or at least, she hoped she looked indifferent. Or insouciant. Gina longed to be insouciant. For now, she tucked the hated high heels under her arm and padded, barefoot, toward her office.

"Great show," Scott said as she walked past, intent on ignoring him. "Adelman loved you."

"He's nuts for you, Gina," Deborah agreed. "He asked me to have a bunch of color publicity stills shot of you tomorrow."

"He did?" Despite her indifferent insouciance, Gina felt her pulse blip.

"Absolutely," Deborah said. "I was just telling Scott, be sure you wear something really neutral tomorrow."

"Neutral?" Regina frowned. "Won't that make my skin and hair look washed out?"

"Not at all," Deborah assured her.

"Hey," Scott said. "Why don't we go catch some dinner and talk it over? If we leave now, I know we can get a table at LaGrotto. I'll call Gino and tell him it'll be the three of us."

"LaGrotto! Yum!" Deborah said. "Are we celebrating already?"

"I don't see why not," Scott said. "I snuck over to the *Vittles* set and watched Tate Moody for a little while this afternoon. I thought Adelman looked bored out of his gourd. I don't think Moody is gonna be towing that double-wide of his to Manhattan any time soon. How 'bout it, Geen?"

"No, thanks," Gina said quietly. "Remember? You told D'John I need to be blonder if I'm going for national exposure? He's going to put the color on tonight."

Deborah looked from Gina to Scott, trying to assess the situation.

"Oh?" she said.

"But don't let that stop you two," Gina said. She wondered what was up with Scott and Deborah Chen. Was he sleeping with every woman in Atlanta? And how had she not noticed before how chummy the two of them had gotten?

"Another time, then," Deborah said.

"Maybe," Gina said. She was getting good at feigning indifference, she thought.

Walking out through the studio's now deserted reception area, Gina realized, when she caught sight of the deepening sky, that she hadn't seen daylight since leaving the town house early this morning.

Morningstar Studios was more glamorous sounding than it was in reality. Located in what had once been a gritty warehouse district off Monroe Drive, in the shadow of the Interstate 85 overpass, the studio, formerly a commercial printing plant, was nothing more than a shoebox-shaped cinder-block affair. The studios took up half the building, and the other tenants consisted of three or four photographers, a caterer, and a wholesale florist.

It was early July, but a faint chill hung in the early evening air. From the clump of pine trees at the far edge of the parking lot, Gina could hear the hum of cicadas, and when she inhaled, she smelled the honeysuckle that grew on the parking lot fence. She was glad of the light cotton sweater she'd thrown on over her sleeveless tank.

The parking lot was mostly empty, with the exception of a dozen cars parked near the far end of the studio, where she saw the glint of sunlight on an odd-looking vehicle.

She walked on past her own car, and toward the vehicle. She passed a crudely lettered sign that read

Vittles with an arrow pointing toward a pair of doors to the studio. As she got closer, she saw that the vehicle was a vintage travel trailer, with quilted aluminum siding and a shape reminiscent of a canned ham. Was this the double-wide that Scott had been referring to? Did Tate Moody really live here?

As she got closer, she could hear . . . something. A high, plaintive keening.

Quickening her step, she bypassed the double doors that led back toward the *Vittles* set and followed the sound.

Now the trailer was directly in front of her. It was hooked up to a gleaming red pickup truck—an old Ford—the kind with the humpback wheel wells and varnished wood truck bed. The gleaming red paint of the pickup truck drew her like a beacon, and in the slanted rays of the late afternoon sun, the highly polished aluminum trailer reminded her of some kind of magic bullet.

But what was that sound?

A blue awning extended over the door to the trailer, leaving it in deep shadows, but as she got closer, she could see that the trailer's aluminum outer door was propped open, leaving a screen door exposed.

Now the keening subsided, and she saw a shape, a medium-size dog—white, with big caramel-colored patches over each eye, and floppy, feathery ears, standing on his hind legs, pawing frantically at the screened door.

"Hey there," she cried, rushing over. "Hey there, sweetheart."

In answer, the dog threw itself against the door, fell over backward, then scrambled back to his former position, tail wagging a mile a minute.

"Poor baby," she crooned, putting her hand up against the screen. The dog licked her hand through the screen, and her heart melted.

She looked around. Nobody was in sight, and clearly, this poor penned-up creature was in dire straits.

"Did the bad man go off and leave you all alone?" she asked, in a singsong, babyish voice.

In response, the dog hurled himself again at the door. He stood up, a little wobbly-legged this time.

She tried the door, but it wouldn't budge. She grasped the handle again and yanked, hard.

The door flew open, and the dog shot out like a rocket.

"Whoa!" Regina cried. The dog ran over to one of the pine trees, lifted his leg, and relieved himself, taking what seemed to her at least five minutes.

"Poor thing," she said again. "I'll bet you were about to explode in there."

When the dog was done, he trotted over to Regina.

"Good boy," she said encouragingly. "Come on. Let's get you back inside."

The dog cocked his head to one side, and she could have sworn he winked at her. She took a step forward, one hand extended, as though she had a delicious treat to offer him.

When she was within a foot of the dog, she reached out to grab his collar, and without warning, the dog took off.

"Hey," she called, as he zoomed across the asphalt. "Come back!"

He appeared to be headed straight for the double doors leading to the *Vittles* set, and he was barking his head off, as if to tell his master he was coming home.

One of the doors opened, and the dog ran inside.

Chapter 13

Tate was demonstrating his grandmother's method for seasoning a cast-iron skillet.

"BoBo, pull the camera in as close as you can get on that," Valerie instructed. "Tate, turn your wrist and look into the camera."

"I'm not double-jointed, Val," Tate griped.

Just then, a medium-size bundle of white-and-brown fur burst onto the set, propped his front paws on the kitchen counter, and snatched the basket of hush puppies that had just come out of the deep fryer.

"Son of a bitch," BoBo hollered as the dog streaked past, spilling the boiling hot fritters all over the floor.

"Moonpie!" Tate yelled, dropping the skillet.

"Cut!" Val screamed. "Cut, damn it."

Beside her at the editing table, she could swear she heard Zeke, the silent assistant, snigger.

"Tate, get that damned dog out of here," Val ordered.

Having managed to corner the English setter beneath the set's rustic kitchen table, Tate was holding out a bit of fried shellcracker, trying to lure the dog out.

"I didn't let him in," Tate said. "Last time I checked, he was locked up safe and sound in the trailer."

"Well, somebody let him in," the producer said waspishly. "And he's just destroyed the swap-out for the hush puppies."

"Get the girls to fix some more," Tate said, just as waspishly. "It's only cornmeal and buttermilk, for Pete's sake."

"Connie?" Val's head swiveled in the direction of her prep cook. "How long will that take?"

The heavyset black woman wiped her face with the edge of her white apron. "It'll take a while. We don't have any more cornmeal. I'll have to send somebody out to get some more."

"For Christ's sake!" Val snapped.

"Here, Moonpie," Tate called softly, attempting to wedge his body under the table. "Come get the nice fish. You love fish. It goes great with hush puppies."

The dog chewed happily on the basket that had contained the fritters and edged backward, away from his master.

"Do dogs like fried fish?" Zeke asked.

"I don't know," Adelman said. "Tate, does that dog of yours like fried fish?"

Tate groaned as he stood up. "Only if I fix it."

Without warning, the dog chose that moment to dash out from under the table, where BoBo, who'd been backing away from the set and the dog, promptly tripped over him, sending his heavy camera clattering to the concrete floor. Moonpie yelped his outrage.

"Christ." Val jumped up from the editing table.

BoBo cradled the camera in his arms like an ailing infant.

Tate's face was ashen. "Is it broken?"

BoBo pointed to the smattering of glass on the floor from the smashed lens. "Kinda."

The producer sat down again and banged her head on the editing table. "This just is not my day. Fuck. Fuck. Fuck."

"Can we . . . get another one?" Tate asked, looking from BoBo to the producer.

"BoBo?" Val gave him a pleading look.

The cameraman stared down at the floor. "It's after six. The rental house we sometimes get equipment from is closed. There's another place, in Nashville. I guess I could give them a call. But even if they're open, and they have one, and they overnighted it to us, we still wouldn't get it till tomorrow at the earliest."

"Call 'em," she said, her lips pressed together in a grim white line. "But in the meantime, get that fucking dog the fuck out of here!"

As if on cue, Moonpie, who was now cowering at Tate's feet, looked up and whined.

"Come on, boy," Tate said softly, grasping him by the collar. "Time to go home."

Instead of trotting along obediently beside his master, as he would have done any other time, the setter decided to do what setters do. He sat, planting his haunches firmly on the concrete floor.

"Moonpie," Tate said, his teeth clenched. "Heel!"

The dog sat.

"Dammit, Moonpie," Tate whispered. Finally, he bent down and gathered the sixty-pound dog into his arms and staggered toward the studio's rear door. He opened it, stepped outside into the dying sunlight, and ran directly into Regina Foxton.

Her face was pink with embarrassment. "Oh!" she said, taking a step backward. "You caught the dog. Good. I was afraid—"

She stopped, seeing the look on Tate's face.

"You did this?" he asked. "You let him out of the trailer? Why would you do something like that?"

"He was howling," she said, taking another step backward. "Scratching at the door to your trailer. He was frantic. I was just going to let him go to the bathroom. But he got away from me. He ran, and I couldn't catch him. And then somebody opened the door from inside the studio and let him in. And it was locked. So I couldn't go after him—"

"You just shut down my show," Tate said, interrupting her. "Big coincidence, huh? The guys from the network are down, taking a look at both our shows. Yours goes just fine. Wonderful. Then they step over to watch *Vittles,* and all of a sudden, my dog gets let into the studio, and all hell breaks loose."

"I didn't intentionally let him in," Gina protested. "I told you, it was an accident."

Tate was crossing the asphalt parking lot in the direction of his trailer at a rapid clip, with Regina trailing behind.

"Oh," he said, abruptly turning around to face her. "Oh, it was an accident," he said, his voice mocking. "That makes it all right that my cameraman tripped over him and dropped and smashed a camera that can't be replaced. All with Barry Adelman and his sidekick sitting there watching."

"Hey!" she said sharply. She ran up beside him and tugged at his arm. "What are you implying? That I deliberately let the dog out to sabotage your show? To make you look bad and me look good?"

He didn't turn and he didn't look at her, he just kept stalking toward his trailer. "That's what happened, isn't it?"

She stopped and planted her aching feet on the still-hot asphalt. "Just a minute, mister," she hollered. "You wait just one dadgummed minute."

Chapter 14

BoBo looked up from the cell phone he'd been hunched over for the past thirty minutes, furiously speed-dialing every professional contact in the phone's memory.

"Uh, Val?"

She looked up from the laptop, hands pressed together as if in prayer.

He shook his head sadly. "Sorry. No go for today. Nothing's available. Not here, or Nashville, not even in New York, until Monday evening at the earliest. You want me to go ahead and have them ship a replacement camera?"

Valerie fumbled desperately on the tabletop for her leather cigarette case. She was down to a pack a day now—and that was with a nicotine patch firmly affixed to each of her upper arms. She shook out one of her ultra-slim menthols, lit up, and inhaled so deeply she seemed to suck all the oxygen from the set.

Exhaling slowly, she nodded through the cloud of smoke wreathed around her head.

Sitting two chairs away, Zeke fanned the air furiously with both hands, making extravagant choking noises. "Really!" he said, pushing his chair away from the table.

Val's eyes narrowed thoughtfully, and she drew deeply from the cigarette again. "Fuck," she said, exhaling at the same time.

BoBo held the phone up, questioning. "So—should I go ahead and tell 'em to ship it? It's the last one they've got."

She reached for her Day Runner, slid out her personal Visa card, and handed it over to her cameraman. "There goes my budget."

She stood up and rubbed the small of her back.

"Okay, everybody," she called loudly. The cameramen, the lighting tech, the sound man, the prep cooks, and the food stylist all stopped and looked expectantly in her direction.

"We're shut down till Monday night. I need everybody back here at four o'clock, no later. Everybody got that?"

The crew gave a collective groan and immediately started to clear the set of food and equipment.

"And, Connie," Val said, her voice rising.

"I know, I know," Connie said, stacking a tray with the mixing bowls and pans Tate had been using. "Cornmeal. Lots of cornmeal. I'll put it at the top of my shopping list."

"What about the fish?" Val asked. "Can it keep till Monday?"

Connie rolled her dark eyes in answer. "Sure. If you want to stink up the whole studio cooking nasty three-day-old fish, be my guest. But don't ask me to cook that mess."

Zeke sniggered.

Val shot him a look. She put her hands on her hips now, mirroring her prep chef's defensive stance.

"Well, what do you suggest? Do we have any more fillets in the freezer?"

"Nuh-uh," Connie said. "Tate fried up everything he caught. Guess you'll just have to send him back out to that pond to catch another mess of fish."

Val frowned. She knew her star's weekend plans, and was well aware that he wasn't planning another fishing trip.

"We can't use another kind of fish as a stand-in?"

Connie frowned and crossed her arms over her chest. "Tate'll be able to tell. And you know how he is about that kind of shit. I'm not gonna be the one to hand him a plate of trout or bass fillets when the recipe clearly says we're cooking shellcracker."

"You leave Tate to me," Val said. "Just do me a favor. Call all your seafood dealers and see what they can come up with that looks like shellcracker. We can use the earlier footage of Tate dipping it in the breading, and nobody will see a thing. Just call me at home tonight, and let me know what you found."

Connie pursed her lips, picked up the tray, and stomped off the set, muttering as she went. "I'm not callin' Atlantic Seafood and askin' them if they got what I know they ain't got. . . ."

Val turned and gave Barry Adelman and his assistant a weak smile.

"Food divas," she said, adding an expressive shrug. "I'm sure you deal with this kind of thing all the time in New York."

Adelman nodded without saying anything, his pen busy jotting something on a yellow Post-it note, which he promptly pressed to the sleeve of his assistant's shirt.

In fact, now that she was standing right in front of him, she could see that Zeke's shirt seemed to be generously papered with a small forest of yellow stickies.

"I'm really sorry about today," Val said, trying not to stare at Zeke. "I hope you won't think your trip was wasted. This was just one of those days. And about the dog . . . what can I say?"

She flicked a long ash onto the floor. "It was inexcusable. I'm going to have a talk with Tate. I myself am a *huge* animal lover. But, well, Moonpie—let's just say he's uncontrollable. I told Tate—"

Barry Adelman leaned over and plucked a Post-it note from a spot directly under Zeke's Adam's apple, and handed it to her.

She read it aloud. "Dog = awesome."

Adelman nodded. "That dog is a natural."

He paused and looked around to see if anyone else was listening. Everyone else, of course, was rushing around trying to make their escape for the weekend.

Lowering his voice, Adelman went on. "I'm not really in a position to tell you this. I mean, it'd be very premature . . ."

Val batted her eyelashes and moved closer to the executive. "Anything you tell me would be totally confidential, Barry."

"Zeke!" he said, snapping his fingers.

His assistant sprang to his feet.

Adelman scanned Zeke's chest, finally picking a slip of paper from the assistant's right shoulder. He smiled coyly and handed it to Valerie.

"Sponsorship tie-in?" she read.

"Exactly," Adelman said.

Valerie wondered what she should gather from this cryptic exchange. Should she hazard a guess? But if she guessed wrong, would Adelman think her some kind of mental defective?

"Ahh," she said finally.

"Dog food," Zeke said, in a conspiratorial whisper.

"Riiight," Val said, grinning. "Of course. It's funny you should mention that. Because I happen to know that the ChowHound folks are looking to launch a whole new ad campaign in the fall. They're crazy to have Tate endorse their premium dog-food line. There's even talk of using Moonpie in some of the ads."

This, of course, was a blatant lie. There was no such talk that Val knew of. ChowHound's corporate offices were located in Atlanta, it was true. Like everybody else in town, she'd stopped and stared at the eight-story headquarters building in Midtown that was shaped like a giant red fire hydrant. But she'd never even met anybody from ChowHound. Still, that could all change. It would change, she vowed to herself.

"Pet-care products," Zeke added knowledgeably, plucking a Post-it from directly above his left nipple. He read aloud from it. "Thirty-eight billion dollars last year."

"My thoughts exactly," Val said, almost purring. "And that's only one of the sponsorship opportunities we see for Tate and Moonpie. Once they're in a national venue. That's why I was hoping we could have dinner this evening. I know Tate is dying to have some one-on-one time with you."

"Hmmm," Adelman said. He looked at his watch, and then at Zeke.

"Can't," Zeke said, handing his boss a yellow Post-it clinging near his left wrist. "Flight's at eight."

"Next time," Adelman said.

Zeke packed up his bulging leather messenger bag and Adelman's laptop case.

"But what about the show?" Val sputtered. "You really didn't get to see what Tate can do."

"We saw," Adelman said. "I'll be in touch. In the meantime, send me that footage of the dog stealing the food, would you?"

"Sure," Val said. As she watched the men walk off, she flung her cigarette to the floor and stubbed it out.

Adelman turned, and Val visibly brightened.

"Just what kind of dog is he?" he called. She could see Zeke's pen poised above the pad of Post-its.

Val had to think fast. "He's a setter," she said. "A Landrover setter. Very rare breed. Tate has the only one in the state."

Chapter 15

Tate whirled around to face Regina, and Moonpie squirmed in his arms.

This woman was truly starting to get on his nerves. At least, he thought smugly, he knew now that she was no threat to his own career ambitions. He had never seen anybody who looked less like a potential network television star. The carefully arranged hairstyle he'd seen created just that morning was now a distant memory. Perspiration plastered her light-brown hair to her forehead. There were dark mascara smudges under both eyes, and a trace of what he guessed was either flour or powdered sugar on her forehead. Also not to mention that she was barefoot and that the neckline of her sleeveless top showed a much more tantalizing view of her cleavage than she surely intended.

"Mister?" he repeated, his voice mocking. "Did you just call me 'mister'? Where the hell are you from, Reggie?"

"Odum, Georgia," she snapped. "Not that it's any of your business. And don't call me Reggie."

"Why not? You don't look anything like a Regina."

She frowned. "Nonetheless, that's the name my mama and daddy gave me. My friends call me Gina. You, however, may call me Regina, if you have to call me anything at all."

"Okay, RE-gina," he said, purposely emphasizing the first syllable. "Excuse me, but now that you've ruined my show and made me look like an idiot to Barry Adelman and his associate, I've got to put my dog back in the trailer. And then I've got someplace I need to be."

He turned and resumed his trek to the trailer, but now she was hot on his heels again.

"I'm sorry about your camera. Truly, I am. But I did *not* sabotage your show," she said, out of breath from trying to keep up with him. "I would never do something like that."

"Because you're such a Girl Scout," he said sarcastically.

That stopped her for a moment.

"I don't like your tone," she called. "And another thing. Stay away from my set when I'm taping from now on."

He turned around again, tightening his grip on Moonpie as a precaution, because the dumb animal seemed determined to rejoin his new friend. Regina Foxton stood in the parking lot with her hands on her hips, glaring daggers in his direction.

"You mean your piddly little regional show? Why shouldn't I watch? Do I make you nervous?"

"No!" she lied. "I just don't want you stealing any of my recipes," she said finally.

"As if."

That really seemed to fire her rockets. She ran right up to him, her jaw clenched in outrage, and Moonpie, the traitor, wriggled in his arms and wagged an enthusiastic greeting.

"So it's a coincidence that you saw me shooting my seafood episode this morning, and then, this afternoon—magically—you happen to also tape a seafood show with Barry Adelman sitting right there in the studio."

She was definitely right up in his face. So close, in fact, that Moonpie stretched out his head and gave her a big sloppy slurp in the face.

He expected her to scream, or jump backward, but the dog's affection seemed to have a softening affect on her. She laughed and scratched his chin, setting off another spasm of heavy breathing and tail wagging—by Moonpie.

"Hey, buddy," she crooned, letting the dog continue his disgusting display of affection. "I like you too. It's not your fault your owner is a big ol' butthead."

"Nice language from a Girl Scout," Tate said.

She continued to ignore him, and to lavish attention on Moonpie.

"What's his name?' she asked.

"Moonpie," Tate said coldly.

"What kind of dog is he? A Brittany spaniel?"

"He's an English setter," Tate said. "Actually, if you want to get technical, he's a Llewellen setter. Are you done now?"

She flicked him a look. "With you, yes."

"It's a hunting and fishing show," he said, desperately needing to have the last word.

"What?"

"*Vittles*," Tate said. "My show."

"Oh, yes," she said dismissively. "So I heard. Kill it and grill it. I get it."

"I cook seafood all the time," Tate insisted. "Today's show was scripted weeks ago. We taped the fishing portion earlier in the week. So, obviously, there was no way I copied your idea."

"If you say so," she said. She gave Moonpie a farewell pat on the head, turned, and walked away, head held high.

Chapter 16

When Gina got home, Lisa met her at the door. She was wearing a vaguely familiar looking, too-tight, low-cut lime green T-shirt and a pair of gray gym shorts with the waistband rolled down around her hips, and the words "POP TART" emblazoned right across her butt cheeks.

"How'd it go?" she asked. "Did those Cooking Channel guys love you? When do you find out if you get the show? Do you want a glass of wine? I bought a bottle of that chardonnay you like. You owe me six bucks."

Regina stashed her laptop on a console table near the door, and allowed herself to collapse into the nearest armchair.

"Is that my shirt?" she asked pointedly.

"Huh? I guess."

"Except that when it belonged to me I seem to remember it had sleeves," Gina said. "And a neckband that did not threaten to expose my boobs to the whole world."

"Yeah. I fixed it for you," Lisa said, twirling around. "Better now, huh? You weren't going to wear it tonight, were you?"

"Never again," Gina assured her. "And how do you know anything about The Cooking Channel?"

"Hello?" Lisa said. "D'John called here looking for you. He filled me in on everything."

"Everything?" Gina asked, dreading the answer.

"All of it," Lisa assured her. "So, Scott was boinking the sponsor's wife? Right under your nose? And he got your show canceled? How trashy is that?"

"Pretty darned trashy," Gina said wearily. "Look, can we not talk about Scott tonight? I am just whipped."

"Okay," Lisa said. "Let's talk about The Cooking Channel. It's a big deal, right?"

"Very big," Gina admitted. "It's what I've been dreaming of since I started writing about food. TCC is only eight years old, and they have ninety million viewers. You know Peggy Paul, that woman who does all the cooking segments on Oprah? She had a little mom-and-pop restaurant in Birmingham. One of Oprah's producers had dinner there one night, and she liked the barbecue so much, she had them overnight ten pounds of it back to Oprah in Chicago the next day. Peggy Paul did one guest shot on Oprah, and within a month she had a cookbook deal with a major publisher, and TCC signed her up even before it came out. Now Peggy Paul has had the number-one best-selling cookbook on the best-seller lists for two years in a row."

"Good, huh? But your cookbook was on the best-seller list too," Lisa said loyally.

"Only a regional best seller," Gina said.

"D'John says you shouldn't worry about getting the new show," Lisa said, plopping down onto the carpet next to Gina's chair. "He says you're a lock."

Gina managed a smile. "He might be a little bit prejudiced. Anyway, it's not a sure thing at all. They do want to add a southern cooking show, but there's another guy in the running."

"No way."

"Way," Gina assured her.

"Who is the turkey?" Lisa asked.

"Nobody you've ever heard of," Gina said. "He does a show called *Vittles*, of all things."

"Oh, my God," Lisa shrieked. "Are you talking about Tate Moody? *The* Tate Moody?"

Gina stared at her sister. "You're saying you know about him? Since when do you watch cooking shows? You don't even watch mine, and I pay the rent around here."

"Everybody I know watches the Tatester," Lisa said unapologetically. "He rocks. In fact, Southern Outdoors rocks. My friends have parties to watch those shows. Like, Andy? This friend of mine? He's in my calculus class? His favorite show is *The Buck Stops Here*. And Sarah? You met her. She loves *Kickin' Bass*. But everybody's favorite is *Vittles*."

Lisa scrambled to her feet, went to her room, and came back with a DVD.

"A bunch of us went in together and bought the first season of *Vittles*, and then Sarah bootlegged copies for all of us."

"I don't believe this," Gina said, holding the DVD gingerly by the fingertips. "My baby sister, who can't even make microwave popcorn without burning it, watches a television cooking show. A show about killing animals, cutting them up, and cooking them. Tell me this. Are any of the recipes he does on his show even remotely edible?"

"Who knows?" Lisa said cheerfully. "He could make Kool-Aid and peanut butter sandwiches and I'd watch. I'm tellin' you, Geen, the Tatester is hot. Not just hot. Smokin' hot. Make sure you watch episode three. That one's my all-time favorite. He's like, on a boat, down on the Gulf Coast, throwing this cast net . . ."

She rolled her eyes and licked her lips. "Without a shirt. Check out the six-pack." She fanned herself with both hands and grinned. "I just totally had an orgasm thinking about it."

Gina stared at her younger sister. "Lisa, that is the crudest, most pathetic thing I have ever heard of."

"Don't knock it if you haven't tried it," Lisa said.

"I think I'll pass," Gina said. "Anyway, I've got to get changed and get over to D'John's."

"Oh, my God," Lisa said. "D'John is so awesome. I love his place. And he always gives me samples of the coolest makeup and stuff. Lemme go too, okay?"

"Deal," Gina said. "Just one thing."

"What now?"

"While I'm in the shower, you change your clothes. We are not leaving these premises with you dressed like some hoochie-mama."

"D'John's gay, Geen," Lisa said. "He *so* is not looking at me that way."

"And I am *so* not going anywhere with you until you put on something to cover your butt cheeks."

Gina had just turned onto Cheshire Bridge Road when she heard the high thin wail. *AAARRRRR.*

She jerked the steering wheel hard right and pulled over the concrete curbing and into the parking lot of a seedy bar with painted-over windows.

"Whoa! What are you doing?" Lisa asked. "D'John's place is two blocks down."

Gina half turned in her seat to look down the street. "Police car. State law says you have to get completely out of the way for an emergency vehicle."

She heard the siren again, but frowned when she couldn't see any flashing lights.

Lisa rolled onto one hip and held up her cell phone.

AAARRRR. The incoming call light flashed off and on.

"Here's your emergency," Lisa said, handing the phone to Gina.

"What in the world?"

"Don't hit the talk button unless you wanna talk to Mama," Lisa warned. "That's her ring tone."

"Lisa! Gina choked back a laugh. "That's awful."

"No. It's efficient. This way, I know without even looking at the readout when Mama's calling. So if I'm at a party or a noisy club, I don't pick up. Saves us both a lot of heartache."

Gina waited a minute, and then punched the button to listen to the message Birdelle surely had left.

"Hello? This is Mrs. Birdelle Foxton, calling for Lisa. Lisa? Is this you? I'm getting kind of worried, honey, because you haven't returned any of my calls all week. And I haven't heard from Gina, either. Anyway, I did want to let you know that I saw that precious Tiffany Tappley last week at church. Well, of course, she's Tiffany Dugger now. She married one of the Duggers from Hazlehurst. He does something for the government. She had the sweetest little boy. I forget his name. And she told me to be sure and tell you to call her next time you're home. Well, that's all for now, honey. You be sweet, you hear?"

Gina pressed the end button and pulled the Honda back onto Cheshire Bridge Road.

"Did you know a girl from home named Tiffany Tappley?" she asked. "Because Mama saw her at church and got the whole rundown on her, and she wants you to be sure to call her when you're home again."

"Tiffany Tappley? That slut? I can't believe she had the nerve to set foot inside a church," Lisa said.

"Well, she did, and Mama got the whole report. You can listen to her message if you want to catch up with good ol' Tiff."

"No thanks," Lisa said. "I haven't talked to good ol' Tiff since she got knocked up at the end of eighth grade."

"Good news," Gina said, turning into the parking lot for D'John's apartment. "She's married to one of the Duggers from Hazlehurst. According to Mama, he's got one of those good government jobs."

"She must be talking about Tommy Dugger. He inspects hog feed for the State Department of Agriculture." Lisa sighed. "Mama thinks that's a great job because he brings home free peanuts that aren't good enough to feed to hogs."

"Eew," Gina said.

"And you wonder why I never return her calls," Lisa said, getting out of the car.

D'John emerged from his kitchen wearing a spotless starched white lab coat with "Dr. Evil" embroidered over the left breast. It was a hot spring night, so he was bare-chested and wearing loose white cotton drawstring pants and white rubber clogs.

Regina eyed the plastic mixing bowl he carried in both hands. She was seated in a high-backed bar stool in D'John's tangerine-painted dining room, wrapped in a matching tangerine-colored plastic cape.

"Just how blond are you taking me?" she asked.

"Geeeeen," Lisa managed, from between lips tightly drawn by the herbal mud mask D'John had applied to her face. "He's a genius. You have to trust him."

D'John blew the baby sister a kiss, and she nodded her receipt. He couldn't wait to complete his work on the braver of the two Foxton sisters. Already he'd cut her hair in a daring jagged bob he'd proclaimed was "Metallica meets Dorothy Hamill." Next up for Lisa, he thought, would be some yummy aubergine highlights.

But in the meantime, Miss Regina was having second thoughts.

"How blond?" she repeated.

Before she could resist, he snapped on a pair of thin latex gloves and quickly began applying the bright gold goo to her hair.

"D'John?"

"Well"—he pursed his lips in thought—"Scott wants you way blonder. This is my own formulation, and I haven't really given it a name yet. I'd say your new color is less slutty than platinum, and more intellectual-looking than a honey blond. Let's just say it's somewhere between Marilyn Monroe in *Some Like It Hot* and Lauren Bacall in *Key Largo*."

"Huh?" Lisa managed. Her idea of a classic movie was *Dude, Where's My Car?*

Regina sighed. "I think he's trying to say that when he gets done with me, I'm going to look like a somewhat brainy bimbo."

"Dingbat!" D'John cried. "I'll call it Dingbat Blond. Oooh. I've got to write down my formulation, because once your public gets a look at your hair, I am going to become Hollywood famous."

"Cool," Lisa said. She plugged her ears with her iPod's buds and immediately began bopping to her own secret beat.

"You'll be fabulous," D'John assured Gina, with a pat on her shoulder. "D'John can do no wrong."

Regina took a sip of her wine and sat back while he applied the strong-smelling chemicals. When her entire head was coated with goo, multiple strands of hair had been pasted to long strips of aluminum foil, and her whole head had then been wrapped in plastic like a leftover Sunday roast, D'John wheeled over a menacing-looking machine and lowered the bullet-shaped hood over her head.

He picked up a plastic kitchen timer and set it. "Twenty minutes till magic time."

The doorbell rang. "That'll be Stephen, the takeout boy from Jade Palace, with our dinner," D'John said. "And he is the most luscious little piece of dim sum you have ever seen!"

Gina shook her head in mild disapproval, and D'John opened the door for Stephen, who, to Regina, merely looked like a surly Asian-American young adult with baggy jeans and a straggly soul patch on his chin.

As the two men opened the white cardboard takeout boxes and the plastic containers of egg-drop soup and arranged them on the tabletop, the smell of sizzling pork wafted through the room and Regina's stomach growled.

D'John whispered something to Stephen, who laughed and blushed, and the men stepped into the kitchen.

Gina's stomach growled again, so loudly she was sure the men could hear it.

Quiet, she thought, patting her tummy. She took a long drink of wine and tried to think of something besides food.

Today, for instance. According to Scott, the taping had gone really well. He was a pig, but he did know television production. Barry Adelman had seemed interested in her concept of fresh, accessible southern food. The prep girls said he'd raved over the shrimp during lunch, and he'd even asked her to e-mail the flounder and slaw recipes to him.

But Adelman had hurried away to watch Tate Moody's taping before she really had a chance to chat with him.

The thought of Moody made her scowl. Stupid creep. Catfish-frying, gun-toting pseudo-foodie. The idea that she would ever stoop to dirty tricks to win this slot on TCC made her blood boil. And that poor sweet dog, Moonpie, locked up in that trailer all day. She took another sip of wine and wondered, idly, if Moonpie's invasion really had ruined the taping, as Moody claimed. She really *hadn't* let the dog loose on purpose, so if things had gone badly for Tate Moody, it totally was *not* on her conscience. At least, that's what she tried to tell herself.

Eventually, she put the wineglass down and felt herself relax for the first time all day. Her eyelids fluttered and then closed.

Such a pleasant dream. She was back at her grandparents' farm in Alma, Georgia. She'd spent the morning picking strawberries from Gram's patch. She was barefoot, and the sun-warmed soil squished between her toes as she popped the sugar-sweet berries in her mouth, eating nearly as many as she plunked into her plastic bucket. Gram had baked her a little yellow butter cake in the special tin tart pans she used only for what she called her "pattycakes" while Gina picked, and she was just taking the cakes out of the oven when Gina wandered into the kitchen, berry-stained face and fingers and all.

Gina heard the oven bell dinging as she sat down at the linoleum-topped table to help Gram trim the tops from the berries and sprinkle them with sugar. Now Gram was reaching into the Frigidaire and bringing out the blue bowl heaped full of sweetened whipped cream. She placed each pattycake on one of her treasured pink Depression glass plates, then spooned a mound of berries on top of the cake, ending with big dollops of whipped cream, and then just a few more berries, their bright red juice dribbling down the edges of the cake and pooling onto the pink plates.

Gram and Gina held hands then, and they sang the special blessing they'd learned at Sunday school before digging into their treat.

There would never be anything that tasted better, sweeter, than those cakes. And after they'd cleaned up the dishes, Gina and Gram went out to the porch to play Go Fish.

She was winning, had all the cards facedown on the green-painted porch floor, when someone touched her shoulder.

"Geen?"

Gina opened her eyes. Lisa was standing in front of her, eyes wide. Her mud mask was dried and cracked in about a zillion pieces. In her hands she held a piece of tin foil with a four-inch-long strand of Dingbat Blond hair dangling from it.

"Huh?"

Gina looked down at her lap. Half a dozen more strips of foil were scattered about the tangerine-colored cape, all of them clinging to similar-size strands of Regina Foxton's very own hair.

Regina shrieked. Lisa shrieked. D'John came running into the dining room, and when he saw Gina, his shrieks drowned out theirs.

Only Stephen, the cute takeout boy, did not scream.

"Dude," he whispered. "Dude, that is *not* cool." He turned and ran for the door.

"OHMYGAWD!" D'John cried. He yanked the hood of the processor into the up position "What happened?" Gina asked.

D'John whipped the plastic from her head and yanked her up and out of the chair in an instant. "Quick. Into the kitchen." He dragged her over to the sink, stuck her head under the faucet, and started spraying her hair with water.

"Lisa!" he called. "Bring me that bottle of shampoo from the bathroom. And the conditioner. Stat!"

Regina could see nothing. She could feel first the cold, and then the warm, water streaming over her head. Her neck hurt and she wanted to stand up, but D'John kept his hand firmly planted on the top of her head.

"Precious Jesus," she heard him mutter. "Precious Jesus Lord."

Then he was lathering her head with shampoo, and her scalp felt oddly cool.

When the water stopped running, he stood her upright. For a minute, she felt dizzy. He wrapped a towel around her head, and tenderly dabbed at her face with another one. Now he was dragging her back into the dining room, pushing her gently down into the chair she'd been sitting in.

"We've got to get you conditioned," he said, squirting a huge glop of conditioner into the palm of one hand.

He patted it over her head, gently working it into her scalp, which still felt strange.

"Tell me what's happened," Regina said. "What's happened to my hair?"

She saw Lisa and D'John exchange a shared look of horror.

"Tell me!"

D'John took a deep breath. "The timer," he said, searching for words. "It must have gone off. But I didn't hear it. I was just in the kitchen, talking to Stephen. I guess I lost track of time. Because I didn't hear the buzzer—"

"No," she said flatly. She stood up and ran into the bathroom. There, in the gold-framed mirror in D'John's bathroom, she stood face-to-face with the truth.

Her scalp reminded her of her granddaddy's cornfield come autumn, once the harvest had started. Ragged strands of damp hair stuck up in random hedgerows.

"Precious Lord Jesus," she whispered, echoing D'John. She sat down on the edge of D'John's commode and began to cry.

Chapter 17

You absolutely sure you wanna do this?" Tate asked, shaking his head in disgust.

"Absolutely," Val insisted. "Hit me."

Tate lifted the cast-iron skillet from the tiny two-burner stovetop and deftly slid the fried eggs onto the stack of pancakes on Val's waiting plate.

"Thanks," she said, pouring a stream of maple syrup over everything, and then tucking into it with an energy that amazed him, slicing the eggs with the side of her fork, then curling a whole pancake around the oozing egg and shoving it into her mouth.

It was Sunday morning. Val called this a production meeting. Tate called it a pain in the ass. He poured himself a cup of coffee and sat opposite her at the red Formica dinette table in what he called the dining area of the Vagabond IV. It was also, when the tabletop was flipped down across the button-tufted red leatherette upholstered benches, and a mattress slid atop it, the guest bedroom.

She chewed furiously, then sighed. "Heaven."

Moonpie, wedged tightly beneath Tate's feet, lifted his snout and whined appreciatively.

"Absolutely not," Tate said sternly. "If she wants to eat a heart attack on a plate for breakfast, that's her problem." He scratched the dog's ears as a consolation prize.

As Val ate, Tate read over the notes she'd made about the upcoming week's shoot, pausing occasionally to sip his coffee.

Her plate mopped clean of every vestige of pancake, syrup, and egg, Val brought out a cigarette, lit it, and inhaled deeply.

Tate swiftly reached across the table, took the cigarette from her fingers, and stubbed it out on the plate.

"Hey," she said.

He got up and rinsed the plate in the minuscule stainless-steel kitchen sink, which also doubled as the bathroom sink, which was why there was a small porthole-sized mirror mounted above it.

"I've told you a million times," he said, scrubbing at the caked-on egg. "You can't smoke in the Vagabond.

This is the original mahogany paneling. The original upholstery. It's forty-two years old, and it's pristine. And it's gonna stay that way."

She lifted her head and blew out one defiant smoke ring toward the pristine forty-two-year-old ceiling. "You let the dog in here."

"He doesn't smoke," Tate said. "He gets washed weekly with a hypoallergenic shampoo, and I brush him outside."

"You're the prissiest damn straight man I ever met," Val said, fiddling with her cigarette lighter.

"I'll take that as a compliment," Tate said. He wiped the thick porcelain plate clean and slotted it into the wall-mounted plate rack that topped the kitchen's only cabinet.

"I'll bet you're gonna tell me those are the original plates that came stocked in the original damn kitchen," Val said.

"Nope. According to the owner's manual, the original plates were green melamine. But they were long gone, and besides, I don't like to eat off plastic. I bought these on eBay. They're from a diner in Pontiac, Michigan, called the Chat 'n' Chew. Same town the Vagabond was manufactured in. The diner closed two years after the factory did, which was 1967," Tate said. "So, the original owner could have replaced the dishes that were included with the optional kitchen package. I know I would have."

"And this stuff is of vital importance to you," Val said, rolling her eyes.

"It is," he agreed.

She sighed again. She'd had a long e-mail from Barry Adelman after he got back to New York on Friday night. Or Saturday morning, actually. The e-mail's time stamp indicated it had been sent at 2:30 A.M. Adelman wrote that he'd liked the show, liked what he called Tate's Q-factor, thought the food was fine. But he really, really loooooved the Vagabond. And Moonpie. Which was a fact she intended to keep to herself.

"All right," she said, glancing down at her notes. "I had a call from Connie on the way over here this morning. And you're not going to like what she said."

"Tell me anyway."

"She's gone to every fish market in Atlanta, called everybody she knows. She was able to find some small white fish fillets, but *she* doesn't think they look anything like the shellcracker fillets we started shooting with on Friday. I don't think it's that big a deal. We'll just have to make do. BoBo called, and the replacement camera should get here first thing tomorrow. When we reshoot, we'll just have him cut away to the oil sizzling in the pan, or the already soaked and floured fillets.

Once they're coated in flour, you can't tell whether they're shellcrackers or chicken breasts. So that's what we'll use. Pounded thin chicken breasts."

"What? No. Nuh-uh. No way," Tate said. "No faking. We start that, pretty soon I'm substituting pork loins for venison, and God knows what comes after that."

"Nobody will ever know, Tate," Val said. "Or care."

"I'll know," he said, crossing his arms over his chest. "And I care."

"Fine," she said, tossing her pen onto the tabletop, and matching him glare for glare. "What do you suggest?"

He stood up, put his authentic heavy vitreous china coffee mug in the sink, and rinsed it out.

"Moonpie," he said.

The dog scrambled to his feet.

"Come on, boy," Tate said, opening the Vagabond's screen-fitted door.

"And where do you think you're going?" Val asked. "We've still got the rest of the week's scripts to go over. We need to decide on a dessert to go with the grilled quail breasts you're doing for Tuesday's show, and figure out what you want to do about the shrimp debacle. We really don't have time for the talent to throw a temper tantrum."

"Okay," Tate said. He jerked his head in Val's direction, and then toward the door. "Like you said, time's wasting. Let's roll."

"Roll where?" she asked, reaching for her purse, patting her pocket to make sure she had her cigarettes. She really needed a smoke.

"Cedar Creek," he said, helping her navigate the Vagabond's fold-down steps. "You just said, I need a mess of shellcrackers. Which means we need to get on the creek in the next half hour, before the sun gets too high, and the water heats up too much."

"But the script," Val protested. "We've got so much work to do—"

"We can talk about it on the drive over there," he said.

"I *don't* fish," she said. "I'm Jewish. We're not a fishing people."

"Whatever. You take notes. I'll fish."

An hour later, Tate pushed the twelve-foot aluminum johnboat into the cool brown waters of Cedar Creek. Val sat in the bow, slathered in insect repellent and swaddled in an orange life jacket that seemed to swallow her small frame. Tate sat in the back. Moonpie, panting happily, sat in the middle.

Using the handle of the nearly noiseless electric trolling motor, Tate steered them to a spot half a mile downstream. He cut the motor, sniffed, and nodded his approval. Quickly, he baited a small hook with a worm retrieved from a Styrofoam cup at his feet, and with a flick of his wrist cast the worm into the shadows of a willow tree on the creek bank. The red-and-white cork bobbed brightly on the surface of the water.

Tate sniffed again. "They're here all right," he said. "Bedded up good."

"How do you know?" Val demanded.

"Can't you smell 'em?" he asked.

She made a face and swatted at a fly. "I smell dirt. And I smell dog. But that's about it."

"That's not dirt you're smelling," Tate said, lifting his rod tip gently to set the bobber rocking. "It's a kind of sour smell, right?"

"It ain't perfume," she said.

"Pan fish like shellcrackers bed up in the cool mud on the creek bottom," Tate said. "It's a real distinct smell. That's how you know they're here."

"Fascinating," she said. She reached down to the pocket of her jeans and brought out the steno pad she'd brought along.

"Now what about the dessert for Tuesday?"

"Peaches," Tate said.

"All right." She scribbled it down. "Cobbler? Pie? Dumplings?"

"Aaahh," Tate said. The rod tip bent sharply, and he reeled with one smooth motion. Seconds later, he pulled in a brilliant orange and yellow fish slightly larger than the palm of his hand.

Moonpie's tail thumped the aluminum bottom of the boat in approval. Wordlessly, Tate slid the fish onto a stringer, placed the stringer in the water, and was soon baited up with a fresh worm.

"You make it look so damn easy," Val said. "Every time out. How do you do that?"

He shrugged. "It's only easy if you know what you're doing. And I've been doing what I'm doing now since I was a kid. Anyway, you know how often I go out and come back with nothing. It's not like this all the time."

"But a lot of the time it is," Val reminded him.

"Right time of day, right weather, right bait, right equipment," Tate said. "After that, I guess it's mostly about luck."

"And you're mostly lucky," she said with a grin. "That's why you're gonna get that slot on The Cooking Channel. Now . . . about those peaches?"

"Yeah," he said slowly. "No pie. Um . . . I'm thinking." He flipped his polarized sunglasses to the top of his head, took out a handkerchief, and wiped his face, which was glistening with sweat in the hot midmorning sun. "Yeah," he said, nodding. "Oh, yeah. Grilled peaches. With a sorghum rum glaze. And homemade vanilla-bean ice cream."

"You can grill peaches?"

"Sure," Tate said. "You split 'em in half, pop out the pit. Leave the peel on. Brush the cut surface with some lemon juice and a little melted butter. Grill 'em for a minute or two, take 'em off, and brush on the glaze."

Val scribbled furiously. "Sorghum. What's that?"

"Southern version of maple syrup," he said. "You could use maple, of course, but since we're talking southern food . . ."

"And the rum?"

"Dark rum," he said decisively. "And you put the glaze on at the last minute, otherwise the high sugar content gives you too much of a char on the grill. And of course, you're gonna serve it with a scoop of home-made vanilla-bean ice cream."

"I dunno," Val said. "That sounds pretty fancy for a show like *Vittles.*"

"What's fancy about it?" he asked, reeling in another fish. "Peaches. Sorghum syrup, or maple if you can't get sorghum. Rum. And, oh yeah, a little grated fresh ginger goes in the glaze for extra zip."

Moonpie scooched forward on his haunches to sniff the fish as it flopped around in the bottom of the boat.

"Moonpie!" Tate said sharply.

The dog lifted his snout and fixed his master with a baleful look.

"You think he'd eat a live fish?" Val asked, fascinated and repulsed at the same time.

"Maybe," Tate said, adding the shellcracker to the stringer and putting it back in the water. "He eats bugs all the time. I've seen him eat a live shrimp, and a minnow. But I'm thinking a live shellcracker would put the hurt on his gut. Anyway, we don't have any fish to spare this trip."

"I don't know, Tate," Val said finally. "Don't get me wrong. The peach thing sounds delicious, but honestly, it sounds to me kind of like something Regina Foxton has done on *Fresh Start*."

"No way," Tate snapped. "I just made the recipe up. Right here on the spot."

"I'm not accusing you of stealing it from her," Val said soothingly.

"Damn straight," he said, casting out again. "I've never even really watched her show."

"We watched several episodes together yesterday, remember?" Val said.

"Yeah, but she never grilled any peaches," he insisted. "Anyway, she's not the only damned person who knows how to cook with fresh stuff. What about that show I did with the tomatoes and fresh basil? And don't I grill fish with lemon all the time? And chives? Hell, I was using chives before chives were cool."

"Hey!" Val said, realizing she'd hit a nerve. "I'm on your side, remember?"

"Regina," he muttered. "Dopiest damn name I ever heard. Probably a stage name. You ever know anybody named Regina in real life?"

"There was a Regina Manoulis in my Spanish class, ninth grade."

"Doesn't count," Tate said. "You're a Yankee. I'm talking about a Regina in the South. She claims she's from the South, right?"

"Somewhere in Georgia," Val said. "And she's sure enough got a believable accent."

"Everything about her is phony," Tate insisted. "Don't you think?"

"I dunno," Val said. "I just thought she was pretty all-American looking."

"Nobody looks like that all the time," Tate said darkly. "Look at you, for instance."

"Thanks," Val said.

"You know what I mean," he went on. "The makeup, the clothes. So buttoned-up looking. Like out of a magazine or something."

"Some men like women who look like that," Val said. "Scott Zaleski sure seems to."

"Who? That producer of hers?"

"Mmm-hmm," she said. "Word is they're an item."

"Figures," he said, grumpily. "Barbie and Ken. The perfect couple. Never a hair out of place on either of 'em."

Chapter 18

Gina!" Lisa pounded on the bathroom door with both fists. "Come on, Geen. Let me in. You gotta let somebody see it. I'm your sister. I'll still love you no matter what."

"Go away," Gina wailed.

"It can't be that bad," Lisa said, putting her cheek to the door frame. "It's Sunday afternoon. You've had on that conditioner D'John gave you since Friday night. He said that would fix you right up."

"Yeah, right," Gina retorted. "He's bald. Why should I believe anything a bald guy says about hair?"

"You can't stay in there forever. You gotta eat. You gotta sleep. And you gotta go to work tomorrow. You've still got more shows to tape, right?"

"Work!" Gina shrieked. "Oh, my God. I can't go to work looking like this. I'm a freak."

"Just let me in. It can't be that bad. Even if it is, we'll fix it. We'll make it all right. I promise."

A moment passed. Lisa heard the lock click. The door swung open an inch. She took a deep breath and stepped inside.

Her sister, Regina Foxton, was sitting on the side of the bathtub. She was wearing pale pink baby-doll pajamas, with a damp towel draped over her slumped shoulders. Her eyes were bloodshot. Her hair was quite blond, what there was of it.

Lisa swallowed hard and tried to think of something cheerful to say.

"It's . . . cute," she said finally. "And it really shows off your facial structure."

"Liar," Gina said glumly.

Lisa sat beside her and slung an arm over her big sister's shoulder. "It's not that bad, really. I mean, it's short, yeah. Shorter than you've ever worn it before."

"Yeah, since I was, like, three?" Gina said. "You've seen the old pictures."

"Come on," Lisa said, getting up and taking her sister's hand. "Come into my room. Will you let me see if I can fix it?"

"Doesn't matter," Gina said dully. "Cut it all off. Shave my head if you want. My career is over. No job, no man. No money. You think they're still hiring at Hi-Beams?"

"Stop talking like that," Lisa said, leading her into her own bedroom, sidestepping the piles of clothing and shoes, dirty dishes, books, and dog-eared magazines. "Sit," she ordered, pointing to the slipper chair in front of her dressing table. She picked up a pair of scissors and walked slowly around Gina. "I'm just gonna even it out a little," she said finally. "It broke off unevenly, especially on the sides, which is why you've got those kinda Bozo the Clown clumps going on. I'll feather it around your face, and trim off that kinda mullet thing you've got going in the back."

"Fine," Gina sighed and closed her eyes. "Whatever."

Lisa snipped and hummed, combed, then hummed some more. She stopped once, picked up the "Sexiest People Alive" issue of *People,* and leafed through it until she found the picture she wanted. "Aha!" she said softly. She picked up the scissors again, snipped some more. "Hold still now," she ordered, wrapping the abbreviated strands of her sister's hair around her curling iron. "I'm not used to working with hair this short, and I don't want to burn you."

"Whatever."

After a few minutes, she put down the curling iron and spritzed Gina's hair with her favorite finishing gel.

With her fingertips, she separated the curls into tendrils, working this way and that until she was satisfied with the results.

"Open your eyes," Lisa said finally.

"I'm afraid."

Lisa gave her shoulder a gentle poke. "Open!"

Gina opened one eye slowly, then the other, quickly. Her hands flew to her face.

"Oh, my God!"

Lisa smiled proudly. "You like it? I was going for a sort of Gwen Stefani look. But not as radical, of course."

Gina leaned into the mirror, then leaned out. The woman in the mirror was a stranger. On Friday night, she'd been what she'd always thought of as average, on-a-good-day-pretty. Shoulder-length brown hair with blond highlights, brown eyes. Good skin, tanned now from a couple weekends at Scott's rented house up at the lake. Button nose with a bump on the ridge from a skateboard accident in seventh grade. Mouth a little wide for the shape of her face, but her first boyfriend had said her lips reminded him of Julia Roberts, which she'd taken as a compliment.

Now she was somebody new. Loose wisps of blond hair curled around her head, and her eyes peeked out from feathery bangs. Her eyes looked bigger. Her cheekbones were more pronounced than she remembered. Her neck and shoulders felt naked.

"Geen? Say something. Do you really hate it that much? I mean, maybe D'John could do it better. He's been calling. He really feels awful about what happened. He said to tell you he can give you extensions. And nobody will be able to tell—"

Gina threw her arms around Lisa and squeezed. "Shut up, fool. It's great. Really. I mean it. You saved my life."

Lisa's mouth flew open. "Really? No shit? You like it?"

Gina blinked back tears. "Really. It'll take some getting used to. And you'll have to show me how you did it. But yeah. It's way better than I could have hoped for. I don't know how to thank you."

Lisa beamed. "That's okay. I mean, you're welcome. But, since you mention it, I'm a little short of cash this week—"

The doorbell rang then, startling them both.

"Are you expecting somebody?" Gina asked.

"Uh," Lisa said. "I think maybe it's Scott."

"Scott!" Gina cried. "What does he want? You didn't tell him about my hair, did you?"

"D'John told him," Lisa said. "We were afraid you'd never come out of that bathroom. You wouldn't answer your cell phone or the house phone, so he started call-ing my cell at the butt-crack of dawn."

"Go to the door," Gina said, giving her sister a shove. "Make him go away."

"He won't," Lisa said flatly. "This is the second time he's come by. Anyway, I think you guys need to talk. Straight up."

"Lisa," Gina moaned. "I can't do this. Not like this. Not yet."

Lisa picked up her car keys and headed for the front door. "Sorry, Geen. It's now or never. I'm going over to Sarah's to play Halo for a little while." She gave her sister a finger wave, then opened the door.

Scott stood on the doorstep, holding a brown paper shopping bag from Whole Foods. Gina ducked back inside the bathroom and slammed the door before he could get a good glimpse.

"Hey, Lisa," Scott said, stepping inside the condo. "Thanks for doing this for me."

His damp black hair still bore comb marks, and he had the Bluetooth earpiece for his BlackBerry in his right ear. Lisa had never seen him without that ear-piece. Scott's blue jeans were sharply creased, the sleeves of his pale aqua button-down shirt rolled up a precise two and a half folds. He wore his Gucci loafers sockless, but spit-polished. His idea of Sunday casual.

Lisa looked him up and down. She was wearing a tight faded army-green tank top with no bra, and she had her hands jammed into the back pockets of faded cut-off camo fatigues that she wore with the fly half-unbuttoned, the waistband rolled down to her skinny exposed hip bones.

"I'm not doing it for you, fuckwad," she said, her voice dripping acid. "I'm doing it for her."

She started to shoulder past him, but stopped short when their faces were only inches apart.

Lisa's blond hair had been dyed a scary shade of purple, and she was wearing it in a bizarre kind of Dutch-boy bob with jagged-edged gel-spiked bangs. She had the same melted Hershey's Kisses dark brown eyes as Gina, but hers were kohl-rimmed and menacing. "And you better not say a damned word about her hair. 'Cuz if you make my sister feel any worse than she already does, I will hunt you down and bitch-slap your sorry ass into next week."

His face flushed, and he started to say something cute, but Lisa cut him short.

"Believe it," she warned. "I'm not sweet like Gina. I'm a South Georgia redneck girl through and through. I'd just as soon cut you as look at you. You don't wanna mess with me."

"I was just going to ask you how she is," Scott said, setting the shopping bag down on the floor.

"She's shitty," Lisa said. "That's how she is. I hope you brought some good news about this Cooking Channel deal along with whatever kinda cheap-ass food you got in that sack."

"Barry e-mailed me this morning," Scott said stiffly. "He's intrigued with the concept of *Fresh Start*. And he loves the tapes I sent. So we are definitely in the running."

"Great." Lisa nodded. She jerked her head in the direction of the bathroom door. "Tell her."

"I will."

"And remember what I said about making her cry."

When Lisa was gone, Scott took the shopping bag and unpacked its contents on the kitchen counter. Cold sesame noodle salad. A small container of chilled grilled honey-lime salmon. Two ripe nectarines. He took out a bottle of Perrier and uncapped it.

He tapped on the bathroom door. "Gina," he said.

"Go away," Gina said. She stood at the bathroom mirror, patting concealer under her eyes.

"I've got good news, honey," Scott said.

"You don't ever get to call me honey again," Gina said. "Save that for Danitra Bickerstaff."

He winced. "I'm sorry. I deserved that. You're right. I screwed up. Big-time. But we really do need to talk. About the show."

"What about the show?" Gina fastened the diamond studs in her ears, then rejected them. With hair this short, she needed statement earrings. She found a pair of Lisa's earrings in a dish on the counter. They were two-inch silver hoops. She screwed them in, and slowly rotated her head from side to side. Yes. Good. Maybe she should get a second set of piercings. Lisa had half a dozen holes in her ears. Why not? It wasn't like her public was going to get a chance to comment on her appearance once she was off the air. Maybe she'd go really punk, and get a tattoo. Like a tiny little shattered heart, right above her breast. Lisa had a red devil tattoo, right above her butt crack. If Birdelle Foxton ever saw that, Gina thought, she would have a myocardial infarction on the spot.

"I need to talk to you face-to-face," Scott said.

Gina took a deep breath and opened the door.

"Jesus!" Scott said, taking a step backward. "What did you do to yourself?"

She tried to bite back the tears. "This was all your idea," she said finally. "You're the one who wanted me to go blonder."

Suddenly, he remembered Lisa's warning. He did not need to upset Gina any more than was absolutely necessary. And he really didn't want to find out what a South Georgia girl like Lisa was capable of in the ass-kicking department.

"It's nice," he said finally, touching one of the tendrils that curled above her earlobe. "It'll just take some getting used to."

Gina felt an involuntary spasm of pleasure at his touch, but she pushed his hand away. She was done with all that.

"You said something about good news?"

"I did," he said. "I brought you some lunch. Let's sit down and talk like two civilized adults, can we?"

"I'm not hungry," she said, but she followed him into the kitchen.

He got two plates from the cabinet, and set them out with the cold noodles and the salmon. He poured two goblets of Perrier. Like he owned the place, she thought bitterly.

She picked up one of the nectarines, sat down, and bit into it.

He took a fork and wound the sesame noodles around the tines. He did it perfectly. "We're definitely in the running with The Cooking Channel," he said, pausing to slurp the noodles.

"You're sure? Even after that catastrophe with the flounder?"

"Positive," he said. "Barry loves the concept of *Fresh Start*. He e-mailed me as soon as he got back to New York. He as much as told me we're a lock."

"As much as? What's that mean?"

Scott took a bite of the salmon and washed it down with Perrier. "He wants us to ship the tapes of this week's shows just as soon as we've got 'em in the can."

"What about Tate Moody? And *Vittles*? Are they still in the running too?"

"Don't worry about it," Scott said. "That guy's a joke. A dog as a sidekick? On a cooking show? It's a health hazard. Anyway, how gimmicky can you get?"

"Have you seen that dog?" Gina asked. "I have. He's precious."

"Listen to me," Scott said, reaching out and taking her hand. She slapped his away. He looked wounded. "You are a natural for this network. You are an amazing cook. We have an innovative, original concept with *Fresh Start*. Now, I know I hurt you. But I swear to God, it was a one-time-only deal. You've got to believe me. I care about you. Deeply."

She looked away. "I can't ever trust you again. It's all so humiliating. . . ."

He sighed. "All right. You're right. Let's not talk about us now. Let's talk about the show."

She took a sip of the Perrier. "What about the show?"

He put his fork down on the edge of the plate. "I brought over some wardrobe for this week. I'd already set it up with ZuZu's in Buckhead."

"What kind of clothes?" Gina asked, frowning.

"Nice ones," he said. "Expensive stuff. Look. This is our big break, Gina. Network television. National exposure. Do you know what that can do for your career? We're talking about a seven-figure contract. Your show will be on the air seven days a week, in every market in this country. Canada too. And don't forget the overseas market. Peggy Paul's show is a huge hit in England. And that's just television. Your cookbooks will be instant best sellers. You'll have endorsement deals. Appliances. Cookware. Tabletop. And then there's packaged food lines. Frozen entrées. Maybe even your own lifestyle magazine."

For a moment, she allowed herself to dream. Her own magazine! And another cookbook. She'd been jotting down ideas for months now. She wanted to take what she called southern heritage recipes, like her grandmother's banana pudding, or Mama's Coca-Cola pot roast, and update them—get rid of the packaged preprocessed ingredients and return to healthy, flavor-filled seasonal ingredients. . . .

The loud ringing of a cell phone brought her back down to earth.

Scott glanced down at the BlackBerry tethered to his Italian leather belt. "Excuse me," he said, getting up. "I've got to take this."

He walked outside. She went to the front window and watched him, pacing around, shouting. She could see the protruding muscles in his neck, his hands chopping the air in agitation. It reminded her of Friday night. When he'd stood over her, totally absorbed in his own rage.

Five minutes passed. Scott came back inside. He found Gina in the kitchen, packing the food he'd brought back into the Whole Foods shopping bag.

"Here," she said, handing him the bag.

"What's this?"

"Your food," she said. "Also your razor, the CD you mixed me for Valentine's Day, the sweatshirt I borrowed from you up at the lake, and a pair of jeans you left here a couple weeks ago."

"That's it? End of conversation?"

Gina gave it some thought. "Pretty much. I'm keeping the diamond earrings, because they're pretty, and I think, all things considered, I deserve them."

He shook his head. "This isn't like you, Gina. I told you, we've got great things ahead of us. We're a team. . . ."

She forced a smile. "This is the new me. The adult me. I hope and pray TCC picks me to be their new southern chef. If they do, I guess we have to work together. That's what adults do. They keep on going, even when things get ugly. If they don't, I guess I'll have to find a new job. One that doesn't involve you."

He put his hand on her shoulder. "Look. It doesn't have to be like this."

"Yeah," she said. "It really does."

Chapter 19

On Monday morning, Gina forced herself to look squarely in the bathroom mirror. The hair fairy had not made an overnight visit. The short blond wisps framing her face were the same alarming length and color they'd been when she finally went to bed Sunday night.

Fine. It was only hair. She'd been telling herself that for the entire weekend. It was time to start believing it. She had a million things to do before taping started later in the day.

In the bedroom, she gathered up the outfits Scott had brought over on Sunday. She grimaced at the olive green satin blouse with the long, billowing sleeves and the deep V-neck that he'd selected for the Thanksgiving show. The olive would make her skin look sallow, and the sleeves would end up dragging in her pie dough. The blouse had a $560 price tag and a designer label she'd never heard of. But then, she'd never even been inside ZuZu's, which was in an exclusive shopping center on West Paces Ferry Road, where she never shopped. It wasn't that she didn't like nice clothes. She did. But she was used to finding them deeply discounted at Filene's Basement, or on clearance at Bloomingdale's. She could have bought three or four outfits for the price of that one blouse, she'd protested.

"Last season's leftovers," Scott had said of her bargain duds. "That's fine for your personal life. But on air, you've got to look up-to-the-minute. Your viewers want to aspire to the kind of life they assume you're leading."

"Anyway," he'd added, "you don't have to pay a dime for the clothes. The folks at ZuZu's are giving them to you—in return for a wardrobe credit at the end of the show."

Gina grimaced again as she crammed a faded blue Atlanta Braves ball cap onto her head. She didn't mind cooking with products and equipment donated by sponsors. But wearing freebie clothes . . . She shuddered a little. It seemed somehow creepy.

Today was not the day to think about this, she decided. She had too much to do.

It was only 6:00 A.M., and she had to get down to the farmers market south of the city to buy the fresh produce and the turkey for the taping, then fight Monday-morning traffic on I-75 to get back to the studio to start prepping.

By the time she'd backed the Honda out of her parking spot, her T-shirt was already sweat-soaked. "Ugh," she said aloud. "Thanksgiving in July."

With an eighteen-wheeler overturned just below the exit to the stadium, and the resulting snarl of fire trucks, ambulances, police cars, and gawkers, it took her an hour to get to the State Farmers Market in Forest Park.

She drove directly to Boyette's produce stand. The Boyettes were her favorite produce dealers. Richard had traded in a successful career as a medical malpractice attorney for the life of a gentleman farmer, while Rachel, his daughter, was a talented artist whose vivid oil paintings of eggplants and sunflowers and rustic farm landscapes were interspersed among the bushel baskets of Silver Queen corn and purple-hulled peas.

Rachel, who she guessed was in her early twenties, was using a dolly to move cardboard boxes of tomatoes toward the stand. She stood up and waved tentatively when she saw Gina's familiar car pull up to the loading dock.

"Gina?" she said, squinting. "Is that you?"

Gina lifted the dark sunglasses. "Hey, Rachel. Yup, it's me. I'm kinda incognito today."

"Guess so," Rachel agreed. "Whatcha need?"

Gina pulled her list from her backpack.

"Everything. We're shooting Thanksgiving today. So, squash, of course, yellow, acorn, pattypan if you've got 'em. Green beans. Sweet potatoes. I need peppers. The prettiest red, yellow, and green you've got, for the beauty shots. Oh, yeah. And pumpkins, of course."

"Pumpkins?" Rachel laughed and shook her head. "You're kidding, right?"

Gina lowered her sunglasses to let Rachel see just how serious she was. "I never kid about pumpkins. We need three or four for the beauty shots, and then, let's see, maybe three of the small Sugar Baby ones to cut up for the actual pies."

"Gina, you're from South Georgia, right?"

"Odum," Gina agreed. "Doesn't get much more South Georgia than that."

"They pick pumpkins in Odum in July?"

Gina shrugged. "I guess. My daddy didn't really farm. Mama keeps a garden. Mostly tomatoes, peppers, cucumbers, and okra. Oh, yeah, and butterbeans."

Rachel giggled. "Gina, you don't harvest pumpkins in July. Daddy's growin' 'em, but they won't be ready till at least the end of September."

Gina felt a trickle of perspiration roll down her neck. She looked up and down the rows of growers' booths in the darkened shed. "What about these other guys? I mean, I hate to give the business to anybody else, but I've really gotta have those pumpkins. They don't even have to be organic."

"Feel free to ask," Rachel said. "Maybe somebody's growing a variety we don't know about. In the meantime, you want me to box up the rest of the stuff on your list?"

"That'd be great," Gina said, handing over the sheet of paper. "I'm really running behind schedule. And I still have to find a couple fresh turkeys."

"In July? Good luck."

For the next thirty minutes, Gina cruised the huge covered sheds in the car, trolling for the elusive summertime pumpkin. Most of the farmers and wholesalers laughed or shook their heads when she inquired about the availability of pumpkins.

Thirty minutes later, she was back at Boyette's.

"Any luck?" Rachel called, as Gina pulled the car alongside the booth.

"Nothin'," Gina said, wearily opening the trunk of the Honda. "I'm screwed."

"Maybe not," Rachel said, starting to load the cartons of produce in the trunk. She crooked a finger at Gina. "Come on inside the office."

Boyette's office was nothing more than a wooden lean-to, with an oscillating fan tacked to a wall, and a couple of sawhorses and a slab of plywood filling in as a desk. Rachel's easel took up one corner of the room.

But there, sitting square on the desktop, was one small-ish but otherwise perfect cantaloupe-size pumpkin.

"Rachel!" Gina gasped, throwing her arms around the younger woman's neck. "How on earth?"

"It was Daddy's idea," Rachel said. "I was telling him about the fix you're in. He had to run home to pick up some more corn, and while he was there, he found that bad boy in the pumpkin patch. The only one with any real size on it at all."

Gina started to pick the pumpkin up.

"Hey!" Rachel said. "Give it a minute. The paint's still wet."

"Paint?"

"Yup," Rachel said. "We were assuming you didn't want a dark green pumpkin. That's what color they are right now, you know. Small, hard, and green. They don't start to yellow up until they get some more size on 'em in the fall. I took some of my acrylics and just kinda painted 'er up."

Gina bent over and examined the pumpkin closer. The body was a rich orange, with subtle shadings of red, yellow, and deep green.

"It's a masterpiece," she said. "I only wish I had half a dozen of them."

"Sorry," Rachel said. "Daddy looked all over. He said the rest of them were mostly softball-shaped, so he didn't even bother to pick any."

Gina sighed. "This will just have to do. I can use it for the counter beauty shots, interspersed with the rest of the produce and the finished pie. I guess, just this once, I'll use canned pumpkin for the actual pie." She winced as she said it.

"It's television, right?" Rachel said. "Nobody at home is gonna know it's canned pumpkin. Heck, my mother always uses the canned stuff. And we grow the real thing."

Gina had heard this a hundred times before, mostly from Scott or the other members of the crew, and always, before, she'd stubbornly insisted on standing by her principles. Today, however, she'd just have to compromise.

She wrote out the check and thanked Rachel effusively. "No problem. It was fun," Rachel said. She carefully placed the painted pumpkin in a cardboard beer box, which they then placed in the trunk with the rest of the produce. "As hot as it is, it should be dry by the time you get to the studio," Rachel promised.

With a wave and a grateful hug, Gina drove off, already ticking off the rest of the items on her grocery list. The turkeys were the biggest thing. She was running too late even to attempt to find the fresh ones she'd hoped for. Frozen would have to do, just this once. Eggs, cream, fresh greens, and citrus to garnish the turkey platter. She'd keep her fingers crossed that maybe she'd find some bags of cranberries in the freezer section. Pecans. Yes, she needed shelled and unshelled pecans for the pies. Oh, yes, she thought, making a rueful face. And canned pumpkin.

Chapter 20

Perspiration trickled between Gina's breasts. Her damp hair was matted to her head, and she could feel a heat rash rising on the back of her neck. The Honda's air-conditioning was usually fairly adequate. But this was not a usual day. The announcer on all-news WGST was predicting the temperature would rise to 102, and there was a brown alert for smog. Since leaving the farmers market she'd managed to inch her way toward the studio at an average speed of twenty miles an hour.

When her cell phone rang, she bit her lip. She knew, without looking, who the caller would be.

"Gina? Where the hell are you?" Scott's voice held a note of high-pitched panic. "The crew's sitting around with their thumbs up their asses waiting on you. We should be taping right now."

"I'm sorry," she said quickly. "I've been stuck in traffic. There was a problem with pumpkins that I won't get into, and then I had to go to three different Krogers to find turkeys."

"Just get here, okay?" Scott said, cutting her off. "How much longer?"

She glanced at her watch, then up again, at the endless line of stalled traffic on all sides of her.

"I honestly don't know," she said. "I can't see anything in front of me. If traffic starts moving, I could be there in maybe ten minutes. Or not," she added lamely.

"Hurry," Scott urged. "I can't even get the prep girls started until you get here with the pumpkins and the turkeys."

She wanted to tell him that wasn't her fault. She wanted to tell him somebody else should be responsible for doing the shopping and delivering the food to the set. Instead she bit her lip again. If she got The Cooking Channel slot . . . No. *When* she got the slot, there would be a designated prep person to do the grocery shopping. But until then . . . at least the frozen turkeys would be fully thawed by the time she got to the studio.

"I'm doing the best I can," was what she said finally.

She clicked the phone off and turned up the volume on the radio. The WGST traffic reporter announced that the three-car pileup that was blocking all northbound lanes on I-75 was being cleared. She sighed with relief and started rummaging in her tote bag for a mirror. She dreaded seeing just how bad she must look.

Just then, the traffic miraculously began to move. She jammed the baseball cap back onto her head, and got the Honda up to speed again. Ten minutes later, she was zipping into the parking lot at the studio, backing into the space nearest the door.

It was after three. Scott would be beside himself. She gathered up the clothing for the day's shoot, and raced for the door. Once inside, she ran to the makeup room.

"I'm here!" she told D'John, who was sitting in the makeup chair, reading a copy of *Cosmopolitan* magazine. "Just let me get the food unloaded and take a quick shower. Can you let Scott know I'm here?"

"Girl!" D'John said, taking in her melted appearance. "What have you been doin' to yourself? You look like somethin' got run over by a MARTA bus."

"Don't mess with me, D'John," she said tersely. "I am *not* having a good day."

"I can *see* that," he muttered. He put the magazine down and began laying out the brushes and bottles and pots and potions for the task ahead of him. "Gonna take some *work* to get you looking right."

There was no time for a snappy answer. In the hallway near the back door to the studio she found the purloined Winn-Dixie shopping cart they used to move props and food and pushed it through the double doors and into the parking lot.

A cherry red vintage pickup truck was wedged tightly into the space beside hers, its rear fender millimeters from the Honda's. The truck's owner stood behind it, glaring at her.

"Hi," she said briefly.

"Hi," said the stony-faced Tate Moody.

She raised an eyebrow. "Problem?"

"You're taking up two spaces," he informed her. "And this one is mine."

He was, unfortunately, correct. In her haste, she'd parked the Honda at a crazy angle that did, indeed, mean that the rear of her car was protruding a good eight inches into the space next to hers.

"Sorry," she said, brushing past him. "I'll have to move it later. I'm in kind of a hurry right now."

She popped the trunk of her car and began carefully transferring the supplies into the grocery cart. The cartons of produce from Boyette's nearly filled the cart. She frowned. There was no time for two trips. She managed to wedge the soggy Kroger turkeys on top of the produce boxes, but she had to take all the canned goods out of the bags and fit them in and around the turkeys.

Tate Moody hadn't moved. He watched as she balanced the beer box holding Rachel Boyette's painted pumpkin precariously atop the pyramid of cans.

"That ain't gonna work," he said.

Before she could respond, two cans of pumpkin spilled out of the cart and rolled, slowly, under her car.

"Told you," he said, not bothering to suppress his satisfaction.

"Dang," she muttered. She flopped down to her knees, inching forward on her elbows to try to retrieve the cans.

"Nice ass," Moody commented.

"Shut up, butthead," she said, reaching for the first can, which was still rolling. Now another can spilled from the cart.

"Dang," she repeated, watching it roll under Moody's pickup. "How 'bout giving me a hand, here?"

She heard, rather than saw, his laconic applause.

"Butthead."

He sighed dramatically and lunged for the errant can, catching the rear wheel of the grocery cart with the heel of his boat shoe.

Slowly, the cart began rolling away. He grabbed for its handles, but before he could stop it, the cart rammed the rear of a gleaming black Mercedes. From its spot atop the peak of groceries, the painted pumpkin bounced from the cart's summit and rolled slowly across the asphalt into the path of an oncoming UPS delivery truck.

The loud grind of the truck's brakes brought Gina crawling, quick-time, out from under the Honda, a can clutched in each hand.

"What happened?" she asked, looking wildly around.

Tate rolled the grocery cart away from the Mercedes, one protective hand atop the turkeys, in the direction of the UPS van. The driver was out now, staring down at the truck's front tires.

"What the hell is that?" the driver demanded. "Was that a cat?"

"It *was* a pumpkin," Tate said.

"My pumpkin?" Gina trotted across the burning asphalt. She looked from Tate to the driver to the pumpkin, or what was left of it. Orange pulp oozed out from under the van's tires.

"My pumpkin," she moaned.

"At least it wasn't a cat," the driver said, wiping his face with the tail of his brown shirt. "You can't believe the paperwork when you hit somebody's cat. Now, a coon, or a possum, you can keep on going, but a cat—"

"Hey!" Gina cried. "That was *my* pumpkin! The only pumpkin in Atlanta. I was going to make a pie with that pumpkin. It was the centerpiece of my show."

"Sorry, ma'am," the driver said. "I tried to stop. I wasn't even going that fast. It just came out of nowhere."

"Forget it," Gina said dully. She snatched the cart away from Tate, sending another can soaring into the air. But she didn't stop to pick it up. She marched back to the Honda and slammed the trunk down.

Tate scooped up the can and ran after her. "Hey, Reggie," he called. "You dropped one."

She ignored him, pausing only to open the studio doors wide enough to allow the cart to pass. Holding the doors with her hand, she gave the loaded cart an ineffective shove with her hip.

"Hang on," Tate said, as he reached her side. He grabbed for the doors. "Lemme help with that."

She froze in her tracks. "Just leave me alone," she said, through clenched teeth.

The knees of her blue jeans were ripped and streaked. Her shirt was grimy, too, and her hair was sweat-soaked, Peter Pan short. She shot Tate a feral look. He took an involuntary step backward, and then stopped short.

"Wait a minute. Why the attitude? It's not like I ran over your friggin' pumpkin. I was only trying to help. Hell, if it hadn't been for me, all your damn groceries would be out there on that pavement."

She sighed and pushed a sweaty strand of hair off her forehead. "I'm sorry," she said finally. "You're right. I'm hot and frustrated, and I forgot my manners for a minute there." She smiled prettily. "Thank you so much for saving my turkey. Now, could you please get the *heck* out of my way? I've got a show to tape."

Chapter 21

U sing long-handled tongs, Tate deftly transferred the cornmeal-coated fish fillets from the iron skillet onto a waiting blue-and-white-speckled enamelware platter that had already been layered with cross-cut slices of grilled lemons and fresh parsley. Ignoring the mosquito buzzing around his chin, he looked directly into the camera and grinned the smile Val called the money maker.

"And that, my friends," he said, "is what we call a nice mess of fish."

"Amen, brother," Val called, from beneath the shade of a jaunty striped picnic umbrella. "That's it, everybody. Take a water break."

Tate slapped at the mosquito on his chin, noting the bloody smear on his palm with a sense of grim satisfaction. "Water break, my ass," he called back, unbuttoning the flannel shirt as he walked toward her. "Gimme a Corona before I pass out."

The camera, sound, and light men put down their equipment and loped over to the caterer's table, where a jerry-rigged tarp provided the only other spot of shade on the set. Large plastic bins of ice held bottles of water, soda, and beer, and there were trays of peaches, grapes, and bananas. They all passed around bottles of water, and Tate rolled an icy bottle of water over his perspiration-drenched chest before uncapping a bottle of Corona and chugging it down.

"Slow down," Val said, joining him under the tarp. "We've still got a lot of taping to do today, buddy boy."

"I'm hydrating," Tate said, but this time he uncapped a water bottle. "Whose idea was it to grill out in this shit?" he asked, looking around at the pale blue, cloudless sky. "It must be a hundred degrees out here."

"It's a hundred and two, if you really want to know," Val said, dipping a handkerchief in one of the ice buckets and using it to mop the back of her neck. "And it was your idea to shoot outside."

"I should be fired," he muttered.

"Never mind," she told him. "We're moving inside for the rest of the week. We're losing time and money with all these breaks, and anyway, the Weather Channel is predicting pop-up thunderstorms all week. As soon as we wrap up with your tomato and Vidalia onion pie, we'll start breaking down the set."

"Inside where?" Tate asked, looking around.

"Right there," she said, jerking her head in the direction of the studio. "I just got it all worked out. There's an empty soundstage available. We can move the Vagabond right through the loading dock. I'll send BoBo to Home Depot for some trees and outdoorsy-looking crap. We hang a blue scrim, and voilà!—the great outdoors. Only indoors and air-conditioned. We can even use the Barbie doll's prep kitchen."

"I don't like it," Tate said. "You know we always shoot on location."

"We're *still* shooting on location," Val said, patting his hand as though he were a cranky toddler. "But this particular location is climate controlled." She leaned over and fanned away a mosquito hovering over his eyes. "And bug-free."

Tate sighed, a sure signal that Val had won this little skirmish. "Does *she* know?" he asked.

"Who? Barbie? Why should she care? *Fresh Start* doesn't own the studio. They lease the time and space just like we do. And our money spends just as good as theirs."

He had a brief, pleasurable vision of Regina Foxton, down on all fours, fishing around on the hot asphalt for a roving can of pumpkin puree, her cute little butt pointed skyward. He flashed an evil version of the moneymaker. "Oh, she'll care. She'll care big-time."

Chapter 22

G ina raced into the dressing room, locked the door, and peeled off her sweat-soaked clothes.

"Gina!" Scott was pounding on the door. "Dammit, we've got a crew waiting on you."

"I know," she called, gritting her teeth. "Get the girls busy prepping the veggies. There's no time to cook the turkey. Have Jess brush it with some soy sauce and run it under the broiler. I'll be right out. Just let me get cleaned up a little. Give me ten minutes."

"More like an hour, I'd say," D'John said, leaning back in her desk chair. "Girl, you look like who-shot-Sally!"

Standing in her bra and panties, she held a towel under the faucet in the mop sink, and proceeded to take what Birdelle, ironically, referred to as a bird bath, dabbing the soapy cloth on her face, chest, arms, and legs.

"Girl, please," D'John said with a deep sigh. He walked over, put his hand on the top of her head, and held it under the running water. She came up sputtering. He grabbed the towel and wrapped it around her dripping head, and guided her to the desk chair.

He clucked and tsked, and squeezed an inch of hair gel out of a pink tube, briskly working it through her short, dampened strands.

"Lisa trimmed off most of the broken ends, and it didn't look too bad yesterday," she said. "Can you make it work?"

"Have to," D'John said, picking up his hair dryer and aiming it at her head. "Otherwise, Scotty-boy is gonna have you wearing that thing over yonder." He jerked his head in the direction of the bookshelves.

For the first time she noticed a Styrofoam head form perched on the top shelf. Pinned to it was a wig—a gleaming, honey blond, shoulder-length wig.

"Oh, God," she gasped, horrified. "Where'd that come from?"

He rolled his eyes. "Wigs 'R' Us? You tell me. I got to work this morning, and he brought Doris Day over there in and told me you'd be wearing it for the shoot today."

"Like hell," she said.

"That's what I said," D'John agreed. "Somebody sees you wearing that thing, they gonna think D'John here been smoking some baaad crack. Don't worry. I'll put a do-rag on your head before I plant that thing on you."

Five minutes passed. He blasted her head with the dryer, tweaking and twisting her short hair this way and that, then finally put his hands over her eyes as he misted her with hair spray.

"Now," he said, handing her a hand mirror. "Behold!"

"It's nice," she said, turning her head to the right and left. "Even better than yesterday."

"I should hope so," he said tartly.

They heard the doorknob turn, and then Lisa's voice.

"Gina? Come on, let me in."

Gina unlocked the door.

Lisa walked into the office and looked at her half-dressed sister, and then at D'John.

"Am I interrupting something?" she asked.

"Shut up," Gina answered. "I'm late already. And why, may I ask, are you here instead of in class where you belong? And what's with the clothes and curlers?"

Instead of her usual tight jeans and tighter T-shirts, today Lisa was dressed in a conservative-for-her pair of black slacks and a red sweater. Her blond hair was wrapped around jumbo hot rollers.

She dropped onto the chair next to Gina's, and stuck out her tongue at her sister. "No class today. My professor's got a stomach bug." She leaned over and gave Gina's desk chair a swivel. "Hey," she said, whistling in appreciation. "Good job, D'John."

"It really doesn't suck?" Gina said, looking from Lisa to D'John.

D'John was unpacking his tackle box full of cosmetics, carefully laying out the pots and tubes and brushes on Gina's desktop. "Drama eyes," he muttered. "Neutral lips. And earrings. We need some big-ass earrings."

"Here," Lisa said, unfastening the heavily beaded Celtic crosses that hung from her own ears. "Wear these."

"Thanks," Gina said dryly. "I was. Until you swiped them several weeks ago."

"Sharing is caring," Lisa said. She looked over at D'John. "Am I next?"

"Next for what?" Gina demanded. "We're working here, Lisa. Not playing beauty shop."

"I know that," Lisa said. "I came down for the Thanksgiving show taping. Scott said it was all right. In fact, he thought it was a great idea. I mean, I'm not gonna try and cook or anything. But Scott said—"

"We'll shoot a family dinner scene at the end of the show," said Scott, walking into the office.

"Can't you knock?" Gina snapped, grabbing the damp towel and draping it across her chest in a futile attempt at modesty.

"Door was open," Scott said. "What's taking so long here?"

He glanced meaningfully at the wig on the book-shelves, and then at D'John.

"I tried," D'John lied. "But she refused to wear it."

"No way," Gina repeated. "I am not wearing a wig. Not now. Not even if every hair on my head falls out." She glared at Scott. "Got that?"

"Fine," he said, returning the glare. "Just get your ass out to the set, will you? We've got no money left in the budget for overtime."

"What's this about a family dinner scene?" Gina asked.

"I was gonna let the crew kids dress up and act like family. And then Lisa called with this great idea of hers. It makes perfect sense. She actually is family. And she's not a bad-looking kid," he said.

"Gee, thanks, Pops," Lisa sniped.

"I thought she could chop onions for the stuffing. Or do the whipped cream for the pie. Like that. Viewers will lap it up."

"See?" Lisa stuck her tongue out again.

"She called you," Gina said. "Gee, there's a news flash. Do you have any other little surprises for me?"

"There is one more thing. Deborah wants to talk to you about some great ideas she's got for publicity. She'll be in as soon as she gets off the phone with New York."

"New York?" Gina's stomach fluttered.

"Yeah," he said enthusiastically. "I'll let her fill you in. They need me out on the set. You too," he added.

D'John patted moisturizer on Gina's face, then handed the bottle to Lisa.

"Isn't this fun?" Lisa asked, applying her own face cream.

"It's a blast," Gina said, as D'John applied a layer of foundation, followed by a blush, concealer, and what he called his "drama eyes"—carefully blended bands of contoured shadow, heavy liner, and the thickest, lushest false eyelashes Gina had ever seen.

"Isn't this a little much?" Gina asked, her left eyelid sagging under the weight of the gunk and the lashes. "I feel like a drag queen."

"Trust me," D'John said, turning his attention to Lisa, but with a lighter hand.

Gina dropped the damp towel and started getting dressed, carefully working her arms into the sleeves of the blouse Scott had brought her.

"Ooh," Lisa said, reaching out to touch the fabric. "How yummy. Is that a Chloe?"

"I guess," Gina said, fastening the buttons. "Scott picked it out. Not my favorite color. It reminds me of the color of cheap olive oil."

"Hmm," D'John said, regarding her critically. "You could be right. Avocado is definitely not your friend."

"I'll take it if you don't want it," Lisa said. "I'd kill for a Chloe."

"Regina Foxton! Is that really you?"

Both women turned to look in the direction of the doorway.

A willowy Asian woman dressed in a form-fitting pink business suit swept into the room.

Deborah Chen's kohl-rimmed eyes took in every detail of Gina's new look. She hugged a thick file folder to her chest. "Very nice," she said finally. "Your viewers will be shocked at the transformation."

Gina frowned, wondering if she'd just been dissed. "Hi, Deborah," she said. "You don't think I look too . . . plastic?"

"Plastic?" Deborah laughed. "Honey, this is television. Plastic is good in our twisted little vid-world."

"Scott said you had some stuff to talk to me about?"

"Oh, yes," Deborah said, sitting down in the chair Lisa had vacated. She crossed her legs, and the hem of her skirt rose perilously high. Although, Gina noted, she had the thighs for short skirts. Deborah rifled through the papers in her folder, found the one she wanted, and put a pair of cat-eyed reading glasses on the tip of her nose.

"Wait until you hear," she said. "First off, we're going to have new publicity stills shot to send to TCC. They're going to publicize the hell out of this grudge match between you and Tate Moody."

"Grudge match?" Gina frowned.

"Absolutely," Deborah said. "We're going to capitalize on the animosity between the two of you."

"There is no animosity," Gina said. "I just don't like him."

"Fine. Go with that." Deborah beamed. "It's great publicity for TCC, and for us, of course. And you'll never guess who the photographer is."

"Annie Leibovitz," Lisa said breathlessly.

"Guess again," Deborah said dryly. "We are talking public television here."

"I don't know," Gina said. "Anyway, why do we have to have new photos made? What was wrong with the old ones?"

"Seriously?" Deborah pulled the offending eight-by-ten publicity still of Gina from her file folder and wrinkled her nose in distaste. She ticked off her complaints one by one. "The lighting was too harsh. Your face looks puffy. Your nose was shiny. You had a cowlick, for God's sake. And that shirt with the pussycat bow . . . unfortunate."

"That was my favorite blouse," Gina said.

"It made you look like a Sunday school teacher," Deborah said. "Other than that, it was perfect . . . for a 4H convention."

"I always hated that blouse," D'John said helpfully.

"Me too," Lisa chimed in.

"Anyway," Deborah went on. "By the most amazing stroke of luck I was able to book Just Joel for the shoot. Isn't that fabulous?"

"Joel who?" Gina asked.

Deborah shrugged. "Just Joel. That's his professional name. I don't know if he has a regular name. It's a real coup that we got him. He's usually booked months ahead of time. He jets all over the country. Print ads, fashion layouts, editorial work. He's the go-to guy for high-society social events. Fortunately for us, the wedding he was supposed to shoot in the Hamptons this week got canceled because the groom ran off with the best man."

"This week?" Gina said nervously. "You don't mean *this* week, right?"

"This week absolutely," Deborah said. "Tomorrow, in fact."

Gina's hands flew to her head. "But my hair," she wailed. "It's still so short."

"That's why we got you that wig," Deborah said. "It's perfect. And the nice thing is, you can take it off when you get done shooting tonight, put it on the stand, and pop it back on tomorrow. No bed-head. No fuss, no muss."

"No wig," Gina said. "And no publicity photos. I've still got more shows to shoot this week."

"This takes precedence," Deborah said briskly. "We'll get the shows worked in, but the publicity is actually more important. It's what Barry wants."

She reached back into the folder for another sheet of paper. "I've already started setting up the print interviews. We're going to do a video conference. Won't that be fun? So far I've got you set up with the television writers from the *Nashville Banner*, the *Memphis Commercial Appeal*, the *Charlotte Observer*, and the *Orlando Sentinel*. I've got calls in to the *Constitution*, of course, since you used to work there. And I'm waiting to hear back from the *Miami Herald*."

Despite her reservations, Gina was impressed. "Those are some pretty big papers. They're interested in doing a story about me? I don't even think our show airs in all those markets."

"It doesn't," Deborah said, dimpling. "But they can't wait to get the jump on this food-fight angle I've dreamed up. Now, I wasn't going to mention this because it's still a long shot, but I guess it won't hurt to tell you I've also had some interest from magazines on this story. Nothing's definite yet. But I really think we've got a shot at *People, US Weekly,* and *Entertainment Weekly.* And the guy from *Hello!* is really hot for the story."

"*Hello!*" Lisa yelped. "Ohmygawd. That's my favorite. It's my bible."

"Wait." Gina leaned forward. "Slow down here. I think I lost you. What food-fight angle are we talking about here?"

Deborah's eyes glittered with excitement. "I knew you'd be surprised. It even took Scott by surprise. Until he thought about it. Then he realized what a natural this story is. Everybody is really pumped."

"What. Food. Fight?" Gina said it slowly, emphasizing every word.

"Why, the food fight between you and Tate Moody," Deborah said. "Over this Cooking Channel competition. We're going to get huge coverage out of this. We'll put you both in satin boxing trunks. Pink for you, blue for Tate. Of course, you'll be wearing a little tank top, but we'll have Tate bare-chested." She paused and licked her lips delicately. "Have you checked out the quads on that man? Not to mention the lats? He is buff, he is ripped, he is divine! And did I tell you I have a call in to *Entertainment Tonight*? It's kind of a long shot, but one of my sorority sisters from Vandy is an assistant publicist there—"

"No." Gina stood up quickly.

"No, what? Sweetie, it'll be in absolutely good taste, I swear. Scott thought we should have you in sort of a wet T-shirt look, but I said—"

"No!" Gina heard herself screaming. Actually screaming. "Hell no. No way, no how, no freakin' way. No."

Deborah's nose got pink. She stood slowly, pursed her lips, and clutched her clipboard even tighter to her chest. "We'll talk later," she said. "After the taping. When you're not so premenstrual."

Chapter 23

J avier Soto eyed the mesh bag of Vidalia onions on the countertop of the prep kitchen with deepening suspicion. The string opening was knotted in a different way. And the bag was not as full as it had been only an hour earlier, when he had unloaded his supplies. Yes, he told himself. It had been opened, definitely. With a scarred forefinger he counted the jumbo sweets one by one.

"*Ocho!*" he said triumphantly.

"Excuse me?" Jenn had positioned herself as far away from Tate Moody's prep chef as she could manage in the studio's small kitchen. Which meant that they were on opposite sides of the brightly lit white linoleum counter.

Jenn and Stephanie had complained bitterly when Scott announced only two hours earlier in the day that they would be sharing the prep kitchen with Moody's crew, and Jenn had even threatened to quit. But they both knew she wasn't going anywhere. How many jobs were there in Atlanta, Georgia, for a CIA-trained food stylist? Jenn put down her rolling pin and scooted her pie pans away from the manic chopping of the surly man at the other side of the counter.

"I say there are only *ocho* onions here," Javier said, raising his voice. "Somebody is taking my onions. Somebody is *stealing* my Vidalias."

"Ignore him," Steph said, under her breath. She quickly dumped a pan of crumbled corn bread into the bowl with the rest of the ingredients for the Foxton family turkey dressing. On top of this she dumped a skilletful of cooked breakfast sausage, along with the pan drippings. She measured out sage, salt, cracked pepper, and chopped shallots, and began folding together the ingredients.

Javier Soto stopped chopping and sniffed the air. His gleaming black bandito-style mustache quivered with each inhalation.

"You!" he screamed with rage, pointing his knife at Steph. "You are the one who is stealing my Vidalias." He ran around the counter and snatched up the mixing bowl. He plunged his hand into the glop and held a handful of it up to his nose. "My onions!" he cried. "My beautiful onions."

"Hey!" Steph yelled. "That's my dressing!" She grabbed at the bowl, but he was too quick.

"Valerie! Tate!" he called, cradling the bowl under his arm. "*Vaya te!* Come see what these thieves are doing to me!"

Val Foster was on the makeshift *Vittles* set, directing the placement of a forest of potted evergreens around the Vagabond. Tate was hooking up the propane tank to the grill, which had been relocated inside the studio.

"What now?" he muttered, turning to see his prep chef stalking toward him with a bright blue mixing bowl under one arm. Trailing close behind were two young women whom he recognized as Regina Foxton's kitchen staff.

"Give it back!" cried the brunette with the short pigtails.

"Scott!" cried the petite redhead with the tattoos. "Scotty! We need you."

Scott Zaleski and Regina Foxton were standing on the *Fresh Start* set, having a decidedly chilly discussion about the pumpkin pie situation, when they heard the ruckus emanating from the set next to theirs.

"What now?" Gina threw her script onto the counter and took off in the direction of her crew's agitated cries. Scott was right on her heels.

The *Vittles* set closely resembled an armed standoff. A stocky, mustachioed Mexican in a white chef's coat, tight Lycra running shorts, and bright yellow rubber clogs was clutching one of Regina's trademark blue mixing bowls and brandishing a large wooden spoon, with which he was fending off the advances of Jenn and Stephanie. Tate Moody stood behind a stainless steel grill of Sherman tank proportions, his arms crossed, looking bemused.

Jenn and Stephanie circled the Mexican, grabbing at the bowl, but being rebuffed by random smacks from the wooden spoon.

"Gina!" Jenn said, spotting her boss. "This maniac was threatening Steph with a knife! Then he grabbed our dressing and ran over here with it. Make him give it back."

"Look at this," the Mexican demanded, thrusting the bowl at her. He held up a fistful of dressing. "You see? You smell? These are *my* onions. My Vidalias. They are stealing my onions."

"Good Lord," Gina said, backing away from the uncooked dressing. "It's dressing. It has onions. I'm sure the girls didn't take your onions. My recipe doesn't even call for Vidalias. We have plenty of our own onions. Right, Steph?"

"Uh, right," Stephanie said.

Tate Moody peered into the mixing bowl. He scooped up a bit of dressing and tasted. "Uh-huh," he said. "These are definitely Vidalia onions." He took the bowl from his aggrieved assistant and held it out to Gina. "Taste for yourself."

"Ridiculous," she said huffily. But she snagged a bit of onion and chewed thoughtfully.

"Sweet," she admitted. She took the bowl from Tate and handed it back to Jenn, raising one eyebrow in an implied question.

"Ladies? Have we been helping ourselves to other people's groceries?"

"It was two lousy onions," Stephanie said crossly. "I don't see what the big deal is. He's got a ten-pound bag. And we just ran out. We've only got one onion left, and we need those for the counter beauty shots. We don't have time to run to the Kroger," she said defiantly. "Scott's already on our case because we're running *way* late."

Gina sighed and turned toward the Mexican. "I'm sorry," she said, her voice soothing. "I'm sure it was an innocent mix-up. I'll see to it that your onions are replaced."

"No!" Javier said stubbornly. He spoke in rapid-fire Spanish.

Tate translated. "Javier says these onions are Vidalia onions. He says he buys a bushel of them in May, takes 'em home, and wraps them individually in his wife's pantyhose, and then he keeps them in the produce drawer in his fridge so they don't rot."

"Oh," Gina said weakly. "I did a whole show on Vidalia onions last spring. Vidalias do have a high sugar content, which makes them sweet, but prone to rotting if not handled properly. That's what I tell my viewers to do."

Tate translated that, and Javier spat out a reply.

"He says he never watches your show," Tate said, his lips twitching with suppressed glee. "He only watches Telemundo."

"I'll replace the Vidalias," Gina repeated. "Tell him that."

But that much English he understood. "Where you gonna get Vidalias in July?" Javier demanded.

"Yeah," Tate echoed. "Where you gonna get Vidalias in July?"

"My produce wholesaler can get them for me," Gina said. "I'll call him in the morning."

"Sorry, man," Scott said. He held his hand out to Javier, who took it only reluctantly. "The girls made a mistake. They won't do it again." He turned to Tate, who shook amicably. He turned to offer his hand to Gina, but she'd already walked off in the direction of the *Fresh Start* set.

Chapter 24

S cott?" Gina closed her eyes as D'John blotted powder on her nose. "Can we talk?" Her voice dripped icicles.

A few feet away, the prep cooks, Jenn and Stephanie, bustled around the set, placing the raw turkey in its roasting pan, and the finished one—a mahogany-hued masterpiece—in the wall oven. At the end of the counter, they'd already lined up the pies—pecan, apple, and even pumpkin—on a carefully draped blue-and-white-checked tablecloth. The girls pretended not to notice that their star seemed to have her panties in a wad over something. Usually a model of cheerfulness and efficiency, she was definitely having an off day.

"All right," Scott called, looking up from the computer monitor where he'd been reviewing the just-taped scenes. "But we need to get Lisa's scene finished, okay?"

Lisa Foxton stood near the pies, holding aloft an electric hand mixer, frowning down at the bowl of whipping cream.

"Nothing's happening," she said plaintively. "It's just, like, milk or something."

Gina stalked over to the counter, dipped the cream with her forefinger, and gave a disgusted snort. "It's not even remotely cool," she declared, looking right at Jenn. "Can somebody please get my sister some new, *chilled* whipping cream? And a chilled bowl? I'd like to get out of here before midnight, if nobody else minds."

"Sorry," Jenn said. She stomped off the set and retreated to the prep kitchen.

"What's up?" Stephanie stood in front of a sink full of soapy water, working her way through a mound of cutting boards, greasy pans, mixing bowls, and measuring cups.

Jenn swung open the refrigerator door and scanned the shelves, looking for the carton of whipping cream that should have been there, right beside the eggs, butter, and cream cheese.

"Gina is *not* a happy camper tonight," Jenn reported, moving the bottles and dishes aside. "I think maybe she and Scott might have broken up. But if she doesn't cut me some slack, she just might find herself with a bad batch of eggnog once we start on the Christmas shoot." She looked over at Stephanie. "What did you do with the whipping cream? The stuff we were using got too hot. It won't set up now, so we've got to start all over again."

"Should be right on the top shelf," Stephanie said, scrubbing at the casserole dish that had held sweet potato soufflé. Bits of burned brown sugar clung tenaciously to the side of the porcelain dish.

"It's definitely not here," Jenn said. "Don't tell me we're out."

"Okay, I won't tell you we're out."

"Not funny," Jenn said, her hands on her hips. "What the hell do I do now? We're ready to shoot the whipping cream thing, but I've got no whipping cream. And I swear to God, I bought, like, three cartons." She held out the grocery list that had been taped to the refrigerator door. "See—whipping cream—three pints. And it's checked off, so I know it got unloaded into the fridge."

Stephanie wiped her hands on a dish towel, opened the refrigerator door, and spent five minutes surveying its contents.

"Jenn, I swear, it was right on the top shelf with the rest of the dairy stuff," she said finally, closing the refrigerator. "I saw it when I got the butter and eggs for the pecan pies."

"When was that?"

Stephanie glanced at her watch. "Maybe . . . an hour ago?

They looked at each other, and then at Javier, who was making an elaborate show of polishing his knives and placing them in a black quilted roll-up case.

"Hey!" Stephanie called. "Hey, you."

He kept his back to them, whistling quietly.

She walked over to him and flicked the dish towel in his direction. "Hey! Did you take our whipping cream?"

He looked up. "*No se.*"

"Whipping cream," Stephanie said, enunciating clearly. "It was in the refrigerator. And now it's gone. Did you take it?"

"*No comprendo ingles,*" he said. He took off the chef's smock and folded it under his arm. He picked up the carrying case of knives.

"Bullshit!" Jenn exploded. "You spoke perfect English earlier today. And we know you took our whipping cream. You were the only other person in here."

He held out his hand and smiled maliciously. "Sorry, man."

Reluctantly, Jenn took the plastic tub of Cool Whip out to the set.

"What's that supposed to be?" Gina asked when she saw it.

"I'm really, really sorry, Gina," Jenn said. "We had two more pints of whipping cream in the fridge. But it's all gone now." She glanced around and jerked her head in the direction of the *Vittles* set. "I think he took it. To get even with us for borrowing his stinking onions."

"Tate Moody stole my whipping cream? You can't be serious," Gina said.

"Not Tate. That guy. His assistant. Javier."

"What's going on?" Scott asked, walking up. "What's the holdup?"

"Sabotage," Gina said. "Moody and his people are deliberately sabotaging my show. They stole my whipping cream. Now there's none left for the pies."

"Ridiculous," Scott said, shaking his head. "Anyway, we don't have time for this." He picked up the tub of Cool Whip. "We'll shoot Lisa whipping the stuff in the bowl, cut away to show you supervising, and when we cut back to her, we'll put the Cool Whip in the bowl. All right? Ready, Lisa?"

Lisa put down the lipstick she'd just finished reapplying, and tucked a strand of hair behind her right ear. She lowered the beaters into the bowl, pressing her elbows together the way she'd practiced earlier, for maximum cleavage. She glanced down and saw a gratifying spillage of breast from the V-neck of the tight red cashmere sweater she'd borrowed from Gina's closet.

"Ready," she said, flashing the smile she'd also perfected after hours in front of the dressing room mirror. Not too much gums, she told herself. The Foxton women all had generous gums. She tilted her chin down, so that she was looking up into the camera held by Eddie, and batted the false eyelashes D'John had painstakingly applied earlier in the day.

"We're rolling," Scott said.

Shortly before midnight, Gina triumphantly placed the platter with her gleaming turkey on the dining room table. Her great-aunt's silver shone softly in the candlelight, and each plate of her grandmother's brown-and-white transferware china was heaped with her lovingly wrought dishes: brussels sprouts in lemon butter sauce; homemade cranberry-orange relish; the bourbon-spiked sweet potato soufflé, mounded with an oatmeal brown-sugar streusel; and on each plate, a mound of creamy mashed Yukon gold potatoes swimming in a pool of herb-flecked gravy. Slowly, Eddie panned the camera around the assembled "family"— Stephanie and Jenn, hastily changed out of their aprons and into jewel-colored sweaters, and Scott, sitting at the head of the table, opposite Gina's own empty chair.

Gina tipped the bottle and poured wine into Scott's outstretched glass, and then Scott took the bottle and began pouring wine for the others.

"Lisa," Gina said sweetly, gesturing toward her younger sister, who'd somehow managed to pull the neckline of her sweater even lower during the hour-long taping, "would you please ask the blessing?"

"I'd love to," Lisa replied, leaning forward to allow Eddie to capture her best angle. She lowered her eyelashes and clasped her hands reverently together. "Bless this food, oh Lord, to the nourishment of our minds and bodies. Amen."

"Amen," the others replied in the chorus they'd rehearsed.

Eddie panned the camera around the table once more, then slowly backed up for the panorama shot.

"And, cut," Scott announced.

Without rehearsing, everyone at the table picked up a wineglass and knocked back the contents.

"Wow," Lisa said, reaching for the wine bottle again. "That was so awesome. I really had a blast today. In fact, I think I'm going to change my major to broadcast journalism."

"Sweet," Eddie said, reaching for the platter of turkey.

"Hold it," Gina said, pinning his hand to the table with the bone-handled carving fork. "You don't want to eat that, Eddie."

"Aw, man," the cameraman said. "Come on, Gina. It's midnight. We're done, right, Scott? I been smelling that turkey all day. I didn't even have any dinner, 'cause I was saving up for this turkey."

"Suit yourself," Gina said, running her fingers through her hair. "But I should let you know, that thing spent nearly an hour and a half in the trunk of my car this afternoon. We only broiled it long enough to get that pretty color. So it's about half raw. After that, it sat on the countertop under these blazing lights most of the day. I'd imagine by now there's a whole buffet of bacteria crawling around that bird. Botulism, salmonella, *E. coli* . . ."

"Oh," Eddie said. "Maybe I'll just have some pie."

While the crew broke down the set, Gina hurried off to her office. She sank down into her chair and popped the top on a can of Diet Coke from the mini-fridge under the desk.

"Can I come in?"

Scott stood in the doorway.

"It's open," Gina said.

"Great show today," Scott said. "That's the first tape I'll show Adelman when he gets here tomorrow."

"Tomorrow?" She set the soda can down on the table with a thunk that sent a spray of liquid all over the tabletop.

He mopped uneasily at the soda with a wad of tissue. "Yeah. Uh, they're all hot about this story angle

Deborah's cooked up. Adelman wants to watch some tapings, and then he wants to sit in on the photo shoot."

Her stomach cramped. When had she eaten last?

"Which tapings does Adelman want to watch?" She really should eat something. Her blood sugar was probably in the single digits.

"Yours, of course. And Moody's." He kept dabbing nervously at the desktop. She wanted to slap his hand away. God, she was hungry.

"But relax," Scott said. "You've got the show in the bag. I know it. I can sense it." He chuckled. "Did you see that lame-ass *Vittles* set they jerry-rigged today? Potted plants, for Christ's sake. It looks like a cable-access show."

"Let's talk about that photo shoot," Gina said. "Deborah has some insane idea about me dressing up in satin trunks and boxing gloves. And actually posing with Tate Moody."

He laughed again. "Yeah, nutty, huh? She's already booked time at a gym down by the airport. Some place professional wrestlers use to train at. Deborah's amazing when it comes to that kind of authentic detail. And can you believe her media contacts? Did she tell you about *People*?"

"Scott!" Gina said. "There is no way I am getting dressed up like Muhammad Ali and posing for pictures with Tate Moody. No way. Ever. Not even for *People* magazine."

He blinked. "Really? I thought you'd love the idea. It's so kitschy. And Adelman is crazy for it. He says TCC could even use the photos for on-air promotion for this food fight thing they've cooked up."

Her stomach growled so fiercely she was sure he heard it. She found a package of Nabisco wafers in her desk drawer and savagely ripped off the cellophane wrapper, scarfing down two cookies in one bite.

Scott stared, openmouthed.

"I'm hungry, okay? I've been running around all day without a bite to eat."

He held up both hands in surrender. "I know. I'm on your side, remember? Now, why don't we go somewhere and get a late dinner? We can have a glass of wine and discuss this calmly."

"I am calm," she said, finishing off the cookies. "Which is why I won't go out to dinner with you. Ever again. And I can't, for the life of me, think of a single reason why it's a good idea for me to have my picture made with that baboon Tate Moody. We're supposed to be promoting me, remember? You produce *Fresh Start*, not *Vittles*."

He nodded agreement and gave her a smile she decided was patronizing. "It is all about you, Gina. But look at it from Adelman's point of view. Television is all about publicity. And the fact that you're up against somebody like Moody makes a great story. Don't you get it?"

"No," Gina said, gulping down the rest of her soda.

"It's a Beauty and the Beast story," Scott said. "We can't buy that kind of publicity."

"Why does this have to be about publicity?" she said plaintively. "I'm a great cook. The sales of my last cookbook were strong. Our ratings were improving, until Tastee-Town canceled on us. If you'd been able to keep Little Scotty in your pants, my ratings would be even higher next year. Why can't it be about that? Why does it have to be some fakey competition with some guy who doesn't know grits from granola?"

He tilted his chair on its back legs and gave her another of those patronizing looks. "This is television, Gina. It is what it is. I didn't make it that way, but I know the rules, and I know how to play the game. So you're just gonna have to trust me on this."

"Trust you?" She balled up the cellophane wrapper and tossed it in the trash.

He opened the door of the fridge and helped himself to a Diet Coke. He drained the soda in one gulp. " 'Fraid so, babe," he drawled. "Like it or leave it, I'm your producer and the co-creator of *Fresh Start*. I'm the one who brought you to Adelman. I'm your ticket. Without me, you're right back at some crappy newspaper, writing fillers about the joys of cooking with frozen Spam."

He tossed the Diet Coke can in the direction of the trash basket, and it clattered off the rim before falling just short.

Chapter 25

As soon as Scott was gone, Gina jumped up and hurried to the vending machine in the staff lounge. She fed the machine eight quarters, and it fed her a stale pimento cheese sandwich.

Her last three quarters went to another Diet Coke. On a normal night, she would have sought privacy in her office. But Scott had swiped her last soda. Besides, everybody was gone for the night. She had the place to herself. She sank down into the chair she'd just abandoned and ripped into the sandwich wrapper.

But wait. The stinkin' satin blouse with the drippy sleeves. She'd somehow managed not to splash anything on it during the taping, but she wasn't going to tempt fate by eating a sandwich while wearing a $560 blouse. It would probably cost twenty-five bucks to have the thing dry-cleaned. She was wearing a perfectly modest beige satin camisole underneath, so she unbuttoned the blouse, took it off, and draped it carefully over the chair back next to hers, enjoying the feeling of the air-conditioning on her bare shoulders.

Gina chewed happily, letting the saltiness of the processed cheese spread wash over her, an absolute balm for her jangled nerves, which she washed down with a hearty slug of caffeinated chemical-laden carbonated beverage.

She reached into her tote bag and brought out the next day's script and her reading glasses. She perched the glasses on the end of her nose and began skimming her notes.

Before all the fuss about The Cooking Channel had erupted, and before her life had been ruined, she and Scott had planned a Valentine's Day segment they were calling a Heart-Healthy Dinner for Lovers. The menu had sounded sexy when she'd concocted it: roast Chilean sea bass with a citrus salsa, cold poached asparagus, and an herb-crusted gallotine of new potatoes. She'd envisioned a dessert of crème caramel—made with reduced-cholesterol eggs, of course, with a garnish of fresh raspberries.

But now, as she chewed and sipped, the menu seemed to lack . . . something. Zip? Originality? She wanted this show, probably her last, to be the best she'd ever done.

Suddenly, she heard footsteps. Somebody was coming this way. Crap! She hoped it wasn't Scott again. Or one of the crew kids. She was too darn tired to deal with their childish problems tonight. She was just crumpling the cellophane sandwich wrapper when Tate Moody strolled into the break room.

"Hey," he said, clearly startled. "I thought everybody had gone home for the night."

"Almost everybody," Gina said.

He stood in front of the snack machine for a moment, studying the offerings, and finally made his selection. An apple.

Uninvited, he sat right down at her table and bit into the apple. He chewed and stared at her.

She blushed violently, realizing for the first time that she was basically sitting there in her underwear. But she was doggoned if she'd make a big deal out of it. Let him think the camisole was a tank top. It looked almost like one.

"Hey, Reggie," he said, when he was finished chewing. "You always go topless around here late at night? Man, if I'd known that, I would have moved in months ago."

"Don't call me Reggie," she said. "And I am not topless. I happen to be wearing a camisole."

"What's a camisole?" he asked, taking another bite of the apple. "Kinda like a bra?"

"Forget it," she said, refusing to be baited by him. "I was just leaving." She swept the script and the crumpled-up wrapper into her tote bag in one swift motion, but in her haste, several pages floated toward the floor.

"Don't go on my account," he said, bending over to retrieve the pages.

But instead of handing them over to her, he leaned back in his chair, took another bite of apple, and to her absolute horror, started reading aloud.

"Hmm," he said. "A Heart-Healthy Dinner for Lovers."

She held out her hand and snapped her fingers impatiently. "Give that to me."

He grinned and pressed the script to his chest. "I would tell you to keep your shirt on, but it's a little late for that, don't you think?"

She grabbed her blouse from the back of the chair and began putting it on. But the left sleeve was turned inside out, and as she struggled to fix it, he stood up and, unasked, yanked her arm out of the sleeve and turned it right side out.

Gina recoiled at his touch, and, of course, he noticed.

"Relax, Reggie," he drawled, sitting back down again. "If I was trying to undress you, I'd pick a better place to do it than here."

"Butthead," she said. Her fingers were shaking as she fastened the blouse's tiny satin-covered buttons.

"Roast Chilean sea bass?" he said, resuming his reading. "With a citrus salsa? Are you for real? Is this what you and Scotty-Wotty consider sexy?"

In answer, she snatched the pages out of his hands.

But it seemed he'd read the whole menu and memorized it instantly.

"You know, of course, there's no such thing as Chilean sea bass. It's really just Patagonian toothfish. And poached asparagus? Reduced-cholesterol crème caramel? Sounds like hospital food if you ask me. Why not serve some red Jell-O and runny oatmeal while you're at it?"

She knew he was deliberately baiting her. Knew she should ignore him and walk away. But the temptation was too great to resist.

"Just what would you consider an appropriate menu for Valentine's Day?" she asked, trying to sound condescending. "Pickled pig's feet washed down with a nice chilled six-pack of malt liquor?"

"Usually I start with oysters," he said, taking another bite of his apple and chewing slowly. "I ice 'em down good, and serve 'em on the half shell, with just a squeeze of lemon juice. You know what they say about oysters, right?"

"I'm aware that they are considered an aphrodisiac," she said.

"Eat seafood, live longer," Moody quoted. "Eat oysters, love longer. You might want to remember that, the next time you're cooking for Scotty-Wotty."

"You're repulsive," Gina said. "And I'm leaving."

"So soon? And just when we were getting to know each another. But maybe it's for the best. You really don't like me, do you, Reggie?"

"I *asked* you not to call me that," Gina said. "Anyway, I don't like or dislike you. I don't know you."

He had to push it. "But if you did know me?"

She considered the question. "I like your dog."

"We're not talking about Moonpie," he reminded her.

"Look," she said, adjusting the shoulder strap of her tote. "We are very different people, you and I. That's fine. My daddy says it takes all kinds to make this world go 'round. You just need to know one thing about me, Tate Moody, and we'll get along famously. This cooking show of mine isn't some hobby. It's not some whim. This is my career here. I have a degree in home economics. I've been a food writer for a major metropolitan daily newspaper, I've taken classes at La Varenne and Le Cordon Bleu. I've been working toward this moment my whole life. I want this TCC show. Period. So you just stay out of my way, all right?"

Head held high, cheeks aflame with emotion, she started to walk out.

"Hey, Reggie."

She whirled around.

Tate put down the apple, which he'd reduced to little more than a core. "I'll stay out of your way. But since we're getting all acquainted here, there's something you need to know about me. You're playin' with the big boys now. This ain't some high school popularity contest. I may not have your fancy chef's credentials. I'm not sleeping with anybody important. But I am damned good at what I do. I want this show just as much as you do. So don't expect me to step aside, or bow out, or play by the girls' rules. It's winner-take-all, baby. And as *my* daddy always says, if you can't run with the big dogs, stay on the porch."

He gave her a dismissive nod, picked up the apple again, and casually tossed it toward the trash can six feet away. She heard rather than saw it hit its mark.

Chapter 26

Tate took the plastic hanger with the baby blue satin boxing trunks, opened the passenger-side window of Val's Audi, and pitched them out onto the roadway. At a speed of sixty miles an hour, the trunks sailed away into the smoggy Georgia air. A truck behind them honked its horn in protest.

From his perch in the back of the car, Moonpie barked a flippant response.

Valerie Foster shook her head. "That's littering, you know."

"Fine with me," Tate said, crossing his arms over his chest.

"Those trunks had to be custom ordered from a company in Hackensack. And FedExed overnight."

"Dock my pay," he said.

"You pay me, remember? It's your production company."

"Okay. I'll dock your pay. In fact, this whole idea is so bad, I may fire you."

She took a long drag from her cigarette. He took it from her and threw that out the window too.

"You *are* in a mood today," she observed. "Anything in particular bugging you?"

"We're supposed to be taping shows," he said. "We're paying a crew just to sit around that studio while I get my nose powdered and my picture taken."

"So. This doesn't have anything to do with the fact that you're getting your nose powdered and your picture taken with Regina Foxton?"

"Gina," he said mockingly. "That's what she likes to be called."

"And you don't like her," Valerie said, glancing down at the clock on the dashboard. They were running late, and as usual, traffic on I-75 was bumper-to-bumper. She'd told that publicist, Deborah, that she'd have Tate and Moonpie at the boxing gym at ten o'clock. He'd thrown a fit when she'd told him about the plan. At first, he'd flatly refused to go. When she'd explained that the photo shoot was approved by Barry Adelman, he'd grudgingly allowed himself to be coaxed into her car for the drive down to the gym. Moonpie, once he'd been given a bacon-flavored chewie treat, had been loaded into the car without protest.

But when Val showed Tate the boxing trunks and explained the whole setup, his reaction had been less than enthusiastic. She'd love to have seen the look on some truck driver's face when the blue satin trunks landed on his windshield, but she'd deliberately sped up and fled the scene after Tate's little tantrum.

They'd have to come up with another idea for the photo shoot, and fast. It was a shame, really. The idea of staging a sparring match between Tate and Regina Foxton was, in her opinion, brilliant. Newspapers and magazines ate up that kind of stuff. And the best part of it was, the publicity would be free for Tate. But it would be useless to try and talk him into it now. She glanced over at him. He was in a filthy mood, all right.

He stared out the window and drummed his fingers on the Audi's dashboard.

"She's got a friggin' degree in home economics. I didn't even know you could get a degree in something like that anymore," he said.

"You're right," Val said. "That's appalling."

Tate gave her a sour look. "We had a run-in last night. In the break room in the studio. The woman's frightening, you know?"

"Regina Foxton? Are you kidding? She's a cream puff."

"No," Tate insisted. "That's all just a facade. I saw the real Regina Foxton last night, and I'm telling you, Val, the woman is a machine. She accused me of deliberately sabotaging her show, and then she basically told me to stay the hell out of her way. She'll stop at nothing to get this TCC show. Last night, she showed me her true colors."

"And which colors were those?" Val asked, jerking the Audi's steering wheel hard left and passing a red minivan full of uniformed Little Leaguers, who all had their faces pressed up against the van's windows. "Beige and taupe?"

He ignored that. "You know what I find most unattractive about her?"

God, would this traffic ever thin out? Val wondered. They were officially thirty minutes late. Adelman and his people were going straight to the gym from the airport. And she was sure that Regina Foxton and her entourage had been there since dawn. That would leave her looking incompetent and unreliable. Not acceptable. She glanced in the rearview mirror to see if there were any law enforcement types in the vicinity. When she saw none, she bit her lip, jerked the Audi hard right into the middle lane, then right again, and finally onto the shoulder of the road. From here, she had a straight shot to the exit ramp less than a mile ahead. She floored it.

"Jesus, Val," Tate said, bracing himself against the dashboard.

She smiled grimly, her mind churning up believable excuses about why the sparring-match photo wouldn't work.

"What were you saying?" she asked. "Something about what you find so unattractive about the real Regina Foxton?"

"Oh, yeah," he said. "She's ruthless. I've never seen anything like it. Naked ambition, you know?"

"Very unattractive," Val agreed.

Chapter 27

G ina looked at herself in the full-length mirror in
the grubby women's locker room at the Southside
Boxing Club and winced. "I can't do this," she wailed.

"Sure you can," Lisa said. She poured some vodka
into the carton of orange juice she'd bought at the Starvin'
Marvin convenience store, swished it around, took a sip
for herself, and handed it over to her sister. "Take a belt
of that," she said. "It'll make you feel better."

"The only thing that's going to make me feel better
is to wake up and find out that this whole morning
has been nothing but a bizarre nightmare," Gina said,
but she took a gulp of the screwdriver, then two more
gulps, and then another.

"I look like an idiot," she said, for the tenth time that
morning. When she'd arrived at the boxing club at nine

o'clock, she'd been positive she'd driven to the wrong place. The address Deborah gave her turned out to be a nondescript prefab metal building in a warehouse district two miles from the Hartsfield-Jackson Airport. But moments after Lisa and Gina arrived, Deborah and Scott drove up in Scott's car.

"Wait until you see your outfit," Deborah had squealed, running over to Gina's car and brandishing a pink plastic garment bag.

Now that she was dressed, she was sure she was in a nightmare.

The white satin tank top had "GINA" emblazoned in six-inch flowing script on the front and back. But the shorts were worse. Much worse. Hot pink satin, and instead of baggy ones, like you saw on boxers on television, these appeared to be two sizes too tight.

"Whoa," Lisa said when she'd seen how they fit. "Crotch cutters. Are you sure you don't have them on backward?"

"I'm positive," Gina said, near tears.

"Put the robe on," Lisa urged. "At least it's the right size."

The hot pink satin robe was barely thigh-length. And it had "KID FOXTON" embroidered across the back.

"Gina? Let me see how you look," Deborah said, sweeping into the locker room. "Oh!" she exclaimed, clapping her hands. "It's just right!"

"It's too tight," Gina said, taking another sip of the screwdriver for courage. "And too short. I'm not having my picture taken in this rig."

"But sweetie, it's all set," Deborah said. "Joel's in the ring setting up his lights and cameras, and Mr. Adelman's assistant just called from the limo. Their plane landed, and they should be here any minute." She looked at her watch. "Val Foster called too. She said they're stuck in traffic, but she expects to be here shortly."

Her gaze swept Gina up and down with practiced measure. "I think you look absolutely adorable. And once you get some makeup on, you'll feel much better."

"I'm wearing makeup," Gina said. "D'John stopped by my condo this morning and did my hair and makeup."

"Oh," Deborah said, tilting her head. "Of course! You go for that natural look, don't you?"

Behind Deborah's back, Lisa bared her teeth and made clawing motions with both hands.

Before Gina could repeat her objections, there was a knock on the dressing room door. "Gina, are you about ready?" Scott asked. "The photographer wants you to come on out so he can get some light readings on you."

"One minute," Gina called. She looked at Lisa. She looked at Deborah. And she looked in the mirror again.

No amount of vodka would make her feel good about what she saw there.

She took a deep breath. "I'll wear the robe," she told Deborah finally. "But I'm not taking it off."

"But—"

"Not under any circumstances," Gina said, her voice steely. "Do we understand each other?"

"Fine," Deborah said with a nonchalant shrug. "As long as you understand that I can't guarantee any of the big newspapers or magazines will be interested in using these photos. The whole concept of the boxing match—the fight between you and Tate Moody—depends on costuming and the set."

"I get that," Gina said.

"Mr. Adelman loved the idea," Deborah said, turning to walk out of the dressing room. "I'm sure he'll be disappointed that you've decided not to fully cooperate."

The Audi's tires kicked up a dust storm of gravel as it made the turn into the Southside Boxing Club parking lot on two tires. Val pulled into the parking space next to Gina Foxton's Honda, which was parked next to a charcoal gray Mercedes, which was parked next to a black Chevy Blazer with a prestige tag that read "JSTJOEL," which was parked next to a black Lincoln Town Car with smoked-glass windows.

"See," Val said, gesturing at the row of cars. "Gina is here. Her people are here. The photographer's here. The network people are here. Everybody's here."

"Fine," Tate said, opening the door and unfolding himself from the front seat. "Now we've called roll. Can we get this thing over with? I've got a show to shoot." He opened the Audi's back door, and Moonpie hopped out, trotted over to the Honda, and promptly relieved himself on one of the rear tires.

"Good boy," Tate said, patting the setter's head. "Piss on all of 'em, right, Moonpie?"

Val shot him a backward glance as she sprinted toward the gym's door.

Inside, she approached the knot of people standing around holding clipboards, cell phones, and BlackBerrys. "Barry!" she exclaimed, grasping both the producer's hands in hers. "And Zeke," she added, turning to the assistant, who today was inexplicably clad in head-to-toe green camouflage. "So good to see you. Did you have a nice weekend?"

"Where's our boy?" Adelman asked, giving Val a nodded greeting. He looked meaningfully at the thin gold watch on his wrist. "The photographer wants to get started with the shoot. And I've got a conference call to the coast in half an hour."

"Oh," she said airily, "Tate's outside. With Moonpie. We got into heavy traffic, and then, wouldn't you know it, Tate insisted we stop to get some water for the dog. So hot, today, you know. And setters sometimes get overheated."

"Can't have that," Barry said. "Viewers are very sensitive to any hint of animal cruelty. That's why we don't ever show whole fish being prepared on any of our shows."

"Or lobsters," Zeke added. "People don't seem to mind if we roast oysters, or steam clams. But they're very sensitive to the rights of crustaceans."

"Crustacean rights?"

Val turned. She hadn't seen Tate walk up with Moonpie at his heels.

She laughed nervously. "Barry was just saying that TCC steers away from any scenes that might be construed as animal cruelty."

"Seriously?" Tate asked, looking from Adelman to Zeke.

"Absolutely," Barry said. "Wendy and I are on the board of Save the Seas, you know. It's one of our passions."

"Wendy was chairman of the Party with a Porpoise Ball in May," Zeke said. "Maybe you saw the photos in *Town and Country?*"

"Honorary chairman, actually," Barry said.

"But we raised sixteen thousand, six hundred," Zeke reminded his boss.

"Have you people ever actually seen my show?" Tate asked. "*Vittles* is about hunting and fishing."

"Oh, not really," Val said quickly. "I mean, yes, technically, in a sense there is *some* limited talk about hunting, but really, *Vittles* is about the human connection to the great outdoors. It's about Tate's commitment to conservation, and his vision for seasonal, heritage-type cuisine."

"I kill things," Tate said flatly. "And then I cook 'em. Moonpie helps. He'll eat a live shellcracker if you don't watch him good. That's what my show's about."

Zeke's face paled. Val fixed Tate with a laser stare.

"People?" The photographer was standing in the boxing ring, his neck strung with heavy cameras. "So sorry to interrupt, but can we get Mr. Moody into his wardrobe? And see about his makeup? I'm losing the light here, people."

"Tate?" Val said it pleadingly.

"Ready when you are," Tate said, walking toward the ring. He turned and gave a sharp whistle. "Come on, Moonpie. Showtime."

Gina squared her shoulders. "I am a network star," she told herself. "I am a network star. I am a network star." She knotted the belt to the satin robe, opened the door, and, head held high, glided out.

The first thing she saw was Tate Moody. He and the dog were in the middle of the boxing ring. Moody was glaring at the photographer, who was glaring right back. The dog was sitting on his haunches, ears back, teeth bared. Deborah Chen and Valerie Foster were fluttering ineffectively around the two men. Scott and the men from the network were outside the ring, each talking on a cell phone while holding a BlackBerry.

Tate Moody was not dressed in a satin robe, and he was certainly not wearing any baby blue satin boxing trunks, as Deborah had promised. In fact, he was wearing pretty much what he wore every time she saw him around the Morningstar Studios, which consisted of a pair of faded blue jeans and a golf shirt.

"Hey," she said sharply, climbing under the ropes and into the ring. "What's the big idea?"

Moody's head swiveled around. All the others simply stared at her.

"You see?" the photographer said, gesturing toward Gina. "This is how you were supposed to dress. Your producer agreed."

The photographer stopped glaring at Tate long enough to smile at Gina. "Just Joel," he said, offering his hand and flashing dimples under both eyes, which were a bright blue, with unnaturally long, doelike black lashes.

"Gina Foxton," she said. "I thought—"

"Nice outfit, Reggie," Tate drawled. "Did you forget the pants?"

Now Scott Zaleski was climbing inside the ring.

"Now, wait just a minute," he said. "Our understanding was that both Tate and Gina would be dressed in boxing gear for this shoot. Our publicist has pitched this story to the entertainment weeklies this way." He lowered his voice a little. "That's what we told the TCC folks we were doing. That's why they flew all the way down here today."

"Our understanding?" Tate leaned back a little, hands in the back pockets of his jeans. "I don't know who cooked up this whole deal, but I never agreed to anything except having my picture taken."

"Uh, Tate," said Valerie Foster, tapping him on the shoulder. "Actually . . ."

"It's supposed to be a boxing match." Now Deborah had jumped into the fray. "Why is this such a difficult concept for you people? That's why we're in a gym today. That's why we rented a boxing ring. And why both of you were supposed to be wearing satin boxing trunks. Pink for you," she said, nodding at Gina. "And blue for you," she said, turning her winning gaze toward Tate Moody. "Now, be a good sport and get dressed, please?"

"Nope," Tate said. "I didn't get any memo about playing dress-up. Wouldn't have agreed to it if I had. Now, I don't mind having my picture made. I don't even mind having it made with Reggie, here. You all can pitch it any way you want." He looked from Deborah, to Just Joel, to Scott, and then, last, to Gina.

"All right with you?" he asked pleasantly.

"Fine with me," Gina said.

She wanted to leap into the air and offer Tate Moody a high five. Instead, she fled into the bathroom to change into her own clothes.

Chapter 28

"All right, people," Just Joel said with an air of bored detachment.

He grabbed Tate by the arm. "You, I want here." He maneuvered Gina so that she was inches from Moody. "And you here."

He raised the big camera and locked it onto a tripod. "I want the two of you to stare into each other's eyes. Really staring. And loathing. Complete loathing. Can we at least do that?"

Gina locked eyes with Tate Moody. He winked.

She clenched her teeth. "Cut it out."

"Make me."

"Tate," Just Joel called. "I'm not buying the hatred. Let me see your killer instinct."

He cocked an eyebrow and growled.

"Oh, for God's sake," Gina said.

"That's it, Gina," Joel said, clicking off three quick shots. "Narrow your eyes like that again."

She narrowed. It came naturally.

"Ooh," Tate taunted. "Now I'm really scared."

"Beautiful, Gina," Joel said, clicking again. "You're a warrior queen. He's invading your territory. Show him who's boss."

"Gladly," Gina said, shoving Tate so hard he fell over backward.

Click. Click. Click.

Moonpie, clamped tightly in Valerie's arms, gave a sharp bark of protest.

"Great stuff," Barry Adelman called from outside the ring. "Let's get some more of that."

Gina glowered down at Tate Moody. Instinctively, he crossed both hands over his crotch. Then, genuinely irritated, he scrambled to his feet.

"You're mad, Tate," Joel coached, circling around the two now. "Pissed as hell. Who does this emasculating bitch think she is? Huh?"

Tate leaned in toward Gina and scowled.

Click. Click.

"Can I ask you a question?"

"What?"

"Have you been drinking?"

She blushed. "A little vodka in my orange juice. It was the only way I could get up the nerve to come out dressed in those stupid boxing trunks."

"Gina?" Joel said, "Are we losing our edge?"

"Wuss," Tate whispered.

She furrowed her brow, balled up her fists, and appeared ready to pummel Tate Moody within an inch of his life.

Click. Click.

"You didn't look that bad in the robe," Tate offered, faking a jab to Gina's chin. "You should show your legs more often."

Click. Click.

This time her annoyance was real. "You sound just like Scott."

"Just one man's professional opinion," Tate said. "Use what you got. That's all I'm saying."

"And that's all I've got?" she retorted. "Good legs? A set of boobs? No brain, no talent?"

"Hey!" Tate said, poking her in the chest. "Don't get all bent out of shape. If you didn't want to wear the stupid outfit, you should have just said so. What? You're so dick-whipped you can't stand up for your own rights?"

He didn't even see it coming.

Cold-cocked, with a roundhouse right to the jaw, Tate staggered backward. Gina clutched her right hand in her left and yowled with pain.

Click. Click. Click.

Chapter 29

I think my jaw is dislocated," Tate said, his fingers gingerly probing the lower half of his face.

"Oh, it is not, you big sissy," Gina countered. "You wouldn't be able to talk if that were the case."

She shifted the bag of ice on her right hand to reveal a bruise roughly the size, shape, and color of a plum forming across her knuckles.

"See what you did?" She held out the hand so he could see the severity of her injury. "It hurts like the dickens. How am I gonna tape a show with my hand like this?"

"What I did?" he sputtered. "You attacked me. It's a clear case of aggravated assault."

"I was aggravated, all right," Gina said. "You deliberately provoked me."

"Shut up, you two," Val ordered. She opened a bottle of aspirin, poured out a handful of tablets and gave half to Tate and half to Regina. She looked around the trainer's room. "Has anybody got a bottle of water?"

"How about some orange juice?" Lisa asked, offering the carton she'd fetched from the women's locker room.

A half smile flitted across Tate's bruised face. "Is this *the* orange juice?"

"Afraid so," Gina said, trying to suppress her own amusement.

"Might as well," Tate said. He swallowed the aspirin with a few ounces and handed the carton over to Gina, who did the same.

The door to the trainer's room opened. Deborah and Scott walked in, their faces glum.

"What now?" Gina asked.

"Well . . ." Deborah said, giving Scott a sideways glance.

He sat down on the trainer's table beside Gina. "How's the hand? Is it broken?"

She wiggled her fingers, wincing. "I'm not going to lie. It hurts," Gina said. "But tell me what happened. Something's wrong."

"Just worried about you," Scott said, patting her leg awkwardly.

"Barry just left," Deborah said abruptly.

"What? He just walked out? Did he say anything?" Val asked.

Deborah tossed her hair. "After these two finished their exhibition match, and while they were getting doctored, Barry finished his conference call, and then he told Zeke to call the hotel and cancel their reservation and book seats on the next flight back to New York. Other than that, no, he didn't say anything. But he didn't have to. You should have seen the look on his face. He was obviously appalled. As was I," she added, with a shake of her head. "What a fiasco."

"I'm sorry," Gina said. "I blew it. There's no excuse for the way I acted."

Deborah fixed Tate with a cold stare. "I have an idea you were provoked. So it wasn't all your fault."

"Screw you, lady," Tate said, jumping up off the table. "This whole boxing match thing was your idea. You engineered the whole thing. The gym, the stupid outfits, all of it. And that photographer. You heard him. He was egging us on. We just gave you what you asked for. I've got no apologies." He jerked his head in Gina's direction. "And neither should she."

Gina looked up and smiled wanly. "Still. I'm sorry I hit you so hard."

He shrugged. "I'll get over it. See you around." He turned to his producer. "Let's roll."

An awkward silence fell over the trainer's room after Tate and Val left.

Finally, Lisa cleared her throat. "I'm, uh, gonna go get our stuff," she told her sister. "Guess I'll drive us home so you can leave the ice pack on your hand."

"Good idea," Scott said.

Cell phone in hand, Deborah started for the door too. "I've got to get started doing some damage control," she said. "I overheard Zeke saying their flight won't leave for another hour. I'm going to call Barry and try to put a positive spin on things. Joel did show me some of the shots on his digital camera. They're actually not bad." She smirked. "I especially like the one of Moody flat on his ass. With a little luck, I think I can still salvage this thing."

Now it was just the two of them. Scott and Gina.

"Guess I blew it," Gina said. "For both of us."

Scott shrugged. "Leave it to Deborah. She's a pro. She'll figure a way to make lemonade out of this lemon." He stood with his hands clasped behind his back. "All this time, I was worried about the other Foxton girl ripping me a new one. You've got quite a haymaker on you, Gina. Remind me not to get on your bad side again."

She shifted the ice pack. "Tate Moody is a redneck jerk. But I shouldn't have let him get under my skin. I wasn't raised like that. If my mama saw what I did out there today, she would be having conniptions."

"You really cleaned his clock," Scott repeated. "The look on your face. I could see he was getting under your skin. What exactly did he say to set you off like that?"

Dick-whipped, Gina thought. What an ugly phrase. She couldn't, wouldn't, repeat it, not to anybody. Anyway, she had stood up for what she believed in. Hadn't she refused to be photographed in those hideous shorts?

"I don't even remember," Gina said finally. "It was all just a blur."

When Lisa slid behind the wheel of the Honda, Gina gave her a searching look. "Are you sure you're okay to drive? How much of that vodka did you have?"

"Not that much," Lisa assured her. "Hardly any. I'm actually more of a Natty Lite girl. Anyway, I only brought the vodka 'cause I thought you might need a little pick-me-up."

"If you're sure," Gina said, leaning back against the headrest. "All I need is for us to get a DUI to make this the hands-down worst day of my life."

"Hands down," Lisa chortled, pulling carefully out of the parking lot. "That's pretty funny. Hands down."

"Not funny at all," Gina said, closing her eyes.

"What did the asshole say after I left?" Lisa asked.

"He thinks Deborah can salvage the mess I made. Doesn't matter. I ruined everything." She turned and gave Lisa a sad smile. "Sorry about your short-lived showbiz career."

"Screw it," Lisa said succinctly. "You can get a new producer. And a new show. Anyway, it was fun while it lasted. I can't wait till everybody at home sees the Thanksgiving show. You think I should start looking for an agent?"

"That vodka of yours is making me really woozy," Gina said, avoiding the subject. "I just want to go home, take some painkillers, and go to bed."

"Tell me one thing before you nod off?"

"Shoot."

"What did the Tatester say to make you deck him?"

Gina yawned dramatically. "It was nothing."

"Then tell me."

She blushed. "It's too crude to repeat. And it's not true."

Lisa guffawed. "Rude, crude, and socially unacceptable? I live for that kind of stuff. Come on. Tell."

"He said . . ."

"What? He said you looked pretty damned hot in that robe?"

"No. I mean, well, yeah, he did say it looked good on me."

"But that's not why you socked him in the jaw."

"Can we just drop this? I'm tired. My hand is throbbing."

"Tell me what he said and I won't say another word."

"He accused me of being dick-whipped. Okay? He said I shouldn't have let them talk me into putting on that outfit if I didn't want to do it. And that's when I punched him. He asked for it. End of story."

Lisa nodded her approval. "Good ending. Especially since the rest of the morning was such a letdown."

"How was it a letdown for you?"

"Helloooo?" Lisa said. "You think I got up at the butt-crack of dawn and drove all this way just to watch you nut up over some tight pants? No offense, but I came because I was promised a chance to see Tate Moody up close and personal. Without a shirt."

She sighed and held up her camera phone. "I didn't get a single shot."

Chapter 30

G ood news, good news, good news," Val sang out,
her footsteps causing the Vagabond to shake with
each phrase.

Moonpie barked a greeting from inside the trailer's
screen door, but there was no sign of his owner.

"Tate?"

Now she heard water running. She stepped inside
the trailer and tapped on the bathroom door. "Tate?
You decent?"

"Go away," he yelled.

"Nope," she said genially. "I've got good news.
Come on out, sport."

The bathroom door opened an inch, and a cloud
of steam emerged, followed by Tate's head. His hair
was dripping wet, and his face was pink from the

heat. "I'm officially on vacation. Moonpie and I are taking the Vagabond and going up to Ellijay for some trout fishing. And you are not invited. Now go away, Valerie."

"Aren't you going to ask me what the good news is?"

"I don't care what your good news is," he said, closing the door in her face. "I'm gone. Call me in a week, and we'll talk."

She unrolled the magazine she'd brought over to the Voyager and slid it under the bathroom door. "Page twenty-eight," she said. "Check it out."

Silence. Five minutes later, the bathroom door opened.

Tate was dressed in clean but threadbare blue jeans. He wore a dark green T-shirt. He was barefoot. He had the *People* magazine open to page 28.

"Did you know *Fresh Start* has been canceled?"

"Not till this morning," Val said. "The rumor going around town is—"

"Jesus!" he said, running his fingers through his damp hair. "What a business. Having your sponsor dump you for NASCAR. Has she seen this yet?"

"Who?"

"Don't play innocent with me. Reggie. Has she seen this?"

"How should I know? Anyway, who cares?" She snatched the magazine away from him and sat down at the dinette. She read the headline aloud.

"FOOD FIGHT HEATS UP DOWN SOUTH. Will hunky outdoorsman Tate Moody be the catch of the day—or will fresh foodie fanatic Gina Foxton win this battle for a prime-time network cooking show?"

Moonpie cocked his head and thumped his tail in approval.

"Not you," Val said, edging the dog's butt off the top of her shoe.

She held up the double-page spread so both Tate and Moonpie could get a look. The color photo took up most of the left-hand page. It showed him face-to-face with Regina Foxton in the boxing ring, looking cocky, self-assured, confident. Gina Foxton's face was contorted in a hideous snarl, her teeth bared, eyes narrowed, one strap of her tank top sliding halfway down her shoulder. The facing page showed a publicity photo of Tate and Moonpie, posed in front of the Vagabond.

"Hunky outdoorsman!" Val repeated. "How fabulous is that? Your sponsors have been calling me all morning. To say they are thrilled is the understatement of the day. Beau Archer started calling at six A.M. He wants to know what it would take to get you to sign with Southern Outdoors for another two years, whether or not you get the TCC spot."

"Who's Beau Archer?" Tate asked, pouring himself a bowl of Rice Krispies.

"Who—who's Archer?" Val sputtered. "Pay attention here, Tate. He's only the president of Southern Outdoors Network. The guy who signs our paychecks. Remember—he flew you out to his ranch in Montana to go grouse hunting with the sponsors last winter?"

"Oh, yeah," Tate said. "Guy couldn't hit the broadside of a barn with a baseball bat. He had a good-looking German shorthaired bitch though."

"His wife?" Val asked, looking shocked. "When did you meet her?"

Tate shook his head sadly. "It's a dog, Val. A German shorthair is a dog. How many times do I have to tell you?"

"Speaking of dogs," Val went on, "I also had a call from a woman at ChowHound dog food. They want Moonpie to be their new spokesdog."

"Hmmm," Tate said, shoveling in the Rice Krispies. "What'd you tell Beau Archer?"

"No deal," she said succinctly. "We're signing nothing till we know whether the Food Fight is still on. They're paying us peanuts right now. But it's gonna cost 'em, big-time, from now on, if this TCC deal goes through."

Val's hip began playing the first few notes of the *Vittles* theme song. She rolled to the right, took the phone out of the pocket of her slacks, glanced at the phone's readout, and grinned widely. "Yes!" she exclaimed, pumping the air with her fist. "It's Barry Adelman. This is it, Tate. He's calling to tell us you've got the show."

Deborah Chen slid the copy of *People* across the desk gingerly, barely touching it with the tip of her fingernail, as though the images might burn her flesh.

"There is no such thing as bad publicity," she told Gina, her voice brisk. "Now, you might not think so right at this moment, but—"

"Oh, no!" Gina said, flinging her reading glasses at the publicist. "This is the worst picture of me that has ever been printed."

"It's not that bad," Scott started to say.

"It's worse than my driver's license picture, and in that one I had a bad perm and a giant fever blister on my upper lip," Gina cried, stabbing the page with her forefinger. "Look at this thing. Tate Moody looks like a rock star. But me? I look like some blood-crazed maniac."

"They could have chosen a more flattering picture of you," Deborah finally conceded, "but I really think you're overreacting. Anyway, as I was saying, this article is actually a godsend. Yes, it does mention that Tastee-Town has withdrawn sponsorship of *Fresh Start*. But now, that opens the way for other, bigger sponsors to step in. It's just a matter of time until they start calling—"

As if on cue, the phone on Gina's desk started to ring. She stared at it without picking up. It rang eight times, and then stopped. A moment later she heard the muted ring of her cell phone, from inside her bottom desk drawer. She picked it up, looked at the caller ID readout, and put it back in her pocketbook. "Mama," she said. "Oh, crap. It's Tuesday. She gets her hair done at the Beauty Box on Tuesdays. They subscribe to everything. Even the *Star*. *People* is the first thing she reaches for when they put her under the dryer."

Now it was Scott's turn. His cell phone rang urgently. He plucked his BlackBerry from the holster on his hip and pressed a button.

"Barry!" he exclaimed. "Yeah! How about that? We were just talking about it. I know! A million bucks worth of publicity for sure. What?" Scott shook his head vehemently. "No, no, *Fresh Start* is not off the air. I'm in negotiations with a couple of other sponsors. No, I'm not at liberty to say just yet . . .

"Really?" Scott's face brightened. "That big a response, huh?"

But now he was frowning. "Utah? I don't see the draw of Utah. I mean, it's not even in the South. . . ."

The smile returned as he listened. "Oh. I gotcha." He was nodding rapidly, reaching for a pencil, making notes. "Well, that's not much notice, but I can talk to Gina, see if she can clear her calendar. She's got a heavy promotional schedule. . . ."

His eyebrows shot upward. "That's our share, guaranteed? Prime time?" He whistled. "Barry, let me just run the numbers by our people, see what we can work out. Today?" He gave a dramatic, beleaguered sigh. "Yeah. I'll get back to you. Absolutely."

Scott busied himself with finishing his note-taking, then looked up at Gina.

"What'd he say?" she demanded. "Did I get it? Why am I clearing my calendar?"

"Whoa!" Scott said. He put his BlackBerry back in his holster.

"Deborah was right," he said slowly. "There is no such thing as bad publicity. As soon as the *People* story hit, the president of TCC was on the phone with Barry."

"What about the show?" Gina begged. "Stop torturing me. Who got the show? Me or Tate?"

"You both got it," Scott said. "In a manner of speaking."

Chapter 31

Valerie Foster was sitting in the Vagabond, going over production notes with her star, when her cell phone rang.

"Barry?" Her face brightened. She got up from the dinette and walked outside. Tate watched her through the window as she talked and gestured, all the time walking in a tight little circle in the parking lot.

After five minutes, she came back inside the trailer and took her seat at the dinette, frowning at the coffee that had gone cold.

"Well?" Tate said. He put his cereal bowl on the floor, and Moonpie obligingly lapped up the last half-inch of milk and soggy cereal. "Who won?"

Val blinked. "Didn't we tape a show at a place called Eutaw Island?"

"Sure," Tate said. "We did it our first season. Don't you remember? You found a tick on your ankle when we got back to the lodge over there, and you screamed so long and loud, you'd have thought we'd have to amputate your leg."

"I knew it," she said. "Eutaw Island. At the very top of my never-again places. Along with Disney World and Gatorland. And let's not forget the Okefenokee Swamp." She shuddered violently.

"Val?" Tate said. "We were talking about The Cooking Channel—remember? What did Barry Adelman say just now? Who won?"

"You both won, sort of," Scott said. "Barry says the network wants to cash in on your sudden notoriety. They've been looking at the popularity of all the reality shows the big networks are running, and he says he's come up with an idea that's a guaranteed out-of-the-park hit."

Gina felt a chill of dread go up her spine. "Like what? No more boxing matches. I mean it, you two," she said, glaring at Deborah. "No more weird getups. I don't care what kind of ratings or money they're offering. I cook. That's it. That's all I do from now on."

"That's what they want you to do," Scott insisted. "They're even calling it Food Fight. They want to take both of you to this barrier island, down off the coast in South Georgia."

"I thought you said something about Utah," Gina said.

"Not Utah as in Salt Lake City," he said. "Eutaw Island. With an E-U. It's some godforsaken sand spit that Barry's research people dug up. Like a dozen people live over there. You have to get there by ferry, and there's only one paved road on the whole island. They'll take us over—our crew, and Moody's. Put us all up at some lodge. Then the two of you will be given a box of groceries—just staples like salt and pepper and cooking oil—and the first challenge. You have to plan, cook, and serve a meal using only what you find on the island. There'll be a couple of judges. Barry says they're still working that part out—and whoever wins the Food Fight wins their own show on TCC's fall lineup. The whole thing will be taped, and they'll show it in three installments during the fall sweeps."

"It's brilliant!" Deborah gushed. "Don't you get it, Gina? The object is to use fresh, natural, native ingredients. It plays to all your strengths."

"She's right," Scott said. "Tate Moody is toast."

Regina Foxton is dead meat," Val declared. "There's no way you can lose. You're a lock."

"Riiight," Tate said, looking dubious.

"Look. The rule is that the meal has to be made of stuff you find on the island. That's what you do every week on *Vittles*. The beauty of it is, we've already been there. We've got the place scouted already. And from what I remember of the place, there were no organic broccoli forests or herds of free-range chicken breast."

"There's just one hitch," Scott warned.

"We leave Saturday," Val said. "I gotta go shopping for snake boots."

Chapter 32

Lisa was sitting on the living room sofa, surrounded by a mound of just-washed laundry.

"What's going on?" Gina asked, sinking down onto the sofa beside her. "Who's dead?"

"Nobody's dead," Lisa said serenely, moving a stack of her thong panties aside. "Can't I do our laundry without you assuming the worst?"

"No," Gina said. "Who told you how to operate the washer?"

"There's a diagram on the inside of the lid," Lisa said. "Plus, I might have asked Mom."

"Mom?" Gina covered her face with the sofa cushions. "Our mom? Why would you talk to her without warning me?"

"We leave for Eutaw Island on Saturday," Lisa said. "You'll have a thousand things to do ahead of time to get ready for the Food Fight. I was just trying to help out."

Now Gina sat up straight. "How do you know about the Food Fight deal? Scott just told me about it an hour ago."

"Zeke? He's Barry's assistant? He called here while you were at the studio," Lisa said airily. "They're couriering over our itineraries and plane tickets, and he wanted to make sure he had the right address."

Gina narrowed her eyes. "What makes you think you're going to Eutaw Island?"

"Of course I'm going," Lisa said, rolling a T-shirt into a tight ball. "I'm your personal assistant. I'm invaluable. And by the way, Mom would really like to talk to you. She's already left two messages on your machine."

"What did she say?" Gina asked, taking the T-shirt away from Lisa and folding it so that it looked factory fresh.

"She said I should hand-wash delicates," Lisa said, frowning at the mangled remains of her best bra.

"I guess she's seen this week's *People*, huh?"

"Ooooh, yes," Lisa said, rolling her eyes.

Gina went into the bedroom. The blinking light on her answering machine reminded her of the twitching her left eyelid had been doing all day. She backed all the way out to the kitchen and poured herself a glass of chardonnay, which she sipped while refolding all the clothing her sister had wadded up.

She turned on the television and flipped channels until she got to The Cooking Channel. Research. For the next two hours, she watched back-to-back episodes of *Light and Luscious*—a dreary diet show hosted by a skeletal gay nutritionist—and *Pizza Power!*, which featured a pair of cheery Italian sisters who traveled the globe in search of the perfect pizza. She made notes about what worked and what didn't work. And when she'd finished that, she made more lists—lists of clothing to take to Eutaw Island, equipment she'd need, questions she had about the logistics of the Food Fight. Shortly after midnight, unable to avoid the inevitable any longer, she crawled into bed and punched the play button on the answering machine.

"Hello?" Her mother's high-pitched quavery voice seemed to have gone up an octave since they'd last talked on the phone.

"This is Mrs. Birdelle Foxton. Regina? Honey? Are you all right?"

The bedroom door opened, and Lisa stood in the doorway, dressed in panties and a severely shrunken T-shirt, swigging from a can of Red Bull. "I told her you were fine," Lisa offered.

"Honey," her mama went on, "I saw that article in *People* magazine today. And I like to have died. The girls at the Beauty Box tore it out of the magazine before I got there today, but afterward, I stopped into the drugstore to pick up your daddy's Gasex, and the girl behind the counter gave me such a nasty smirk, and then she gestured toward the magazine right there, and asked if you'd be moving home to Odum now that you were out of a job! Did you ever? Naturally, I just smiled and said 'We'll see' and then I bought it, and when I got home and saw the story, and that unfortunate picture of you, and well, I like to have died."

"She like to have died," Lisa said helpfully.

"Of course, you know, everybody down here in Odum is just real proud of you," Birdelle said. "Except for some un-Christian types whose names I won't mention, who are just jealous of how sweet and smart and successful you were."

"*Were?*" Gina repeated. "*Were?*"

"Now, Regina, honey," Birdell said, a little hesitantly, "I wish you had told us that you lost your job. It is nothing to be ashamed of. We would have completely understood. I swannee, I don't know what those people at Tastee-Town were thinking. What could have gotten into them, canceling your show like that?"

"I heard it was Scott Zaleski's getting into Danitra Bickerstaff's drawers that made them cancel the show," Lisa said. Gina responded by throwing a shoe at her.

"Anyway, the girls at the Beauty Box, and my Sunday school class, and Laura Anne across the street, and your aunt Opal, we are mounting a letter-writing campaign to Tastee-Town. We are going to give them a piece of our minds, believe you me. And, of course, we are completely boycotting Tastee-Town. Well, except Laura Anne says she can't be expected to give up her Tastee-Town frozen biscuits."

"Can't blame her," Gina said ruefully. "They do have the best frozen bagged biscuits. Better than Mama's even."

Birdelle's voice droned on. "Now, don't be mad at me, sweetheart, but I put a little box together for you. It's nothing much, just some coupons for canned goods, and some toiletries, and a package of my Coco-Nutty Toffee Bars."

"Sweet," Lisa said. "Dibs on the cookies."

"Your daddy tucked in some mad money for you too," Birdelle said. "Just a little something until you get yourself back on your feet. Well, I'll let you go. I'm sure you have a lot more important things to do than listen to me run on. You be sweet, now, you hear?"

Gina punched the stop button on the answering machine and pulled the covers up over her head.

"There's one more message," Lisa pointed out. She sat down on the bed beside her sister, patted her back, and punched the play button.

"This is Birdelle Foxton calling again," her mother said. "Gina, honey? Your daddy wants to know can you get that nice Tate Moody to autograph a cookbook for him. We're just crazy about *Vittles* down here. We never miss a show."

Chapter 33

Val Foster looked dubiously at the sixty-foot launch idling alongside the dock at Darien. The *Belle of the Seas* had once been painted white, but now most of that paint was gone, and its hull was streaked with green mold and clumps of dying barnacles.

The passenger "cabin" had a rickety roof and open sides, and the deck was littered with huge coils of oily ropes and vaguely nautical-looking machinery. Its engines spewed foul black smoke into the sticky summer air. The *Belle* had seen better days.

"Oh, no," Val said, backing away. "I don't think so."

"Don't be such a weenie, Val," Tate said, clapping a hand on her shoulder. "It'll be fine. She's perfectly seaworthy. And it's only a forty-minute crossing to Eutaw."

"Seaworthy," Val said, reaching into the pocket of her slacks for her cigarettes. "Isn't that how the *Titanic* was described on her maiden voyage?"

One of the deckhands, a wizened old geezer wearing greasy white pants and a yellowing undershirt, blew an air horn. "Fifteen minutes," he hollered. "Fifteen minutes till departure."

Val lit up the cigarette and inhaled deeply, her eyes narrowed behind their dinner-plate-size sunglasses.

Tate plucked the lit cigarette from her mouth and tossed it into the water. He picked up the canvas tote Val had dropped on the dock and hefted it onto his shoulder. "Come on," he coaxed. "Barbie and Ken and Company are already loaded aboard."

"Good," Val said, planting her feet firmly on the planks beneath them. "I'll wait till the real boat gets in."

"This is the real boat," he told her, tugging at her arm.

She allowed herself to be helped on board by the granddad grease monkey, and she even reluctantly handed over her other suitcase to be loaded with all the rest of the party's luggage.

Tate sat down on a rough wooden bench and motioned for her to join him. BoBo and Javier and the rest of the crew were milling around at the back of the boat, laughing and having a grand old time.

Once she'd settled herself, Val looked over her shoulder. Sitting on the row of benches behind her was Regina Foxton and her entourage. Her producer, Scott, was two rows back from her, engrossed in a paperback thriller, and, with his deep tan and casually rumpled khaki slacks and pale yellow polo shirt, he looked like something out of a Ralph Lauren catalog.

"You folks all set?" the geezer hollered, and without waiting for an answer, he gunned the boat's engine, and it lurched away from the dock.

"You okay, Moonpie?" Tate asked, leaning down to check the dog's crate.

The dog's answering thump said that he had fewer misgivings about the *Belle of the Seas* than Val.

"Hang in there, buddy," Tate said, scratching the dog's nose through the crate's metal mesh.

He hadn't been happy at hearing the news that the launch captain required all pets to be crated on board. He'd argued and whined and even threatened to cancel, but the girl at the ferry dock had been adamant. No dogs—or cats—were to be loose on the boat.

In fact, Barry Adelman's assistant, Zeke, had been required to get special permission from the family foundation that owned Eutaw to take Moonpie over at all.

Tate glanced over his shoulder at Gina, who quickly looked away when their eyes met. What was up with that woman? He thought they'd negotiated a truce after that fiasco at the boxing match, but she'd been distinctly edgy around him ever since.

Like this morning, when he'd run into her in the motel's diner. He replayed their brief encounter in his head.

She'd been seated alone, at the counter, dumping packet after packet of artificial sweetener into her coffee, when he'd wandered in with the Atlanta newspaper tucked under his arm. There were only two other people in the coffee shop.

"Mind some company?" He perched on the stool next to hers, not waiting for an answer.

She'd shrugged. Not exactly a warm welcome.

The waitress poured him a cup of coffee and disappeared into the kitchen.

"Should be pretty good weather today," Tate said, searching for some kind of an icebreaker. "Highs in the mid-eighties, lows down to the sixties tonight."

"That's nice," she'd said, concentrating on the packet of nondairy artificial creamer she was trying to puncture with her fingernail.

"Here," Tate said, taking it from her and ripping off the foil tab top before handing it back.

"I could have done it myself," she said.

"Just trying to help," Tate said.

She stirred the creamer into the coffee.

Something occurred to him. "Hey, Reggie. Aren't you the one who's always harping on natural this and seasonal that?"

"I'm an advocate of fresh, seasonal ingredients," she said cautiously.

"And yet," he said, picking up the discarded creamer packet and reading from the ingredients label, "you're using hydrogenated dexo-whatever, and blahblah chemicals in your coffee this morning. So, I'm assuming you'll be having those fresh, seasonal ingredients with the rest of your breakfast?"

Before she could answer, the waitress slid a plate onto the counter in front of her. Two runny fried eggs swam in a pool of bacon drippings, flanked by three bright red sausage links and a mound of buttered grits. Two cat's-head-size biscuits perched on the edge of the plate.

"Your side of bacon'll be out in a minute," she told Gina, whose face was getting pinker by the second.

"Healthy, seasonal," Tate agreed. "You sure walk the walk, all right."

"My plane didn't get in to Savannah till ten, and then there was an issue with the rental car, so we didn't get down here to Darien till after midnight last night," Gina said, dipping her fork into the grits. "I had no lunch or dinner. I'm famished. Anyway, we're in a diner in Darien, Georgia. It's not like they're gonna have something like a fruit plate on the menu."

The waitress came back with Gina's bacon, then tilted her head and gave Tate a friendly smile. "Ready for breakfast, hon?"

"You got anything healthy and seasonal like a fruit plate?" he asked.

"Sure," she said. "We got strawberries, cantaloupe, and peaches this morning. Anything else?"

"Maybe some low-fat yogurt?"

"Show-off," Gina said, doing her best not to laugh at him.

The waitress brought his fruit plate and a bowl of plain unflavored yogurt. He looked at it with undisguised displeasure.

"Yum," Gina said, reaching over and snagging one of his strawberries.

"Double yum," Tate said, staring down at the canned peach slices.

Taking pity on him, Gina sliced one of the biscuits in half, loaded it with jelly from the bowl on the counter, and laid two slices of bacon across it before topping it off with the other half.

"Here," she said, placing the biscuit sandwich on his plate. "You're breaking my heart."

"For real?" he asked. "Aw, Reggie, you really do like me."

She snagged another of his strawberries and sliced the top off with her butter knife. "Just don't make a move on my red-hot links, or you'll be drawing back a bloody stump."

They ate in companionable silence. He sipped his coffee and tried not to get caught staring at her.

"You're staring at me," she said, mopping up the last bit of fried egg with a bit of biscuit. "Do I have egg on my face?"

"Literally? No."

"What?"

He propped his chin on his elbow. "I'm trying to figure out what that Zaleski character sees in you."

"Thanks," she said dryly.

"I mean, you're so obviously not his type," Tate said, struggling to explain himself. "Not showbizzy, if you know what I mean. I mean, you're pretty, but not in an obvious, conventional way."

"You really know how to flatter a girl," Gina said.

"I suck at this," he said.

"Boy, howdy," she agreed.

"I'm usually great at pickup lines," Tate said, frowning. "Girls love me. They fall all over me. When I go to Bargain Mart, I have to fight 'em off with a stick. I think it's your fault. I think you throw me off my game."

She picked up her napkin and delicately dabbed at her mouth. "Maybe you should stick to trying to pick up girls in Bargain Mart. Instead of women in diners. You ever think of that?"

"How come you bleached your hair and cut it so short?"

She threw down the napkin, reached for her billfold, and took out a five-dollar bill. "This has been fun," she told him, with a crooked half smile. "We should definitely never do it again."

"Aw, Reggie," he drawled, spinning around on his stool so that his knees were touching hers. "Don't leave. You know I don't mean it like that. I like your hair. I really do. I liked it when it was long and brown, and I like it now." He reached out and touched a tendril that had fallen over her forehead, and to her surprise, she didn't stop him.

"Scott wanted me to go blonder so I'd look more glamorous for this TCC thing," she heard herself telling him. "D'John accidentally left the color on for too long because he was flirting with the cute Chinese takeout boy, and it burned my hair, and half of it broke off, and my little sister cut off the rest of it." Her eyes got very wide. "I can't believe I just told you all that."

"And I can't believe you let a jerk-off like Zaleski tell you what to do," Tate said. "Let alone sleep with him."

"I'm not," Gina said quickly. "Anymore."

And then she spun around on her stool and walked quickly out of the diner.

Chapter 34

As the dappled green waters of Eutaw Sound slid by, Tate slung an arm around Val's shoulder.

"See?" he said companionably. "Isn't this cool? Don't you love the fresh air and the open sea? Isn't this going to be great?"

"I fuckin' hate fresh seas and open air," Val said. "Always have. Makes me queasy."

"You'll get used to it."

"Never," Val said. "My next job, I'm thinking about game shows. Yeah. Game shows. You never leave the studio."

"Wait till you see Eutaw again. Miles of unspoiled beaches. Windswept dunes, gnarled oaks. Remember the herds of wild ponies? And that sea grass, ruffling in the breeze? And what about the whitetail deer? And there's what, thirty different kinds of birds? I wanna go back over to the other side of the island, see that blue heron rookery again. And you know my favorite part? Not a soul around, hardly. No condos, no suburban assault vehicles, no traffic jams. Spectacular."

Val turned and gave him an appraising look. "You're sure little Johnny Sunshine today. What's going on with you?"

"Nothing," Tate told her. "The tides and the moon are perfect. Fishing should be great for the next couple days."

"That's my boy," Val said, nodding approval. "We're gonna win this thing."

Gina Foxton could feel Tate watching her from two rows ahead. Her cheeks still burned from the memory of her blurted-out confession in the diner.

God! She shook her head, trying to dislodge the whole stupid scene from the place where it had embedded itself in her brain cells.

"Smile, girl!"

D'John trained a tiny, handheld camcorder inches away from her face.

"D'John, no!" she wailed. "I'm not even wearing any makeup."

"I know," he said, leaving the camera rolling. "This is for my Before file. Give D'John a smile so he can see where we gonna be shootin' the Botox on you."

Instead she showed him the back of her head.

He clucked his tongue in disapproval. "Bed-head! Didn't I teach you anything? Did you just roll out of bed and forget to look in a mirror this morning?"

D'John put the camera down and started fluffing her hair. "You can't be walkin' around in public looking like this, Gina," he fussed. "If you don't care about yourself, think about how it reflects on *me*. People see you, and they're saying, 'Damn! D'John did that? He musta been trippin'!' "

He picked up the camera again and pointed at her. "Tell the folks at home that you will never be seen in public again without full makeup and hair."

Gina rolled her eyes, but mugged for the camera as she was told, and, satisfied, he put the camera away and sat back to enjoy the scenery. She rested her head on D'John's shoulder and watched the sweep of sky and sea as it flowed past. "Beautiful, huh?" she murmured. "I think I'll go up on the bow in a little bit and get some sun."

"Can you say squamous-cell carcinoma?" D'John said, biting out the words. "Here." He reached into his straw beach bag and brought out a pink baseball cap and a tube of sunscreen. "I don't wanna see you step-ping foot out of the shade unless you're covered head to toe in this stuff."

D'John himself was dressed in a Moorish-inspired, ankle-length, pale yellow cotton tunic with black embroidery at the neck and hemline, matching draw-string pants, and rope-soled espadrilles. The brim of a huge floppy straw hat drooped over his shoulders. And he'd taken the precaution of coating his nose with a paste of white zinc oxide. His favorite white plastic Jackie O sunglasses shaded his eyes.

Lisa sat on the other side of D'John, already deep asleep, snoring with her mouth open. She'd disappeared the night before, shortly after they'd checked into the Riverside Inn, and had crept back into their shared room around dawn. Gina had no idea how her sister had managed to find nightlife in a tiny little town like Darien, but obviously she'd found somebody to party with, because when she'd finally managed to drag her-self down to the boat dock minutes before their depar-ture this morning, she was still dressed in a spangled black halter top, filmy black chiffon miniskirt, and lace-up, high-heeled black sandals.

Gina looked discreetly around, trying to figure out where Barry Adelman and the rest of the TCC people were. Zeke, Barry's assistant, had already unzipped his laptop computer from its carrying case and was busily tapping away on the keyboard, oblivious to the spectacular scenery flowing by.

Gina got up and made her way to the bow of the boat, tugging the bill of the cap down in deference to D'John's dire warnings about skin cancer.

The sun beat down on her shoulders, and the wind whipped at her hair and hat so that she had to hold them down with one hand. If she squinted, she could barely make out a dark shape in the distance. Seagulls cawed and dipped in and out of the water ahead of them, and suddenly, off to the right side of the boat, she saw the sleek dark gray backs of a pair of dolphins as they surfaced for air. Now, as she watched, two more smaller fins joined the other two, and then there were two more, close enough that she could hear their snorts as they surfaced. The dolphins reminded her of children at play, circling and, yes, leaping into the air, spraying droplets of water as they hit the water again.

"There's a school of fish they're feeding on." She turned, and Tate Moody was standing right beside her at the bow rail.

"I love watching dolphins," Gina said. "Before Lisa was born, my daddy used to take me with him to the coast, on fishing trips. We'd rent a little boat in Brunswick, just the two of us, and go out into the creek.

Sometimes when the tide was in, dolphins would swim right up beside the boat. Daddy'd always toss 'em some of our bait. It was like they were hanging around waiting on us for a handout."

"Do that now, and you'd get arrested," Tate said. "Dolphins have protected status in Georgia. It's against the law to do anything to lure them closer to boats. The experts think that's how a lot of 'em get injured and die."

"Oh, well," Gina said with a sigh.

"That's Eutaw up ahead," Tate said, pointing. "If you look over there to the right, in a minute, you can see a little bit of the lodge and the plantation house through the treetops."

"You've been here before?" Her voice was sharp.

"Yeah. Of course. I did a show here a couple years ago."

"I should have known," Gina said bitterly. "I thought this was supposed to be some big mystery destination. It's not really fair. Is it?"

"I had nothing to do with picking the spot for the Food Fight," Tate said. "I've been doing my show for two years. We've been all up and down the East Coast filming. But that doesn't necessarily give me an advantage. I've got no idea of what these clowns have up their sleeves for us."

"Guess I'll just have to be a better cook than you," Gina said, keeping her gaze on the approaching island.

"You think I'd cheat?" Tate asked.

"You're a man," she said, as if that settled the question.

"Zaleski cheated on you, is that it?" he asked.

"Like you hadn't already heard the whole tawdry tale?"

He tapped her on the shoulder, and reluctantly, she turned toward him.

"I'm kinda out of the loop on local gossip. Though, to tell you the truth, it doesn't surprise me."

"He *says* it was a onetime deal," Gina said, turning so her back was to the island and the wind was out of her face.

"Moron. You mind if I ask who it was?"

She shrugged. "Danitra Bickerstaff."

"Who's she?"

"You really are out of touch. She's married to Wiley Bickerstaff III, the owner of the Tastee-Town supermarket chain."

He grimaced. "Aren't they . . ."

"Yeah. My sponsor. Or, they were my sponsor. Wiley caught 'em in the act, and so now, come spring, my show's off the air. Unless—"

"You win the Food Fight," he finished for her. "And get a shot at the big leagues."

She gave him a sideways look. "Make you feel guilty?"

"Nope," he said. "This is a whole separate deal here. May the best cook win. Anyway, I'm not the one who cheated on you. See, that's one big difference between me and Zaleski."

"What? You're smart enough not to get caught?"

"I'm not all that smart," Tate said. "But if we were together, I'd never cheat on you."

"Sweet," she said, touched.

"Geen?"

Lisa lurched toward her, her face a grayish shade of green.

Gina moved aside just in time for her sister to hang her head over the rail and puke her guts out.

D'John leaned over the side of the boat to catch the action on camera. "Lisa, baby," he called. "Look this way."

"Ohhhh." Lisa moaned, pressing her face to the rail. "Get me off this boat."

"You okay?" Gina asked, pulling a tissue from the pocket of her shorts to wipe her sister's face.

"Noooo," Lisa said. "I need this thing to stop moving."

Gina looked up. They were only a few yards from a long wooden dock extending out over a stretch of salt marsh and sea grass. Parked under a covered pavilion at the end of the dock were half a dozen golf carts.

"Five minutes," Tate assured her. As they watched, a golf cart trailering a string of luggage carts came bumping over the dock toward the end. "The guys from the plantation will get the baggage and equipment unloaded, but we'll take those carts up to the lodge for check-in," he said.

"Gina? Lisa?" Scott strode toward them. "I'll get you guys up to the lodge." He put a proprietary hand on Lisa's elbow. "Come on, Lisa. You'll feel better once you're out of the sun."

Lisa groaned, pressed both hands to her mouth, then barfed all over Scott's Ralph Lauren polo shirt.

"Got it! D'John said triumphantly, neatly sidestepping the mess as he panned the camcorder for a wide-angle shot of the disaster.

Chapter 35

L isa!"

Zeke rushed up and put his arms around Gina's retching sister. He tenderly helped her back to her seat and proceeded to mop her up with the roll of paper towels fetched by one of the crew members.

Scott stared down at his ruined shirt and his spattered shoes. "She did this on purpose," he said, his voice low and furious. He pointed his finger at Gina. "You told her to do this."

"Me?" Gina sputtered. "You think I can make my sister barf on command?"

Tate had to move away, his shoulders heaving with suppressed laughter.

Sensing the tension, D'John quietly followed, his camera switched to off.

Scott watched them walk away. "You think this is funny too?" he asked Gina. "This was a Purple Label Ralph Lauren. It cost a hundred and eighty-five dollars," he said, stripping it off and flinging it into a nearby trash barrel. "It was a gift from a very special friend," he added, with more than a touch of malice.

He looks good shirtless, Gina thought idly. All those hours on the rowing machine, on the elliptical, at the weight bench, and on the beach had paid off. His shoulders rippled with muscles, his golden chest hair glinted against the deep bronze of his skin. He was flat-bellied. He was buff, he was tan. He was soulless.

"Maybe if you play nice, she'll buy you another one," Gina offered.

His eyes clouded. "I'm sorry," he said, running his hand through his hair. "That was way off base. Danitra did give me the shirt, but I swear, it was just that one time, when we were at the Ritz."

"None of my business," Gina said lightly, feeling a faint stabbing in the vicinity of her left ventricle.

"I want it to be your business again," Scott said. "I want you to know I haven't seen her or talked to her since that night." His voice faltered. "I . . . don't know why I wanted to throw that in your face. I was mad at Lisa. And maybe . . ." He gazed into the distance, and she saw he was watching Tate, sitting beside Val Foster, deep in conversation. "I was jealous. I saw you this morning, in the diner. With him. You looked pretty friendly. And just now . . ."

"We were talking," Gina said coldly. "About dolphins. And then we were talking about the island. He's been to Eutaw before. I think it gives him an unfair advantage."

"Shit!" Scott said, suddenly energized. "That sucks. I'd never even heard of the place before."

The sharp bleat of the air horn sounded, and suddenly the launch bumped hard against the dock.

"Debarkation point, Eutaw Island," the deckhand called.

"People?" Zeke was standing beside the deckhand now, his laptop and briefcase strapped across his chest, bandolier-style.

"Everybody?" he repeated. "This is Eutaw Island. Before you depart the boat, I've got dossiers for everybody." He reached into the briefcase and pulled out a stack of shiny orange vinyl packets, which he started passing around.

Gina grabbed one of the packets. "Food Fight!" read the label on the packet. "An Adel-Weis Production for The Cooking Channel."

She opened it up and scanned the first page, but she needn't have bothered, since Zeke had already started his briefing session.

D'John stood against the boat's deck rail, panning the camera at the crew, and then focusing on Zeke's big moment.

"Eutaw Island is the southernmost coastal barrier island in the state of Georgia," he began. "The name is thought to be derived from a Creek Indian word that, translated loosely, means 'damned good oysters.' "

That drew a faint round of laughter from the surprised crew. Zeke adjusted his reading glasses on the end of his nose and plowed onward in his lecture.

"Before the Civil War, the entire island was owned by Colonel Bradyn Nathaniel Hooker, a wealthy cotton planter. Colonel Hooker built a plantation home here, called Rebeccaville, named for his only daughter.

"At one time, nearly one hundred slaves lived and worked on Rebeccaville, which produced the highest quality Sea Island cotton on the Georgia coast. The old tabby-shell slave quarters have been preserved and are sometimes rented—"

"Slaves!" D'John lowered the camera. His voice was indignant. "I'm not staying in any damned slave quarters."

Zeke blanched. "We'll all be staying in the lodge while on the island."

"Fine," D'John said, gathering up his belongings. "As long as we've got *that* settled." He came and stood beside Gina, listening for more details.

Zeke cleared his throat. "The island and the plantation remain today in the hands of Brady Hooker's heirs, who operate it as a conference center, wildlife preserve, and corporate retreat.

"The entire building complex was completely restored and modernized by the Hooker family five years ago. At the lodge, you'll all have access to the living areas, which include a living room and dining room, library, and of course, a screened porch that looks out over the plantation's grounds, much of which have been allowed to return to their natural, unspoiled state."

"Does that mean bugs and snakes?" D'John asked. He poked Gina in the ribs. "You know this queen does not mess with bugs and snakes."

"Where will we be doing the actual cooking for the Food Fight?" Gina asked, hoping to quiet D'John.

Zeke beamed his approval. "I'm glad you asked. We've had a crew over here all week, building a state-of-the-art kitchen in the ruins of the mansion's old ballroom. I haven't seen it myself yet, but Barry says it's stunning."

"A kitchen?" Tate frowned. "We don't each have our own kitchen? We have to share?"

"Barry feels it'll make for great television," Zeke said. "And there will be plenty of room for both of you."

"I don't like it," Scott said, folding his arms across his chest. "Nobody said anything to me about shared facilities."

Valerie yawned loudly. "Can we just get the hell off this boat? I've got to pee. And I'm hungry."

"And I don't feel so good," Lisa said, wobbling as she stood.

"Fine," Zeke announced, throwing her a sympathetic look. "The golf carts will take you all up to the lodge, and the caretaker will meet you in the lobby and give everybody their keys and room assignments." He glanced down at his watch. "Our lunch should be ready when we get there, and the dining room will be open until one thirty."

"Is there a bar?" Val asked pointedly.

"I believe wine and beer will be available after five o'clock," Zeke said. "After lunch, we'll have a meeting to go over the rules and procedures for the Food Fight, and we'll discuss the taping schedule."

"Let's go," Scott told Gina, moving toward the ramp that had been lowered from the ferry to the dock. "I want to start getting the lay of the land as soon as possible. Moody's already got a head start on us."

Gina nodded in agreement and looked around for her younger sister. But Lisa was already being helped off the boat by Zeke.

Chapter 36

Val watched Gina Foxton and her producer/boyfriend climb into the first golf cart lined up at the end of the dock at Eutaw Island. Scott Zaleski swung himself behind the steering wheel and patted the seat beside him. But Gina shook her head, motioned to D'John, the makeup artist, to take that seat, and instead sat on the backward-facing backseat. Val chuckled at the look on Zaleski's face. A moment later, he was flying down the dock in the direction of the island.

Tate sat back in the passenger seat of their cart and watched them go.

"Trouble in paradise?" Val asked.

"Yeah," Tate said. "You could say that. The dickhead got her show canceled because he was screwing the sponsor's wife."

"Ow," Val said. She backed the golf cart away from the pile of baggage mounded on the dock, and then steered the cart down the dock, her head bouncing as the cart sped along on the weathered board planks.

"She's pissed that I've already been on the island," Tate said, hanging on to his seat with both hands. "Seems to think it's cheating."

"Tough," Val said.

The woman who opened the front door at the Eutaw Island Lodge was as tall as she was wide, with short silvery hair and bright blue eyes set into a deeply tanned and lined face. She wore khaki slacks, a pink T-shirt with "eutaw island" embroidered in script over her left breast, and weather-beaten leather deck shoes.

"Welcome," she said, shaking hands with D'John, Scott, and Gina as they walked into the lodge's entry hall, Lisa trailing slowly in their wake. "I'm Alice McLemore, but everybody around here just calls me Sis." She put a sympathetic hand on Lisa's shoulder. "You okay, shug? Usually the boat ride over from Darien is pretty smooth."

"It was very smooth," Gina said. "It's not seasickness. She's just a little . . . hung over."

Sis looked from Gina to Lisa. "You two are the sisters? I've got you sharing a double. It's two beds. I hope that's all right."

"Fine," Lisa mumbled.

The door opened again, and Tate and Val and the rest of both crews stepped inside the lodge's living room.

"Welcome, everybody," Sis said. "Lunch is in the dining room in fifteen minutes. That'll give you time to drop your stuff in your rooms, and then meet back down here. Please don't be late, because I promise you, you do not want to get off on the wrong foot with Iris and Inez."

"No lunch," Lisa said, groaning. "Bed."

While everybody else was stepping up to the counter to check in and pick up their keys, D'John was strolling around the lodge, camcorder in hand.

"So, this is the lodge at Rebeccaville," he said, in a golf commentator's hushed voice.

It was a large, pleasant room, Gina thought. Low ceilings with heavy age-blackened beams, polished heart-pine floors scattered with worn Oriental rugs, and furniture that reminded her of the living room of any well-bred Atlanta matron. The overstuffed sofas and squashy armchairs were covered in a bright flowered chintz, and the tables and cabinets were good antique reproductions in the expected mahogany. Around the walls were nicely framed bird and botanical prints, with a large, well-done oil seascape hung over the mantel of the large fireplace that took up most of one wall.

D'John didn't seem overly impressed. "Hmm," he said, panning the camera across the room. "I'd call it very Buckhead wannabe. Not really shabby, but it's not a *Veranda* magazine cover, either."

"Shh!" Gina hushed him. "I'm going to go look in on Lisa. See you down here in ten minutes. I don't know who Iris and Inez are, but I know I don't want to get 'em mad at me."

She found her room on the second floor of the lodge. Lisa was sprawled out facedown on one of the queen-size beds in the room, dressed only in her panties and bra, her clubbing ensemble left in a heap on the floor.

"Lisa?" Gina bent down to check on her younger sister. "Are you all right?"

"Hot," Lisa said. "No air-conditioning."

Gina stood up and looked around the room. There was a set of triple windows on the wall facing the bed. The windows were open, and the frilly lace curtains moved slightly in the breeze coming off the marsh.

"It's not so bad," Gina said. "We've got a nice sea breeze, even though it's midday."

"No AC," Lisa mumbled.

"I'll see if Sis will send up a fan," Gina said. She stepped into the bathroom to wash her hands and face, and then hurried downstairs to the dining room.

She met Scott on the broad stair landing between floors.

"How's your room?" he asked solicitously. "Everything okay?"

"Fine," she said. "No air-conditioning, but there's a decent breeze coming in. Lisa's not too happy about it, though."

"She all right?" He didn't even try to look concerned.

"She'll be fine," Gina said. "I'll take her some ginger ale and saltine crackers after lunch. That usually perks her up."

Barry Adelman stood outside the entrance to the dining room, beaming at them as they approached. He was dressed in what Gina guessed was a Manhattanite's version of island-wear, a scientifically pressed Tommy Bahama shirt adorned with parrots and hibiscus blossoms, soft banana-colored silk trousers, Italian leather loafers, sans socks, and a black ball cap bearing the Adel-Weis Productions logo.

"Gina!" he exclaimed. "And Scott! How are you two?" He took Gina's hands in his. "Isn't this great? Are you two as excited as I am?"

"Absolutely," she said, accepting the kisses he landed on both cheeks. "I'm thrilled to be here, Mr. Adelman."

"It's Barry," he corrected. "Come on into the dining room and meet the rest of the kids. We'll bring everybody up to speed on what we've got planned for this week."

The dining room had faded chintz wallpaper, a long, polished mahogany table, and a dozen good repro Chippendale chairs arranged around it. A huge brass chandelier held candles instead of lightbulbs. Seated around the table were "the kids," as Adelman referred to them: gaffers, cameramen, sound and light techs, and two or three other assorted crew members whose names Gina couldn't remember and whose job description she didn't quite understand.

Tate Moody and Val sat at the far end of the table, and Adelman pointed Scott and Gina to two chairs beside D'John, who was already seated near the door, chatting away with one of the New York crew members.

"All right, everybody," Barry announced, standing at the head of the table like the patriarch of his newly formed clan. "Let's get some lunch under our belts, and then we'll have our powwow."

He sat down, and as he did so, two scrawny, dour-faced women in their early sixties entered the room, each balancing an enormous food-laden tray on one shoulder.

The women wore black slacks and the same pink T-shirt as Sis. With their high cheekbones and gray hair pulled back into tight knoblike buns, they appeared to be identical twins.

"Miss?" one of the women said, pausing beside Gina's chair. "You want da swimp or da chicken salad?"

"Uh . . ." Gina paused, trying to decipher the server's question.

"Get the shrimp salad," Tate called from the far end of the table. "Inez makes the best shrimp salad on the Georgia coast."

Inez flashed a dazzling smile in Tate's direction and giggled girlishly. "Oh, you hush up, you," she retorted. She turned to Gina. "He's a mess, ain't he?"

"A big mess," Gina agreed. "I guess I'll try the shrimp salad."

The thick white crockery plate held a mound of shredded iceberg lettuce and a huge scoop of pale pink shrimp salad, along with two slices of dead-ripe tomato and a handful of Town House crackers.

She loaded a cracker with a forkful of the shrimp salad, tasted, and nearly swooned. The shrimp were sweet and moist and perfectly cooked, finely diced, and mixed with mayonnaise that could only have been homemade. She could taste a hint of lemon juice, and a bite of green that she identified as chopped capers. She was superbly happy and deeply disturbed.

Tate Moody was right. Again.

Talk swirled around the table. Barry Adelman and Scott had a long discussion about wine, and college basketball, and some kind of digital technology that Gina did not understand. When Gina looked up, she saw Tate, down at the end of the table, idly chatting with his producer when he was not giving her that cocky told-you-so look of his.

Gina managed to finish her lunch and restrain herself from picking up her plate to lick clean the last remnants of the shrimp salad. Iris came back around the table, offering small dishes of dessert—some kind of cake, peach cobbler, or butterscotch pudding.

"No, thanks," Gina said, sipping her iced tea. What she really wanted was another scoop of that shrimp salad. And the recipe. She'd kill for that recipe.

Suddenly, Barry was tapping the side of his glass with his spoon. "Everybody," he called, getting to his feet. "I know you've all been on pins and needles, so let's get down to business."

Gina sat back in her chair, arms crossed.

"*Food Fight*"—Barry said, pausing to add dramatic effect— "is going to be the biggest hit of the fall season."

He looked around the room, nodding thoughtfully. "And you people are going to make that hit."

"Yeah!" Scott said, pumping the air with his fist as the others applauded politely.

"You!" Barry said, pointing at Tate, "are going to go mano a mano against the South's leading lady of healthy regional cuisine!

"And you," he said, turning to Gina with a flourish, "are going to have to figure out how to catch and cook a dinner in the wilds of Eutaw Island, competing against the wiliest outdoorsman on land or sea.

"And I," he said modestly, "am going to make that magic happen."

He turned toward Zeke and snapped his fingers. Zeke peeled a yellow sticky from his shirtfront and handed it to his boss.

"Logistics," Barry announced. "Tomorrow morning at oh-eight-hundred, you'll each be assigned your kitchen space over at the old ballroom at Rebeccaville. Each refrigerator and pantry will be stocked with identical ingredients. You'll be given staples—salt, pepper, a limited amount of seasonings, flour, sugar, cornmeal, cooking oil, eggs, butter, cream, and the most basic of vegetables: onions, carrots, celery, and potatoes. Your kitchens will have the most modern appliances available—all provided, of course, by our sponsors, Viking."

Barry turned toward Zeke again, and was handed yet another yellow sticky note.

"Oh, yes," he added. "Makeup and wardrobe call will be at oh-seven-hundred."

"Makeup?" Tate started to object, but Val put her hand over his mouth.

"This isn't regional television," Barry said blandly. "Our audience expects our chefs to look like the entertainment stars they are."

"Uh-huh," D'John agreed, nodding vigorously. "I heard that."

"Time and task," Zeke whispered.

"Right," Barry said. "When we start taping, you'll be given your cooking task for the day, and the time limit. Taping will start immediately afterward."

He crossed his arms over his chest, looking pleased with himself. "Any questions?"

"Uh, Barry," Gina ventured. "Where, exactly, will we be getting the rest of the ingredients for this mystery meal we'll be preparing?"

"From the bounty of the sea and the land," Barry said, throwing his arms out in an expansive gesture.

"Catch it or kill it," Tate said smugly.

"Fine," Gina snapped. "Will we have fishing tackle, that kind of thing, available?"

Zeke handed Barry a yellow sticky. He read and then crumpled it and stuck it in the pocket of his slacks.

"You'll have what you need," he said. "Obviously, we want to leave you in the dark about some elements of the competition, in order to heighten the suspense for our viewers."

"Judges?" Tate asked. "Who decides the winner?"

Barry blinked. "The judges decide, of course." He held up a hand.

"All right, everybody, that's enough for now. We'll want the crew members to stay here after the lunch dishes are cleared, for our production meeting."

"You two," he said, nodding toward Gina, and then Tate, "will have the afternoon to familiarize yourself with the beauty of Eutaw Island. You'll each have a golf cart at your disposal."

"And a two-way radio," Zeke added. "Cell-phone reception is pretty poor over here."

Immediately, Scott and Barry seized their Black-Berrys and started madly thumbing.

"No service," Scott said bleakly.

"So you'll want to make sure you have your radios with you anytime you leave the lodge, just in case something happens while you're out in the wilds," Zeke said.

"Don't want to lose track of our stars," Barry said.

"Oh," Zeke said, standing up and gathering his clip-board and file folders. "One more thing. There are cart paths all over the island. Stay on the paths, and you shouldn't have any problems."

Gina stood up too and stretched. She was eager to get outside and try to start catching up to the unfair lead Tate Moody already had over her.

"And one more thing," Zeke called. "Stay away from the alligators."

"Alligators!" D'John shrieked. "Jesus, Lord!"

Chapter 37

Tate bolted from the dining room, but Val managed to grab his arm before he broke into a run.

"Hey, hang on a minute," she said. "What's the hurry?"

"You heard what Barry said," Tate said. "I want to get out and ride around the island, scope out the possibilities for tomorrow. It's been almost two years since I was here last, you know."

"It's an island," Val said. "What could have changed? It's not like they've opened a new supermarket or restaurant."

"You're kidding, right? You haven't really spent two years on this show without figuring out that everything takes advance planning."

Val shrugged and gestured toward the door. "Be my guest."

"You're not coming with me?"

"Hmm. Let me think. It's summer, we're on an island, and it's Africa hot. There are bugs, snakes, and yes, alligators. No. Thanks for the invite, but I think I'd rather have a root canal. You go do your homework. I'm gonna go sneak a smoke, and then I'm headed for the beach to work on my tan."

Gina opened the door to her room and tiptoed inside. "Lisa?" she whispered. The room was in half darkness and was now, officially, stifling. Her sister was still facedown on the bed, fast asleep, a tiny trickle of drool pooling on her pillowcase.

Gina set the plate of saltines and the can of ginger ale on the bedside table. She went out into the hallway and brought in the portable fan Sis had loaned her. She set it up on the dresser, pointed it toward her sister's bed, and turned it on.

The fan hummed quietly, and the fringed edge of the chenille bedspread ruffled in its breeze.

From outside the bedroom window, Gina could hear the raucous calls of a blue jay sitting on the branch of a sweet gum tree, and the thrum of cicadas. A faint floral scent wafted through the room. She was operating on only a few hours' sleep, and the adrenaline of the food fight was fast running out. She was sorely tempted to join her sister in an impromptu nap.

She stood and stretched. A movement outside the window caught her eye. She went over and peered out, just in time to see Tate Moody careening away on a golf cart.

"Crap!" She jammed her cap on her head, grabbed a bottle of water from the dresser, and was out the door before she did an about-face. "Bug spray," she chided herself. "Don't want to go on camera with bug bites."

She found her golf cart parked outside the front porch, with the promised two-way radio stashed in a cup holder that also held a map of the island. She slathered the insect repellent on her arms, legs, neck, and face while studying the map.

Eutaw Island, she discovered, was shaped roughly like a large thumb with a wart extending on each side. On the inland side of the island, facing Eutaw Sound and, across the sound, the mainland and Darien, the wart held the ferry dock where they'd landed earlier in the day.

According to the map, on the ocean side of the island, the wart was the site of the Eutaw Lighthouse. The cart paths seemed to form a network throughout every part of the island. All she needed to do was figure out where she wanted to go first. Tate Moody had headed east. Gina decided she would go north.

The day was already a scorcher, with the sun blazing down white-hot on the top of her ball cap. She was glad of the insect repellent as a cloud of gnats rose up from the tall grass on the roadside.

The branches of huge old live oaks lined the crushed oyster-shell cart path on either side, their low-lying branches extending to form a canopy dripping with Spanish moss. Riding down the path, Gina suddenly felt herself in a cool, green tunnel. Squirrels scampered up and down the trees, and twice she saw armadillos scuffling through the fallen leaves and palmettos. She was maybe a quarter of a mile away from the lodge when she spied a woman walking along the path up ahead. She wore a pink T-shirt and black slacks, and a pair of sturdy black shoes were slung by their knotted laces over her shoulder.

"Inez?" she called, coming up alongside the woman.

"I'm Iris," the older woman said.

"Sorry," Gina said quickly. "Can I give you a ride somewhere?"

Iris hesitated only a moment. "Guess that'd be awright," she said, climbing in beside Gina.

"Where to?"

"Up yonder," Iris said, pointing forward. "They's a fork in the road. When you get to that, go on to the right."

"I'm Gina Foxton," Gina said, groping for a thread of conversation.

"TV lady," Iris said, nodding in recognition. "You right cute, ain't you?"

Gina laughed. "Well, my mama and daddy seem to think so."

Iris studied her for a moment. "Mr. Tate Moody thinks so too."

"Oh, no," Gina said quickly. "I'm sure you're mistaken about that."

"I know what I seen," Iris said. "He cut his eyes away when he see you lookin', but he like what he sees."

"He's just watching me because we're in competition for this network show," Gina explained.

"You say so," Iris said, unconvinced. She took a handkerchief from the pocket of her slacks and mopped her sweat-dampened face with it.

Anxious to change the subject, Gina pointed at the older woman's bare feet. "Don't your feet get cut up walking on these oyster shells?"

Iris's laugh sounded like a honk. She wriggled her toes. "Me 'n' Inez, we been goin' barefeets on this island our whole life. Shoes is what hurts my feets. But Sis, she want us to wear 'em at work."

"You and Inez are twins?" Gina asked.

"Yes'm. She's the older one," Iris said. "Think she knows it all too. Like I can't make swimps as good as her!"

"About that shrimp salad today," Gina said, seizing the moment. "That really was the best shrimp salad I have ever tasted in my life."

Iris nodded. "You seen Inez actin' like she made that up her ownself? That swimps was our mama's recipe. Inez, she take the credit, but Mama the one made that up."

"The chicken salad looked delicious too," Gina said.

"It ain' too bad," Iris conceded. "Me and Inez, we come up with that. Just use the same dressin' we put on the swimps, but with some pecans and a little bit of honey and some chopped-up celery."

"Homemade mayonnaise?" Gina asked.

"Oh, yeah," Iris said. "Mama didn't have hardly no money for store-bought."

They were at the fork in the road. "Right here you turn," Iris directed. "You could let me off here, if you want."

"Oh, no," Gina said. "I'll take you all the way. Now. About that shrimp salad. Do you catch the shrimp over here?"

"Yes'm," Iris said. "Up in the creek. My daddy, he used to knit nets, sell 'em over there in Darien. We got a good net he made us."

Gina handed her the map of Eutaw Island. "Could you show me a good place to catch shrimp in the creek?"

Iris gave her a quizzical look. "You studyin' gettin' you some swimps? City gal like you?"

It was Gina's turn to laugh. "I grew up in Odum. You know where that is?"

"Over there 'round by Waycross?" Iris said.

"That's right," Gina said. "My daddy taught me to shrimp too. He didn't knit nets, but he taught me how to throw a cast net as good as a boy. I didn't have any brothers," she added. "Just a younger sister."

"Yeah, sisters is a trial and a tribulation," Iris said with a dramatic sigh. She picked up the map and squinted down at it. With a long bony finger she stabbed at a squiggly line. "That right there is Fiddlercrab Creek. That's da place me 'n' Inez goes for swimps."

Gina studied the map. "Is it hard to get to? I don't see a cart path marked near it."

"You got a boat?" Iris asked.

"I don't know," Gina admitted. "They haven't told us too much yet. All we know is that tomorrow, they'll tell us our challenge, and then we have to go out and gather food for a meal and cook it."

"Hmm," Iris said. She leaned over the edge of the cart and spit a stream of brown chewing tobacco into the soft sand.

"We never had us no boat neither," she said.

Suddenly, the golf cart hit an exposed root in the road and nearly bumped then both off their seats.

"Whoa, Nelly!" Iris hollered.

"Sorry," Gina said.

"Right up here," Iris said, grabbing Gina's arm. "Stop the car."

Gina did as she was instructed and stopped the cart at the edge of a clearing among the oaks and palmettos.

Sitting behind a bleached-out cedar post fence, Iris's house was a tidy wooden cottage with a tin roof and a tiny covered porch crammed with potted plants. A large tree shaded one corner of the house, and a row of hydrangeas with huge blue mopheads extended across the concrete block foundation. The yard was neatly swept sand, edged with rows of sun-whitened conch shells. A satellite dish poking up from the roof of the house was the only reminder that this was the twenty-first century.

"How pretty," Gina exclaimed. "Have you lived here long?"

"Me 'n' Inez lived here our whole life," Iris said, beaming with pride. "Our granddaddy built this house. We grow'd up here, went to school here. The other chirren went off to the mainland, got jobs and families, but when Mama got sick, me and Inez moved in here and took care of her and Daddy till they died."

"You never married?" Gina asked gently.

"No'm," Iris said, climbing out of the cart. "Had me some boyfriends, but wadn't none of 'em as good a man as my daddy, so I just never did jump the broom. Now, Inez, she was boy-crazy for sure. Had her two different sorry husbands, and buried 'em both a long time ago."

"That's too bad," Gina said.

"Too bad for them." Iris cackled. "Folks said my sister wore them mens slap out!" She looked over her shoulder at her house. "You like to come in, have a glass of buttermilk?"

"I'd love some. I don't know when I've had a glass of fresh buttermilk," Gina said. "Don't tell me you keep a cow here on the island."

"Not no more we don't," Iris said sadly. "We got store-bought."

Gina edged the cart into the sandy edge of the yard and followed her hostess inside a rusty iron gate. As soon as she set foot in the yard, she was assailed with a cacophony of clucks and cries and flapping wings. Half a dozen large brown-and-white chickens rushed toward her.

"Guinea hens!" Gina cried. "My grandmother always had guinea hens on her farm."

"Yes'm," Iris said proudly. "We've always had 'em too. Seem like the only old-timey thing left on this island."

Iris pushed the door to the cottage open. "Well, this is it," she said, hanging back shyly. "It ain't nothin' much, but it's ours, free and clear."

It was cool and dim inside. The cottage's main room was a combination living room, dining room, and kitchen. An ancient brown sofa and a black vinyl recliner with duct-taped arms were positioned in front of a modern-looking television in one corner of the room. The wall above the television held rows of framed family pictures.

The other half of the room was a throwback to the old-timey times Iris had spoken of. An ancient cast-iron cookstove had pride of place in the kitchen. A collection of battered tin pots and pans and cast-iron skillets hung from nails pounded into the bare wooden walls, and a box fan held the only window propped open.

"Sit down right here," Iris said, pointing to a wooden kitchen table with two chrome and vinyl dinette chairs.

She went over to a rusted refrigerator and brought out a carton of buttermilk, poured a glass for her guest, and sat down beside Gina.

"Now," Iris said, sighing contentedly. "Lemme tell you 'bout catchin' you a nice mess of swimps."

Chapter 38

Val Foster managed to make it through the communal dinner that night by sheer willpower—fueled by two strong gin and tonics and three surreptitious smoke breaks.

She hadn't seen her star since he'd left the lodge sometime after lunch. She'd gotten back from the beach—as if you could call it a real beach; there were no daiquiri bars on this godforsaken island, no lounge chairs, and certainly no cabana boys—and found that Tate was AWOL. She'd tried repeatedly to raise him on the two-way radio, with no luck.

At dinner, Barry Adelman had quizzed her closely about Tate's whereabouts.

"Oh," she said, trying to sound unconcerned, "he's getting himself in the zone for the Food Fight. He always does this the night before we tape. He goes off into the wilderness and gets his chakra in harmony with the universe."

"Chakra?" Barry looked to Zeke for translation.

"I'm Presbyterian," Zeke said apologetically. "We don't have chakras."

"Just a technical question," Scott said, leaning forward to catch Barry's attention. "If Moody's not back by morning, we win the Food Fight by default—right?"

"He'll be back," Val said. "We came to play. And win."

"Glad to hear it," Barry said. "Our judges are flying into Savannah tonight, and they'll be over on the first ferry in the morning." He turned to Zeke for confirmation. "Right?"

"As far as we know," Zeke agreed. "The last e-mail I had from Deidre said that we should pick them up at the ferry dock tomorrow at eight."

"Deidre?" Scott pounced on the name. "Do you mean Deidre Delaney?"

"Oops," Barry said, rising to his feet. "You didn't hear that from me." He turned and gave Gina an abbreviated bow. "You folks have a nice evening. I'm expecting a call from Wendy, and then I've got a conference call with the coast."

"Uh, Barry . . ." Zeke said, shaking his head sorrowfully.

"What? Still no phone reception?" Barry's face darkened. "That's absurd."

"Here, Barry," Scott said, thrusting his BlackBerry at Adelman. "Try mine. It's the beta version. My electronics guy in Taiwan says you can get reception on Mars. But I did have to go out to the end of the ferry dock earlier today to get a call through."

"You got through?" Barry said, snatching up the phone. "Great! I'll bring it back when I'm done."

"No problem," Scott said, throwing a triumphant glance Val's way.

"Shall I drive you down there on the golf cart?" Zeke asked, pushing his chair away from the table.

"No, no," Adelman said quickly. "I feel like taking a spin by myself, before it gets dark."

As the dishes were being cleared by two high-school-age girls, Sis came into the dining room with a tray holding a silver pitcher and half a dozen tall ice-filled glasses.

"It's a tradition at the lodge to have Arnold Palmers out on the porch after dinner," she announced. "Or, if you'd like something stronger, we can manage that too."

"Have you got any Natty Lite?" Lisa asked.

Sis nodded.

"Make it two," Zeke added, following Lisa out the front door.

"An Arnold Palmer sounds great," Gina said, getting up from the table and stretching.

"What's an Arnold Palmer?" Val asked.

"Iced tea and lemonade," Sis told her.

"Great," Val said. "I'll have an Arnold Palmer and gin."

On the porch, Val staked out a rocker on one side of the front door, and Scott and Gina took rockers at the opposite end. Lisa and Zeke had already claimed the wicker swing, and Gina could hear her sister's laugh from where she sat.

Dusk was settling over the island. The last remnants of a peach-hued sunset filtered through the canopy of oaks and pines, and already Gina could see the tiny sparks of fireflies in the shrubbery at the edge of the porch. In the distance, she heard the soft hooting of an owl.

"I wonder what Moody's up to," Scott said, rocking animatedly.

"Who cares?" Gina said. "Right now, I just want to look at the sky and relax. I'll worry about him tomorrow."

"I'll worry about him right now," Scott said. "He's up to something, I guarantee."

"Scott?" Gina asked. "Who's Deidre Delaney?"

His rocker abruptly stopped creaking. "You really never heard of her?" her producer asked incredulously.

"Nope. Should I have?"

"She's the Deidre of Deidre's on South Beach," Scott said. "She's just the hottest celebrity chef in Miami. Hell, the country, just about."

"Oh," Gina said, feeling slightly out of touch. "If she's from Miami, what's she know about southern food? Isn't that what we're supposed to be doing here?"

"She's a top-gun foodie," Scott said. "A tastemaker. Her presence as a judge ups the ante that much more. It means Barry's really going all out for this Food Fight."

Now she felt queasy. "Miami? What if she doesn't like my kind of food? I mean, here on Eutaw, I won't have access to papayas or mahimahi or cilantro or anything trendy like that."

Scott reached over and laid his hand on top of hers. "Neither will Moody," he said, trying to sound reassuring. "Unless . . ."

Gina stared pointedly at his hand. "I don't like Tate Moody. But I don't think he's the type to cheat."

"And I am, is that what you're saying?" he asked, his voice low and full of heat. "What's it gonna take to convince you how sorry I am, Gina? You want me to crawl on my belly? Write an apology in my own blood?"

"Forget it," she said. "Let's change the subject. Keep things on a professional level, all right?"

"All right," he said. "Let's talk about your plan for tomorrow, then. I'm assuming you have one?"

"I do," she said simply. "And I think it's a really good one. You remember those cute little ladies who served us lunch? Iris and Inez? Well, I gave Iris a ride home in the golf cart today. Can you believe it? They're seventy-two! And they've lived on Eutaw their whole lives."

"Fascinating," Scott said, yawning.

"I think Iris was jealous of all the attention Tate Moody was giving Inez," Gina said, giggling. "Iris knows everything about Eutaw. After she showed me her adorable little cottage—she still cooks with a woodstove, do you believe that?—she took me on a tour of the island. And she showed me her favorite spot for shrimping. With any luck, if the tide's right tomorrow, I can wade out and cast for shrimp. And then we rode over to the ferry dock. Those pilings around the ferry dock should be loaded with blue crabs. The ladies on Eutaw are famous for their deviled crabs. Iris says her mama used to make grocery money selling deviled crabs to tourists who came over on the ferry."

"Shrimp, deviled crab," Scott repeated. "Sounds good, but I wonder, isn't that what the judges will find predictable?"

"Not the way I'll fix it," Gina promised. "Besides, I'm not done. Iris showed me her favorite blackberry patch. It's right around the corner from her cottage, and the berries are the fattest, prettiest things you've ever seen. They'll be perfect for a cobbler. That's something the judges won't be expecting."

"Maybe not," Scott said.

"Hey, Geen?" Lisa stood at the edge of the porch steps. "Is it okay if we take your golf cart out for a ride around the island? I haven't really gotten to see it yet, and Zeke says the beach is awesome at night. Did you know there are wild ponies?"

"I saw some of the ponies today," Gina said. "You'd have seen them too, if you weren't passed out on the bed."

Lisa stuck her tongue out at her sister. "Cut me some slack, okay?"

"All right," Gina said, relenting. "But don't stay out late again. We've got an early call in the morning."

"We?"

"You're my assistant, remember?"

As Lisa and Zeke were zipping away from the lodge, another golf cart rolled slowly past and up to the porch.

Tate Moody sat in the cart, motionless, for a moment.

"Tate!" Val called, hurrying over to him. "Where in the name of God have you been? I've been trying to raise you on the radio."

"Battery's dead," he said wearily, slowly easing out of the cart.

"Jesus!" she said, getting a good look at him.

He smiled ruefully. "Not so pretty, huh?"

Tate Moody looked like he'd done battle and lost. He had a cut over his right eye and a huge bruise on his left cheekbone. His face and arms were scratched and bleeding, and his jeans and shirt were torn and bloodstained.

He took a step toward the porch, staggering slightly.

Gina saw her rival's condition and was shocked. "Are you all right?" she asked, hurrying over.

"Fine," Tate said, giving her a wide, if somewhat weary grin. "Just superficial wounds. I accidentally did a little off-roading in the golf cart. Got stuck in some mud and had a hell of a time getting out."

"Here," Val said, taking his arm and putting it around her shoulder. "Lean on me. Let's get you into the house and get you doctored up. You look like crap."

"Like I got shot at and missed, and shit at and hit," he agreed, complying with her commands. "You think there's any supper left? I'm starved."

"We'll find something," Val promised.

Scott and Gina watched as Tate limped slowly into the lodge.

"I don't care what you think," Scott said. "He's up to something. He's all beat to hell, but did you see the look on his face? If I didn't know better, I'd think he was drunk."

"Not drunk," Gina said slowly. "Happy. Like a pig in slop."

All right," Val said as soon as they were inside and out of earshot of the competition. "Cut the crap. I know you, Tate Moody. What have you been up to all day and all night?"

"Oh, nothing," he said innocently. "I just locked up the contest, that's all. We can stick a fork in Little Miss Sunshine. She's done."

Chapter 39

The air in her room was as hot and sticky as a tar-paper roof. Gina couldn't breathe, let alone sleep. She kicked the sheets off her clammy skin and stood in front of the little fan, letting it billow the folds of her cotton nightgown. She glanced over at the clock on the nightstand. It was only midnight, but she had to be in the makeup room at seven in the morning. How was she ever going to get some sleep in this toaster oven of a bedroom?

Lisa's bed, of course, was empty. Should she worry about her sister, out this late on an island in the middle of nowhere with a man she hardly knew? Hah! Zeke was the one she should worry about. Lisa Foxton could hold her own, anywhere, anytime.

She heard hushed voices drifting in from the window. Shamelessly, she stepped over and peeked out.

Moonlight spilled over the grassy area in front of the inn. Lisa and Zeke stood there, her head resting on his shoulder. Gina smiled despite herself. It was so sweet, the way he wrapped his arms around her waist, nuzzled her neck.

She felt sad. Sad for herself, that all the sweetness had gone so quickly from her own romance, replaced by bitterness and resentment.

She should quit spying, should go to bed and get some sleep. If her personal life was in ruins, at least she could now concentrate, exclusively, on getting what she wanted professionally.

And she would do that, she promised herself, but right now, the only breeze entering the room was coming from this window. A moment later, when she peeked out again, the lovers had disappeared.

She saw a slight movement at the edge of the small clearing that served as the lawn, and held her breath as a doe stepped daintily into the pool of light near the porch. Slowly, two small fawns joined their mother. They nibbled at the grass, and the moonlight shone on their dappled brown and white backs.

A moment later, the doe raised her head, startled by something. And as quickly as she'd come, she was gone, bounding into the darkness, the fawns springing away right behind her.

As Gina watched, a man emerged from the darkness of the porch. He was holding a huge flashlight in one hand and a baseball bat in the other. A white dog with brown freckles and a distinctive feathered tail dutifully followed in his wake. The bill of his cap shaded the man's face, but Gina knew the dog and its owner.

Tate Moody. He glanced around, then limped painfully to the golf cart he'd parked earlier in the evening.

The dog stood motionless on the same spot where the deer had stood earlier, his muzzle quivering, his tail up, in a perfect point.

"Moonpie," Tate called. "Come! Come on, boy!"

The dog turned, looked at his master, then longingly into the darkness where the deer had vanished. But he padded over to the cart and jumped up into the passenger seat. Within seconds the two were zipping off, down the path, into that same darkness.

She heard footsteps outside the hallway. Lisa. She scampered back to bed, forcing herself to play possum as her baby sister crept inside and began hurriedly undressing.

Chapter 40

Gina was sitting in the makeshift makeup room—in reality, a small downstairs bedroom in the lodge—sipping coffee when D'John stuck the lens of his minicam around the door frame.

"Behold!" he said, zooming in on her, "the lovely Regina Foxton—ready, willing, and *oh my God, what are those suitcases under your eyes?*"

Gina managed a wan smile. "It was so hot last night, I couldn't sleep. I finally got up and went downstairs and slept on the sofa in the parlor around two."

"That's where you went?" Lisa said. "Damn. I thought you were sneaking off to see a man."

"Not quite," Gina said, her voice dripping sarcasm.

Now D'John turned the camera on Lisa. "And speaking of sneaking—what time did you and your man-candy get back last night?"

"Midnight," Gina said, before Lisa could answer.

"I thought you were asleep," Lisa said accusingly. "Spy-girl!"

"I just happened to be standing near the window, trying to catch a breeze, when you and Zack drove up to the lodge. It was more an act of ventilation than espionage."

"That is *so* not cool," Lisa said. "You're acting just like Mom. And, oh, by the way, she called. She wants to talk to you."

"No way," Gina said. "I happen to know there's no cell-phone reception on Eutaw."

"Think again," Lisa countered. "It comes and goes. Anyway, she text-messaged me."

"Who the heck taught her to text-message?" Gina demanded. "Why would you do that?"

"Girls, girls," D'John said, "play nice, now."

The door to the makeup room opened then, and Tate Moody sauntered in.

"Hey, Reggie," he said, hopping into the chair next to Gina's. "What's shakin'?"

"Don't call me that," she said.

Tate looked at Lisa and gave her a conspiratorial wink. "Is she always this cranky in the morning?"

"No sleep," Lisa said. "And she's only had one cup of coffee. But as long as you don't poke her with a stick or make any sudden moves for *her* coffee, you should be safe."

D'John trained the minicam on Tate. "Good Lord," he exclaimed. "What have you done to yourself?"

Tate put his hand to his face, which, although freshly scrubbed, was still crisscrossed with cuts and scratches. "You mean this? My golf cart got stuck in the mud when I was out tooling around the island yesterday. Then Moonpie ran off, and I had to go after him, right into a blackberry bramble."

He gave Gina a wide smile. "Blackberries—excellent, right? They'll be great in the dessert I'm fixing to make for the first round of the Food Fight today."

Gina forced herself to smile, although she could feel her molars grinding into sand. "That's a pretty nasty bruise, too. Did a tree fall on you while you were in that blackberry bramble?"

"Aw," Tate said. "You're worried about me. That's so sweet." He turned again to Lisa. "I think I'm growing on her."

"Like a fungus," Gina muttered. "D'John, will you please put that silly camera down long enough to slap some makeup on me? I'm sure Tate's gonna need a lot more work than me today, to cover all his war wounds."

"She wants me, bad," Tate announced. "You guys can tell, right?"

Lisa and D'John sniggered in unison, but D'John put the camera down, picked up his makeup brushes, and set to work on Gina's face.

"You've got to start getting more sleep," he fussed. "There's only so much concealer can do, you know."

"Well, save some for Tate here," Gina told him. "Doesn't look like he got much sleep last night either." She turned to Tate and gave him a chilly smile. "We missed you at breakfast this morning."

He didn't bother to look up from his magazine article. "Moonpie and I got restless last night. It was pretty hot in our room. So we went for a midnight spin on the cart. Went down to the dock, and it was so nice and cool, I just curled up and went to sleep right there. Inez gave me biscuits and gravy before I came in here. I'm fixin' to marry her, unless you come to your senses about me pretty quick."

The door opened again, and Deborah Chen poked her head in.

"Toodles, everyone!" she trilled, walking inside. "Gina, you look fabulous." She put her hand under Gina's chin and turned her this way and that. "Even your hair has grown in. The color isn't nearly as alarming."

"Uh, thanks," Gina said dutifully. "I didn't know you were coming over, Deborah. When did you get in?"

"Just now," Deborah said. "I hitched a ride over on the ferry with the judges. And wait till you find out who they are! I'm not supposed to say," she said, giving Tate and Gina an exaggerated wink, "but suffice it to say, they are all three amazing. TCC has really gone above and beyond to make this a first-class competition."

"Great," the contestants said, accidentally in unison.

"Well, I've got to run along," Deborah said, after giving Tate a curious glance. "Press releases to write, phone calls to be made." She toodled herself right out the door.

It was nearly nine by the time Barry Adelman entered the dining room of the lodge with Zeke and the three strangers. The crew was all set up. The lights were lit, boom mikes aimed, cameras rolling.

About time, Gina thought. She'd been standing around, hair and makeup done, dressed and ready to go, for nearly an hour. Her nerves were shot. It was time. She was ready to stop talking and get cooking.

It was obvious that the hour she'd spent waiting had been spent readying Barry for his date with the cameras.

His already tanned face was coated with thick pancake, his eyelashes were so heavily mascaraed that they resembled Cher's, and wait . . . yes, his hair color had definitely been touched up since the night before. He was dressed in black.

"Everybody," Barry said, clapping his hands to get the crew's attention, which he already had, "I want you to meet our distinguished panel of judges."

That did get her attention. And Tate's.

"This," Barry said, gesturing toward the woman on his right, "is Deidre Delaney. Deidre, as anybody who hasn't been living in a cave for the past three years knows, is the owner-chef at Deidre's on South Beach. She's a graduate of the Culinary Institute of America, has been named 'Chef on the Rise' by *Bon Appetit* magazine, and her restaurant just became Miami's first five-diamond restaurant."

Deidre Delaney was as tall and willowy as a fashion model, with striking white-blond hair that fell nearly to her waist, a deep, golden tan, and an unfortunate beak-like nose that might have been the reason she'd become a success in a kitchen, rather than on a runway.

The group applauded politely, and Deidre smiled and nodded modestly.

"Now," Barry said, gesturing toward the man standing next to her, "meet Beau Stapleton. Beau is the brains behind the hottest restaurants in Atlanta, including Bleu Plate, Sizzle, and Drizzle."

Beau Stapleton! Gina's heart sank. She'd never met the rock star of Atlanta's haute cuisine world in person, but she knew his restaurants all too well. She had, in fact, given Sizzle a lousy review back in the days when she'd been a food writer at the *Constitution*. Looking at him now, preening before the cameras, she remembered all too well the adjectives she'd used to describe the menu at Sizzle: *pretentious, silly,* and, oh God, worst of all, *icky.* She'd called his warm Stilton and apple crème brulee "an oozy, icky, barely edible pot of glop."

Stapleton had responded by having a beautifully gift-wrapped dead rat messengered over to her office.

Beau Stapleton had a long, greasy gray ponytail hanging down his back, which was only accented by his rapidly retreating hairline. His face was pale and puffy, and a potbelly jutted out over his checked chef's trousers. It occurred to Gina that he looked exactly like his crème brulee had tasted.

Get over it, she told herself, forcing a warm smile.

Barry had his hand on the shoulder of a petite, round-faced black woman with close-cropped silver hair.

"And of course," he added, "we're thrilled to round out our distinguished panel of judges by introducing Antoinette Bailey, of the award-winning Toni's Country Kitchen in Mountain Brook and Point Clear, Alabama."

Toni Bailey wore a long cotton print skirt that swirled around her ankles, a simple white peasant blouse, multiple beaded necklaces and bracelets, and huge silver hoop earrings. Her unlined coffee-colored face glowed with goodwill.

"The *New York Times* has called Toni's Country Kitchen the true mothership of authentic southern cooking," Barry went on.

"At least they didn't call it the grandmother!" Toni quipped, drawing a laugh from everybody on set and momentarily cutting the obvious tension.

"And when we come back," Barry announced to the camera, "we'll have our Food Fight contestants in their fifty-thousand-dollar dream kitchen, and I'll announce the first of their three challenges."

"And cut," announced a production assistant standing in the background.

"That's good, everybody," Barry said, beaming. "Beautiful. One take. That's what we like."

"All right," the production assistant said. "You've got fifteen minutes, and then we want everybody over on the kitchen set."

"About time," Tate whispered in her ear. "Reggie, are you ready for a good, old-fashioned butt-kickin'?"

She whirled around. He was standing right behind her. D'John had managed to cover the worst of the scratches and bruises with concealer, but his face had an unnatural orangish glow to it.

She started to comment on it, but thought better. "I'm watching you, Tate Moody," she said, her eyes narrowed. "I know you're up to something."

"Just cookin'," he assured her. "And may the best man win."

Chapter 41

Valerie was watching Tate as the judges were introduced, and as soon as Deidre Delaney stepped into camera range, his face went very, very still. Earlier in the day, he'd been unbearably cocky, but once he saw this blonde, his whole demeanor changed. Literally, the wind went out of his sails.

She had to run to catch up with him as he hastened out of the lodge and toward the ballroom.

"What's up?" she asked, grabbing him by the arm to slow him down.

"Nothing," he said, his face conveying just the opposite.

"I know better," she said. "Come on, Tate. I saw your face when Barry introduced Deidre Delaney."

He sighed. "I know her, okay? And not in a good way."

"What kind of way do you know her? Not, for God's sake, in the biblical sense. Right?"

He rubbed his bruised cheek with the back of his hand, smudging his carefully applied makeup.

"We met at the Miami Food and Wine Festival, last year," he said finally, glancing over his shoulder to make sure they wouldn't be overheard. But he needn't have bothered, because Regina Foxton and her producer were making tracks toward the ballroom and the kitchen. For once, Little Miss Sunshine didn't look too sunny. She looked, he decided, absolutely murderous.

Not that he was feeling all that cheery himself. Not now.

"How do you know this woman?" Val repeated.

"It was after one of those huge, bloated dinner things," Tate said reluctantly. "A fund-raiser for some charity I never heard of. They had celebrity chefs at all these different stations throughout this gigantic ballroom in this swanky hotel down on the beach. I was doing conch fritters, and this Delaney broad's station was next to mine. She was doing some kooky dessert with papayas and guavas and pomegranate syrup. I struck up a polite conversation."

"You made a pass at her!" Val said, slapping her forehead in disbelief.

"The hell I did," Tate protested. "We chatted a little bit during the evening. She came over to watch me making the fritters. Said she was interested in my technique."

"I'll bet," Val said.

"She kept touching me while she was talking to me. Man, I hate that when people can't keep their hands to themselves."

"Oh, me too," Val said, rolling her eyes.

"I'm being serious," Tate said. "Then, I'm breaking down my station, and she wanders over and asks if I want to go get a drink. But I was beat from standing on my feet for four hours frying up fritters for the beautiful people—who, incidentally, treated me like I was some kind of glorified busboy. I politely begged off, told her I was going back to my room to get a shower and hit the rack. Which is what I did. Next thing I know, I'm climbing out of the shower, there's a knock at my hotel room door, and she's standing there—wearing nothing but the hotel's complimentary bathrobe—holding a bottle of Veuve Cliquot."

"A gorgeous blonde. In a bathrobe. With a four-hundred-dollar bottle of champagne. Are you sure you're not making this up?"

"I wish I were," he said.

"And you did what?"

"She caught me off guard. I don't even like champagne."

"Don't whine," Val said. "It's not attractive on you."

"I just stood there, staring at her. Eventually, she says, 'Aren't you going to invite me in?' I kinda stammered around, and I guess I just blurted out the first thing that came to mind."

"Which was?"

He winced. " 'No, thanks.' And then I shut the door and locked it. I guess I didn't handle it too well," he admitted.

"Ya think?"

Chapter 42

Each Food Fight kitchen was a stainless steel symphony. Side-by-side mirror images, they took up one end of the Rebeccaville plantation's old ballroom.

Gina trailed her fingertips across the polished countertops. Large wooden cutting boards had been dropped flush with the stainless steel countertop work surfaces. Each station held a commercial-size Viking stove with six burners and a built-in grill. There were double ovens on each side, and separating the workstations was a glass-doored walk-in refrigerator. All the comforts of home—if your home happened to be a state-of-the art commercial kitchen.

Propped at eye level above each stove was a foot-high digital time clock, each set at 6:00. The red LED display light was blinking on and off.

Before Tate Moody could establish a beachhead, Gina quickly chose the station on the right-hand side of the set and began unrolling the case that held her knives.

"Good idea," Scott said, his lips close to her ears. "Be aggressive from the get-go. Let him know you won't be pushed around."

"You're sure you want to wear that color top?" Deborah asked, fussing with the strap of Gina's tank top. "I really think red, rather than pink, is your power color."

"I'm sure," Gina said firmly.

On the short walk over to the ballroom, Scott and Deborah had peppered her with a barrage of suggestions and questions. Was she sure of the menu she'd dreamed up? Yes, but she might have to make substitutions on the fly. Could she gather ingredients, cook, and style the final dishes in the allotted time period? Absolutely. What did she think Tate Moody had up his sleeve? She had absolutely no idea, but she did have a sinking feeling in the pit of her stomach.

One thing she didn't share with Scott was her unfortunate history with Beau Stapleton. There was no point in it, she decided. Maybe he'd forgotten all about her.

And maybe, if a frog had wings, it wouldn't bump its butt every time it hopped around.

While the TCC crew fiddled with lights and cameras and boom mikes, D'John flitted back and forth between Gina and Tate, powdering noses, combing hair, and reapplying Tate's smudged makeup.

"Hey, Reggie," Tate called over, as D'John was reapplying her lip liner. "Looking pretty good over there. You want me to come over, give you some cooking tips?"

"Bite me," she said, without moving her lips.

Neither of them dared look over at the panel of judges, who were in a small set off to the side of the kitchen, all of them seated in sleek swivel chairs behind an electric blue console with the *Food Fight!* logo emblazoned across it.

"What's with that Beau guy?" D'John asked. "He keeps staring at us. He looks familiar, but I can't figure out how I know him."

"Maybe you saw him in one of his restaurants," she suggested.

"Hmm," D'John said.

"Is he gay?" she asked.

"He's giving off mixed signals," D'John said. "I can't tell whose team he plays on. But I'll tell you one thing—he's definitely a player."

"One minute," the floor director called, sending D'John scurrying off set. "Barry, can I have you over here on the kitchen set?"

Barry Adelman strode onto the set. "C'mere, you guys," he said.

He put one arm around Tate's shoulder, the other around Gina's. "Before we start shooting, I just want to say you kids look fantastic. The network is behind this in a major way. Everything is golden. Now, cook your fuckin' brains out!"

He moved smoothly into place.

"Ready?" the director asked.

"All set," Barry said.

"Good evening, everybody, I'm Barry Adelman, and welcome to beautiful Eutaw Island, Georgia, and The Cooking Channel's first ever Food Fight!"

Gina blinked a little in the glare of the camera lights, and then smiled her brightest smile.

Tate glanced over at Deidre Delaney. She caught his look, winked, and licked her lips.

He looked away, groaning inwardly.

"After an extensive talent search across the entire South for the region's best chef, TCC's talent scouts narrowed the field to two contestants," Barry said. "Join me now in welcoming Regina Foxton and Tate Moody!"

Barry extended both hands, and, on cue, Gina and Tate walked over from their respective stoves to join their host–slash–master of ceremonies.

"Are you ready to rumble?" Adelman asked, laughing at his own joke.

"Ready," Gina said.

"Bring it on," Tate agreed.

"All right then," Adelman said. Reaching behind him, he brought out a massive iron dinner bell. "Listen carefully, as I detail the first of your three challenges. You'll have exactly six hours from starting time, till I ring the dinner bell, which signifies time is up. During that time, you'll be expected to gather, prepare, style, and plate a southern supper—using only the staples you'll find in your pantries, and whatever foodstuffs you can gather right here in and around Eutaw Island. Is that understood?"

The two nodded in unison.

"For you viewers at home—Tate and Gina's task will be especially challenging, because there are no stores and no restaurants on the island. There are also no automobiles and no paved roads. However, each of them has had an opportunity to roam the island and study its amazing bounty of natural resources. Each will have a golf cart for transportation and, on that golf cart, some very basic equipment to help them gather ingredients."

"A cast net," Gina prayed silently. "Please let them give me a cast net."

She glanced over at Tate, who looked supremely, annoyingly confident.

"To your kitchens," Barry said. A buzzer brayed from somewhere off set, and the next thing she knew, she was sprinting over to her kitchen.

She poked her head inside the glass-doored cooler and surveyed its contents. Milk, cream, eggs, butter. No cheeses, she noted, disappointed. On the wire shelving unit, she found glass jars marked FLOUR, SUGAR, CORNMEAL, GRITS, BAKING SODA, and BAKING POWDER. She found salt, pepper, paprika, red pepper, and half a dozen spices and herbs you would encounter in any halfway well-equipped home kitchen. No seafood seasoning mixes, but that was fine; she could concoct her own, as long as she had salt and red pepper. There were bottles of olive oil, vegetable oil, Worcestershire sauce, Tabasco, and vinegar.

In baskets lined up on the countertop she was relieved to find onions, carrots, celery, and green and red peppers. Another basket held lemons and limes.

Under the counter, she found an empty basket and a small six-pack-size cooler.

She grabbed both and, making a mental list of what she'd need to gather, glanced at the clock on the counter. Five minutes gone. She glanced over at Tate's kitchen. Empty. He had another head start on her. She ran for the door.

Chapter 43

As promised, a lone golf cart was waiting right outside the door. A plastic milk crate had been bungeecorded to the back. Inside it was a long-handled dip net, a collapsible fishing rod with a child's plastic Zebco spinning reel, a lethal-looking sheathed knife, a ball of twine, some bottled water, and a can of insect repellent. There was a brown paper sack too. Peering into it, she found a ham sandwich neatly wrapped in waxed paper, an apple, and what appeared to be a couple of homemade oatmeal cookies. Her fingers clutched a scrap of paper. "Good luck, girl!" was penciled in crabbed print. "XO Iris."

"Thanks, Iris," Gina said softly. "I've got a feeling I'm gonna need it."

She felt a bead of sweat travel down her spine, dampening the back of her shirt as it moved toward the waist of her jeans. She swung behind the steering wheel and floored the cart's accelerator.

As she bumped along the cart path away from Rebeccaville, she heard the thrum of cicadas in the high grass, and birds trilling from the tops of the live oaks. Not even ten o'clock, and the sun was already high overhead, promising a scorcher of a day. Gina forced herself to rethink her options. No cast net. There went her shrimp dishes. True, she had a fishing rod—of sorts. But she had nothing for bait. And no boat.

Fine, she thought, just fine. Her mama and daddy had not raised any sissies. She would find a way.

She steered the cart toward the inland side of the island, and followed the crudely painted wooden stakes that acted as the island's road markers.

She doglegged right onto Burned Church Road, made a quick left onto the first unmarked path after that, and followed the oyster-shell path deeper into a palmetto thicket that seemed to close in on her from either side. The jagged palm fronds scratched her shoulders and arms as she lowered her head and powered on through.

Half a mile in, she glimpsed a stretch of shining water through the gnarled and twisted limbs of a wind-bent grove of oaks.

The oyster path gave out abruptly at a tall stand of sweetgrass. A fire circle—scorched earth surrounded by moss-covered chunks of broken concrete—and a pile of discarded soda and beer cans told her she'd found Runaway Creek.

The smell of the marsh—the deep gray pluff mud redolent of a place where land and sea melted into one oozing expanse of netherworld—rose up to meet her nose.

"That grass look tall, honey," Iris had told her. "But you look around, you see a lil' trail goin' in there. Oyster shells, some boards, like that. My daddy drug all that out there, cuz we din' have no bateau when I was a kid. Just you follow that, like a lil' bridge, that'll take you out to the creek bank."

She could see the gleam of Iris's gold-capped front teeth as the old lady smiled knowingly. "That there is my daddy's honey hole. They's a deep spot right offa there. You wade out when the tide's out, catch you some swimps, throw a line, maybe catch you a spot-tail."

"Spot-tail?"

Iris's smile widened. "Redfish, girl."

"All right, Iris," Gina said aloud. "I'm counting on you." She uncapped a bottle of water and took a deep swig. Her watch told her nearly an hour had passed. Her stomach told her she'd been too keyed up to eat breakfast.

She reached around and fetched the brown lunch sack Iris had packed for her, and her fingers closed over the apple.

Gina bit in, savoring the cool green sharpness of the fruit. She finished it off in scant minutes, and considered the carefully gnawed core. Would a fish bite a bit of apple? How about a blue crab? Doubtful.

Then she remembered the ham sandwich. Her daddy had always used chicken necks or stinky fish-heads for bait. This time, though, she'd have to rely on something else.

She rolled the legs of her jeans above her knees, and slathered her bare arms, chest, and legs with the insect repellent. Ruefully she looked down at her shoes— gleaming white Tretorns. She'd bought them back in the spring, a lifetime ago, when her career wasn't in the pits, when she hadn't paused for a second over spending $250 for a pair of tennis shoes. The pluff would ruin them. Still, she didn't dare risk going barefoot because the oyster shells would cut her feet to ribbons.

In the milk crate, Gina found a baseball cap with "Food Fight!" embroidered on the bill, and jammed it on her head. She took the knife and cut off a length of string, which she wound around her waist. She carefully put the knife back in its sheath and tucked it in the waistband of her jeans.

When she picked up the Zebco, she discovered a small flat plastic box underneath it. It was a cheap, ineffective tackle box, the kind unknowing Yankee tourists bought at any tourist trap on the southern coast, convinced that with it, they would catch the kind of trophy fish that would be the envy of the folks back home in Buffalo or Bayonne.

Opening the tackle box, she nearly cried with frustration when she saw the contents: a small plastic envelope of shiny gold hooks, some tiny lead weights, a plastic bobber, some gigantic fiberglass lures, and a package of neon-green-and-pink rubber worms. Useless crap, most of it. But she shook a hook and a weight into the palm of her hand and attached them to the line on the fishing reel, with the bobber positioned eight inches above them, then tucked the rest of the hooks into her pocket.

She picked up the ham sandwich and, lacking any other safe place to stash it, tucked it into the neckline of her top.

Then, shouldering the rigged fishing pole and dipnet over her shoulder, she stepped gingerly out of the cart and into the marsh. Fiddler crabs skittered away into their holes, and a startled marsh hen rose from its hiding place in the grass with a sharp, remonstrative cackle.

"Hi ho, hi ho, it's off to work we go," Gina sang softly.

Iris's walkway was narrow—three feet at its widest, and made of whatever cast-off materials her father had access to: chunks of broken concrete, weathered and rotting boards, discarded rubber tires—even, in one place, what appeared to be a sun-bleached tree trunk. Gina stepped cautiously, looking out at the undulating expanse of greenish gold marsh grass.

A hundred yards out, she saw the faded red paint of a wrecked bateau riding jauntily atop a bleached clump of driftwood. A boat, she thought. What she wouldn't give for a boat right now.

Five hundred yards out, she found herself standing on a solid mound of oyster shells—with the gray-green waters of Runaway Creek lapping at its edges.

The tide was out.

Holding her breath, she stepped into the creek. The water swirling around her ankles was warm as bathwater. Her shoes made a sucking sound as they sank into the mud, and it was an effort, with each step, to keep them from being sucked right off her feet.

When the water was almost up to her hips, she decided it was time to fish or cut bait. Reaching into her neckline, she brought out the sandwich, pinched off a bit of ham, and threaded it onto the tiny gold hook of her fishing line.

The opposite side of the creek bank was maybe two hundred yards away. She cocked back the bail of the reel and cast her line, letting her wrists flick it, as her daddy had taught her all those years ago.

The bobber landed with a soft *plonk*, ten yards away. Not her best effort. But the wind was blowing toward her, and the light weight of her tackle and line would not send it any farther.

The little red-and-white bobber did its job, riding gently atop the slow-moving current of the creek.

She watched it intently. 'Come on, baby," she whispered, willing it to sink—a signal that she had a bite. "H'yah, fish!" she called.

Within a minute, the bobber dipped below the water's surface. She felt a gentle tug on the line, and her spirits soared.

The line zigged quickly off her reel for a moment, before she jerked back hard, setting the hook as she'd been taught.

"H'yah, fish!" she called triumphantly, reeling as quickly as she could. In her mind, she was planning her catch. A nice spot-tail, she hoped. There was a cast-iron skillet in her designer kitchen back at Rebeccaville, and with the cayenne pepper and other seasonings she had on hand, she could quickly and easily blacken it on high heat. She'd seen some tomatoes and yellow banana peppers in Iris's little kitchen plot, and perhaps, if she could talk her out of a couple of them, she could make a quick salsa with them and the onions and peppers from the countertop basket. She would slide the blackened redfish out of the skillet and onto a bed of buttered grits, and ladle the salsa over the redfish.

The fish fought, zigging away from her despite her crazed reeling, and she jerked the pole again, making sure she'd set the hook.

The line slackened a little, and she reeled in quickly. She caught a flash of silver through the greenish murk of the creek water, and then she reeled it up and out.

"Durn!" she cried, as the fish's silver scales glinted in the sunlight. There was no telltale black spot near the fish's tail. It was not a redfish. It wasn't a fat sea trout. It was, she thought, a lowly, stinking, no-good, totally inedible pinfish.

It wriggled enthusiastically on the end of her hook, and she gritted her teeth, clamped her hands around the fish, and carefully extricated the hook from its mouth. She tossed it back into the creek without ceremony, and rebaited and recast.

An hour passed. She caught five more pinfish, each the exact same size as the first. The ham from her sandwich was nearly gone. The sun beat down, and the wind picked up. Something brushed against her ankles, and she let out an involuntary shriek.

Time to go, she thought. She'd wasted two hours, and had nothing to show for it except a nasty sunburn. As she trudged back to shore, she tried to cheer herself up. She still had four hours. Plenty of time.

Time to go to Plan B. She would ride over to the ferry dock and use the string as a crab line, tied around the last bit of her ham sandwich for crab bait. Now she frowned. Why hadn't she saved one of the pinfish to cut up and use for bait? What had she been thinking?

The mud sucked her tennis shoe clear off her foot. She reached down into the water to retrieve it, and a tiny wave caught her by surprise, knocking her off her feet and into the water.

She came up sputtering, and another wave broke over her head. Perfect. She reached back down into the water. Her $250 shoe was gone, washed away, probably even now providing shade to a whole school of redfish.

Gina struggled to her feet and limped forlornly back to the creek bank and her golf cart. Four hours to go. It was going to be a very long day.

And what about the enemy? What about Tate Moody? She'd seen no sign of him since he'd sprinted out of the ballroom earlier that morning. If there was any consolation, it was in knowing that somewhere on Eutaw Island, Tate Moody was faced with exactly the same equipment—or lack of it—and the same predicament.

Chapter 44

Tate gazed up at the pig hanging from the lowest limb of a hickory tree deep in the interior of the island. Thank God, it was untouched since he'd had to return this morning to the lodge.

Moonpie was untouched too—unconscious was more like it. He slept now, curled up at the foot of the tree. "Some guard dog you are," Tate said. The dog, hearing Tate's voice, raised his muzzle sleepily, wagged his tail twice, then went instantly back to sleep. Tate patted his head approvingly. Moonpie had done his job, driving off any marauding animals that would have liked to have dined on that fine wild pig hanging from the tree.

The two of them had spent the previous night beneath that same tree, bunked down on a hastily assembled bed of pine needles and Spanish moss, with only a sheet and blanket swiped from Tate's room back at the lodge as bedding. It had been one extremely long night. The island's nighttime creatures—foxes and raccoons—had crept close to where they slept, drawn by the scent of the fluids draining from the pig's body. Moonpie had barked and growled and driven off the would-be diners who'd come and gone all night long—meaning they'd had next to no sleep.

There was no time to think about that now. He had work to do—lots of work.

Luckily, the pig was a young one—maybe two years old—so its meat shouldn't be as tough or gamey as that from one of the gigantic feral hogs that roamed the wilder parts of the island, uprooting everything in their paths. From what Inez had told him, wild hogs had roamed Eutaw for as long as anybody could remember.

"My granddaddy hunted hogs here, his granddaddy too," Inez had said. "The old folks say they's livestock escaped from the days when Rebeccaville was still farmed. My mama and daddy always had a cow, and some chickens and two-three pigs they raised up for meat, but Daddy still hunted the hogs 'cause they bad to dig up folkses gardens. What he'd do is, our neighbor-man Jimmy, he had a fine coondog. That coondog would get up on the smell of a hog and chase him down, then Daddy, he'd get his dog, BooBoo, you know, BooBoo was one of them pitbulls, and BooBoo would wait till the other dogs flat wore out that hog, then he would run in, catch the hog by the ear, then Daddy and one of the boys would run up, get the hog, tie it up, and carry it home. They'd pen it up, fatten it up with peanuts and such, and come spring, we'd have us a fine pig-pickin'."

No time for a pig-pickin' now, Tate thought. He cut the hog down from the tree and, staggering a little from the weight of it, loaded it onto the back of the golf cart. One whistle, and Moonpie was jumping in alongside him in the front of the cart.

Inez was waiting for him at her cottage, dark eyes shining with anticipation.

"Whoo-eee, that's a fine fat pig," she exclaimed as he rode up into her yard. "Bring him on around back. I got everything all ready."

"This here was my daddy's fish-cleaning table," Inez said proudly, gesturing toward the scrubbed board-top table that extended out over a porch railing.

Unrolling the chef's knives he'd brought with him, Tate made quick work of the pig, handing each sectioned piece off to Inez, who was ready with dishpan and a roll of freezer paper.

"Mmm-mmm," she said, deftly wrapping the various cuts. "Pork chops, ribs, hams. I'll make me a fire from hickory wood and smoke us a butt. And I got mama's meat grinder right inside, I'll make up some sausage. We gonna have a freezer full from this here pig."

He kept only the tenderloin for himself.

"That all you gon' take?" Inez asked incredulously.

"It's all I've got time for," Tate said, laughing. "I've still got the rest of my dinner to take care of." He leaned over and planted a kiss on her cheek. "Thanks, Miss Inez. I don't know what I would have done without your help."

"Get on out of here then," she said, giving him a playful push off the porch. "That little gal will be back up there at the lodge, firing her oven up while you stand around here messin' with an old lady like me."

He paused at the edge of the yard, tentatively reaching up to touch the branch of a towering bush that shaded one whole corner of the property.

"Figs?" he asked as a fat greenish brown fruit fell into the palm of his hand.

"Best on the island," Inez told him. "Mama took a slip from a tree over there at Darien. Iris, she babies that tree somethin' awful. Every day, she puts a dishpan full of soapy water on that tree. Last year, she canned up near a hundred jars of preserves."

Tate bit into the fig and savored the grainy, honeyed taste of the ripe fruit. "Think she'll miss a few?" he asked.

Inez put both hands over her eyes. "I ain't seen nobody stealin' no figs."

As he plucked figs, he planned his meal out loud. "I'll simmer these with some sugar, and make a glaze with some cracked peppercorns for the tenderloin. But I don't have a clue about what I'll serve as side dishes."

"Sweet potatoes would be good," Inez remarked.

"You know a potato patch I could raid?" Tate said playfully.

"Nosirree," Inez said. "Iris, she picks those sweet potatoes in August, and she don't overlook a single one. After they're cured, she banks 'em up out in the garden. Later on, she wraps 'em up in croker sacks and puts 'em in the smokehouse out yonder." With a jerk of her head she gestured toward a crude structure of weathered silver boards at the edge of the sisters' back property. "They ain't but a few left now from last year.

"Well," she said after an exaggerated pause. "I'm goin' on in the house now. And if I hear them guinea hens settin' up a ruckus, I'll just figure it's a stray cat crossing the yard."

She wiped her hands on her apron, gave him a wink, and walked slowly inside.

Gina looked down at the blue crabs scuttling around inside her plastic bucket. She had maybe two dozen crabs. Big and fat, they were what her daddy called jimmies—males. On another day, she would have been more than happy about her catch. But this wasn't just any day. She'd spent the day on and around the marsh, desperately trying to catch a supper worthy of winning the Food Fight. And these crabs were all she had to show for it.

She walked dejectedly down the length of the dock and placed the bucket on the floor of the golf cart. She had only two hours left, but that should be plenty to boil the crabs, pick out their meat, and fix her own version of deviled crabs. She had no idea what else she could serve. The sun had fried her brain.

She was headed back to the lodge when she had an idea. Iris's garden. Maybe, Gina thought, she could scavenge a tomato or a cucumber—anything to supplement her pathetic offering of deviled crabs.

The cool air rushing past felt good on her sunburned face and shoulders, and her spirits lifted a little when she caught sight of the little cottage and the stoop-shouldered woman standing at the edge of the yard, picking figs from a huge tree.

"Lookee here," Iris said, setting her plastic dishpan down on the dirt of the yard. "You got you a mess of fish, I hope."

"Not quite," Gina said ruefully. "They just weren't biting. But I did get some blue crabs." She held out the bucket for Iris to inspect.

"That's fine!" Iris said. "You done good." She looked around at the house. "Course, that boy Tate, he ain't done too bad hisself."

"You've seen him?" Gina asked eagerly. "When was that?"

"Little bit ago," Iris said. "He was headed to the lodge, fixin' to start cooking up that pig meat of his."

"A pig?" Gina was dumbfounded. "Where did he get a pig? How did he get a pig? They didn't give us any guns."

Iris shrugged. "He didn't say. Inez let him do the butchering out on the back porch here. She's sweet on that white boy! Course, I'm kinda sweet on him now my ownself, since we got us most of a pig now, packed away nice in the freezer. Onliest thing he kept was a tenderloin."

"A pork tenderloin," Gina wailed. "And all I've got are these stinkin' crabs. I don't have a chance against him now."

Iris stared down at the bucket. "What you fixin' with these here crabs, girl?"

"I thought I'd do deviled crab," Gina said half-heartedly. "I don't have the ingredients for anything else."

"Hmm," Iris said, pulling at her bottom lip. "You ever fix crab and corn chowder?"

"Sure," Gina said. "But I don't have any corn."

"Look back yonder in the garden there," Iris said. "I got me some Silver Queen ready to be picked."

"Really? You wouldn't mind giving me some of your corn?"

"Don't see why not," Iris said. "Inez done give that boy the last of my sweet potatoes out of the smokehouse. And I know he picked some of my figs. You see anything else you want out there, you pick that too. There's some pretty 'maters out there. Got some cukes, and some sweet red peppers and some of them little bitty hot finger peppers. Get you some of them. But be quick about it, 'cause Inez is taking her a nap, and I don't want her knowing what I'm up to out here."

"Oh, Iris, thank you," Gina said, throwing her arms around the old woman's neck. "You have saved my bacon."

"Bacon! If you had some bacon for real, you'd be all set," Iris said, smacking her lips. "I like to fry me up some green tomatoes in bacon grease. Fry corn in it too. . . ."

"Well, Tate may have bacon, but I don't. But it's just about all I lack, except for some herbs to put in the chowder and the deviled crabs," Gina said.

"Don't grow no herbs," Iris said. "But, tell you what. You go on down this same road here, and you come to a burned-out old house. Burned clear down to the concrete block pilings. That was Miz Chessie's house. She was from away, and she was all the time growing stuff nobody else around here messed with. When that place burned down last year, she took herself back to where she came from. Ride on down there and walk around back where she kept a garden, maybe there's something left the hogs and deer didn't get a hold of.

"Here," Iris said, reaching in the pocket of her apron and handing her a worn plastic grocery sack. "Use this for your pickin's. And be quick now!"

In ten minutes, Gina had filled her sack. She had six ears of Silver Queen corn, three huge ripe tomatoes, a cucumber, three or four hot peppers, and a red bell pepper, and just as she was leaving the garden, she spied the bright yellow blossoms of a squash vine clambering over the picket fence surrounding the plot. She added them to her stash and ran for her golf cart.

When she climbed in, she found another plastic grocery sack on the floor, beside her crab bucket. Opening it, she found two jars. One held what she decided were fig preserves. The other, which appeared to be an old wine bottle, held a dark liquid and was stopped with a wine cork. She uncorked and sniffed, then tasted. Scuppernong wine!

She glanced toward the cottage and saw a curtain move slightly.

Half a mile down the road, she came to what she decided had to be Miz Chessie's house. Scorched earth surrounded equally scorched concrete pilings, and a pile of mostly burned furniture. A rusting bedspring marked the entrance to the yard.

She pulled the golf cart up to the remains of the house, got out, and walked quickly to the back of the property.

Although Inez had said the fire had been only a year ago, the former garden was already returning to a wild place. Mimosa trees had sprung up in the middle of the plot, and a network of vines clambered across still-standing corn stalks and whittled sticks that had probably held Miz Chessie's tomatoes and pole beans.

Nothing edible grew here now, Gina decided. But as she was walking back to the cart, she spied some bright green shoots near the burned-out foundation. She bent down to look closer. Chives! She snatched up a handful and looked around again. More shoots, these broader. She pulled up the whole clump and found herself holding wild onions, the sandy soil still clinging to the white onion bulb.

She inhaled deeply and smiled. Suddenly she found that success smelled sweet—and oniony.

Chapter 45

The camera crew and her own entourage were waiting on the porch of the lodge when Gina drove up in her golf cart. One of the cameramen ran toward the cart, followed by the sound man, who was wielding an ominous-looking boom mike aimed right at her.

"And, rolling," Barry called.

"Noooo!" Gina cried, shielding her face with both arms. "Not like this! I'm a mess. I look like who-shot-Sally."

"Exactly," Barry said, walking over to the cart, trailed by all the others. "Reality is the new reality, sweetheart. We want the viewers to see that you've really had to battle in this food fight. And believe me, that's obvious right now."

"Ohmigod, Geen," Lisa said, lifting up a lock of Gina's salt-stiffened hair and dropping it just as quickly.

"What happened? I mean, no offense, but you look like Swamp Thang."

"I got wet," Gina said, climbing wearily out of her cart. "And before that I got sunburned, and bit by bugs, and pinched by crab claws, and then slapped in the face with every branch and blade of saw grass on this island."

"We were starting to get worried about you," Scott said, taking the bucket of crabs from the cart. "Moody got back here thirty minutes ago. The man is unbelievable. He killed a pig. An honest-to-God pig. Hey, what happened to your shoes?" he asked, looking down at her bare feet, which were scratched and filthy.

"Okay, people," Barry said, clapping his hands for attention. "We can play twenty questions later. Right now, I need everybody out of camera range, because we have got a show to shoot."

"Oh, no, no, no, no, no," D'John said, elbowing the others aside as he wielded a spray bottle and a comb. "You are not letting the world see this tragedy until I do something with this hair and makeup. Not D'John's client. Oh, no. I'm not having people associate my name with a woman who looks like she got beat up with a homely stick."

"Flatterer," Gina muttered under her breath.

"You can do something about her hair and wipe some of the crud off her face, but other than that, I want her left as is," Barry said, relenting a little. "And you've got five minutes. I want her in the kitchen, cooking, in five minutes. So hurry."

"Hurry," Scott said tersely. "The clock's running." He grabbed Lisa's arm. "And could you please get your sister some shoes?"

"Hurry," Gina said, as D'John combed watered-down conditioner through her tangled hair. "I'm so far behind, I'll never catch up. What did Tate look like when he got here?"

D'John shuddered. "He looked ghastly! Blood all over his clothes, and those cuts and bruises. If I were the type for rough trade, honey, I would have been all over him. But I'm not, and I wasn't."

Lisa hurried over with a bowl of hot water and a soapy cloth, and began gently dabbing at her sister's face. She stepped out of her sandals and slid them onto her sister's feet. "It was awesome, Geen. He looked kinda like Mel Gibson in one of those battle scenes from *Braveheart*. Only Tate's taller than Mel. And hotter. Much hotter. You know, his shirt was kinda ripped open and his hair was all wild and windblown. I swear to God—"

"Enough!" Gina said.

"Enough," Barry decreed. "Stand back, every-body."

———

The smell of roast pork greeted her when she finally made her way to the ballroom and the kitchen set.

Tate looked calm and collected—and clean—as he nonchalantly chopped onions and added them to a sauté pan.

"Hey, Reggie," he said, taking in her disheveled appearance. "Long day, huh?"

"The longest," she agreed. "Heard you're serving pork for dinner. Not bad."

He shrugged. "I got lucky. What about you?"

She had already resolved not to ask him how he'd managed to kill a pig. No, she would not give him that satisfaction.

"Not that lucky," she admitted. "I managed to catch some blue crabs and scrounge up some vegetables. So don't count me out yet."

"Never."

She bustled around the kitchen, putting a stockpot full of water and seasonings on to boil for the blue crabs, shucking the corn and putting it on to boil, and lining up all the ingredients she'd need for the menu she'd assembled in her head on the ride back to the lodge.

"Nice-looking tomatoes," Tate murmured from his side of the kitchen.

"Quiet," Barry thundered. Turning to the camera-men, he looked annoyed. "Cut here. And Tate, buddy, no more chitchat. You guys are supposed to be mortal enemies, right? I don't want our viewers suspecting collusion."

"I don't know about her viewers, but mine wouldn't know collusion if it bit 'em on the ass," Tate said.

Gina shot him a surprised but grateful look, and then the cameras were rolling again, and the big digital clock was ticking off the minutes.

The rest of the hour was a blur. She whisked to-gether a quick topping of crumbled sugar, butter, flour, and cinnamon to top the dewberries she'd spotted only a few hundred yards down the path from the lodge. She sprinkled sugar on the berries, added the topping, and thrust the cobbler into the oven.

When the crabs had finished boiling, she dumped them on the counter and began furiously picking the meat from the shell, setting the heat-reddened backs aside.

Gina's hands shook slightly as she diced celery and onions and dropped them into a skillet to sauté. In the pantry, she found a box of saltines, grabbed a sleeve of them, and pounded them into crumbs with the bottom of a can of tomatoes. She folded the cracker crumbs into the softened vegetables and added half the crabmeat, an egg, and some of the crab boil seasonings.

She carefully spooned the crab mixture into the crab backs, and placed them on a baking sheet. Just before placing them in the oven, she sprinkled the chopped chives over each deviled crab, and dribbled melted butter over each one.

When the corn had cooled, she scraped the kernels from the corncobs and dumped them into a pan of simmering cream and butter, then added in a cup of the crabmeat, salt, pepper, and nutmeg. Her stomach growled at the tantalizing smell of cooked pork wafting from Tate's kitchen. If only, she thought, she had a bit of pork fat to throw into her chowder. And maybe a hit of sherry to give some depth to the chowder's flavor.

She shot Tate a surreptitious look. He was peering into his oven. "You got any sherry over there?"

"Nope," he said, not looking up. "But I saw a bottle in the bar in the library."

"No time," she said with a sigh, cutting up the tomatoes, cukes, and peppers for a southern version of chopped salad.

"I've got five minutes till my tenderloin comes out," he said, and then he was running off the set, headed for the library.

"Hey!" Barry called. "Where the Christ do you think you're going? We're shooting a show here, dude."

"Library. Be right back," Tate called over his shoulder.

Less than a minute later, he was back, a bottle of bourbon in one hand and a bottle of sherry in the other.

"Thanks, Tate," Gina said softly, hoping the boom mike wouldn't pick up her words. "Really. You didn't have to do that."

"I know. But I'd been thinking about grabbing that bourbon anyway, to use in the glaze for my pork tenderloin," he said.

"Five minutes," Barry intoned. He was on camera now, standing in front of the kitchens, supplying commentary to the furious action going on right behind him.

"Our chefs are at the make-or-break point right now," he said in a golf whisper. "Tate Moody appears to have his dishes out of the oven and ready to plate. Right now he's whisking some bourbon into the pan his pork tenderloin cooked in, deglazing the pan drippings. With the remnants of the fig and cracked pepper glaze, that should make a unique sweet-and-savory pan gravy for the pork."

Gina heard Adelman's commentary, but she didn't dare look up from her own kitchen to see her rival's progress. She yanked open the oven door and took out the dewberry cobbler, setting it on the counter to cool. But when she grabbed the baking sheet with the deviled crabs, one went skidding off the pan and onto the floor.

"Oh, too baaad!" Barry crowed. "Party foul for *Fresh Start* chef Gina Foxton." And now the cameras and mikes were aimed at her. "She's got three judges to feed, and only five deviled crabs now," Barry observed. "Can she turn this tragedy into a triumph?"

Gina forced a smile. She placed three of the remaining crabs on three dinner plates, then scooped the crab out of the two extra shells and divided the extra crabmeat between the three plates, mounding the crab higher now on each. She spooned the chopped salad onto the plates alongside the deviled crabs, and quickly showered each dish with a confetti of chopped chives.

"One minute left," Barry said breathlessly. "Can she do it? Can she get everything plated and on the judge's table with so little time left?"

"Bite me!" she wanted to scream. But instead, she ladled the corn and crab chowder into shallow soup bowls and splashed a little sherry into each bowl. Grabbing a tray, she ferried the plates and bowls to the judge's table, then ran back to retrieve the cobbler.

The buzzer went off just as she placed the steaming hot cobbler onto the table.

"And . . . time!" Barry yelled.

Chapter 46

Tate watched the judge's faces carefully. Their dishes had been delivered to the judges for what Adelman called a blind tasting, and he fervently hoped that justice would, indeed, be blind.

Deidre Delaney lifted a tiny forkful of the tenderloin, held it in front of her nose, and sniffed delicately. She turned the fork this way and that, put the fork down, made a note on a clipboard beside her plate, picked the fork up again, and finally took a bite.

She chewed slowly, closing her eyes, nodding thoughtfully. She made another note, then took a tiny bit of the sweet potato fritter and tasted, nodding some more.

"Overcooked," she pronounced. "Not to mention clichéd."

At least, Tate thought, she wasn't holding her nose or gagging.

Beau Stapleton had taken a knife and was quite deliberately separating out all the elements of his dishes before tasting, like a kid pushing the peas aside from the mashed potatoes on a school lunch plate. He'd take a bite, chew, take a healthy swig of the wine on the table by his plate, and then take another bite.

Toni Bailey, on the other hand, pulled her plate toward her and happily dug in, attacking the pork and sweet potatoes with reckless abandon, the way southern cooking was meant to be approached, he'd decided.

"Nice," she said aloud, scribbling a note on the clipboard at her place. "The meat is tender and flavorful, and I love the fig and pepper glaze. I'm gonna have to steal that idea, for sure."

"Looks like you've got at least one fan," Gina said.

They were sitting off camera, watching the judges from a couple of folding chairs they'd dragged up to one of the monitors at the assistant producer's table.

"Thanks, Reggie," he said, glancing over at her.

Adelman had called for a break between shots, and she'd hurried off the set. Fifteen minutes later, she was back, showered and changed into clean clothes—a brightly flowered cotton sundress and sandals. She wore little or no makeup, and with her still-damp hair and sunburn, she looked like a teenager just back from spring break in Panama City Beach.

Zaleski was hovering around her, trying to get her to eat some of the sandwiches and fruit that Iris and Inez had sent over for the cast and crew, but she just waved him away.

"I can't eat anything. I'm too nervous. And all your fluttering around isn't helping. So please, just leave me be."

When Zaleski had wandered away, Tate yawned widely. "You're not hungry? I'm starved. I could eat that whole cobbler of yours."

"Maybe later. Not that it matters. You've won this round," she said, not taking her eyes off the judges. "But don't count me out yet."

"I wouldn't be so sure of that," he replied. "Check out Deidre's face. She doesn't look overly impressed. And she's hardly touched anything."

"Yeah, but Toni Bailey's digging on your stuff."

"What's with this Stapleton dude?" Tate asked. "I can't tell whether he likes it or hates it. Do you know anything about him? Ever eaten in one of his restaurants?"

"Just once, unfortunately," Gina said, tucking a strand of damp hair behind one ear. "Let's just say it was a memorable experience. For both of us."

"Look," Tate said. "They're starting in on your soup."

"It's probably cold by now," she fretted.

Deidre Delaney lifted a spoon to her lips and tasted. "Beautiful presentation," she said, lifting up one of the chive blossoms Gina had floated on top of the soup bowl. "And the silkiness of the corn doesn't overwhelm the delicacy of the crabmeat. Although I would have liked a little heat to the finish."

"Daggumit," Gina said. "I should have added one of Iris's peppers. But I was worried about repeating too much of the deviled crab flavors."

Toni Bailey wasn't stopping to make notes. She was lapping up the soup like a contented kitten, not stopping until her bowl was empty.

"Now that's a winner," she declared. "The essence of southern summer flavors. It's easy to get too precious with all this layering of flavors that's the hot ticket right now. But this chef understands that simple, fresh ingredients don't need any embellishments."

Gina let out the breath she'd been holding and beamed proudly. "She really gets my food," she said.

"You must be joking," Beau Stapleton declared, pushing his nearly full bowl aside. "I can't believe either of you liked the chowder. It was watery, insipid. Lacking in imagination. And," he said, holding out his spoon with a flourish, "I found a huge chunk of crab shell in my bowl. If a line cook in one of my restaurants pulled a rookie stunt like that, I'd fire them on the spot."

Gina clapped her hands over her mouth. "Oh, my God," she whispered. "I was in such a hurry, I must have missed it. That's it," she said, shaking her head sadly. "He's right. I blew it."

"Hey, don't be so hard on yourself," Tate said, patting her knee. "It's just one dish. And the other two seemed to love the chowder."

"No," Gina said, shaking her head emphatically. "He knows which dishes are mine. And he won't let me win. It's not fair, but that's how it is."

"Huh?"

"I'm not saying you don't deserve to win this round," she said quickly. "I mean, you went out with a kid's fishing pole and a glorified butter knife and somehow managed to come back with a pork tenderloin. It was totally MacGyver."

"Shh," one of the sound tech guys told them. "We're rolling here."

"Sorry," they both whispered.

Beau Stapleton reached for the next plate on the table. "Crab again?" he said nastily.

Gina jumped up. "I can't watch any more of this. I'm about to jump out of my skin."

"Shhh!" Barry Adelman glared at her.

———

He found her on the front porch of the lodge, prowling back and forth.

She stopped in her tracks when she caught sight of him. "Is it over? What did they say?"

Tate had to laugh. "Would you relax? They finished deconstructing your deviled crabs, and Barry gave everybody a break before they come back to dessert."

"What'd they say?" she asked. "No, don't tell me. I don't want to get any more depressed than I already am."

"Toni loved 'em, Deidre would have liked 'a little more heat.' The woman probably puts jalapeños on her oatmeal."

She had to ask. "And Beau?"

"Can't understand why you used so much breading. 'A little seasoning and a lot of crab—that's all they need.' That's the gospel according to Beau."

"I only used the barest minimum of cracker crumbs!" she wailed. "You've got to have something as a binder. Anyway, that's the authentic Eutaw Island recipe for deviled crabs."

He shrugged. "I think maybe you're right. The dude just doesn't like you. Or your food. But don't let it bother you. Deidre Delaney's not exactly president of the Tate Moody fan club."

"Really? She knows you?"

"We've met," he said succinctly.

"What's that supposed to mean?"

"Nothing. Just that we're probably in a draw. Deidre hates my guts, Stapleton's got it in for you. That makes Toni the wild card."

"You're just trying to make me feel better," Gina said, pacing again. Then she stopped and whirled around. "Hey! What's up with that? Why are you suddenly on my side?"

"It's not so sudden," he said.

They heard a horn beeping then, and turned to see D'John speeding toward them on a golf cart.

He pulled alongside the porch. "All right, you two," he drawled. "Barry wants you back at the set ASAP. The judges are ready to score the first round. But first, I have got to find a way to make both of you look presentable."

Tate bowed in Gina's direction. "Age before beauty," he said with a grin.

Chapter 47

D'John was brushing powder over Gina's face—a shame, Tate thought, to cover up those freckles—when Lisa strolled into the makeup room.

"Hey!" she started.

"You don't have to tell me," Gina said glumly. "I lost."

"Who knows?" Lisa said, hopping into the empty chair next to her sister and uncapping a bottle of water. "The judges have been bickering for an hour now."

"What are they saying?" Tate asked.

"I can't really hear anything. But that Deidre chick threw a glass of wine in Beau Stapleton's face a little while ago. And not long after that, the black lady—Toni? She got so mad she stomped off the set and Zeke had to go get her and beg her to come back."

"But I thought you said they were ready for us," Gina said, blotting her lips on the tissue D'John offered her.

"That's what they told me," he said. "Barry's exact words were, 'Get 'em ready and get 'em on the set.' "

"Yeah," Lisa said. "I'm supposed to take you back over there now."

"Lisa! Why didn't you say so?" Gina asked, unfastening the plastic cape D'John had placed around her neck.

"You didn't ask. Anyway, I still don't think there's any hurry."

Zeke was standing outside the door to the ballroom when they pulled up in the golf carts.

"All set?" he asked.

"I'm good," Tate said.

"Me too," Gina said. "Where do you want us?"

"Actually, we're not quite ready for you yet," Zeke said, glancing down at the clipboard he held in his right hand. "We're changing the lights around, and Barry decided to give the crew a dinner break so we don't go into overtime."

"So, what now?" Tate asked.

"You could get dinner—it's set up in the lodge—"

"No," Gina said quickly. "I can't eat."

"Or you could hang out in the production trailer. I think that's where Val and Scott are." Zeke walked around to the side of the ballroom and gestured toward a big white mobile home that had the TCC Network logo painted in red and black on the side.

"Where'd that come from?" Gina asked.

"Barry had it brought over this morning," Zeke explained. "He wants to go ahead and do some of the postproduction work here before we all head back to the mainland." Zeke opened the trailer door and motioned them inside. "I'll be back in a few minutes," he promised. "Can I get anybody anything?"

Lisa giggled and whispered something in his ear, and his fair skin flushed a vivid pink.

The inside of the trailer was nothing like a mobile home. One whole wall was taken up with television monitors and a control board with what looked like more switches, dials, and buttons than a NASA cockpit.

Opposite the electronic gear, four leather swivel chairs were bolted to the floor, surrounding a small table littered with coffee cups, water bottles, and paper.

Scott Zaleski sat in one chair, Val Foster in the one opposite him. They were both madly typing away on their BlackBerrys.

"Hi," Scott said, looking up from his PDA. "Is it time?"

"Nope," Lisa said, stepping inside right behind her sister and Tate. "The crew's taking a break."

"Sit here," Scott said, getting up and gesturing toward his chair.

"Thanks," Tate said, dropping down.

Scott glared. "I meant Gina."

"Let him be," Gina said. "I'm too nervous to sit."

"I'm not," Lisa said, sitting beside Val.

"This is cozy," Val said, looking around the room before going back to her BlackBerry.

"I thought you couldn't get service over here," Gina said, peering over Scott's shoulder.

"You can in this thing," Scott said, tapping away. "Did you see the size of that antenna?"

Gina sat down at a chair in front of the control panel. "It looks like they're still arguing," she said, tapping at a monitor that showed the judge's table.

Tate got up to look for himself. The three judges did indeed seem involved in some kind of heated debate.

"They've been at it for two hours now," Scott commented, not looking up.

"We figure it's a stalemate," Val added. "Deidre hates Tate. Seems like Beau's got it in for Gina. Toni Bailey's the wild card, but she can't seem to get either one of them to budge."

"Wait! That's totally unfair. Does Barry know about this?" Lisa wanted to know.

"We told him. He thinks it's great. Says it adds 'intrigue' to the food fight," Val said.

"Prick," Scott muttered.

Tate spun around in his chair. "So what do we do now?"

"We wait," Val said. "But at least I can get some work done on the shows we start taping once we go home." She went back to her BlackBerry. Scott did the same.

Time passed. Tate found a deck of cards and dealt a hand of solitaire. Gina and Lisa shared a two-year-old back issue of *People* magazine Lisa found in the trailer's postage-stamp-size bathroom.

"I'm bored!" Lisa announced after an hour.

"Can't dance, and it's too wet to plow," Gina said mildly.

"What the hell does that mean?" Scott asked, finally putting aside his BlackBerry.

"I don't really know," Gina admitted. "Our granny used to say it when we were visiting her and we didn't have anything to do."

"I don't get it," Scott said.

"My grandma used to always say, 'All dressed up and no place to go,'" Tate volunteered.

Val sighed deeply and exchanged a sympathetic look with Scott. "Don't you just love all these folksy southern sayings?"

The door swung open, and Zeke stuck his head inside. "The crew's back, and we're ready for you."

Val and Scott were out the door like a shot, and Lisa was right behind them. Gina hung back for a second, reluctant, it seemed, to face the music.

Tate held the door open for her, and she went slowly down the folding stairs. She turned to thank him, and he stuck out his hand. "Good luck. And I really mean it."

"Thanks. I'd say the same to you, but for this first round, anyway, I don't think you're going to need it."

"Gina!" Scott called. "Get in here, will you? D'John needs you again."

Val was waiting for him just outside the trailer, her arms folded across her chest. "What do you think you're doing?" she demanded. "Why are you sucking up to her? I almost died when you trotted off set in the middle of the shoot to fetch that sherry. Are you deliberately trying to sabotage our chances to win?"

"I'm just being a nice guy," he protested. "Is that a crime?"

"This is television," she shot back. "As far as I'm concerned, nice is a felony."

Barry Adelman put an arm around each of the contestant's shoulders.

"Okay, you guys, you both did great. Sorry about the wait, but you know chefs." He shrugged. "Talk about a bunch of prima donnas. Anyway, we're all set now. So here's how it's gonna go. You two are each gonna be in your kitchen. The judges will be at their table. They'll give us their opinions on the dishes, and then their scores. Then the camera will cut over to each of you, in turn, to catch your reactions."

"Oh, no—" Gina started.

"Now, don't worry about a thing," he reassured her. "I want you to just be yourself, no matter what happens. Show your emotions. If you're disappointed, lemme see that. Pissed off, excited, whatever. I'm looking for honest, gut reaction. Got that?"

"Yeah," Tate said. "Honest."

"Of course," Barry added, "it goes without saying, no profanity. No high fives, no gloating. No hysteria."

"Just honesty," Tate said, rolling his eyes.

"Our judges have tasted, they've talked, they've argued, and they've debated," Barry said, speaking smoothly in front of the camera. "Now it's time to see how they scored the first round of the Food Fight. So, judges, how did you like the dishes submitted by contestant one?"

Deidre Delaney flipped her long blond hair over one shoulder and smiled wanly. "Contestant one's food left me cold, to be honest. I'll give the chef credit for managing to kill a wild pig, but really, aside from that, I was disappointed."

Beau Stapleton groaned dramatically.

"Let me continue, please," Deidre said, glaring at Stapleton. "The chef had a whole pig to work with, right? A pork tenderloin . . . I mean . . . please. If it were me, I would have done pork belly braised in wild greens. Spare ribs. I would have done pork cheeks. They are wonderful, moist—"

"But it's not you," Toni Bailey pointed out. "Just judge what the chef did, for Pete's sake."

"Fine," Deidre said, flipping her hair again. She held up a card with a "2" scrawled on it. "The dishes were generic. And I'm being generous even giving a two."

"I disagree," Stapleton blurted. "Deidre, what does it take to impress you? This chef basically killed a wild boar with his bare hands, butchered it, and prepared an amazing meal. I'm giving him a five." He held the card up over his head, then pointed at Tate. "You rock, dude!"

Toni Bailey smiled serenely. "As much as I hate to agree with Beau, I have to say that he's right. The pork was outstanding. The fig and pepper glaze was a playful and inventive way to work indigenous ingredients into the menu, and the sweet potato fritters were a nice surprise. For me, the only thing keeping the meal from being perfect was the need for a more assertive vegetable. That said, I'm scoring it a four."

Tate nodded thoughtfully but gave no other reaction.

The camera switched over to Barry Adelman. "All right. It seems the judges have correctly divined that chef one is Tate Moody with his wild hog supper, and given him a combined score of eleven out of fifteen. Now, let's see how Regina Foxworth's seafood sampler fared with the judges."

Deidre Delaney tossed her hair again and beamed in Gina's direction. "Gina, your menu struck all the right chords with me. I loved the crab-corn chowder with that lovely little chive blossom garnish. It was simple but creative. I did want more heat to the soup, but that's a personal preference. The fresh-vegetable chopped salad was perfect, and I adored the little deviled crabs, which were the essence of low-country southern cuisine. The dewberry cobbler was a lovely end note to a perfectly balanced symphony of flavors." She flipped her card up triumphantly. "Five!"

The cameras switched to Gina and caught her letting her breath out slowly, and finally giving a tentative smile.

"Beau?" Barry prompted. "What's your take?

Stapleton grimaced. "Well, Barry, I don't know what dishes our esteemed chef Deidre was tasting, but it can't have been the same meal I sampled."

"Oh, please," Deidre said, giving him a dismissive wave.

"This chef had all the right ingredients, and yet she managed to do all the wrong things. As I said before, the chowder wasn't a proper chowder at all—in fact, it's an insult to honest chowders to call it that."

Barry Adelman laughed. "Hey, Beau! I didn't know you could insult a soup."

"She seems to have a special knack," Stapleton quipped. "Or should I say, lack. Whatever. Those vegetables Deidre loved? Tired. Dull. In short, forgettable."

The camera cut quickly to Gina, who had her hands clasped in her lap and her teeth clenched behind a pasted-on smile.

"He's a dickhead," Tate whispered without moving his lips.

"And now we get to those deviled crabs Deidre so 'adored,'" Stapleton said, his voice mocking. "One word. Gimmicky. All in all, I'd have to say the entire menu was a huge disappointment."

Toni Bailey leaned forward. "But what about that cobbler? Are you just ignoring that?"

"Again," Stapleton said, "no surprises there. I want a fresh fruit cobbler with some zing to it, some spark. A hint of ginger, some lemon zest or orange liqueur, some little something that makes my tongue tingle."

"I'll make his tongue tingle," Tate muttered. For a fleeting moment, Gina's smile took on an authentic warmth.

Stapleton yawned widely, not bothering to cover his mouth. "The cobbler was forgettable. Amateurish. As was the entire meal." He offhandedly flashed his score-card, and the entire crew gasped.

"Only a one!" Barry crowed. "Ow! That's gotta hurt."

Gina felt tears welling in her eyes. Her jaws ached from pseudo-smiling, but the camera, unrelenting, was aimed right at her.

"Shake it off," Tate whispered. "You knew he was gonna screw you over."

"So, Toni Bailey," Barry said. All eyes on the set were focused on the third judge. "It all comes down to you now. Our other two judges were at extreme odds in their scores of Gina Foxton. What did you think, Toni?"

The petite black woman's hoop earrings jangled as she shook her head in dismay at Stapleton's harsh comments.

"Honey, don't you fret," Toni soothed, looking directly at Gina. "You are a fine young cook. And that meal was so good, it made me wanna slap my mama."

Gina laughed ruefully.

"See?" Tate whispered.

"I agree completely with Deidre about your chowder. Some folks," she said, inclining her head toward Stapleton, "like a gloppy, floury mess in a chowder. Not me. No, sir. Me, I just want honest flavors. Over in L.A."—she glanced at Stapleton—"that's Lower Alabama to you, you add that other mess when you don't have the real thing, say if you were using frozen corn, or canned crabmeat. But when you got the honest-to-goodness thing—fresh-picked corn, crabs right out of the creek—you don't need that other junk. Same thing with those chopped vegetables, and that wonderful dewberry cobbler of yours. They were real nice. I don't hold with people who wanna mess around with the conventions of southern cooking."

She gave Stapleton a look that Gina's grandmother would have called the skunk-eye. "And that is what we're supposed to be looking for here on Eutaw Island. The best *southern* cook."

Gina felt her spirits rise.

But Toni sighed. "Baby, the only thing keeping me from giving you a perfect five was this." She held up the index finger of her left hand. A tiny fragment of white gleamed against the mocha color of her skin.

"Yeah," she said sorrowfully. "A little bitty old piece of crabshell no bigger than a pea. That's how come I had to give you this." She held up her scorecard, with a bold "4" scrawled on it.

Gina felt a tear working its way down her cheek. She swiped at it, blinked, then turned to Tate.

"Congratulations," she said, her voice shaky.

Chapter 48

Well, that's it for round one of The Cooking Channel's Food Fight!" Barry said, reading from the teleprompter. "Our esteemed panel of experts awarded round one to Tate Moody for his unique take on a wild hog supper, but only by a slim one-point margin. Don't forget to tune in tomorrow night for round two of our Food Fight, when Regina Foxton has vowed to come out of her kitchen hotter than hot!"

The number-two camera flashed on Tate, who nodded politely, and then at Regina, who, at Barry's direction, brandished a giant cast-iron skillet in what he assured her would be a menacing gesture.

"Okay, let's take a break," Barry called. The lights switched off, and the cameramen trotted off to the craft table.

Gina exhaled slowly. She closed her eyes and rolled her neck clockwise and then counterclockwise, trying to diminish the tension knots in her upper body. When she opened her eyes, she saw Zeke escorting Beau, Deidre, and Toni off the set.

She noticed with grim satisfaction that the three judges looked just as bedraggled as she felt. Deidre Delaney's mascara seemed to have melted off, and Toni Bailey's perky demeanor had finally faded. Beau Stapleton's shirt was dark with perspiration, and even his ponytail looked waterlogged.

"Christ, the humidity here must be two hundred percent," he griped. "It's like a damned steam bath in here."

Zeke handed Beau a cold bottle of water and murmured something reassuring about the air-conditioning in the production trailer, and then they were all gone.

She was about to leave herself when she felt a large hand clamp her shoulder.

"Great show, you two," Barry exclaimed, clamping his other hand on Tate's shoulder. "No kidding, guys, this one had it all. It had drama, it had comedy, it had suspense—"

"And tragedy," Gina said wryly. "At least from my point of view."

"Will you stop?" Barry said. "Forget about the crab shell thing. It was nothing. Coulda happened to anybody."

"That's what I told her," Tate said, gently easing his shoulder out from under Barry's grip.

"It shouldn't have happened to a pro," Gina said.

"That's the point of this show," Barry said. "Don't you get it? The audience at home will love that about you. You think Sally Subdivision in Horseplop, Arkansas, hasn't dropped a hunk of eggshell in a birthday cake? Of course she has. Everybody has! And that's why they'll love you. You let them see that even a pro messes up sometimes. People are gonna relate to you, Gina. They'll relate to both of you. Because you're real. And that's what we're looking for. Real cooks with real personalities. We're not looking for polish and perfection."

"Tell that to Beau Stapleton," Scott said, striding onto the set with a cold Diet Coke for Gina. "What a jerk! Barry, are you aware of how biased he is against Gina? It's so blatant. I can't believe you let him get away with that crap."

"But what about Deidre?" Valerie chimed in. She uncapped a bottle of Heineken and handed it to Tate. "She crucified him—and why? Because he politely declined her offer of a free fuck!"

"Val!" Tate exclaimed, slamming the bottle down on the countertop, "For God's sake—"

"People, people, people," Barry said soothingly. "Yes, I am aware that there are some undercurrents. Some creative tension. But as I told you before, conflict makes for drama. And that's what entertainment is about, right?"

He looked from Val to Scott to Tate to Gina for affirmation.

"It's still not fair," Scott grumped. He tugged on Gina's hand. "Come on, Geen. It's after ten."

Gina nodded and yawned. "I gotta get some sleep. Good night, everybody." She trailed dutifully behind her producer. On the way out of the ballroom she stopped at the craft table, where Lisa was laughing and joking noisily with the crew, cutting her eyes every so often at Zeke, who pretended not to notice.

"I'm headed for the room," she told her sister. "Are you coming up soon?"

"Yeah," Lisa said vaguely. "Soon. I just want to unwind with the guys a little. Don't wait up for me, though. I'm a big girl, I can handle myself."

"She worries about you, okay?" Scott said, glaring at the younger sister. "As long as you're out partying your ass off, she won't sleep. So for once, could you just think of somebody else?"

Lisa glared right back. She took a long sip from her beer and wiped her mouth with the back of her hand. "Fuck off, Scott, will you? My mama's alive and kickin' in Odum, so I sure as hell don't need you to tell me what to do."

"Don't!" Gina interjected. "I'm too tired to play referee." She turned to Scott. "You don't need to walk me to my room. I want to sit on the porch for a minute, get some fresh air."

"I'll come with you. We need to discuss the plan for tomorrow."

"Not tonight," she said gently. "I really just want to be alone for a while, to think about what went wrong today and regroup. We can talk in the morning. I'll meet you downstairs for breakfast. Is seven too early?"

He shrugged in a way that telegraphed his hurt at what he perceived as a snub. "Fine. I'll see you at seven." He hurried out of the ballroom without looking back.

"Night-night, Scottie," Lisa sang out.

"Lisa!"

Unrepentant, her younger sister put down her empty bottle and reached for another beer from the open cooler on the table.

"Why do you even put up with his crap?" she asked. "You broke up, didn't you?"

"He's still my producer," Gina said. "And in a crazy way, I guess he still thinks he cares about me."

"But you're over him—right?"

Gina bit her lip and nodded. Out of the corner of her eye, she saw Zeke, bent over his open laptop at the director's console.

"What's with Zeke?" she asked. "Did you two have a fight or something? He looks like somebody stole his lollipop."

"Let me ask you something," Lisa said, running her fingers through her hair. "Why does a man think it's his job to boss a woman around?"

"I don't know," Gina said. "Is that what Zeke's trying to do?"

"Trying? He's becoming a major pain in the ass," Lisa said.

"In what way?"

"He thinks I drink too much."

"Do you?"

"I have a good time, that's all," Lisa said. "It's not like I'm hurting anybody. I have a few beers, I party. I'm not an alcoholic, for God's sake."

Gina stared pointedly at the line of empty beer bottles on the table. "I think Zeke is sweet. And I think it's sweet that he worries about you."

"You would," Lisa said, swaying ever so slightly. "You always think you have to have a big ol' man to look after you, don't you? Well, not me, sister. I can take care of my own damn self."

"I see that," Gina said. "Just make sure that you do take care of yourself. Or I'll have to answer to Mom."

"Mom!" Lisa said, her eyes widening. She reached in the pocket of her capris, brought out her cell phone, and handed it to Gina. "She wants you to call her. She's left half a dozen messages on my phone. Text and voice."

Gina dropped her clothes on the bathroom floor and stepped into the shower. The shock of the ice-cold water on her sweat-soaked skin was delicious. She put her face into the full force of the spray, soaped up, rinsed, and then soaped and rinsed again. She patted herself dry, slathered night cream on her face, and slipped into a pair of faded cotton jeans, a worn but clean T-shirt, and a pair of hot pink flip-flops.

Stifling a yawn, she got out the research materials she'd brought with her. Spiral-bound cookbooks from various coastal church and community groups—including her favorite, *Soul Stirrin'*, from the ladies' circle of the Darien Church of God in Christ—natural history books, and a well-thumbed field guide to coastal Georgia plant life. Somewhere in these books, she knew, was the inspiration—and the recipes—that would lead her to success in the second round of the Food Fight.

She dug a bag of pork rinds out of the bottom of her suitcase and crammed one into her mouth, trying not to chew too fast. Her stomach growled loudly. She quickly ate half a dozen and was reaching for another when she heard her sister's voice outside the bedroom, telling somebody good night. She shoved the empty bag under her mattress just as Lisa stepped unsteadily inside.

"Hey!" Gina said. "You're in early."

Lisa threw herself down on her bed. "Everybody else wimped out on me. Claimed they have to work in the morning. And I thought TV people were supposed to be such party animals."

"What about Zeke?"

"Zeke!" Lisa said, wriggling out of her pants and tossing them onto the floor. "All he does is look at me with those big ol' puppy-dawg eyes. Talk about a buzz killer."

Lisa pulled a sheet up over her bare shoulders and looked over at her sister. "What are you doing? Studying? I thought you were dead tired."

Gina yawned widely. "I'm wiped," she admitted. "But I've got to figure out a way to win tomorrow. It's my last chance. Otherwise, I go home to Mama and Daddy."

They shuddered in unison.

"Lord, I'm so tired, I could sleep for a year," Gina said, standing up to stretch.

"Then go to bed. That's what you told Scott you were doing."

"I just didn't feel like being fussed over anymore," Gina said. "If I leave the light on, will it bother you?"

"Nope," Lisa said. "Nothin's botherin' me."

"I think I'll go downstairs and see if there's any more coffee left," Gina said, standing up and stretching. "I've gotta find a way to stay awake for a while."

"Coffee? Nah," Lisa said. She swung her legs out of bed and went to her canvas tote bag, which she'd slung onto the back of a chair.

She reached inside, brought out a bright red-and-black soft drink can, and popped the top. Dipping into the bag again, she brought out a small pill bottle and dropped two capsules into the can.

"Here," she said, thrusting the can at Gina. "Drink this."

"What is it?" Gina asked, with a mixture of horror and fascination.

"Red Bull and NoDoz," Lisa said. "The kids at school call it a Raging Bull. We drink it when we have to cram for a final."

"Is it legal?" Gina asked, sniffing the can.

"Who cares?" Lisa said, flopping down on her bed again. "Call Mom, okay? She's driving me nuts." She turned over, sighed loudly, and moments later was softly snoring.

Gina sighed and put Lisa's cell phone in the pocket of her jeans, deciding she would call her mother later—much later. She looked down at the pile of books on her own bed, and then at the soda can.

"What the hell." She held her nose and chugged the Red Bull. The taste was odd, vaguely citrus, with undertones of chemicals. Definitely an acquired taste. But if it would keep her awake long enough to do her research, she decided, it was worth the weird aftertaste.

The old lodge was quiet as she padded down the worn wooden stair treads, down to the lobby, and to the front door. She opened the door and peeked out. The porch was empty. Bliss.

She settled herself into one of the rockers and opened her copy of *Soul Stirrin'*.

At first, all was serenity. She watched moths flickering around the yellow globe of the porch light, and once, unbelievably, she saw a bat swoop in and snatch an unfortunate insect in midair. She heard the croak of tiny green tree toads from a palm tree at the edge of the porch, and when the wind wafted in just the right direction, she smelled the exotic scent of Confederate jasmine and honeysuckle from the vines that threaded their way up the trunk of an ancient oak near the driveway.

Gina worked on, leafing through her books, making notes on ideas for the next day. Oysters? Conventional wisdom—and Birdelle Foxton—had always declared that oysters were inedible in summer months. But her field guide begged to differ, stating that though summer oysters would be somewhat smaller, they were definitely edible. She'd spotted a promising-looking shell bank earlier in the day, during her unsuccessful fishing expedition. If not oysters, perhaps she'd walk along a sandbar and dig her toes in, searching for the quahog clams that the book said should be abundant in the summertime. Fried clams—let Tate Moody top that, she thought.

If the field guide was to be believed, there were wild greens to be had on barrier islands like Eutaw—something called sea purslane, which grew on sand flats in the high marsh. The guide had a small, fuzzy photograph, which she tried to memorize. If she could find the sea purslane, maybe she could fashion her own version of oysters Rockefeller. Oysters Eutaw, she'd call them.

Gina blinked. Suddenly, she could feel the adrenaline pumping through her bloodstream. Her pulse raced.

Her eyes and mouth were dry. She put her hand over her chest and could have sworn her heart was beating so hard it lifted her hand up and off her body.

"Holy crap," she whispered. She'd been gored by a Raging Bull.

She rocked faster, slapping her flip-flops rhythmically on the porch floor. She tried writing, but her hand was too shaky. She had to get up, had to move, go somewhere. She was hungry. She glanced down at her watch. After midnight. Would the kitchen be locked up? More importantly, would there be any food?

The kitchen was dark, bathed in the eerie blue-gray light of the microwave's digital readout. She yanked open the refrigerator door, and silently blessed Iris and Inez.

A large platter of neatly sliced sandwiches, blanketed in plastic wrap, rested on the top shelf of the fridge, beside a huge glass pitcher of iced tea—also swathed in plastic.

She put the platter on the old-fashioned marble countertop and lifted the plastic to investigate. Chicken salad. Thinly sliced turkey, and ham with Swiss cheese. Her stomach growled so loudly, she was afraid she'd awaken the entire house.

Gina helped herself to half a chicken salad sandwich and half a ham and cheese on whole wheat, placing both on a paper towel. She put the platter back and poured herself a tall glass of tea.

There was a tin breadbox on the island, in the same funny jade green color as her mother's breadbox. She lifted the lid and was rewarded with a bag of potato chips, clamped shut with an old-fashioned wooden clothespin, the same way her mother fastened opened bags of food.

She added a handful of potato chips to her sandwich and sat down on a wooden stool pulled up to the counter.

Gina thought it might have been the best food she'd ever tasted. But maybe that was just the bull talking. She took a swig of tea and a bite of potato chip, and in less than five minutes—she knew it was only five, because she was watching the readout on the microwave—she'd polished off her whole dinner. Mortifying—but tasty.

She was sponging off the counter—erasing any clues about her presence there—when she heard soft footsteps coming down the stairs.

When the footsteps headed away from the kitchen and toward the front door, she decided to investigate. Was the midnight traveler Lisa—off for an assignation with Zeke? Unlikely—her sister was passed out upstairs. Could it be Scott? And if it was, who was he slipping out to meet?

Without stopping to think, she tiptoed out of the kitchen and down the hall, pausing again when she heard the slight creak of the front door opening.

Peering around the edge of a grandfather clock, she saw a familiar feathery tail—and the spotted butt of Moonpie—going out the front door. Tate Moody was right behind him, stopping at the door and looking warily around. She ducked down behind the massive carved oak console table in the hall to avoid being discovered. A minute later, she was back at the door, peeking out from the sidelight to see Tate going down the porch steps. Her heart was still pounding and her brain was obviously fogged, because the next thing she knew, she was slinking onto the porch, hiding behind one of the columns, peering into the darkness to see where Moody and Moonpie had gone.

A moment later, she heard the high-pitched whir of a golf cart, and saw the cart's headlights flash past.

Crap! He was off on another of his midnight hunting expeditions. But she'd be darned if she was going to let him get away with it this time. Tomorrow was her time to shine, not his.

She crept off the porch and ran—as best she could run in flip-flops—to her own golf cart. She turned the key and headed off into the night, bumping along the shell path, staying back as far as she could and still keep Moody in her sights. She left her own headlights off, praying that she wouldn't run off the path and into one of Eutaw's alligator-infested ditches or ponds.

Chapter 49

Tate looked down at the crude map he'd drawn earlier in the day and stared off into the darkness. The paths weren't marked this far from the lodge, but the landmark—and the turnoff he was looking for— was a palm tree with most of the top sheared off. In the dark, though, nothing looked familiar.

He stopped the cart once, got out, and played his flashlight over a palm tree, but on closer examination, he discovered it was not the right tree. He heard a noise on the path behind him. Moonpie whimpered. Tate ruffled the fur on his neck. "It's okay, buddy, probably just an armadillo bumping around out here in the dark like the rest of us."

He got back in the cart and traveled another five hundred yards before spotting a palm tree he was sure was the right one. The flashlight confirmed it, so he veered hard right when the road forked.

"Gettin' close, buddy," he told the dog. He was so close to the water now, he could hear waves lapping on the shore.

Finally, maybe half a mile down the path, he sighted the strip of his own white T-shirt that he'd tied to the branch of a hunk of driftwood on the left side of the path. He stopped the cart, got out, and stretched.

From out of the darkness he heard a faint humming noise, then nothing. Moonpie whimpered and got out of the cart, his tail raised as though he were flushing a quail.

"Stay, boy," Tate told him, grasping the dog's collar. He took a few steps away from the cart and played the flashlight over the path, but could see nothing, except a couple of tree toads engaged in what looked to him to be toad-humping.

"Nothing there but a couple horny toads," he told the dog, grinning at his own pun. "Come on, let's see if she's still here."

Tate walked to the edge of the path, to the point where the oyster shells seemed to merge with marsh grass. He felt mud squishing beneath his sneakers, then water seeping up to his ankles. Holding the flashlight over his head, he shone it in the direction of the marsh.

"Jackpot!" he said smugly.

There, snagged in the trunk of a dead tree, was an old aluminum johnboat, maybe fourteen feet long, that he'd spotted bobbing in the water earlier in the day at high tide. From where he'd stood then, it had appeared that the boat was snagged on something beneath the water's surface. And now, at the ebb tide, he could see that, yes, the boat was still there, and, yes, its bow appeared to be wedged into the crotch of an old dead tree on a sandbar.

He took a deep breath and looked back at Moonpie, who sat very straight, looking out at the water. "You stay here," he told the dog. "Don't let those toads steal our cart."

"Let me give you a hand there, old buddy." A woman's voice came out of the darkness, startling him so that he dropped the flashlight into the water.

"Oopsie," the voice came again.

He whirled around but could see nothing in the now total darkness.

"Dammit, Reggie, is that you?"

"Yup."

"You made me drop my damned flashlight."

"So I see."

He fished around in the knee-deep water but, finding nothing, let out a stream of colorful expletives.

"You always talk that way around an impressionable dog?" Gina called.

"If Moonpie could talk, he'd say a lot worse," Tate yelled. "Dammit, this was my one chance to grab that boat."

"You could come back in the morning," she suggested.

"It'll be high tide in the morning. I'd have to swim out—and that's only if it's still here. It's snagged on something, and I'm afraid it'll float away by then."

"If you had another light, say right now, could you get to it?"

"Hell, yeah."

A tiny beam of light hit him in the face. He put his hands in front of his eyes to shield them.

"Great," he said. "How about bringing the flashlight out here to me?"

"In the water?"

"It's only knee-deep."

"I don't think so."

"Afraid you'll drown?"

"I don't like snakes. Or alligators. This place looks like it could be crawling with both."

He sighed. "If I come back up there, you'll give me the flashlight, right?"

"We can discuss it."

He muttered another string of colorful phrases, but slogged slowly back through the marsh muck until he reached the shell bank.

"Give me a hand up," he said.

She considered it. "You wouldn't pull me down into the mud, would you?"

"The thought hadn't entered my mind," he lied.

"I'll bet."

She stuck her hand out, and helped him up the bank.

"Hi," she said.

"You followed me here."

"No, I was just out for a midnight joyride and bumped into you and your dog out here in the middle of nowhere."

He took the flashlight out of her hand and flashed it in her face. Her eyes were huge, her face flushed. She had a loony grin on her face that was most un-Reggie-like.

"Are you on some kind of dope or something?"

She blinked. "It's not dope. I was trying to stay up so I could research and get myself ready to whip your butt tomorrow, but I was tired, so Lisa gave me a can of her Red Bull."

"Red Bull. That's all?"

"Well. It's sort of a college cocktail the kids all drink when they're studying for exams. Lisa calls it a Raging Bull."

"What else is in it?"

"NoDoz."

"NoDoz and Red Bull? Jesus H. Christ on a crutch, Reggie. That's a heart attack in a hurry. You mean to say you drank some?"

"Just one can."

He shook his head. "I want to beat you fair and square, but I can't do it if you're dead."

"I'm fine," she insisted. "Finer than fine."

"You're amped out of your gourd. You just up and followed me out here in the dead of night? Didn't even put the headlights on in the golf cart?"

"I wanted to see where you were going. Find out what you were up to. And now I have."

"Yes," he agreed. "What do you intend to do now?"

She gave it some thought. "I'll hold the flashlight and shine it on the boat, while you go out and drag it back here."

"And then?"

"And then tomorrow, we'll go out in it and catch some nice fresh fish."

"We? No. No way. It's my boat. I found it, and I'm gonna go out there and drag it back up here. And that'll be the end of it."

"Fine," she said. "I'll just take my itsy-bitsy old flashlight and go home." She grabbed the flashlight back and turned to leave.

"Wait," he called. "Let's see if we can figure this out."

"We?"

He swore quietly. "You and me. I'll play fair. I swear."

Chapter 50

Safely back in her room at the lodge, Gina did not sleep.

She read all of her reference books. She took notes. She tiptoed downstairs to the library, found an old copy of *The Yearling*, and read it in one sitting, crying, as she always did, at the end of the book. She filed her nails and washed out her underpants in the bathroom sink. Then she washed her sister's underpants. She even considered, but only briefly, calling her mother, but at six thirty, she decided it was time to get ready for the big day.

Showered and dressed in khaki slacks and a tank top with a blue cotton work shirt thrown over it, she looked at herself in the mirror. Her eyes still looked, as Tate had pointed out, a little loony. But her heart had finally stopped pounding, and her pulse seemed to have slowed down to the rate of a moderately hyperactive gerbil.

She went bouncing down the stairs to the lobby, but stopped, mid-bounce, when she saw Scott standing there, looking up at her.

"You're in a great mood," he observed.

"Today's the day," she agreed. "Today I win. Or die trying."

"That's kind of extreme, Gina," he said, frowning.

"But true. Let's face it. My show has been canceled, and so far, not a whole lot of people are banging on my door begging to put me on television."

"They will. I told you that. Even if, God forbid, you lose today, your career is far from over. I promised you that, didn't I?"

"You promised me a lot of things," she said.

"I'm sorry—"

"Don't," she said, stopping him. "It's in the past. I'm just saying, it's up to me to make my own career path. I can't count on you—or anybody else—to do it for me. And that's fine. It's great. I believe in me."

He put his finger under her chin and lifted it up and gazed into her eyes. "You've changed in the last week, you know that? You're, I don't know . . . tough, I guess, is the word. How did that happen?"

"Resilient," she corrected. "Let's go get some food. I could eat a horse."

It was only seven, but the rest of the production crew was already sitting around the long polished mahogany table, passing an oversize basket of bread.

"Biscuits?" Gina swooped down and short-stopped the basket before it could reach Zeke. She folded back a checked cotton napkin and nabbed a biscuit, still warm from the oven.

She took the vacant seat next to Zeke's, pulled the biscuit in half, and proceeded to slather it with butter and honey.

Scott looked on openmouthed. "You're eating carbs? And butter? And honey? All in the same meal? In front of other people?"

"Hungry," Gina said between bites. "Very hungry."

"Uh, Gina," Zeke said quietly. "Is Lisa up yet?"

"Not yet," she said, turning toward him. "But don't worry, I'll run up and get her after I've had my eggs and bacon."

"Good God," Scott said, clutching his chest. "Who are you?"

"Lisa's mad at me," Zeke said, his eyes downcast.

"She'll get over it," Gina said, filling her glass with orange juice. "My baby sister has the attention span of a toddler. Trust me, she's probably already forgotten what you were fussing about."

"I told her she was drinking too much," Zeke whispered. "And she *was*. She called me an old lady."

"Don't worry. She calls me that all the time. And worse."

"Did she say anything about me last night?"

"She thinks you're sweet," Gina said, patting his hand reassuringly. "We both do."

"Zeke!" Barry Adelman stood in the dining room doorway, dressed in a sky blue silk tropical print shirt and cream silk slacks. He had paper napkins tucked around the collar of the shirt, to keep his orange pancake makeup from ruining it. "The meter's running, sport. Production meeting in five minutes."

He looked at his crew members, at Gina and Scott and the others. "Big day, everybody," he boomed. "Round two. Let's go make some television!"

Chairs were pushed back and forks put down midbite. The crew members rushed for the door.

Scott took Zeke's vacant seat next to Gina.

"Did you have some time to figure out a plan for today?" he asked.

"I was up all night," she said simply. "It's taken care of."

"All right," he said slowly. "What are your thoughts?"

"Oysters, if I can find them. Or flounder. If the tide's right. Maybe both, if I get really lucky."

He frowned. "Oysters? You can't do oysters now. They're poison or something. Nobody eats oysters in the summertime."

"*Au contraire*," she said. "I can, and I will, if I can find them."

"What about the flounder?" he asked, deciding to let the oysters drop for the moment. "You didn't have any luck fishing yesterday. What makes you think today will be any different?"

She smiled serenely. "I've got a whole different approach today."

"Moody did pork yesterday. So he'll for sure be doing fish today," Scott said. "I think you should do some counter-tactics. Maybe chicken. Something homey like that. Everybody always loved that show you did with the fried chicken."

"I've got it under control, Scott," Gina said, standing up. "I gotta go get made up. See you on set."

She hummed as D'John did her comb-out.

"Stop that," he said. "You've never hummed before."

She hummed another bar. The song was her own off-key version of "Brick House," although she would readily admit it was nothing the Commodores would recognize.

"Shake it down, shake it down, shake it down now," she sang.

Tate slid into the chair next to hers.

"Is that supposed to be 'Brick House'? Because if it is, it's the worst version I've ever heard. I was at a wedding reception in Pittsburgh once, and the polka band did a better version."

Gina sang on.

In defense, D'John carpet-bombed her entire head with hairspray.

She quit singing.

She glanced around the makeup room to make sure that nobody else was listening.

"Are we all set?"

"Yes."

"You checked? It's still there?"

"As of half an hour ago."

"All systems go?" she asked.

"Roger that."

The makeup room door opened, and Zeke walked in, followed by an unhappy-looking Moonpie.

"D'John?" Zeke said, his voice tentative.

"What are you doing with that dog in here?" D'John demanded.

"Uh, Barry wants Moonpie in the shoot today."

"What?" Tate asked. "Just in the stand-up part? That should be all right. He's used to being on camera with me."

"Uh, well, that, and uh, Barry wants you to take Moonpie out with you today. And afterward, he wants him in the kitchen with you."

"Hell, no!" Tate exploded. "He's a dog. He sees a mockingbird or a squirrel, and he thinks it's time to go hunting. I love my dog, but I don't have time to go chasing after him when we're on a deadline like this. When we shoot my show, we always have somebody off set tending to him while we finish the shoot."

"Aw, come on, Tate," Gina said, laughing. "Moonpie wants to go. Don't you, Moonpie?"

The setter put his front paws on Gina's lap and thumped his tail happily.

"Absolutely not," Tate said, crossing his arms.

"Afraid so," Zeke said. "And uh, D'John?"

The makeup artist rolled his eyes. "Don't tell me . . ."

"Barry wants to know if there's anything you can do to emphasize Moonpie's eyes more. Like uh, eyeliner or something? Also, he wants you to trim the droopy stuff around his ears, and maybe fluff up his tail a little. He suggested a blow-dryer."

Tate started to argue, but then thought better of it. He climbed down off the makeup chair and thumped its padded seat. "Here, boy," he called. "Your turn."

The day was hot, but overcast. Barry decreed it the perfect weather for an outdoor shoot.

He guided Tate and Gina toward the front door of the lodge, an arm over each of his would-be stars' shoulders.

"All right, kids," he said. "The crew's out front, waiting for you. Here's the plan:

"We've already shot an interview with the judges back in the ballroom. And P.S., before we started taping, I did mention to Beau and Deidre that you two are concerned about their impartiality. They both swear they have no biases against either of you."

"Riiiight," Tate said.

"I'm gonna give them the benefit of the doubt," Barry said. "So. I'll go outside and do my stand-up about how it's the second round of the Food Fight, blasé, blasé, blasé. Zeke is going to stand inside the door with you two, and at his signal, I want you both to come bustin' full-tilt boogie out this door. Then, I want you to run to your golf carts, get behind the wheels, and glare at each other. Got it?"

"Glaring," Tate said. "Check."

"Full-tilt boogie," Gina answered. "Got it."

"Knock 'em dead," Barry said, slapping their backs.

Zeke took his station beside the front door, with the freshly groomed Moonpie's leash wrapped loosely around his wrist. The dog sat patiently waiting for his cue. Zeke glanced at the yellow sticky note posted on his left forearm, and then at the watch on his right wrist. He wore a headset and a worried expression.

"Lisa still hasn't come downstairs," he told Gina. "Do you think she's all right?"

"She was in the shower a few minutes ago," Gina told him. "Aren't you supposed to be giving us a signal to go out?"

"Oh. Yeah. Right."

He spoke into his microphone. "Barry? Are we ready?"

He nodded.

"Two more minutes," he told Gina. "On the signal, I'll hold the door open, and you guys go charging out. Barry wants to do it all in one long shot, so try not to mess up.

"Should I go up and check on Lisa?" he asked. "Or is that too old-lady-like?"

"Concentrate on this shot," Gina suggested. "Lisa's not really a morning person."

They could hear Barry's voice through the door. "And now, let's get our chefs out here and ready to rumble," he said loudly.

Chapter 51

As they'd planned the night before, Gina and Tate each took different forks in the road at the end of the Rebeccaville driveway. And as planned, Gina took the loop path that followed the island's coastline, then cut across the island to meet Tate at the spot she'd followed him to the night before.

The sky was a dull gray this morning, and there was not a hint of a breeze to dispel the damp, sticky humidity that seemed to close in around her body as she bumped over the oyster-shell cart path. She could feel her energy starting to flag, but shook her head violently, as though to shake off any doubts about the day's outcome.

Ten minutes later, she arrived at the palm tree with the shorn-off top, and two minutes after that, she saw

Tate standing beside his parked cart, unloading his fishing equipment. Moonpie stood at the edge of the marsh grass, nose in the air, tail erect.

"He saw a heron," Tate said as a greeting to her. "Talk about an incurable optimist, he actually thinks he's gonna flush and fetch me a three-foot-tall blue heron."

Gina leaned over and rubbed Moonpie's ears. "Go get 'em, boy."

Tate made a face and started down the shell bank. He looked back at Gina, who stood motionless, her cheap plastic spinning reel in one hand, her cooler in the other.

"Come on, then, if you're coming," he said, glancing up at the clouds. "I think we may be in store for some rain."

"Did you check the boat to see if there are any leaks?" she asked, stepping daintily down into the mud before getting in.

"It's floating," he said, handing her a weathered oak oar. "It probably has a little seepage, but nothing major."

Tate stepped out of the boat, whistled, and Moonpie jumped in. He shoved the boat's bow off the shell bank, and waded it out until the water was nearly waist high before climbing in and taking a seat at the front.

"You know how to row, right?" he asked.

"Of course," she said indignantly. "Did you say something about seepage?"

"It's an old boat," he said, dipping his oar into the water and pulling it forward with one fluid motion. "The rivets are probably a little loose. But if it wasn't seaworthy, it would have sunk long ago. I pulled all kind of gunk out of it before you got here. It's been sitting on that snag for some time now."

Gina dipped her own oar into the water on the other side of where Tate's was. "So, this boat probably belongs to somebody. Somebody who'd probably consider us as thieves, since we're taking it without their permission."

"You could always hop out," he suggested. "Before you become an accessory to grand theft, boat."

Instead, she kept rowing, working to get her strokes in rhythm with his. She hadn't rowed a boat in years. She could already feel blisters rising on the palms of her hands, and after fifteen minutes, the muscles in her shoulders were protesting.

They didn't talk. The dark water flashed by, and red-winged blackbirds rose out of the tall marsh grass as they glided along. She could see shrimp popping at the point where the water met shell banks, and occasionally a mullet would jump and slap the water, causing Moonpie much excitement.

"Hey, we're getting pretty good at this," she said at one point, marveling at their relative speed.

"Tide's going out," he said, deliberately bursting her little bubble.

In thirty minutes, when she turned around, she could barely see the point in the marsh where they'd left the carts. They were out of the creek, she thought, and in the ocean. The thought made her pulse race again.

"Do you actually know where you're going?" she asked anxiously. "I mean, this creek just seems to curve and meander, and it all starts to look the same to me."

"I know what I'm doing," he said simply.

Her feet were wet. There was half an inch of water in the boat.

"Uh, Tate," she said.

"It's just a little water. You won't drown."

"I was just saying . . ."

He grunted and kept rowing, so she did the same. She could feel beads of sweat rolling down her face, and her shirt was damp with perspiration. She wanted to take a break, have a sip from the bottled water she'd stowed in her cooler, but she didn't want Tate Moody to think she was a slacker. Or worse, a girl.

Thirty minutes later, he put his oar down and frowned. They could see the dark green shape of Eutaw

Island behind them. The sky had darkened to a pale pewter shade, and the wind whipped little whitecaps on the dark green sea. "This looks like the place Iris told me about."

"Inez told me about a place too. Where her daddy used to take her to catch spot-tail bass. But if it's the place, why are you frowning?"

"No anchor," he said, slapping his thigh in disgust. "How could I not have thought of that?"

She hadn't thought of it either, but she didn't intend to volunteer that information.

"We've got that rope up in the bow," she said. "Could we tie up to something?"

He gestured toward the creek bank, which seemed half a mile away. "You see anything we can tie up to?"

"What do we do now?" she asked. "Go back?"

"Hell, no," Tate said. "We'll just have to take turns. One can fish, while the other keeps rowing us back toward the island."

"What do we use for bait? I'm used to fishing with shrimp. Or minnows."

"There's that *we* thing again," he said, reaching for the plastic tackle box. He pawed through the contents. "Most of this stuff is worthless," he said. "But there's a couple halfway decent jigs in here. It's better than nothing."

He busied himself rigging his fishing line, and in a moment, he'd cast out in the direction of the creek.

"I take it that means I'm on rowing duty first?"

He nodded, not taking his eyes off the water. "Keep trying to move us back toward the island. You'll have to work at it too, the way the tide's moving."

She had just put her oar in the water when Tate grunted. His rod tip bent. He jerked hard on it, then casually started reeling.

"Hey, fish!" he said happily. Moonpie gave a happy bark, and in what seemed like a very short time, Tate was reeling in a fish.

"Nice one," he said. "Three pounds, easy."

"What kind is it?" she asked, glancing down at the silvery fish flopping around on the bottom of the boat. Moonpie bent down, sniffed, and thumped his tail in approval.

"Spot-tail," he said. "Redfish, you'd call it. Good eating."

"Hope so," she said, setting her oar down. "Now it's my turn."

She picked up the rod he'd just discarded.

"Hey," he protested. "That's mine. You can't use my stuff. It's against the rules."

"Screw the rules," she said, casting out in the same direction where he'd just caught the fish. But the wind had picked up, and it blew the light line right back toward the boat, landing almost beside it.

"Hah! You fish like a girl."

She glared at him. "You deliberately turned the boat so that would happen. Come on. Play fair."

He shook his head and dipped his oar in the water, rowing hard to turn the boat so the wind was at their back. It had picked up considerably, and twice she had to grab her baseball cap to keep it from sailing away. She cast out again, and this time her line landed right where she wanted it.

"Take the slack out of your line," Tate instructed. "Reel in, then let the spinner drop, so the fish'll think it's a wounded minnow."

"I *know* how to fish," she said, insulted. But she did as he'd instructed, remembering it was the exact same advice her daddy had always given her on their fishing trips to the coast.

She felt something bump her hook and then, suddenly, give a sharp tug, bending her rod tip sharply downward.

"Got one," she reported happily, watching the line unspool.

"Reel!" Tate called. "Come on, reel it in, Reggie."

She propped her feet on the side of boat to give her leverage, and reeled for all she was worth.

"It's a big one," she gasped, struggling for control.

"Give it a little line," he coached, reaching forward and flipping the bail on her reel.

Line zigged out, and the fish made a run for it.

"Now, set the hook," he told her. "Jerk it hard, then reel like you mean it."

She flipped the bail with her thumb and yanked for all she was worth. The fish responded by zooming away.

"Reel!" he called.

"I . . . am . . . reeling." She propped her elbows on her hip bones, leaned back, and struggled to get control of the fish, which seemed to be zigzagging away, and then, suddenly, without warning, turning and running toward the boat.

"Reel fast now," he instructed. "Bring in the slack." With the fish coming toward her, she was able to bring in the line, and soon she saw a flash of silver beside the boat.

"Bluefish!" Tate called. "Can you boat it by yourself?"

"Got it." She grunted and, with an effort, jerked the fish out of the water and into the boat, where it seemed to fill the whole vessel, thrashing violently against the aluminum hull.

Moonpie barked at the fish until Tate swung around in the seat and clamped a shoe on the fish to still it.

"Holy shit, Reggie," he said, looking up in admiration. "That's a big damn bluefish."

She grinned, ridiculously pleased with herself. "It is, isn't it? How big, do you think? Ten pounds?"

"Ten!" He guffawed. "Dream on, little girl. It's maybe eight, but that's still a huge bluefish. You ever caught one before?"

"Never," she admitted. "I've had bluefish in restaurants, of course, but this is the first time I've ever even seen one alive."

She bent down and studied the fish. Its vivid blue and silver coloring were in stark contrast to the mud-streaked boat bottom. "It's really beautiful."

"Good eating too," he said. "Ideally, the best-tasting ones are much smaller, but fresh-caught, grilled or pan-fried, it's hard to beat a bluefish."

"Grilled," Gina said, already envisioning her menu. "I'll brush it with some olive oil, and—"

She felt a drop of water on her shoulder and looked up, surprised. The sky had darkened another shade, and the wind-whipped whitecaps rocked the boat.

"Damn," Tate exclaimed. A sudden sheet of rain swept over them, and the wind caught Gina's baseball cap and sent it sailing off.

"We better get back," he said, picking up his oar.

Gina turned around and for the first time realized she could no longer see Eutaw.

"I screwed up," Tate said grimly. "So busy telling you how to fish I didn't notice how far out we'd drifted."

"But we can get back—right?"

"We can try," he said, swinging an oar into the water.

Five minutes of furious rowing got them exactly . . . nowhere. The tide and the wind drew them inexorably out and away from the shore. The rain slashed down on them, and Moonpie huddled in the bottom of the boat, his snout tucked under his paws, as though he were too afraid to look.

Gina hunched her shoulders against the rain. "Now what?" she asked, trying not to let Tate see her growing fear.

"We go where the tide takes us," he said, letting his oar rest across his knees.

"Out to sea?" she asked, panicking. "In an open boat?"

"Look over there," he said, turning around and pointing off into the murk.

She saw the faint outline of a faint grayish green hump off in the distance. "What's that?"

"Rattlesnake Key," he said. "We'll let the wind take us there, beach the boat, and see if we can sit out the storm."

"Good," she said, her voice saying she did not really think this was so good. "An island, right?"

"A small one," he said. "People come out on their boats sometimes and camp overnight."

"Good," she repeated. "That's a good thing to know. But what I don't want to know is why they call it Rattlesnake Key."

Chapter 52

Rattlesnake Key loomed before them, a forbidding-looking dark green spit ringed with a collar of grayish sand. As the rain slashed at her shoulders and hatless head, Gina was eying it with trepidation when the boat, which had been rising and falling with the pounding waves, suddenly lurched to a stop.

"What's wrong?" she asked, panicking. The island was still several hundred yards away.

Instead of answering, Tate hopped out of the boat—into ankle-deep water. "Sandbar," he said. "I forgot about it. Come on, jump out. We'll have to walk it across to the deeper water."

She hesitated.

"Come on. It's not like you're going to get any wetter."

This was true. She was soaked to the skin. She stepped out, and Moonpie came right behind her, leaping with abandon into the water.

Tate didn't look concerned. He grabbed the bow of the boat and started trudging across the sandbar, which was maybe a hundred yards wide.

"Can he swim?" She asked, glancing worriedly at Moonpie, who seemed to struggle somewhat to keep his head above water.

"Well, he's no Chesapeake Bay retriever, but yeah, he can swim. He loves the water."

As if to prove it, when the dog reached shallow water, he romped joyously through the waves, running alongside his master, and barking at a single seagull that swooped and called from a wind current above.

The wind tore at their clothes and the waves tossed the empty boat as, together, they walked it over the sandbar. When Tate finally pronounced the water deep enough, they climbed back into the boat and let the tide drift them onto the island.

Just as they stepped onto the beach, lighting struck behind them, a wicked, jagged bolt lighting up the deep gray sky.

"Crap!" Gina cried.

"Come on," Tate said, hoisting the boat onto the sand. "We've gotta pull it all the way past the high-water mark to beach her and make sure she doesn't drift off when the tide changes again."

They half dragged, half carried the heavy aluminum vessel onto the beach and up to a line of seaweed and dried-out seashells.

"We're good here," Tate decreed, dropping his side of the boat.

"Shouldn't we drag it up there toward those trees?" she asked, hanging on and pointing toward a stand of gnarled oaks and cedars. "We could tie it to one of those trees, just in case this storm makes the tide higher than usual."

Tate shrugged. "What? You're that afraid of being marooned alone on an island with me?"

"I'm just being careful," she said, wiping her face with the sleeve of her shirt. "It's my curse. Lisa is naughty by nature. I'm, well . . . careful."

Lighting zapped again, closer, so close she could have sworn it struck the sand at her feet. But Gina didn't wait to find out. Without thinking, she dropped the boat and ran for the tree line, followed again by Moonpie.

When Tate caught up with her, she was leaning against the trunk of one of the cedars, bent over double, trying to catch her breath. The thick canopy of oak and cedar limbs seemed to shelter her somewhat from the rain. She sat down abruptly and hugged her knees to her chest.

"You all right?" he asked.

"Tired," she said, yawning, her eyelids fluttering. "No sleep . . ." Without warning, she slumped back against the tree. For the first time all day, her face relaxed. A moment later, she was snoring.

While she slept, he worked. This squall, which he'd at first assumed was just one of the typical summer thunderstorms that swept through the Georgia coast and was quickly gone, did not seem to fit the stereotype.

The wind and rain lashed Rattlesnake Key and did not abate. The waves pounded the sand and crept up to the high-water mark and past, which alarmed and chagrined him—Gina had been right to worry about the boat.

Cursing, he ran through the rain, grabbed the bow rope, and dragged the boat almost to the tree line. He picked up the fish—his own spot-tail and her bluefish— and put them into the cooler he'd brought along. He'd been trying to ignore his own hunger pangs, but it was getting late in the day, and he'd had nothing to eat since breakfast. If nothing else, they would at least be able to eat the fish—assuming he could find a way to make a fire. He took the fishing equipment and Gina's cooler and his own and dropped them under the trees, not far from where she slept.

Satisfied that the boat was out of harm's way, he stepped out of the tree line and surveyed his surroundings. Tate had fished in the waters off Rattlesnake Key for a taping previously, but he'd never actually been on the island before.

"Moonpie," he called softly. The dog, stretched out alongside the slumbering Gina, looked up, blinked, and then looked expectantly at Tate.

"Come on, boy," he said. "Let's go explore."

The dog stayed put.

"Slacker," Tate said. He decided to let the dog stay with Gina.

He trudged through the fine white sand, down to firmer footing below the high-water mark, and headed for what looked like the tip of the island.

He stopped occasionally as he walked, stooping to pick up whatever useful bounty the waves brought his way. He found a piece of lumber resting in a tangle of seaweed and shells at the tip of the island. It was a two-by-four, maybe five feet long, sun-bleached and too soggy to be of any use for firewood, but he had another use in mind for it anyway.

He left the board and walked on, wading out once when he caught sight of an object bobbing at the water's edge. As he got closer, he saw that it was part of a six-pack of beer—with only two cans remaining in the plastic ring pack. He grabbed it up, hoping for the best. The cans—Miller Lite—were undamaged and appeared to be full. "There is a God," he said, pulling the cans from the plastic ring and tucking each in a pocket of his cargo shorts.

The tree line seemed to extend around to the island's tip. He walked on and was surprised to find a small clearing in the trees. A mound of oyster shells marked the edge of the clearing, and there was a fire ring in the center of it, with a rusty metal grate that had obviously been used as a grill. He frowned when he saw what careless campers had left behind—empty plastic soda bottles, smashed beer cans, cigarette butts, and what he believed was a pile of soggy disposable diapers. His lip curled, he skirted the edge of the makeshift campground, hoping to salvage something useful from a larger trash pile.

Tossed on top of the pile was a discarded plastic inflatable raft—bright blue with a SpongeBob SquarePants design across the top. He grabbed it up and, with the toe of his shoe, stirred the pile some more. There were empty cardboard cigarette cartons, more beer cans and bottles, and a faded red plastic Zippo lighter. He picked it up and, hoping against hope, gave it a flick. A tiny flame licked out, giving him the biggest thrill of the day.

Tate pocketed the lighter and again kicked at the debris with his toe, sending a surprised lizard skittering away. When his toe hit something solid, he bent over to get a closer look. It was one of those citronella candles in a jar. The jar was soot-streaked, and held an inch of water, but when he dumped it out, he discovered there was at least two inches of candle inside.

"Excellent," he said. He wrapped the candle and the grate in the inflatable raft and walked for another thirty minutes, occasionally stopping to add more finds to his makeshift raft-tote. Then he reversed course and headed back through the rain to the boat, stopping again to retrieve the two-by-four, which he hefted over his shoulder.

Feeling unaccountably pleased with himself, he trudged back to where he'd left Gina and Moonpie.

He gave a soft whistle, and Moonpie trotted out from the tree line.

He ruffled the dog's damp ears. "Worthless mutt," he said fondly.

Tate looked out at the water. The tide had receded some, but the water was still choppy, and now thunder boomed off in the distance. A steady drizzle fell.

Gina was still sleeping. He squatted down beside her and stared into her face. Her damp hair was plastered to her cheeks, and the makeup so carefully applied hours ago by D'John was mostly gone—with the exception of some dark streaks of mascara leaking from the corners of her eyes, which gave her the comic look of one of those Italian clowns. She was oddly vulnerable and completely, sweetly lovely. He put out a finger and gently wiped at one of the smudges.

Her eyes fluttered open. "Hey," she said sleepily, sitting up.

"Sorry," he said. "Didn't mean to wake you."

"It's okay," she said, yawning hugely. "How long have I been asleep?"

"Maybe a couple hours," he said. "You didn't miss much. Rain and more rain."

She struggled to her feet and walked to the edge of the tree line, taking in the dark skies and wind-whipped waves.

"Oh," she said, slumping a little. "I was hoping maybe the storm had blown through. Like they do at home this time of year."

"No such luck," he reported. "I think it's some kind of front, and it's just stalled out—right on top of us. The good news is that there hasn't been any more lightning in a while."

Gina used the hem of her shirt to wipe her damp face. She sighed. "All right. Now, tell me the bad news. Like, how and when do we get back to Eutaw?"

He pointed out at the churning sea. "No sense in even attempting anything until the tide changes. The wind and waves would just drive us right back here to Rattlesnake. We'd literally be spitting in the wind."

She bit her lip. "How long before the tide changes?"

"Another six hours," he said. "But it's three now. That would put us at nine o'clock. Nearly dark, and it's a new moon, so no help there."

"Six hours," she repeated. "On this island."

"At the very least," he agreed. "Realistically? I'm thinking we're looking at not getting back to Eutaw until tomorrow morning."

It took her a while to process it. She wrapped her arms around herself for a little warmth. "Overnight. On this island."

"No food, no phone, no phonograph. Not a single luxury," he sang from memory. After all those years of *Gilligan's Island* reruns, the words and tune came easily. "Like Robinson Crusoe, it's primitive as can be."

Chapter 53

Gina pointed at the stack of debris Tate had hauled back to their campsite. "What's all this junk?" She picked up the SpongeBob raft. "Were you planning to blow this up so we could float back? Did you happen to notice this big gouge in the plastic?"

"This junk," he said haughtily, "is what's going to help shelter and feed us until we can get off this island."

He picked up the two-by-four and began digging a hole in the sand to stand it in. "Give me a hand, will you?" he asked. "Hold this upright."

This time she asked no questions. He dragged the johnboat over to where he'd planted the beam, laid the boat on one side, and used the beam to prop it up.

"It's a lean-to," he announced. "To keep out the rain."

Gina ducked under the boat and sat in its shelter. "Not bad," she admitted, crawling back out again.

Now Tate picked up the plastic raft.

"And what's that supposed to be?"

Tate smoothed the raft over the wet sand. "It's a priceless Oriental carpet," he said testily. "I thought you might like to let your butt dry out at some point tonight."

It dawned on her that she'd unwittingly hurt his feelings.

"I'm sorry," she said quickly, scrambling back under the lean-to to test it out. "That's a great idea, Tate. I swear, I've been in these wet pants so long, it feels like I'm getting diaper rash."

He grunted and went back to his stash of treasure. He began piling up the bits of driftwood and pinecones and downed tree limbs that he'd gathered on his scavenging expedition, piling it under the far end of the lean-to. He opened his cooler and rooted around until he found what he was looking for. He brought out the map of Eutaw Island that he'd stored there the day before, and began tearing off thin strips of paper, which he twisted tightly.

He placed two of the paper twists at the bottom of his pile of kindling and set the Zippo to the edge of one of the twists. He held his breath while the edges of the paper blackened and then began to burn. "Come on," he coaxed. "Burn, baby, burn."

The wicks flamed briefly, and just as quickly died out.

"Damn," he muttered, tucking more twists under the firewood.

Gina duckwalked over to where he worked. "Looks like everything's wet," she said helpfully.

He gave her an exasperated look. "We're in a monsoon," he pointed out. "Dry wood's kinda hard to come by right now. The store was fresh out."

She said nothing but went back to his treasure trove, which he'd also placed out of the rain, under the shelter of the boat. She pawed through the junk, then brought back the citronella candle, and held it out to him.

"What were you going to do with this?" she asked.

"Insect repellent," he said. "When and if this storm dies down, I've got a feeling we're gonna have a hell of a swarm of gnats and mosquitoes."

"Good thought," she said, shaking her head in agreement. "Can I borrow that?" She held out her hand for the Zippo. "Please?"

He handed the lighter to her reluctantly. "We need to conserve it. No telling how much lighter fluid is in there," he warned. "Somebody left it at a campsite up at the end of the island, along with a lot of other garbage."

"I'll be careful," she promised. "Can I borrow your knife too?"

She sat down beside the fire pit Tate had dug in the sand, and began slowly working the knife's edge around the edge of the candle. A minute later, she popped a bowl-shaped hunk of the candle free of the glass jar. She carved off a pie-shaped chunk of the wax and set it on top of the driest-looking piece of driftwood on the fire.

"May I?" she asked, pointing to the pile of paper twists Tate had manufactured.

She took one of the twists, lit it with the lighter, and set it under the chunk of candle. The twist sputtered momentarily, but soon set the candle ablaze. She then repeated the process, scattering chunks of the candle at various points in the fire pit, then lighting them with a twist that she'd designated as her candle lighter. Within five minutes, the wood had begun to burn.

"Damn," Tate said admiringly. "I never would have thought of using the candle that way. Where'd you learn a trick like that?"

"Girl Scouts," she said, holding her right hand in the three-fingered Scout salute. "Before we went on camping trips, our leader would have us save empty tuna fish cans. We'd cut up strips of corrugated cardboard, coil them up and put them in the can, then pour melted paraffin over the whole thing. We called them a buddy-burner. Now, if you've got a big ol' empty lard can, I could cut a little door on the top of it, put the buddy-burner under it, and we'd have a hobo stove. Just like a miniature griddle."

"Not bad," Tate admitted. "I should have known you were a Girl Scout."

"And a 4-H'er," Gina said, laughing. "Want me to tell you how to get your laying hens to produce better? Or maybe demonstrate the proper way to hem an apron? Mama was a home ec teacher before Lisa was born, so she made me get involved in all that kind of small-town useless South Georgia stuff."

"I wouldn't call it useless," Tate said. "You did get the fire started."

"You would have thought of something. Weren't you in Scouts too?"

"Not me," he said. "I was way too cool for anything as dweeby as Boy Scouts. Misspent youth and all that."

He stood up and fetched the coolers and set them down beside the fire.

Tate opened his own cooler and brought out the redfish. Moonpie wandered over and sniffed the fish appreciatively.

"You hungry?" he asked Gina, wiping the candle wax off the blade of the knife.

"Starved," she said, without hesitation. "But . . . your redfish. The Food Fight—"

"Forget about the fight," Tate said. "We're on this island, and we may not get off till morning. We're hungry. And unless you've got a steak packed in that cooler of yours, this is looking like our best bet for supper."

Gina reached for her own cooler. She opened it and began inventorying its contents. "Insect repellent and an apple," she said. "Three bottles of water. A turkey sandwich." She blushed as she held out the final item in the cooler. "Jumbo bag of fried pork rinds."

He cocked his head and looked at her. "You're just full of surprises, aren't you?"

She flashed the Girl Scout pledge sign again. "Be prepared."

While Tate cleaned the redfish, Gina wandered over to reexamine Tate's salvage pile. She held up a faded yellow plastic child's sand pail. "Any plans for this?"

"Figured we could use it as a bail, once we get back on the boat in the morning," he said.

She nodded. "Okay. I'll bring it back." Then she set out on foot through the rain.

"Dinner in an hour," he called to her retreating back. "Don't get lost."

Gina turned and shot him the Girl Scout salute.

Keeping the wind at her back, she headed north, until she could no longer see the dull shine of the upended aluminum boat. The rain had diminished to a soft but steady drizzle. She was going toward the tip of the island. She walked at the water's edge, stopping occasionally to examine a broken seashell or a bit of driftwood tossed up by the storm.

At one point, she turned and looked at her own plodding footsteps in the sand. With each step she took, she thought, her chances of winning the Food Fight competition were eroding, just like her own footprints in the sand, which took only a moment to fill with water and disappear.

She could walk the length and breadth of this island, she thought, and there would be no sign that she'd been there. The wind and the surf would wash everything away.

And what would it matter? Forget the damned Food Fight, Tate had advised. That was fine for him—he still had his own show, even if he somehow managed to lose the competition. She, on the other hand, would soon be jobless—and homeless.

During their discussion that morning, Scott had assured her he had a plan for both their careers. But wasn't that plan predicated on her making a respectable showing in the Food Fight?

How would Barry Adelman react to her disappearance? And what about Scott? He'd be concerned for her safety, she felt sure. But what would he make of the fact that Tate had gone missing at the exact same time?

She smiled at the delicious irony of it. Scott already disliked Tate intensely. Would it occur to him that she and Tate had snuck off together for some kind of romantic tryst?

God no! She was appalled that the idea of a romance with Tate had even crossed her mind. But, she had to admit, it had crossed her mind. And more than once, especially after she'd awakened back there at the boat and found him caressing her face. His touch was gentle, tender even. Literally an eye-opener.

Suddenly, her wet clothes felt unbearably clammy against her skin, and the gritty sand that had sifted up into her sneakers chafed at her feet. She took her shoes off and hooked their shoestrings through the belt loops on her pants, and after a moment of hesitation, unbuttoned her soggy shirt and tied it around her waist.

She stood motionless for a moment, enjoying the sensation of the rain on her bare shoulders and back. She caught herself glancing furtively around, as if to make sure no prying eyes were watching. Idiot! she thought. They were alone on this island. Tate was half a mile away, cleaning fish and tending the fire. And Mama?

Mama and her cell phone and text messages were far, far away, in a place called Odum, Georgia.

Feeling wildly adventurous, rebellious even, she peeled off her pants, and after just a little more hesitation—she was the careful Foxton sister, after all—she stripped off her tank top and everything else, right down to the buff.

She stood like that—nekkid as a jaybird, her grammy would say—very still, on the beach at Rattlesnake Key.

Gina Foxton was almost thirty years old, and she couldn't remember if she'd ever been so naked before. She hugged the bundle of wet clothes to her chest, not quite ready yet to give them up.

Prude! She shook her head, disgusted with her inability to totally liberate herself from convention. What would her wild-child sister do if she found herself in the same situation? Lisa? Her sister would have tossed her clothes to the wind, Gina felt sure. She would have run and romped in the wind and the rain, danced naked on the beach, danced naked by the fire.

But that was Lisa. She was Gina, the firstborn. The careful one, who'd refused to let her daddy remove the training wheels from her bike until long after all the other kids her age were riding solo.

"Screw that!" she said aloud, surprised at her own fierceness. She tossed the ball of clothing on the sand and dashed into the waves, screaming at the shock of the cold water on her bare skin. She dove under, splashed, screamed some more, it felt so good. Then she ran up, onto the beach, and let the rain rinse off the salt water. She shook her wet hair from side to side, the way she'd seen Moonpie do in an effort to dry off.

She felt different. Lighter. She could feel the burden of her worries wash off her skin as easily as the salt water. Her show was over. She would most certainly not win this competition for her own cooking show. She and Scott were history. But it would all work out. Gina felt sure of this.

To celebrate, she needed to do something bold. Something extraordinary.

She yelled like a banshee, ran down the beach to build up a head of steam and, pumped full of adrenaline, planted first her left palm and then her right palm in the sand. She flung her legs up, up and over her head, and it wasn't until the exact moment when she literally turned her world upside down that she remembered she'd never had any talent for gymnastics, especially for a cartwheel. But it was too late. She felt herself overbalance. Her arms collapsed in on themselves, her legs spun wildly, and she felt herself go crashing onto her back. As she lay sprawled out on the sand, feeling like a crippled cockroach, she was uncomfortably aware of another sensation from childhood. She was naked. With sand in her crack.

Chapter 54

He was admiring the fillets he'd cut from the red-fish when he noticed how uncharacteristically quiet Moonpie had gotten. Glancing over, he saw what was preoccupying the dog. Moonpie was crouched beside the fire, happily gnawing away on the Zippo.

"Moonpie, no!" Tate shouted. He lunged for the dog, and the dog bounded away, the lighter clenched firmly between his jaws.

"Moonpie, come!" he yelled. But the dog was in full retreat.

Tate sighed. This was a game the English setter never tired of playing. Call it tag, or chase, or keep-away, it didn't matter. Once Moonpie got something in his mouth that Tate wanted, the game was on. Tate had no choice but to play.

He scrambled to his feet and went after the dog. Moonpie dashed for the beach, stopped once to make sure his master was following, and then sped across the dunes.

As he ran after Moonpie, Tate cursed his own inability to make the dog do anything he damned well didn't want to do. The setter was a skilled hunter, good at finding quail and pheasant in any kind of cover. He'd find downed birds, and he had a light mouth. But he retrieved birds only if he felt inclined to do so, and would deliver them to Tate with infuriating irregularity. He was the best dog Tate had ever had.

If Moonpie had stolen a bone, or a shoe, or something inconsequential, Tate might have quit the chase and returned to the campsite. Sooner or later, the dog would grow bored of the game and give it up if his master refused to play along. But it would be dark soon, and he needed that lighter. More importantly, if Moonpie chewed through the Zippo's plastic casing, which he surely would do, given the opportunity, Tate feared the dog would be poisoned by the lighter fluid. And he couldn't let that happen.

Tate ran as fast as he could—and even in his mid-thirties, he prided himself on being pretty damned fast—but he was no match for the dog, which Moonpie knew. Every once in a while the dog would double back, run straight at Tate, then peel away at the last second and reverse course again.

Now Moonpie headed away from the water, up to the dunes, toward the tip of the island. It was slow going in the floury white softness of the sand, and he soon lost sight of the dog. He ran in the direction Moonpie had gone, and when he reached the oyster-shell mound that marked the abandoned campground he'd visited earlier, Tate stopped to catch his breath.

"Moonpie," he called softly. "Come here, boy. You win, okay? Come here, and I'll give you a treat."

He heard a rustling in the underbrush, and spotted Moonpie, rolling happily on the pile of disposable diapers.

"Come here, buddy," he coaxed. The dog stood up, tilted his head this way and then that way, considering his options. He still had the lighter in his mouth.

"Here, Moonpie," Tate called. "Good boy. You win, okay? Let's go get your treat."

The dog's ears perked up at the mention of his favorite word. He trotted over, sat on his haunches, and dropped the lighter at Tate's feet.

"Good boy," Tate said, snatching it up with one hand and grabbing the dog's collar with the other.

Tate squatted down and put his face right in Moonpie's. He shook the Zippo. "No! Bad! Understand? Bad!"

Moonpie thumped his tail enthusiastically.

"Incorrigible," Tate muttered, scratching the dog's ears anyway.

"Let's go home," he told him. "We gotta get supper on."

He was walking back down toward the dunes and the beach when he heard an earsplitting scream.

He ran without thinking, toward the beach, but stopped in his tracks when he saw where the scream was coming from.

At first, he wondered if he could be dreaming. Or hallucinating. Through the thin gray mist of rain, he thought he saw a woman. She was naked, running down the beach, arms spread joyously wide. And she was yelling bloody murder.

"Whoa," he whispered.

The woman was Regina Foxton. She was totally oblivious to him. Without thinking, he dropped down into the sand, hoping to stay unnoticed. Moonpie sat down beside him.

Tate knew he should look away. Or leave. He should definitely leave. And give her some privacy for whatever demented ritual she was performing. But he couldn't move. She was so lovely, unfettered by clothes, her slim body glistening with the rain. She ran and dove into the waves, yelling again, and then diving under the water again. Frolicking, that was what she was doing. It was very un-Reggie-like behavior, and it was totally captivating.

He glanced over at Moonpie, who was panting hard. Tate nodded in agreement.

Suddenly she ran out of the water, and he threw himself flat on the dune. Now would not be a good time to advertise his presence. A moment later, he raised his head, just in time to see her go running full-tilt down the beach.

It was a lovely sight, Regina Foxton sprinting naked through the rain, her face the essence of pure, unadulterated bliss. She was the most beautiful thing he had ever seen, prettier than a trophy bass, prettier even than Moonpie as a puppy. He could spend the rest of his life remembering this vision of her.

Wait. What was she doing now? Oh, God. Oh, no. She let out another scream, and one minute her body was hurtling through the air.

And the next, she was flat on her ass in the sand. He couldn't bear to look anymore. He covered his eyes with his hands.

Poor Reggie.

Chapter 55

After making a mental note to give up all forms of gymnastics in the future, Gina waded back out into the waves to try to rinse away all the sand. When she reached the shore again, she felt suddenly chilled—and vulnerable. She hastily scrambled back into her damp clothing, finger-combing her wet hair into some semblance of order.

The rain had almost let up, and she could see the sun valiantly trying to break through the low-lying cloud cover.

She resumed her trek, rounding the tip of the island. Suddenly, she found the visibility clearing. Off in the distance, across the sound, she saw a long low shape that she decided had to be Eutaw Island. How far across was it really? she wondered. Less than a mile? If the tide weren't running in the wrong direction, if they'd had a boat with a motor, she bet she could be back on dry land in less than an hour. But right here, right now, she felt like she was hundreds of mile from civilization. From the Food Fight. From Scott.

She saw an object moving slowly across the water, and when she squinted, she could just make out the shape of a boat with nets extending out on booms from both sides. A shrimp trawler.

Feeling ridiculous, she stepped out into the water and waved her arms wildly over her head, but only for a moment.

What was she thinking? Rescue me? From what?

Her foot scraped something sharp. She reached down into the water and pulled out an oyster. It was small, but tightly closed and intact. She reached down, and by groping cautiously with her fingers and toes, managed to unearth another, and then another.

Oysters! She ran to the beach, slipped her shoes on again, grabbed the plastic bucket, and waded back out to the same spot. She filled the bucket almost to the brim before deciding she was cold and wet and tired.

Slogging back to the beach, she stood and faced the sound—but now the clouds and mist had obscured the island so that all she could see of it was the faintest gray suggestion of a faraway landmass. The shrimp boat, too, had disappeared.

So that was it, she thought, heading back to the campsite. She was on this island for the night, and she wasn't getting off. *And what was so bad about that?*

Moonpie heard her coming before he did. The setter went bounding off to greet her, jumping up and planting his paws on her chest, then sniffing anxiously at the bucket, before racing back to Tate to announce her arrival with a short, sharp bark.

He glanced up from the fire, trying to act casual. "Hey," he said, half standing, half crouching under the shelter of the boat. "You're back from exploring."

What a totally lame thing to say. She was dressed now, of course, which too bad, because she looked sort of bedraggled, in a drowned-rat kind of way. Well, not a rat, really, more like a drowned mouse. But a cute drowned mouse.

Gina held out her bucket. "Look what I found. Oysters!"

"Oysters?" Tate reached down into the bucket and held one up. "Pretty dinky. And you can't eat oysters in June. They're poisonous. Or something."

Wounded, she snatched her bucket back. "Wrong. That's an old wives' tale. I read up on it last night. The

Geechee people on these islands always ate oysters in the summer months. They preferred the fatter, juicier ones from colder months, but there's absolutely nothing wrong with oysters in June, as long as they're harvested from clean waters, which these were."

He stuck his nose into the bucket and sniffed doubtfully. "They smell okay. Where'd you say you found 'em?"

"Over on the other side of the island," she said.

That would be the naked side of the island. He slapped his forehead, trying to dislodge the image of her, which was stuck there now, in the permanent data bank in his brain, a mental photo album where he filed other memorable images.

Like the forty-pound snook he'd caught on ten-pound test on a blistering day in Sarasota, the twelve-point buck he'd bagged as a nine-year-old, and, yes, he wasn't proud of it, but the first set of naked breasts he'd ever seen outside *National Geographic*, which belonged to a girl named Khandee, Miss December 1989, who, come to think of it, also liked long walks on the beach.

"Something wrong with you?" Gina asked, looking at him oddly.

"Sand gnat," he said, scratching a nonexistent bite. "You hungry?"

"Starved."

"The fire's almost ready," he told her, gesturing toward the grill he'd rigged with the odds and ends from the trash dump.

He'd scrubbed the grease-and soot-caked metal grill with a bit of rag dipped in wet sand, and propped it up on a couple of sand-filled Mr. Pibb cans over the fire. He'd also flattened out a wadded-up piece of aluminum foil, which he laid over the grill.

As Gina watched, he carefully placed the redfish fillets on the foil.

She leaned back on her elbows on the plastic mat and enjoyed the novelty of having somebody else cook for her.

Tate had stripped off his wet shirt and draped it over a piece of driftwood he'd stuck into the sand, near the fire. His cargo shorts rode low on his hips, and it occurred to Gina that he was, as Lisa would put it, "going commando." Why hadn't she thought of that? No underwear was supremely superior to damp ones. She flicked her eyes over him, appreciating the view. He was deeply tanned, and he was, as Lisa had aptly put it, "Fine." Very fine, in fact.

He sat down beside her on the mat. "I cleaned your bluefish, and put the fillets in my cooler. There's only a little bit of ice left, but maybe they'll keep till we get back to Eutaw in the morning."

"Thanks," she said. "I should have thought of that myself. My daddy always says it's best to clean oily fish like mackerel and bluefish just as soon as you catch 'em, to keep them from tasting too strong."

He was sitting so close that his bare shoulder touched hers, and his bent knee knocked casually against hers, and the thrill of it nearly sucked the breath out of her chest.

"The morning," she said weakly. "You think we'll be able to get back by then?"

"If the wind doesn't change again, and the rain quits," he said.

Let it rain, she thought.

Her hair smelled like rain, and her wet shirt clung to her body, and he could see the faint outline of her nipples beneath the undershirt sort of top she wore beneath the work shirt. He was trying hard not to stare at that work shirt, at the buttons, all six of them, wishing he had supernatural comic-book powers, like martian mind-meld, that could magically unfasten the pesky mother-of-pearl buttons, one by one.

Tate found himself suddenly loopy, unaccountably tongue-tied by her proximity. "What do you want to do with your oysters?"

Mental head-smack.

His question brought her abruptly back to reality.

"I'm a sissy," she admitted. "I don't do raw oysters. How 'bout we grill 'em?"

"Be my guest."

She heaped the oysters on the edge of the grate, and soon the smell of roasting fish and grilled oysters was wafting out from under the overturned johnboat.

Her eyes watered from the smoke, and her stomach growled in appreciation. When Moonpie ventured too close to the fire, Gina coaxed him away, emptying one of her bottles of water into her empty cooler. He lapped it all down in moments.

"Hey," Tate said, ashamed that he hadn't thought of it himself first. "Thanks. That was nice of you."

She reached over and scratched the dog's chin, which he obligingly stretched out for her. "He's my bud. Aren't you, Moonpie?"

Tate took the blade of his knife and flaked the fish fillets, grunting with satisfaction. "Just right," he said, sliding the foil off to the side of the grate.

When he stood and stretched, Gina noticed an odd bulge in his cargo shorts. She motioned to the pockets of his shorts. "What ya got there?"

He actually found himself blushing. "Uh . . ."

And then he remembered. Reaching into both pockets he whipped out the cans of beer, brandishing them like an Old West gunslinger's pearl-handled Colts.

"These were floating in the water, over near the abandoned garbage dump where I found the raft and the grill. Some fisherman's cooler must have tipped overboard." He extended one to her. "I was saving 'em for dinner."

She took one of the cans and considered it. "Warm beer?"

He popped the top of his own can and took a swig. "The English drink warm beer all the time. They think Americans who insist on beer being ice cold are barbarians."

"These are the same people who eat cold baked beans on toast for breakfast," Gina pointed out.

She set the beer down and helped herself to an oyster. "Not bad," she said. "But I'd kill for some cocktail sauce and lemon slices."

Tate tipped an oyster into his mouth and followed it with a swallow of beer.

"Perfect," he pronounced. He opened another shell with the tip of his knife blade and tossed the oyster to Moonpie, who caught it in midair.

They lingered over their dinner, sitting close together on the plastic mat, as much for companionship as for the warmth of the fire, eating with their hands. The fish was tender and flaky, perfectly sweet and fresh.

"This was great," Gina said finally. "I take it all back. You really can cook."

"Of course," he said, annoyed. "What did you think?"

She considered whether to tell him the truth. Which was that she'd assumed he'd gotten his hit cooking show because of his great butt and killer abs, which she'd been staring at off and on all day.

"Who taught you to cook?" was what she actually said. "Your mama?"

That made him laugh out loud. "My mama? No, sweetheart, my mother didn't teach me how to cook. She barely knows how herself. She just retired as vice president of corporate communications for the Bales Group. You heard of them? Insurance, banking, securities?"

She shook her head. "Nope. So who did teach you how to cook?"

He lifted the last of the fish from the grill and set it out on the lid of a cooler for Moonpie, who greedily scarfed it all down.

"Different people. My dad liked to hunt and fish. We belonged to a fancy hunting club that had a quail plantation down near Tallahassee, so I learned a lot from the women who worked in the kitchen there. In college, we had an old guy, Gilbert, who did all the cooking at my frat house. He'd been a cook in the navy. I'd hang out with him, watching the way he fried chicken, how he made sawmill gravy. Like that."

She took a tentative sip of the beer. It wasn't so bad after all. "You never went to cooking school?"

He grinned. "You found my shameful secret."

"And you're not really a redneck, are you?"

He leaned back on his elbows and lazily stretched out his legs. "Never said I was. Just because I drive a pickup truck with a gun rack and live in a trailer with my bird dog—you're the one who made that assumption, Reggie."

"So you're not exactly what my mama calls po' white trash. You're college educated. . . ." She stretched herself out beside him, hip to hip, and rolled over so that their faces were only inches apart. "Since you're sharing all your secrets—what about telling me how you managed to kill that pig?"

"Swear you won't tell another soul?"

She flashed the Girl Scout pledge again. "I'll take it to my grave. Now give."

"Pure dumb luck," Tate said. "I hit it with my golf cart."

"No way!" she exclaimed, giving him a playful punch.

"Afraid so," he said, laughing. "It just ran out in front of the cart, and boom—next thing you know, me and Moonpie are knee-deep in hog. I managed to get it on the cart the next day and take it over to

Iris and Inez's. I swore 'em to secrecy in return for a year's worth of pork chops and fatback. Now it's your turn. Tell me all about the secret life of Regina Foxton."

"Nothing else to tell. I'm Birdelle Foxton's oldest girl, thoroughly boring, predictable, and white-bread, through and through."

He stared right through her, and the image came back, unbidden.

"I know about your secret life, Reggie," he said quietly. "I saw you on the beach today. Earlier. On the other side of the island."

The color drained from her face. "You saw me?"

"I didn't mean to spy on you." His words came rushing out. "Moonpie took off with the lighter, and I went running after him, and well, there you were."

"Naked." Her voice sounded strangled. She closed her eyes. "Oh, God. I thought I was alone. You saw me making a fool of myself."

"Hey . . ." He touched her cheek. "I'm sorry. It was a private moment, and I spoiled it."

Her eyelids flew open. "You were watching the whole time?"

"Kinda. Look, I swear, I'll never say another word on the subject. I've forgotten it already. Swear to God." He held up the three fingers on his right hand, in his own version of the Scout's oath. But behind his back he crossed the fingers on his left hand. Forget, hell.

Gina rolled onto her back and concentrated on the night sky. She'd never seen so many stars. A tear rolled from one eye and slid off her cheek.

"I saw a shrimp boat out on the sound over there. Earlier. While I had my clothes on. And at one point, the clouds cleared and I could actually see Eutaw. I had no idea we were so close."

"Yeah, we're not far from it at all," Tate said, glad for the change of subject. "Only thing keeping us over here tonight, like I told you, is the tide and the wind. Once the tide changes, we should be able to row back across with no problem. Long as the boat holds water."

"You're gonna think I'm an idiot when I tell you what I did when I saw that boat," she said, helping herself to another sip of beer, which really was beginning to taste better and better.

"Oh?"

"When I saw that shrimper, I waded out into the water and actually tried to flag it down," Gina said. "As if they could even see me over here. Dumb, huh?"

"Scott is probably pretty worried. You did disappear. At the same time as me."

"Yeah," she agreed. "What about your producer? Won't Val be worried?"

"Nah," he said. "She knows I can take care of myself. She'll be pissed that I messed up the shooting schedule, that's all. What about your sister? What'll she think?"

"Lisa?" It was the first time she'd considered how her sister would take her disappearance. "She'll probably assume I ran away with you. Deliberately. She'll think . . . I mean, just because we were alone together like this, that we hooked up. Lisa thinks you're totally hot."

"Hooked up?"

"Her word, not mine. It means—"

"I know what it means," he said, chuckling. "She doesn't know you very well, does she?"

"What's that supposed to mean?" Gina sat up so suddenly she felt dizzy. She chugged the rest of the beer in one swallow and wiped her mouth with the back of her hand. "What? It's so hard to believe somebody like you would go off with somebody like me—and that we'd hook up?"

He frowned. "I hate that phrase. It's . . . crude."

"Crude?" She hooted, and scooched over closer to him, peering into his face. "Who *are* you, Tate Moody? You see me naked on the beach, alone, and you just turn around and walk away? Is there something wrong with me, or is it just you?"

"There's nothing wrong with you," he said, sitting up now too. "You're gorgeous. Amazing. And there's nothing wrong with me. I'm not somebody who just . . . anyway, it doesn't matter, 'cuz Reggie, you sure as hell aren't the kind for a hookup."

"How do you know what I would or wouldn't do?"

"You said it yourself. You're the cautious sister. The apron-sewing, cake-baking, training-wheels-on-the-bike nice girl."

She didn't let him finish. Instead, she climbed onto his lap and wrapped her legs around his waist. "Nice? I'll show you nice!"

Her kiss was fierce at first. She wanted to show him the new, improved Gina Foxton. The one who'd been born on that island. Who didn't care about appearances, who did exactly as she pleased. No inhibitions.

But his response wasn't what she was expecting. Not by a long shot.

"Hey," he said, pulling away. He held her face between his hands, studying it in the orange glow of the firelight. "What's this about, Reggie?"

She pulled him closer. She kissed the hollow of his throat, warm from the fire. He tasted salty. "This is me . . . being nice," she whispered in his ear.

"Oh."

He ran his hands slowly up her back, and she shivered.

She kissed him again, and this time managed to part his lips with her tongue. He kissed her back, telling himself it was the polite thing to do. And then, because he was nothing if not polite, he helped her with the buttons on that shirt of hers.

Gina wriggled out of the shirt and flung it aside. He kissed her neck, and her shoulders, and he thoughtfully pushed aside the skinny little straps of her undershirt, and then he cupped one of her breasts in his hand, and he realized she hadn't done such a good job of sand removal. . . .

And the next thing he knew, she was tugging at the waistband of his cargo shorts.

"Wait."

She looked up from her work. "Wait?"

"Is this really what you want?"

"No," she said flatly. "What I want is a bubble bath and air-conditioning and Porthault sheets and Marvin Gaye on my iPod singing 'Let's Get It On.' Preferably in a suite at the Ritz-Carlton in Buckhead. But we're on an island. I've got no job and no boyfriend and no future. So we'll have to make do with SpongeBob here. Improvise. Now, are you gonna take off your pants, or do I have to do all the work?"

Chapter 56

Lisa Foxton squinted through the salt-flecked window of the trawler's cabin, but night had fallen, and despite the running lights mounted on the shrimp boat's bow, all she could see was the inky blackness of a night at sea.

"I can't see anything," she wailed. "Don't you people have a searchlight or something?"

"A searchlight!" Mick Coyle snorted. The wiry, sunburned captain of the *Maggy Dee* ran his hand over his bloodshot eyes to make sure they were still open. He still didn't quite know how he'd gotten mixed up with this crazy crowd he'd met up with on Eutaw Island. Especially this chick. "We're shrimpers, not the Coast Guard," he reminded her. "Anyway, there's nobody out on the water tonight. We've been all around Eutaw twice, talked to other boats out of Darien, nobody's seen any sign of your sister. Diesel fuel ain't cheap, you know."

"She's out here someplace," Lisa said fiercely. She clutched at the sleeve of his grimy T-shirt. "She's gotta be. We've looked everywhere else. You've gotta help me find her." She turned those big brown eyes of hers on him and blinked back tears.

"Shit," Mick muttered. It was the eyes that had gotten to him. He'd tied up at the ferry dock at Eutaw shortly after the storm started kicking up. His intention was to sell some shrimp to the woman who ran the lodge at Rebeccaville, maybe sit out the weather. He'd just popped a cold beer when the girl came running down to the dock, screaming that her sister was missing, caught out in the storm.

Pretty soon she'd been joined by two more men, a squirrelly-looking guy in his early twenties, dressed head-to-toe in black, and the older one, kind of a bodybuilder type dressed in what he probably thought was foul-weather gear—an expensive-looking raincoat, khaki slacks, and mud-spattered loafers.

The bodybuilder seemed to be the self-appointed sheriff of the search party.

"How much to charter the boat?" he'd demanded, pulling a fancy ostrich-skin billfold from his back pocket and flashing a platinum American Express card.

Coyle ignored the credit card and took another sip of his beer.

"Well?" the sheriff repeated. "What about it?"

"You wanna go shrimping? In this weather?"

"Zeke, Scott, make him listen," the girl cried, stepping between them. "We think she's out there—in a boat. You've got to help us. Please?"

"Lisa, please," Scott had said, pulling the girl aside. "Just calm down. Let me handle this."

Lisa crossed her arms over her chest and glared at him.

"My girlfriend is missing," he went on.

"Ex-girlfriend," Lisa piped up. "Gina is so over you, Scott."

Zeke, the one dressed in black, cleared his throat. "Gina is Lisa's big sister," he'd said apologetically. "We're all staying here at the lodge, shooting a television show, and this afternoon, Gina—that's the sister—just disappeared."

"I'm her executive producer, Scott Zaleski," the older man said. He pulled a business card from the wallet and handed it across to Coyle, who nodded, but didn't take it. "Maybe you've seen our show—*Fresh Start with Regina Foxton*?"

"Nope," Coyle said. He jerked his head at Zeke. "What makes you think she's not still on the island?"

"We found her golf cart parked by a shell bank on the creek, but there's no other sign of her," Zeke said eagerly.

"She's been gone for hours," Lisa wailed. "I *told* Scott there was something wrong when she didn't come back on time—"

"Gina's very focused on winning this competition," Scott said. "There was no reason to get alarmed, especially since Moody also missed the deadline."

"That's the other thing," Zeke added. "We found Tate's golf cart parked right beside Gina's. Their fishing equipment is gone, and their coolers, so we're thinking—"

"Tate?" Coyle said. "You mean Tate Moody?"

Zeke's glasses slid down his nose. He pushed them back up. "Well, yeah. Tate's missing too. Nobody's seen either one of them since this morning, and one of the women who works at the lodge seems to think they might have found a boat and decided to go off together. Although I think that's highly unlikely—"

Mick put his beer down and headed for the *Maggy Dee*. "Why didn't you say it was Tate missing to begin with? We never miss *Vittles*. Man! My old lady would kick my ass if she knew I turned down a chance to meet the Tatester."

The three of them had followed him down the dock to the boat, ready to board, until Coyle held up two fingers.

"Two of ya can come, but that's all. This ain't no cruise liner."

"She's my sister, and I'm going," Lisa had said, and without further ado, she nimbly jumped from the dock onto the deck of the *Maggy Dee*.

Scott Zaleski looked down at the waves slapping up and over the deck of the shrimp boat, and seemed to have second thoughts about this mission. "Maybe it would be better if I stayed on the island, just in case she turns up," he said. "I can coordinate things from here."

"Wuss," Lisa called. She held out a hand to the other man. "Come on, Zeke."

The younger man took a deep breath and jumped. His foot slipped when he hit the wet deck, and he went sprawling on his ass at the girl's feet.

"Christ," Coyle said, stepping over the man in black. "Gonna be a long night."

Lisa picked up a pair of binoculars from the *Maggy Dee*'s console. She stepped out onto the deck and swept them slowly to the right and to the left. Zeke drifted over and put an arm around her shoulder.

"Don't worry," he said. "We'll find her. Barry had me put in a call to the Coast Guard earlier. They had a Liberian tanker grounded on a sandbar down near Jacksonville, but as soon as they get the crew transported to land, they'll have a cutter on the way. And when it turns daylight, we'll send out a spotter plane."

"Daylight!" Lisa shrieked. "It's nearly ten o'clock. We can't wait till morning to find her. Anything could happen if she's out here. Mama's been calling nonstop since this morning." She clutched Zeke's collar in both hands. "Do you want to be the one to tell Birdelle Foxton that the Coast Guard was too busy rescuing some stinking old *Liberians* to find her daughter?"

"Nooo," Zeke admitted. Lisa had replayed some of the messages Birdelle had left on her cell phone. She sounded formidable, to say the least.

"Go!" Lisa urged, pointing toward the *Maggy Dee*'s cabin. "Talk to the captain. You're a man. He'll listen to you. Make him understand that we have got to keep looking. Gina's out here, somewhere, I just know it."

Zeke hesitated. The only reason Mick Coyle had agreed to this particular search-and-rescue mission was that he was a huge fan of Tate's. That and the five crisp hundred-dollar bills Zeke had folded into the man's grubby fist before they'd left the dock. Coyle made him nervous. This shrimp boat made him nervous too. Not to mention seasick. He'd already logged serious time hanging over the side of the *Maggy Dee*, tossing his cookies. He was a rising star in the galaxy of culinary entertainment. What was he doing out here in the middle of nowhere, on this oil-belching garbage scow?

"Zeke." Lisa wrapped her arms around his neck, stood on tiptoe, and pressed her body close to his. "Please, lover. Help me find my sister."

Oh, yes. Now he remembered.

He sighed and went into the pilothouse to have a word with Captain Coyle.

The boat's radio crackled with ghostly disembodied voices, men's voices, checking in from boats like the *Little Lady*, the *Craw Daddy*, and *Hellzapoppin*.

"*Maggy Dee, Maggy Dee*," a man's voice called. "This is the *BadDawg*. You folks still lookin' for that party missing out of Eutaw?"

Coyle flipped a button on the boat's console and spoke into a microphone. "Roger that. You got something?"

"Could be," the voice came back. "We're headed back to port, but just went by the south end of Rattlesnake Key. I didn't see it, but my mate swears he saw a light out there."

"Light?" Coyle repeated. "On Rattlesnake?"

"Roger that," the voice repeated. "He says maybe a fire, something like that. Could just be campers. Teenagers out of school for the summer. Or maybe it's them folks you're looking for."

"Thanks, *BadDawg*," Coyle said. He flipped the switch again, and put his own binoculars to his face.

"Rattlesnake Key," Zeke said eagerly. "How far off is that?"

Coyle shrugged. "Not far. We've been by there twice tonight, but I didn't see nothin'. We'll check it out, though." He swung the boat's steering wheel hard right and shoved the throttle forward, sending the trawler surging through the waves.

Chapter 57

It occurred to Tate that he was living every red-blooded American man's fantasy. He was alone, on an island, with a gorgeous, willing woman who was urgently trying to undress him.

And yet . . .

He hesitated.

"What?" Gina saw the uncertainty in his eyes.

He hardly knew how to articulate what he was feeling. But he had to try to explain himself. Somehow.

He took her hands in his and kissed them gently. "You're ready to make love to me tonight—but why? Is it because we're out here in the middle of nowhere, and you think nobody will ever have to know?"

"No!" She snatched her hand away from his. His rejection felt like a bucket of icy water had been splashed over her head. She scrambled to her feet. "I thought . . . you wanted to . . . as much as I did. I'm attracted to you, damn you, Tate Moody."

He stood up too, and reached for her, but she pulled away again, turning her back to him.

He grabbed her by the shoulders and turned her around so that they were facing each other again, but she wouldn't look at him. "Don't get me wrong, Reggie," he said. "I want you. Here. Now. Wherever. In case you haven't noticed, I've been working really hard not to want you. But it's no good. Hell, I think I loved you even when I didn't like you."

She was crying now, dammit. "Then why . . ."

"I don't want to be your last resort," he said. "I won't be that. I won't ever be a hookup. Not for you or anybody."

"That's not what I want, either," she insisted. "I've changed, Tate—"

Suddenly Moonpie, who'd been drowsing by the fire, leaped to his feet. He dashed to the edge of the campsite, barking ferociously, his tail up, on point.

"Stay here," Tate told Gina, glancing around in search of something to use as a weapon. "There's something out there on the beach—"

"Uh, people?" a voice called from the darkness. "Tate? Gina? Is that you? If it is, could you please call off the dog?"

"Moonpie!" Tate's voice was sharp. "Here!"

The dog sat on his haunches, his ears quivering with anticipation.

"Who's that?" Tate called.

Slowly, a slightly built figure crept toward the firelight, dressed all in black, water streaming from his clothes and every orifice. The creature's eyes loomed unexpectedly large and dark without their customary horned-rim glasses.

Gina blinked in disbelief. "Zeke?"

Chapter 58

They're coming!" Lisa leaned so far over the bow of the *Maggy Dee*, Mick Coyle feared she'd fall over. He'd have hauled her back over the rail, if he hadn't been so thoroughly enjoying the view of her cute little ass, complete with a cute little tattoo. . . .

"A rope!" Lisa yelled, turning toward him. "We need to throw them a rope or a life ring or something."

"Christ," Coyle muttered. It had been more than an hour since he'd left the little twerp off on the sandbar that surrounded Rattlesnake Key. He'd tried to explain to the chick that the *Maggy Dee*'s hull was too deep to make it over the bar, but she wasn't exactly a rocket scientist when it came to such things.

By then, they could all see the glow of firelight coming from the key's south end, and Lisa had been insistent that her sister and Moody were on the key. She'd been ready to dive overboard and swim to the key herself, until Coyle had inquired about her swimming skills.

"Oh." She'd hesitated.

"You can't swim worth a damn, can you?" Coyle asked.

"I'm more like a dog-paddler than a swimmer," Lisa admitted.

"I'll go," Zeke had volunteered. "I rowed crew five years in prep school."

In the end, Coyle inflated the *Maggy Dee*'s never-used navy-surplus life raft, fitted Zeke with a neon orange life vest, and instructed him on how to use a signal flare once he'd reached Rattlesnake Key to let them know he was safe.

Despite Coyle's deepest doubts, Zeke had apparently not only reached the island unharmed, he'd also managed to ferry the two marooned sailors, plus a dog, back out to the *Maggy Dee*.

Coyle flipped the trawler's rope ladder over the side of the boat and barked orders to Zeke, and against all odds, not to mention the tide and the wind, which kept driving the life raft away from the *Maggy*, soon the three sailors were hauling themselves over the trawler's bow rail.

Tate Moody carried the dog under his arm. He set him down on the deck, and the dog immediately shook about twenty gallons of water on the rest of them.

"Gina!" Lisa cried, throwing her arms around her sister. "Oh, my God. I can't believe it. You're safe! You didn't drown."

"I'm fine," Gina insisted. "We were never in any danger of drowning."

"Zeke!" Lisa cooed, turning toward the kid in black. "You saved them." She draped herself on him, even though he was soaking wet, and covered him in kisses, which he didn't seem to mind at all.

Coyle watched the reunion with an amused air of detachment. Ever since he'd heard the details of the couple's disappearance, he'd wondered just exactly what Tate Moody was up to.

The guy was no dummy. He'd been in and around these waters a lot. If he'd gotten himself marooned on an island, he clearly had something in mind for the little lady who'd accompanied him.

The big sister was kind of a surprise. Coyle had been expecting some really hot television babe—after all, Tate Moody could have any woman he wanted. Coyle's own wife had frequently commented that she'd happily hop in the sack with the Tatester, given the opportunity.

It wasn't that Gina Foxton wasn't attractive. Even soaking wet and sunburned, she was more than pretty, although clearly not in the same foxy category as Lisa, Coyle thought.

As soon as he laid eyes on her, and on Tate Moody, he knew the two of them had done the deed. They tried to be discreet, but Mick Coyle was a man of the world. He knew what was up.

Once the *Maggy Dee* got under way again, Gina allowed herself to be hustled into the pilothouse and wrapped in a blanket from his bunk, although she wisely refused a cup of Coyle's two-day-old reheated coffee. The two sisters huddled together in the pilot-house, carrying on a heated, whispered discussion.

Tate Moody and the kid, Zeke, wrapped themselves in some old jackets Coyle had dug out of a gear locker and dried the dog off with a towel. The men stayed out on deck, well away from the women. Moody and the girl stayed as far away from each other as possible on a forty-four-foot shrimp boat. But they couldn't fool Mick Coyle. Oh, yeah, the Tatester had definitely hooked himself a piece of tail on Rattlesnake Key.

The filthy blanket the shrimper had fetched her stank of dead fish and rancid grease, but Gina welcomed its warmth. What she didn't welcome was her sister's sudden and astonishing transformation into the world's most annoying mother hen.

"Oh, my God," Lisa repeated, for about the tenth time. "Do you have any idea of what you've put us all through? I was going crazy! When you didn't show up this afternoon, I was sure something awful had happened. I even called Mama, just on the off chance she'd heard from you. She went apeshit when I told her you were missing."

"You called *Mama*? Are you insane? Lisa, why in God's name would you do something like that? I'll never hear the end of this now."

"Why in God's name would you go off in some leaky piece of crap—in the middle of a storm, yet—without telling anybody?" Lisa retorted. "And with Tate Moody, of all people?"

"It wasn't storming when we got into the creek," Gina said. "The water was perfectly calm—unlike you."

"Easy for you to say. You weren't the one searching every inch of Eutaw Island, expecting to find your sister's broken and bleeding body at any minute."

"I'm fine!" Gina repeated. "Nothing bad happened, except that we missed the deadline. I'm sorry everybody got themselves all worked up about me, but the bottom line is, I'm not dead." She sighed. "Not dead. Just deeply, deeply humiliated."

Lisa stared at her. "Something happened on that island. Between you and Tate."

"Nothing happened, believe me."

"You lie like a rug," Lisa said. "You think I'm blind? After all the crap you put me through today, you owe me, big-time. So spill it, Sis. Was he better than Scott? What am I saying? Hello—we're talking about the Tatester, so it had to be like, ten times better. Was he totally amazing? I want all the dirty, smutty details."

"Lisa, look at me," Gina said, grabbing her sister by the chin and swiveling her head until their faces were only inches apart. "Read my lips. Absolutely nothing happened between me and Tate. Okay? He was a perfect gentleman. And I was a perfect . . . fool. End of story."

"Whatever." Lisa gave her a knowing wink.

Gina leaned back against the pilothouse wall and closed her eyes. The *Maggy Dee*'s diesel engines churned, and the boat rose and fell over the waves. She would not allow herself to think about the day's events. She wanted sleep. And a long, hot bath. And a one-way ticket off this shrimp boat.

Chapter 59

The cell phone clipped to Mick Coyle's hip rang loudly enough to be heard over the drone of the *Maggy Dee*'s engines.

Coyle jerked the phone off his belt and flipped it open. "Who the hell is this?" he bellowed.

"Who?" Coyle asked. "Barry who?"

Lisa and Gina had dozed off, and Zeke and Tate had just come into the pilothouse to get out of the wind. At the mention of Barry Adelman's name, everybody was on full alert.

"Yeah," Coyle said. "That's right. We got 'em. The girl, Tate. Even the friggin' dog. Although, if he takes another leak on my deck, we might come back minus the dog."

Coyle listened, and his belligerence quickly dissipated.

"Well, sure," he said enthusiastically. "Yeah. Well, thanks, Barry. I think that would about take care of my time and expenses." He listened again, then held the phone out to Zeke.

"Barry would like to have a word with you."

Zeke took the phone, nervously wetting his lips.

"Hello? They're right here, Barry. They were on Rattlesnake Key, this little island less than a mile from Eutaw. They found a boat and got caught out in the storm. . . . Oh, yeah. They're both fine."

Zeke listened. He held his hand over the phone for a moment. "Barry's thrilled that you guys are all right," he told Gina and Tate.

"Yeah. I agree. Absolutely," Zeke said. "Yeah. It does have all the elements of excellent television. Drama, suspense. Danger . . ."

"We were never in any real danger," Tate said, through gritted teeth.

But Zeke was listening to his boss again. He made a writing motion with his hand, and the suddenly cooperative Mick Coyle handed him a clipboard and a stub of a pencil.

Zeke scribbled furiously. "Um. That's a thought. Of course. I think that's a brilliant idea. But let me check."

He held the cell phone to his chest. "People? Barry wants to know if you did, in fact, catch any fish on this nutty excursion of yours."

"I did," Tate said wearily. "A spot-tail bass."

"And I caught a bluefish," Gina put in.

Zeke scribbled again. "A spotted bass and uh . . ."

"Bluefish," Gina repeated.

"Bluefish," Zeke said. He was listening and frowning.

"Gee, Barry, I don't know. They've had kind of a long day. No, they're not injured or anything. It's just that everybody's wet and kind of sunburned—"

He frowned again. "All right. Yeah. Okay." He clicked the phone closed.

"So," he said cheerily. "Here's the plan. Barry has the camera crew on their way down to the ferry dock at Eutaw. They'll be all set by the time we get back. And they'll start the cameras rolling when we tie up, and then you guys will just step off the boat.

"Barry will give a little recap of the day's events, and then he'll interview you both. You'll tell the story of your adventure—"

"And the thrilling rescue," Lisa added. "That part was my idea, wasn't it, Zeke?"

"Absolutely," Zeke said. "Oh, I almost forgot. Barry says you'll do a little cameo, too, Lisa. And Captain Coyle, too, of course."

"Ohmygawd!" Lisa shrieked, jumping up and down on the bench where she and Gina had been napping.

She dug into the pocket of her shorts and triumphantly brandished a tube of lip gloss. "I knew this would come in handy."

"Great," Zeke said. "And then," he said, gesturing to Tate and Gina, "the plan is, you'll go right over to the kitchen at Rebeccaville, and start setting up to cook. Barry says the judges are gonna be a little peeved about having to schlep over there in the rain, but—"

"No," Tate said, crossing his arms over his chest.

"No way," Gina agreed, crossing her own arms in solidarity.

"People, please," Zeke pleaded. "Barry is really, really excited about the potential for this."

"Not happening," Tate said.

Zeke sighed and flipped the phone open again. He punched in the producer's number and waited for an answer.

"Barry?" he said, his voice apologetic. "They're having some reservations about the idea."

Tate stalked over to the production assistant and held out his hand. "Gimme."

Zeke handed the phone over.

"Adelman? There is no way in hell. No. I don't care. Anyway, we got nothing to cook. We ate my fish for dinner, and we left the cooler with Gina's fish back at the campsite at Rattlesnake Key. So you can just forget—"

He listened some more, glowering at what he was hearing. "All right, put her on, not that it'll make any difference."

Hi ,Val," he said.

"Tate? You're okay? No injuries—right? The last thing we need right now is for you to go on the disabled list."

"I'm fine," he assured her. "Really. Just kinda sunburned. And fed up. Now, about this bullshit idea of Adelman's—"

"It's not bullshit," Val said quickly. "And I need you to be a team player. So just suck it up and get on board."

"This is nuts!" he exploded.

"It's a guaranteed ratings bonanza," Val said. "Deborah's back here right now, working the press angle."

"I don't give a rat's ass about ratings," Tate said bitterly.

"You signed a contract," she reminded him. "There's a lot on the line here, Tate."

"Yeah, I know I signed a contract, but nobody ever said anything about—"

"Listen to me," Val said urgently. "You're not the only one affected by this thing. You walk away now, your credibility takes a big hit. Mine too. And let's talk about Gina, while we're on the subject. If you walk away, they're gonna have to use what they've got so far. That's you, Tate Moody, winner of the Food Fight. Gina Foxton gets nothing. *Fresh Start* is history. She's history. And why? Because Tate Moody, selfish bastard that he is—"

"Fine," he said finally. "I get the picture. You win."

He glanced over at Gina, who quickly looked away.

He closed the phone and handed it back to Mick Coyle. Without another word, he turned and walked out of the pilothouse. He put his forearms on the bow rail and looked out at the foaming waves below.

"Shit!" Despite the howl of the wind, they all heard it clearly.

Chapter 60

L ook," Zeke said, grabbing Lisa's elbow. He pointed to a bright white light glowing in the distance. "That's Eutaw. Barry's already setting up the cameras."

"Cameras?" She ran over to Coyle. "A mirror. We need a mirror. Also, some concealer, hot rollers, and a hairbrush. Stat!"

His answer was a guffaw. "We got a mirror, and there might be a comb somewhere around here. In the head." He jerked his thumb in the direction of a narrow door set into the opposite wall of the pilothouse.

"It's not just in my head," Lisa said hotly. "I'm a wreck. And just look at Gina. We can't go on camera looking like this."

Gina gently pulled her sister away from the boat captain. "The head is what they call a bathroom on a boat."

"Oh." Lisa walked over and opened the door to the head. Blanching, she took a step backward. "Ick."

"Mouth-breathe," Gina instructed, shoving herself and her sister inside the cramped cubicle.

The *Maggy Dee*'s claustrophobic head consisted of a grimy porcelain sink set beneath a fly-specked mirror, a commode, and a rusted sheet-metal shower stall.

"Oh," Gina said, cringing at her reflection in the tiny mirror. She sighed. "Doesn't matter. My television career is officially over."

"Screw that," Lisa replied. "Sit," she ordered, flipping the commode seat to the down position. She picked up a lank lock of Gina's hair. "Nothing we can do about this," she said briskly. She reached over and turned on the shower. "Strip and get in."

"No way," Gina said. "Not without a tetanus shot."

But Lisa wasn't listening. She opened the door and edged out. "Be right back," she promised.

When she came back five minutes later, she had a crumpled Kroger grocery sack under her arm, and Gina, showered and wrapped in a faded blue towel, was sitting on the commode, right where she'd left her.

"Here," Lisa said, dumping the bag's contents in her sister's lap. "Put these on."

Gina held up a white cotton T-shirt and a pair of worn, time-shredded blue jeans. "Where did you get this stuff?"

"One of the boat's mates left them behind after he was unfortunately incarcerated for public drunkenness, according to Captain Coyle," Lisa said. "Don't worry. They passed the sniff test."

"But they're a mile too big." Gina stretched the waistband of the jeans over her own much smaller waist.

"Got it covered," Lisa said, flashing a roll of duct tape and a handful of safety pins. "But hurry, the captain says we'll be docking in less than fifteen minutes."

While Gina finger-waved her hair into soft curls, Lisa tucked, pinned, taped, and tied. "Good thing I've never missed an episode of *Project Runway*," she said, running a length of rope through the belt loops of the jeans and cinching it around Gina's waist. She grabbed a hunk of the T-shirt, whose hem hung almost to her sister's knees, and, with a fishing knife, slashed off the bottom eight inches. Then she pulled the fabric tight across Gina's chest, and knotted it in the back.

"Lisa, no, you can see my nipples," Gina cried, reaching to undo the knot. But Lisa slapped her hand away.

"Nipples are in this year," Lisa said.

"Tell that to Birdelle Foxton," Gina said. "Mama would just die if I let myself be seen on television this way. Do something. Gimme your bra."

"What bra?" Lisa said. "Wait. Hold it." She reached for a white first-aid kit sitting on the commode tank. Opening it, she found a box of Band-Aids, extracted two, and handed them to her sister.

"Instant bra," she proclaimed.

Finally, Lisa applied a coat of lip gloss to Gina's lips and pronounced her camera-ready. With Gina's sunburned face and shiny hair, and the blue jeans, with their safety-pin-tightened back seam and rolled-up hem, plus the tight white T-shirt, she looked like a fresh-faced, all-American, small-town goddess.

"You look good," Lisa said, critically appraising her sister. "Sorta haute shipwreck. Wait till Scott gets a load of you."

It was the first time Gina had thought of Scott since boarding the shrimp boat.

"Where is Scott?" she asked. "Why didn't he come out here with you guys?"

"He didn't want to get shrimp guts on his Burberry," Lisa said with a sneer.

"Was he . . . worried? I mean, when I didn't show up on time?"

"I guess so. He went out looking with the rest of us, well, that is, he and Deborah went out looking for you. And he did try to charter the shrimp boat, with his American Express card—"

There was a knock at the bathroom door, and when Lisa opened it, Zeke stuck his head inside. His eyes lit up when he saw Gina's transformation.

"Wow," he said, adjusting his glasses. "You look terrific. Both of you."

"Thanks," Gina said. "This is all Lisa's doing."

Zeke looked adoringly at the younger sister. "Awesome." And then he remembered the rest of his mission. "Captain says we're docking in five minutes. So, you guys are ready?"

"As ready as I can get," Gina said, exiting the bathroom. "But tell me this. Just how, exactly, does Barry plan for us to cook a meal with nonexistent fish?"

Zeke's cheeks reddened. "Barry's a logistical genius. Don't worry. He'll have it all worked out."

"Hey, assholes!" Coyle's voice boomed out. "Somebody get up there and take care of the bowlines." He raised his voice even louder. "And for Christ's sake, turn off those gawddamn camera lights. I can't see shit with them shining right in my eyes."

Once the *Maggy Dee* was snugged up to the ferry dock and a wooden gangway was lowered to the boat's deck, Gina could see the camera crew waiting for them.

"I want Gina to be the first one off the boat," Barry called. "Then Tate, then Lisa, Zeke, and the shrimp guy, whatever his name is."

"Captain Coyle," Coyle yelled. "Mick Coyle."

"Whatever," Barry called. "Okay, we're rolling tape. Come on, Gina."

Gina took a deep breath and stepped onto the gangway. She straightened her shoulders, looked backward, and caught Tate's eye.

"Traitor," she whispered.

Harsh white lights bathed the end of the dock in artificial light. Barry Adelman, dressed in a yellow vinyl rain slicker, hip waders, and his ever-present Adel-Weis Productions ball cap, folded her into his arms.

"Thank God, you made it back," he said, looking past Gina and into the cameras. "Now, Gina Foxton, in the past twenty-four hours you've survived a storm at sea and a harrowing rescue by valiant Food Fight production assistant Zeke Evans. I think it's fair to say there's just one question America wants to ask." He paused dramatically. "What's for dinner tonight?"

Gina gazed coolly at the producer and then at the camera pointed at her. "Well, Barry, I guess America will just have to see what I've got up my sleeve." And with that, she walked away and out of camera range.

"Cut!" Barry bawled. "That was brilliant. Gina, sweetie, you're a natural. Honest to God. I couldn't have come up with a better line myself."

"What are we going to be cooking, Barry?" she demanded. "I won't fake it. I don't care what Tate does, but I am not going to cheat on my audience."

"Cheat?" He thumped his fist over his heart. "Gina! Barry Adelman does not cheat. My shows are all about authenticity. We would never ask—no, *allow*—you to fake it. What we are going to do is simply come up with a different challenge. We've got everything all set up in the kitchen for you guys. And let me tell you, that crew of ours have really humped it to make that happen."

"A different challenge?" Gina narrowed her eyes suspiciously. "What kind of challenge?"

"Tate Moody!" Barry called, gently pushing her away as he turned to greet his other Food Fight contestant.

"Wait, I want to know—"

But Barry was already busy conducting his next interview.

Scott met her on the steps of the plantation house. "Gina!" he exclaimed, folding his arms around her. "My God! I can't believe you made it back in one piece. I've been worried out of my mind."

She wriggled out of his grasp. "Really? Out of your mind?"

He frowned and looked over her shoulder at Lisa, who was parking the golf cart. "What kind of crap has Lisa been telling you?"

"She didn't have to tell me anything. Actions speak louder than words," Gina said, walking straight past him.

"That damned boat captain wouldn't let me come with them!" Scott said, his face reddening. "I tried everything. I even called the Coast Guard."

She stopped on the porch, turned, and gave a grave smile. "I'm sure you were deeply concerned. But it looks like I've got a show to tape, so maybe we could just concentrate on that for now."

"Fine," Scott said, following her inside. "Did Barry explain the setup to you?"

"No."

"He's only got the lodge and plantation location booked for one more day," Scott said. "And the crew's got to get back to New York for another shoot too."

"I still don't see how we can pull this off," Gina protested.

"The guy's brilliant," Scott continued. "He's cleaned out the lodge's kitchen for ingredients. You and Tate will both have the exact same grocery list, and you'll have two hours to come up with a meal incorporating everything you've been given. Brilliant, huh?"

Gina pushed an errant strand of hair out of her eyes. "Maybe if I'd had a little time to process all that's gone on today, I'd appreciate his brilliance. But right now, Scott, what I really want is eight hours of sleep and my own clothes."

"Later," he said, pointing to the ballroom and her kitchen. "Right now you've got a Food Fight. It's yours to win or lose, Gina."

Chapter 61

Gina stood on the kitchen set, staring down at the counter, which was covered with a white bed sheet. "What's this supposed to be?" she called.

"Don't touch that!" Barry hustled onto the set. He'd left the rain suit behind and was dressed in his customary black shirt and pants. Zeke trailed not far behind, dressed in dry clothes—also black.

Barry took her by the arm and ushered her to a quiet corner of the ballroom, set up with folding tables and chairs. "Your surprise ingredients are under those sheets," he told her. "I don't want either one of you to see what you have to work with until we start taping. I gotta tell you, Gina, I like this challenge even better than the first one. Don't you?"

"Honestly? Barry, we're exhausted. Do we really have to do this tonight? I'm dead on my feet. And I look like crap. Where's D'John?"

He patted her cheek. "You look fabulous. Fresh as a daisy. Which is why I told D'John we won't need him tonight. I want you and Tate to look just the way you do—fresh from a brutal confrontation with the elements."

"But," Gina sputtered, "I can't work looking like this. These aren't even my clothes, Barry—these jeans have got a row of safety pins running up the butt. And this T-shirt—"

"You look awesome," he said, getting up to leave. "You'll start a new fashion trend. The day after this show airs, you wait, every chick in America will be wearing jeans just like those." He glanced down at his watch. "Okay, cookie. Since you're so tired, I'm gonna give you a break. Ten minutes, then I want you on set. Okay? Terrific."

Hey," Tate whispered. "Are you pissed at me?"

She refused to look over at him. The sound tech snaked a mike up underneath her T-shirt and clipped it to the neckline.

Despite Barry's edict, D'John hovered at her side, makeup kit in tow. "I'm just going to powder her nose a little," he told Adelman. "To take the shine down, that's all. And I'll put a little gel in her hair, to make her color more dramatic."

"What's going on between you two?" D'John whispered, cutting his eyes from Tate to Gina. "And don't even try to stonewall D'John."

"Nothing's going on," she insisted.

"He hasn't taken his eyes off you since he walked onto the set," D'John said. "He's looking at you like he looks at that dog of his. And you're treating him like dog—crap. What's the story? I thought you two made nice after the first Food Fight."

"He sold me out," Gina said stonily. "If we'd presented a united front on this thing, we never would have had to do this crazy taping tonight. But Barry insisted, and Tate folded, like a cheap tent. He'll do anything to win this thing."

D'John squirted styling gel into his hands and began working it into her hair. "The two of you, marooned alone on an island. It's crazy sexy."

"You weren't there," Gina said.

"Ooh, but I wish I had been," he said.

"All right, everybody," Barry called from his seat at the production table. "Let's get this thing cranked up. I'm going to come out, detail the challenge, and unveil your secret ingredients. You'll have two hours to cook up a storm, using as many of the ingredients as possible. You can also draw from the supply of kitchen staples that are already in each kitchen. But you'll have penalty points subtracted from your total if you don't use one of the surprise ingredients. When the food's done, we'll bring the judges back and do the presentation and the scoring. Everybody good with that?"

Tate cleared his voice. "Uh, Barry? What exactly are we supposed to be cooking? A southern meal, or what?"

"Whatever you think will tickle the judge's taste buds," Barry said, chuckling at his own cleverness. "Use your imagination. Go nuts. *Comprende?*"

"*Comprende*," Tate said sourly.

Gina stared down at the groceries assembled on her kitchen counter in disbelief. She glanced over at Tate, whose reaction was even stronger than her own.

"What the hell?" He pointed at the boxes and bags. "I can't make a meal out of this crap. Is this somebody's idea of a joke?"

"Cut," Barry said. He strode onto the set, his customary cheeriness gone. "It's not a joke," he said tersely. "We're trying to emphasize the kinds of ingredients the average Joe Sixpack has in his home kitchen. And the crew and I would appreciate it if you would just do your job, without any editorial comments. You're not the only one who's had a long day today."

So, Gina thought. The teacher's pet had his hand smacked with a ruler. She smiled sweetly to herself, and then started taking stock of her raw ingredients.

A one-pound sack of Martha White flour. A dozen eggs. A can of Campell's cream of tomato soup. A tin of Hershey's cocoa. A pound of sugar. A box of Frosted Flakes cereal. Containers of salt, garlic powder, chili powder, and black pepper. A can of Crisco. A package of defrosted chicken parts, thighs, drumsticks, breasts, and wings. A pound of bacon. A huge head of cabbage. A bag of confectioner's sugar. A jar of Duke's mayonnaise.

She heard pots and pans being rattled and slung around from Tate's kitchen, and plenty of muttering. But she tuned it all out. Scott, damn him, was right. This challenge was hers to win or lose.

This time around, she couldn't lose. The foodstuffs on her kitchen counter could have been straight out of Birdelle's kitchen back home. Right out of the aisles of Tastee-Town, in fact.

She closed her eyes and tried to remember the shelf of stained and tattered cookbooks in her mother's daisy yellow kitchen. The red-and-white-checked *Better Homes and Gardens* was her mother's biblical authority on culinary theory. It sat beside the faded green metal file box full of recipes, clipped from *Southern Living*, the Savannah paper, and the *Atlanta*

Journal-Constitution. But the go-to cookbook, the one her mother and her grandmother had cooked from day in and day out was *Simply Sinful: Recipes from Tabernacle Baptist Church Women's Missionary Circle*—or *Sinful*, in her grandmother's shorthand.

Gina had learned to cook from that cookbook, with its cheerful pink laminated cover and its spiral-bound spine. Later on, after college and cooking school, where she'd flirted with the works of Julia Child, Paul Bocuse, and Pierre Franey—not to mention every Junior League cookbook published in the South—she'd sneered at *Sinful*'s reliance on convenience and processed foods, its two dozen recipes for congealed salads, its reliance on gimmicky recipe titles, but now, she thought, *now* was the time to bring back *Sinful*.

Gina reached for the can of tomato soup and stepped back twenty years in time. For the next two hours she sifted and stirred, chopped and crushed, fretted and frosted.

She was just taking her chicken dish out of the oven when she heard the Food Fight buzzer go off.

"Time's up!" Barry announced from his place at the director's table. He stood up, stretched, and yawned. "Gina, Tate, why don't you guys take a little break, then we'll come back and show you plating up your food."

Scott rushed onto Gina's kitchen set. He looked at the dishes assembled on the counter, his forehead wrinkled in concern. "It looks . . . interesting," he said. "Did you manage to use all the ingredients?"

"I think so," Gina said numbly. She yawned hugely and glanced over at her opponent's kitchen. Tate had disappeared. As far as she could tell, his counter held only two dishes, a baking pan that seemed to contain a casserole, and a plate of cookies. Her own counter held half a dozen dishes.

"You've got Moody beat by a mile," Scott said smugly. "He made barbecue sauce with the tomato soup and poured it over the chicken, and then he mashed up some of the Frosted Flakes for some bizarre kind of cookie. Look over there," he pointed. "Half his ingredients haven't been touched."

Her pleasure at the prospect of besting her rival suddenly dimmed.

"Wow!" Lisa wandered over and handed her a cold Diet Coke. "Geen—I've never seen anybody cook that hard or that fast. It was like you were in some kind of trance or something."

"It kinda felt that way," Gina admitted. "Come on, I need to sit down before I fall down."

Deliberately ignoring Scott, Lisa led her to the makeup room. When she opened the door, the first thing she saw was Tate, sitting in one of the chairs, leafing through a newspaper. He looked up when she walked in, and then, quickly, back down at the paper.

"Hey, Tate," Lisa said cheerfully. "Are you as tired as we are?"

"Yes."

Gina dropped into the chair next to his, while Lisa perched on the edge of a table.

"You think they'll let us eat some of that food once the judges have finished?" Lisa asked, desperate to fill the awkward silence in the room.

"Why would you want to?" Tate flipped the page of the newspaper.

"I haven't eaten in hours," Lisa said plaintively. "And everything smells so good. My stomach was screaming the whole time you were cooking. Geen, what was that chicken thing you made?"

"Oven-fried chicken," her sister said. "Mama used to make it when I was little. You weren't even born yet. The original recipe called for crushed up cornflakes and buttermilk. But I only had Frosted Flakes, and since they're way too sweet, I added chili powder to the crushed cereal. I just dipped the chicken in a mixture of the mayonnaise and egg, instead of buttermilk, and then coated it with the cereal. God knows how it'll taste."

Tate laughed despite himself. "Frosted Flakes and chili powder. Damn. Wish I'd thought of that. I used the Frosted Flakes for cookies—it was the only thing I could think of."

"Too bad," Gina said. She finished her drink and stood up. "Come on, Lisa. We better get back before Barry sends out another search party to look for us."

"You're still mad at me," Tate said, tossing the paper in the trash. "Why?"

"I'm not mad at you," Gina said coolly. "I don't care about you one way or the other. I have a job to do, and I'm doing it."

She had her hand on the door, but Zeke pushed it open and stuck his head in. "Time, people," he said excitedly. "The judges can't wait to get started."

Chapter 62

Gina was halfway to the ballroom when Tate caught up with her. He tapped her lightly on the shoulder. "Can I have a word with you?" he said, his voice low.

Lisa took the hint and sped ahead, linking her arm through Zeke's.

"What is it now?" Gina asked. Her tone was light, but her heart was beating a mile a minute.

Tate opened the nearest door and pulled her inside what turned out to be a broom closet.

"Hey!" she protested, nearly tripping over a mop bucket.

"Shut up." He leaned back against a set of metal shelves. "Did I get hit on the head on that island tonight? Maybe suffer a brain injury without even realizing it?"

"What's this about?" Gina asked.

Tate ran his hand over the stubble on his chin. "Just a few hours ago, we were alone on Rattlesnake Key. Did I just imagine it, or did you jump me and insist that you were ready to—how shall I put it delicately—have your way with me?"

Gina felt her cheeks burning. "I'd appreciate it if you would forget about what happened on Rattlesnake Key tonight. It was a big mistake."

"A mistake? That's what you want to call it?"

"Yes."

"Even though I told you that I'm in love with you?"

"We've both been under a lot of strain in the past few days," Gina said. She hesitated. "I, uh, want to thank you for not taking advantage of me at a time when I was extremely vulnerable. You were right. I was feeling desperate. But now that we're back on Eutaw, I would like to focus on the competition."

His dark eyes glittered, and his smile was sardonic. "This is bullshit, Reggie. You want me, I want you. It's that simple. Forget about the damned Food Fight. This whole thing is a joke. You saw how Adelman treats us. Like cattle. He was halfway hoping we had drowned—think of what a ratings sensation that would have been."

"No," she managed. "It's easy for you to call it a joke. You've still got your show. Even if you lose, you win. It's different for me."

"It doesn't have to be," he said. "You're great. Adelman's said it a hundred times. You'll get another show."

"I want this one," she said stubbornly. "Look, Tate. Despite what you think, I'm not really like the woman you were with on Rattlesnake Key tonight. I, uh, regret that I let things get out of hand."

He leaned in closer, his lips grazing hers.

"You regret this?"

"Yes." She tried to back away, but the closet was too small—there was nowhere to go.

Tate pulled her to him, kissing her harder, his hands roaming down her back, cupping her rear end. He kissed the hollow of her neck and her shoulder blades, pulled the neckline of her T-shirt down and kissed the top of her breast. "You regret this?"

"Yes," she said, moaning. She was dimly aware of the scent of Pine-Sol, of something damp pressing against her back, but her head was spinning.

He kissed her deeply one more time, and this time she was kissing him back, giving in, giving up, wrapping her arms around his neck, burying her fingers in his hair, still salty from the sea.

"Liar." His voice was fierce.

And then he was gone. She heard the closet door open, then slam shut behind him.

Chapter 63

People, please!" Zeke pleaded, pacing back and forth on the *Food Fight* set. "We have got to get this taping started. We need Tate, we need Gina. . . ." He glanced at the doorway from the veranda, where Val Foster had appeared, reluctantly cutting short her smoke break.

"Have you seen him?" Zeke asked.

"He's around," Val said vaguely. "I think he was just taking Moonpie for a short walk. I'll go see if I can round him up."

She was starting down the hallway toward the makeup room when Tate burst out of a doorway and came storming down the hall toward her, murder in his eyes.

"Hey!" she said, stepping in his pathway. "Remember me? Your producer?"

"Gotta go," he said, trying to sidestep her. "Adelman's ready for us."

"I know," Val said. "Zeke just sent me to fetch you." She took a step closer, brushing at something on the collar of his shirt. She held up a fingertip and examined it. "Translucent powder," she said.

"D'John insisted," Tate said. He did another quick sidestep, but again she was too quick for him. With her thumb, Val wiped at a smudge on his chin. She held up the thumb. "Very Berry lip gloss. Not really your shade, Tate."

"You've made your point," he said gruffly. "Now can we get on with this damned charade?"

She fell into step beside him. "How do you think you did on this round?"

"You saw how I did. I sucked. What the hell was I supposed to do with tomato soup and a jar of mayonnaise?"

"Gina Foxton found plenty to do," Val said. "God knows what the judges will make of it, but she does have quantity, if not quality, on her side."

"Fine," he snapped. "Let's just get it over with, okay? This place is really starting to get on my nerves."

"I completely agree," she said. "But if Gina wins this round, it complicates things. She ties it up, we have to go through one more challenge. Which you will have to win, if you want to win the whole shooting match."

"Remind me why I agreed to go along with this insanity?" he said irritably.

Val stopped dead in her tracks. She felt panicky. She'd been panicky ever since she set foot on Eutaw Island. No good could come of a place without off-ramps, smog, or a single Starbucks. The wheels were starting to come off the well-oiled *Vittles* machine.

"I shouldn't have to remind you. You're doing this because they're going to give the winner his own prime-time network cooking show. You're doing this because it means no more cooking demonstrations in the parking lot at the Peach County Feed 'n' Seed. It means more money and more prestige. It means a Porsche Carrera for you, a Mercedes for me, and a Louis Vuitton collar for Moonpie."

He sighed. "That's what I was afraid of." He started to walk away.

"Do you even know what a Louis Vuitton dog collar costs?" Val called after him.

"Don't wanna know," he called back.

There you are," Lisa cried, spying her sister lollygagging around outside the ballroom. "Where have you been? Zeke's had me looking all over for you."

"Lipstick," Gina said cryptically. "D'John forgot to fix my lipstick."

"Well, come on then," Lisa said, pushing Gina through the door to the ballroom. "Everybody's been standing around for the past ten minutes waiting on you."

"Sorry," Gina said, starting for the set.

"Wait." Lisa grabbed Gina's arm. "You can't go out there like that."

"Like what? Do I have lipstick on my teeth?"

Lisa patted her sister's butt. "Eeew. You're all wet. And you smell like Pine-Sol. What happened? Did you pee in your pants?"

Gina reached around and felt the damp seat of her pants. "Crap," she muttered.

"Gina! Come on, come on," Barry stood at the director's table, motioning her forward. "Time is money, cookie. You don't want to keep the judges waiting."

"Coming," Gina said, tugging her T-shirt down over her wet butt.

Contestant one," Barry announced, setting trays in front of the three judges.

Toni Bailey clapped her hands with delight after tasting the first of Gina's dishes.

"Tomato soup cake!" she exclaimed. "Oh, my mercy, I bet I haven't had a chocolate layer cake this dense and moist since my mama died."

Gina blushed with delight.

"Tomato soup cake?" Beau Stapleton lifted a forkful of the layer cake to his quivering nostrils and sniffed. He slid the cake in his mouth, chewed, and nodded reluctantly. "It's actually quite good," he said.

Deidre Delaney leaned forward, holding out a plate with a chicken thigh. "Taste the oven-fried chicken," she urged. "It's beyond weird—Frosted Flakes and chili powder—but I actually like it."

Stapleton gnawed on the end of a drumstick. "I'd never dream of serving this in one of my restaurants," he said.

"They're not asking you to serve it in one of your hooty-snooty joints," Toni retorted. "We asked them to come up with dishes using everyday ingredients, and this is what they fixed. I, for one, applaud this contestant's inventiveness and creativity."

"This bacon-sauteed cabbage is awfully good," Deidre said. "Although I don't want to think of the fat and carb count on any of these dishes."

"Definitely not what you'd serve to your South Beach patrons," Stapleton said.

"Don't be so sure," Deidre shot back. "I can see doing this as a small plate. Of course, I'd do it with apple-smoked pancetta and organic kale, maybe throw in some pan-toasted fennel seed, but the concept is really a winner."

Stapleton stabbed a piece of pie on the plate in front of him. "What's this?"

Toni nibbled a piece. "Vinegar pie! My goodness, what a trip down memory lane."

Deidre scribbled something on her scorecard and looked around at the others. "Did the contestant use all the ingredients?"

From off camera, Barry nodded yes.

"No points deducted," Toni said. "Contestant two is going to really have to step it up a notch to beat this performance."

Barry made a show of sliding the next round of dishes onto the judge's table.

"Contestant two," he announced solemnly.

"This is it?" Deidre said, looking around expectantly.

"Looks like it," Stapleton said. He speared a piece of the barbecued chicken and chewed.

"Nice and moist," he said. "Got a tang to it that I wouldn't have expected."

Toni and Deidre each helped themselves to a piece of Tate's barbecued chicken.

Deidre wrinkled her nose after one bite. "Too sweet."

Toni spooned up a bit of cabbage from the bottom of the chicken casserole. "It's an unexpected pairing," she said charitably. "I think I would have done a coleslaw instead."

"But we're not judging on what you would have done," Beau reminded her. "You two just applauded the first contestant for originality, but you're slamming this contestant for taking a chance with adding shredded cabbage to a chicken dish."

"Contestant one's dishes worked," Toni said. "This one just doesn't. Not on any level."

Val closed her eyes and shook her head. What had Tate been thinking? He'd made dozens of variations of coleslaw on his show. He'd made braised cabbage, stuffed cabbage. How the hell could he be stupid enough to dump cabbage into a dish with barbecued chicken?

She glanced over at Tate, who seemed perfectly relaxed, sitting off camera, staring into space. He had Moonpie at his side, and was absentmindedly scratching the dog's ears.

Gina Foxton, on the other hand, seemed to hang on the judge's every word, leaning forward, fists tightly clenched at her side. Occasionally she would sneak a peek at Tate, and then instantly glance away. He was making quite a show of not looking back.

She could wring Tate's neck. He had women of all ages following him everywhere, throwing themselves at him. He could have his pick of any girl, any time. He'd had girlfriends since the show started, yeah. But they never lasted any longer than a month at most, and he somehow managed to part friends with every girl whose heart he broke into a million tiny pieces.

But why now? Why this Susie Homemaker with the bad dye job? The one woman in America whose ass he needed to kick—and he was obviously, pathetically, head-over-heels in love with her. He had this thing in the bag, and he was going to blow it, all for her.

Toni Bailey, bless her heart, was trying to even the odds. She picked up one of Tate's heinous-looking Frosted Flakes cookies and broke off a piece. Gamely, she chewed, smiled, and swallowed.

"Interesting," she said, dabbing her mouth with a paper napkin. She didn't fool Val, who could see Toni covertly spitting the rest of the cookie into the napkin.

Deidre Delaney didn't trouble herself to make nice. "I'd give these to Tate Moody's dog," she said, after one bite. "But I happen to be an animal lover. Cocoa and Frosted Flakes? It's almost worst than the barbecued chicken with cabbage."

Beau Stapleton did his damnedest to sway the others to his side. "I don't see what your problem is with the cookie," he said, reaching for another while still chewing the first cookie. "The texture is great. Crunchy with a chewy middle. And I like the chocolate undertones."

"You mean aftertaste," Deidre sniped.

"All right, you two," Toni said. "Let's see if we can come to some kind of decision—it's been a long hard day for all of us."

"It's no contest as far as I'm concerned," Deidre said. "Did contestant two even use all the ingredients?"

"No." Barry mouthed the words.

"So, there's a deduction right there," Deidre said, looking to Stapleton and Toni for a consensus.

The three judges took only a moment to scrawl their scores on their clipboards.

Barry strolled onto the set, collecting the scores, while turning toward the camera. "The suspense is killing us all," he said, sotto voce. "But we're just going to have to wait until after the break to see how the judges have scored round two of our exciting Food Fight."

You're going to win!" Lisa trilled, hopping up and down with excitement. "I just know it. Did you see those judges? Even that snotty Beau Stapleton had to admit you rocked it with the chocolate cake and the fried chicken."

Gina nervously rotated her shoulders, desperately trying to relax. "They did seem to like everything," she admitted.

"Like it? They loved it!" Scott said. He stood behind Gina and rubbed her shoulders. "No way you can lose this time," he said. "Moody blew it. We're going to New York, baby!" he exulted.

Gina wondered why she felt so numb. Scott and Lisa were right. She had definitely dominated in this round. She should be celebrating. So why did she feel like crying?

"All right, people," Zeke called a moment later. "We need Tate and Gina on their kitchen sets in two minutes."

D'John hurried over to give Gina a last-minute freshener. He fussed with her hair for a moment, brushed more powder on her nose and cheeks, and touched up her lipstick. He had Lisa hold his minicam while he interviewed her sister.

"Gina Foxton, you're about to win the second round of the Food Fight. How does that feel?" D'John asked in a plummy radio voice.

"We don't know that I've won," Gina corrected him. "It could go either way."

"No way," Lisa said. "Chicks rule!"

Gina's stomach was doing flip-flops as Barry approached the kitchen set. She took a deep breath, tried to remember the relaxation exercises she'd learned in yoga class. But her mind was mush. It kept wandering back to that damned broom closet, to the feel of Tate's beard scraping against her cheek, the feel of his hands on her body, and to the appalling realization that no matter what he'd said, her own actions had betrayed her.

Barry had a piece of paper he was reading from. He was thanking the judges, thanking Tate and Gina for an outstanding performance, even thanking Zeke and Lisa for rescuing them from Rattlesnake Key. His voice droned on and on. She felt her eyelids drooping.

Wait. Barry had his arm clamped around her shoulders, was beaming at her.

"Gina Foxton, what a stunning comeback tonight," he said. "Our three celebrity judges unanimously named you winner of tonight's Food Fight. Tell our audience at home—how do you feel?"

"I'm, I'm . . . stunned," she said, forcing a smile. She wanted to cry.

Chapter 64

T ate!" Val saw him walking rapidly toward the front of the lodge, Moonpie close by his heels. "Tate, wait up," she called again, but if he heard, he was ignoring her.

She heard the front door closing, and when she went to the front windows, she was just in time to see him shooting off into the darkness on his golf cart. Let him go, she thought.

Val sat on the steps of the porch and lit a cigarette. She leaned back on her elbows and surveyed the grassy lawn. Gigantic bugs flitted around the coach lanterns flanking the sidewalk, and she could see fireflies twinkling in the treetops. She inhaled deeply and smiled. One more day. Tonight's loss was a setback, but tomorrow, Tate would be on his game again. She'd make sure of it. And then, she would gladly trade the deep green scent of fresh-mown grass and magnolias for insects whose names she knew, and the comforting smell of the hot asphalt and carbon monoxide fumes of Peachtree Street.

And if all went well, not long after that, they would be packing for New York. All she had to do was find a way to talk her pigheaded star out of thinking he was in love. She tilted her head back and blew a smoke ring, watching it dissipate into the soupy night air. One more day.

Lisa's ebullient chatter was a welcome distraction. "Can you believe it? All you have to do is win tomorrow, and we're a lock. Zeke won't say anything, he's got this crazy idea he has to be impartial—I mean, what is he, a friggin' Supreme Court Justice—but I can tell he thinks you should win."

"That's nice," Gina said wearily, dropping her clothes to the floor of their room.

"Where do you think we'll live in New York?" Lisa went on. "Zeke lives in Brooklyn. I always thought Brooklyn was kind of a ghetto, but he says it's actually very nice. He takes the subway to work every day. Can you imagine—he doesn't even own a car. I told him, no way am I giving up my car, but he says nobody in New York owns a car. I mean, how do you get to Target?"

"Don't know," Gina managed.

She showered and put on a cotton voile nightgown, and when she came out of the bathroom, Lisa was propped up in bed, a pair of reading glasses perched on the end of her nose, a book open.

"You're reading? When did this start?"

"Very funny," Lisa said, not bothering to look up. "I read. Sometimes."

"Since when?"

With an exaggerated sigh, Lisa held up the book. It was a thick hardback tome—Robert McKee's *Story*. "Since Zeke gave this to me. It's about screenwriting. And it's amazing. All the big Hollywood producers and writers have studied with this guy."

"Not to mention Lisa Foxton," Gina said. "Are you actually interested in screenwriting?"

"Oh, yeah," Lisa said. "Zeke thinks I should go to film school. He says I have a natural talent for storytelling."

"Is that the same thing as being a gifted liar?"

"Zeke says UCLA has the best film program in the country," Lisa went on, ignoring the dig. "But NYU is very well respected too. If I went there, I could keep working part-time as your personal assistant while I go to school."

"Don't count your chickens before your eggs are hatched," Gina warned. As soon as the words were out

of her mouth, she realized with regret that she sounded
just like Birdelle. She dropped down onto her bed and
stretched out on top of the bedspread. Even though it
was nearly midnight, their room was stifling, the fan
merely stirring up the hot stale air.

"I almost forgot," Lisa said. "Mama called while you
were in the bathroom. She nearly popped a gusset when
I told her you won tonight. She wants you to call."

"Maybe tomorrow," Gina said. She reached over
and turned off the light on her nightstand. Lisa's voice
trailed off.

"Oh!" she said. "One more thing. I know what
tomorrow's challenge is. I heard Barry and Zeke talking
about it while you were AWOL tonight."

"Lisa!" Gina interrupted. "Don't tell me. I don't
want to know. It wouldn't be fair to Tate."

"Oh, pooh, fair," Lisa said. "How fair was it that
he'd been to Eutaw before?"

"I don't care," Gina said. "Don't say another word.
I've got to get some sleep."

"Have it your way," Lisa said airily. "But it wouldn't
matter if you did know what the challenge was."

Barry Adelman ushered Tate and Gina onto the
kitchen set. Once again, their counters were covered
with white sheets.

"Now, no peeking," he said, wagging his finger.

"Fuck that," Tate said, lifting the corner of the sheet with his little finger.

"Hey!" Barry said sharply. "I'm not kidding around here. We've gone to a lot of trouble to make this competition strictly fair and on the up-and-up. TCC's reputation is on the line here, my friends."

"For God's sake, Adelman. It's television, not the Olympics," Tate said. "Who really gives a rat's ass?"

A vein twitched on Barry's forehead. "Who gives a rat's ass? Is that what you just said to me?"

"We all do," Val said, materializing at his side. "We all care deeply, Barry. Don't mind Tate. He's just overtired."

"Look around you," Barry said angrily, gesturing toward the crew. "You see anybody here who isn't sleep-deprived? You see anybody who isn't giving one hundred percent so we can make a piece of quality entertainment?"

"No, Barry," Val said soothingly. "This crew is amazing. The whole production is amazing. Food Fight is going to be a ratings sensation. I just know it."

"Goddamn right it is," Barry muttered, shooting a sidelong glance at Tate.

"We're ready to roll," Zeke called from the production table. "On five."

Val hustled off the set. Barry's sullen expression faded. His shoulders lifted, and he seemed to smile with his whole body.

"Welcome, everybody, to our third and last challenge of our exciting and first-ever Food Fight. If you've been watching for the past couple nights—as I'm sure everybody in America has—you've seen our contestants, Regina Foxton, of the award-winning public television series *Fresh Start with Regina Foxton*, and Tate Moody, the host and star of Southern Outdoors Network's *Vittles*, face off over two difficult, and yes, dangerous even, challenges.

"On the first night of the competition, our challenge for these star southern cooks was to gather and cook a meal, based only on what they could find here in the beautiful wilds of Eutaw Island. Tate Moody astonished the judges with his wild hog dinner and won that first round. But then Gina Foxton came roaring back the second night, when we asked the competitors to prepare a meal with the kind of mundane everyday contents they might find in any ordinary kitchen. Gina wowed the judges with a chocolate tomato soup cake, oven-fried chicken made with Frosted Flakes cereal and chili powder, bacon-braised cabbage, and an unusual vinegar pie."

The cameramen panned from Gina, rested and relaxed after a full night's sleep, to Tate, who stood with his back to the stove in his kitchen, not bothering to suppress a tonsil-baring yawn.

"What's he doing?" Val whispered to nobody in particular. "Stop that!" Sitting beside her at the production table, Scott Zaleski smirked his appreciation.

"Tonight's challenge is both simple and deceptively complex," Barry said. He whisked the sheet from Gina's counter and then Tate's.

"We're asking our contestants to prepare the exact same recipe," Barry said. "They have all the ingredients necessary to make a dish that's a staple in every southern cook's repertoire—bourbon pecan pie! They can, of course, do their own twist on the recipe, but only using the ingredients they have available in their kitchens. Gina, Tate, you have two hours—starting now."

The starting buzzer sounded, and Barry stepped away from the set.

Gina looked down at the counter and couldn't help but smile. She'd been baking pecan pies since she was eight years old, and had, in fact, once taken second prize at the Ware County Fair with Birdelle's aunt Ludie's pecan pie recipe. Of course, since Great Aunt Ludie was a foot-washing Baptist, her recipe had never called for bourbon. Which was a good thing, since Ocilla, where she lived, had been a dry county.

She managed a sidelong glance at Tate, who caught her eye for only a second before turning away. For a second, she actually felt sorry for him. He might be a whiz at barbecuing and frying, but just how good was he at baking? Was it really fair to ask a man to bake a pie?

Yes, she thought grimly. It was just as fair to expect Tate Moody to bake a pie as it was to ask Regina Foxton to catch and cook her own dinner on an island. She rolled up the sleeves of her shirt and reached for the sack of White Lily flour. The game was on.

He hadn't missed that pitying look. He wanted to laugh. Or maybe not. He had a job to do. He skimmed the recipe and the list of ingredients. It was, as Adelman had explained, a pretty basic recipe for pecan pie.

Lined up on his counter he had flour, a pitcher of ice water, salt, sugar, butter, eggs, a bowl of shelled pecans, dark and light corn syrup, vanilla, and yes, even a pint bottle of bourbon.

He grabbed a mixing bowl and dumped in flour, salt, and sugar, mixing them with his fingertips. Tate took a knife and cut the stick of butter into cubes, which he then dropped into the bowl of flour. Looking furtively about, he uncapped the pint of bourbon, took a swig, and set it aside.

He found a pastry cutter and began cutting the cold butter into the flour. Butter! He shook his head. Trust a bunch of Yankees to supply them with butter instead of lard for pastry. Well, at least somebody had the good sense to buy unbleached all-purpose White Lily flour.

He still remembered a kitchen assistant Val had hired to help with his first season's show. He was doing smothered quail and gravy over biscuits for an episode called "Early Bird Special." Val had sent the assistant, who was fresh from a fancy California cooking school, to the grocery store with a shopping list. While he prepared the biscuit dough on camera, the girl was busily working away in the prep kitchen, fixing the dough that would be used to make the biscuits that would actually get baked. Unbeknownst to all of them, this particular California girl had gone out and bought self-rising Betty Crocker flour. The resulting biscuits looked fine, but when the time came for him to split them and cover them with the smothered quail on camera, the biscuits had been so hard he would have needed a hacksaw to cut them in half.

Heather, the girl, had sobbed for hours after the catastrophe. He'd gently taken the time to explain the difference between "soft" southern wheat flour and "hard" bleached flour, and she'd perked right up. They'd had some good times together after that, and the show's raw footage had been his favorite scenes in the "best-of, worst-of" bloopers tape Val always compiled for the end-of-season crew party.

Tate paused from cutting the butter into the flour and took another sip from the bottle of Jack Daniel's.

Using his fingertips again, he made a well in the middle of the bowl of flour and dribbled in some ice water, which he quickly worked into the dough. When the dough looked right, he sprinkled more flour onto the countertop, gathered the dough into a thick, round disc, and flopped it onto the countertop. After coating both sides of the disc with flour, he dumped it onto a piece of waxed paper and put it in the refrigerator to chill.

Wiping his hands on a clean dish towel, he snuck a peek at Gina, who, it happened, was doing the exact same thing. He smiled smugly and shot her a thumbs-up. Her returning smile puzzled him. What the hell was she thinking? He raised the bottle of Jack Daniel's in a salute and sipped again.

"Cut!" Barry called. He gave Zeke a meaningful look.

"All right, people," Zeke said, "let's take a break."

Uh, Tate." Zeke cleared his throat and looked down at the yellow Post-it on his shirt sleeve. "Barry's a little concerned."

"About what?" Tate was sprawled out on the porch steps, Moonpie at his feet.

"Well, uh, he wants to make sure you understand that this is absolutely our last night of taping. The judges will pick a winner of the Food Fight based on this last challenge, and then we're all packing up and leaving in the morning."

"Got that memo," Tate said, yawning. "I'll see you at the ferry dock bright and early, right?" He slapped Zeke on the back. "It's been real, buddy."

Zeke peeled the Post-it off his sleeve and crumpled it up. "The thing is, Tate, we can all see that you've been dipping into that bottle of Jack Daniel's on the set, while we're taping."

Tate scratched Moonpie's ears. "There a rule against that? Because that's one memo I didn't get."

"Barry feels . . ." Zeke pushed his glasses back up to the bridge of his nose. "Oh hell, Tate. You can't be drinking during the show. You know that. Our demographic for this show is strictly Middle America. Our sponsors for Food Fight are the American Dairy Council and the all-new Subaru Forester. Think about it—milk and mid-size imported SUVs. We can't have our contestants cooking under the influence. Our sponsors will freak if they see something like that. Barry *is* freaking."

"Riiiight," Tate drawled. He stood and stretched, and swayed just slightly. "Tell Barry to relax. The Tatester has everything under control."

For the fourth time since she'd put her pie in the oven, Gina opened the door and peeked in. She couldn't understand it. She'd set the oven at 375—just as the recipe had specified. The baking time should have been forty minutes, tops. But the pie was nowhere near done. Her crust hadn't browned, and when she gave the pie pan a slight jiggle, the unbaked pecan bourbon filling sloshed over the sides and onto the baking sheet she'd set the pie on. The filling definitely was not setting up.

The big time clock ticked off the seconds and minutes. Thirty minutes. She had only thirty more minutes to get the pie baked, cooled, and ready to serve to the judges. And pecan pie took a notoriously long time to cool and set. How many times had her daddy tried to rush things by cutting a pie and been rewarded with a burned tongue?

Gina looked over at Tate. "Psst. Hey," she whispered.

Tate, who was lolling around beside his oven, looking bored out of his mind, glanced over.

"Hey," he whispered back.

"Is your pie done?"

"Nope." He didn't look concerned. Come to think of it, he barely looked conscious.

"Did you set the oven at 375?"

"Yup."

"I think something's wrong," Gina said. "We both put the pies in at approximately the same time. They should have been done ten minutes ago. But my crust still looks raw."

He bent down, opened his oven door, and surveyed its contents.

"Ditto," he said.

The crew had taken a break, and Barry and Zeke were sitting at the production table, heads bent together.

"Barry," Gina called.

He looked up. "Yes, cookie? Those pies smell incredible."

"They're nowhere near done," Gina said frantically. "I think something's wrong with my oven."

"Yeah, me too," Tate called.

"Hmm." Barry strolled over, opened the door to Gina's oven and looked inside. "Yep. I think you could be right."

"Well, what do we do? We only have thirty minutes left on the time clock. Can you bring somebody in to fix the ovens? Or reset the clocks?"

"Don't think so," Barry said affably. "I guess you'll just have to figure out something else. We're bringing the judges back in thirty, and then we wrap it all up."

"That's not fair," Gina cried, running her hand through her already sweat-dampened hair. "You can't expect us to be able to bake with an oven that's messed up."

"Sorry," Barry said with a shrug. "Improvise."

"Schcrew that," Tate said, slurring the words. "Hey. You guys did this on purpose. You knew the ovens were schcrewed up. I bet you did it yourselves."

Now Zeke hurried onto the set. "Is there a problem?"

"They've discovered that the ovens aren't properly calibrated. And I've explained that they have"— Adelman glanced over at the clock—"twenty-six minutes to figure it out." He nodded at both contestants and went back to the control table.

"Hey!" Gina said angrily. "Tate's right. You guys did this to us deliberately."

"One of the qualities we're looking for in our Food Fight winner is the ability to think on his or her feet," Zeke said. "Consider it part two of your challenge."

"My ass!" Gina said angrily. She stomped back to her kitchen and turned the oven's heat up to 425 degrees. Then she rolled up a strip of aluminum foil, fashioned a protective collar for the edge of her neatly crimped crust, and put the pie back in the oven. She had no idea if it would keep the crust from browning too much—or what the higher heat would do to her filling—but she didn't know how else to salvage the situation.

In the meantime, she went to the refrigerator and found a carton of whipping cream. She dumped the cream into a bowl and attacked it with the hand-held electric mixer she found in a drawer of her kitchen, adding a teaspoon of sugar and a tablespoon of the bourbon to the cream. When she was satisfied with the whipped cream's consistency, she slid the bowl into the refrigerator.

Now there was nothing left to do but wait. She paced back and forth in the kitchen, coming face-to-face with Tate more than once.

He seemed completely unfazed by any of the ongoing drama. He puttered around his kitchen, straightening things up, washing the dishes he'd used, wiping down the counter, literally whistling while he worked. Once, she thought she saw him take a giant gulp from the bottle of Jack Daniel's. She tried not to look shocked. What was he thinking?

After ten minutes, she could bear it no longer. She took the pie out of the oven. The higher heat seemed to have helped. The filling seemed set, and the crust, once she'd removed the protective foil, seemed to have browned up a little too. Not perfect, by a long shot, but better. She had only ten minutes left. She cut the pie into slices, slid the slices onto individual plates, and set them in the freezer to allow them to cool quicker.

Five minutes later, she removed the slices and proceeded to chop each slice into healthy chunks. Then she took the pecan pie chunks and dumped them into tall-stemmed parfait glasses that were probably just meant to be pretty set dressing. She was dropping generous dollops of the sweetened bourbon whipped cream into the last of the glasses when the buzzer went off.

"Time's up!" Barry announced, stepping onto the set. "Everybody step away from the ovens!"

Chapter 65

Val rushed onto the set and looked down at the charred pie on Tate's countertop.

She grabbed her star's wrists. "What the hell happened?" She pushed at the pie with her fingertip. "What the hell do you call this?"

Tate's grin was wobbly. "It's an old Cajun specialty. Blackened pecan pie."

"That's all you have to say for yourself?" She leaned forward and sniffed his breath, then fanned the fumes away from her face. "I don't believe it. You're plotzed. Totally, stinking drunk."

"I prefer to think of my current condition as pleasantly buzzed." Tate got a butcher knife and began hacking at the pie, haphazardly slapping the misshapen pieces on the plates he'd set out on the counter.

"You can't serve this crap to the judges," Val said. "They'll laugh us right off the set. Off the show, for damned sure."

Ignoring her, he opened the refrigerator, took out a bottle, and painstakingly placed a maraschino cherry on the top of each hunk of pie.

"Plate appeal is nearly as important as palate appeal," he said, flourishing the finished product.

"All right, people," Zeke said, joining them in the kitchen. "Five minutes. I've got the judges coming over right now."

He looked down at the plate Tate held out and blinked. "Are you serious?"

"Never more serious in my life," Tate said. He gestured toward the pan. "There's plenty more. Would you like a taste?"

Zeke sighed. "You're not making this easy for me, Tate. What am I supposed to tell Barry? And the judges?"

"Tell them my oven was broken," Tate said. "Tell them you people deliberately sabotaged our equipment. *Tell them Tate Moody does not fuckin' appreciate bein' fucked with, you moron!*"

Zeke shook his head and held his hand out to Val. "I'm sorry, Valerie. You know I have nothing but respect for you and your abilities." He gave Tate a pitying glance. "I respect him too. Most of the time."

Val took Zeke's hand in both of hers. "Thanks, Zeke. I appreciate that. And the chance to compete. I'm just sorry, well, you know. For all of it."

Wow!" **Barry** said, glancing down at the judge's tally sheets. "Talk about a drama-packed evening. After two riveting rounds of competition, everything came down to one night—one show—one dish. Our contestants were asked to prepare a favorite southern dish— bourbon pecan pie. They were given the recipe, and all the ingredients necessary, and a two-hour time limit."

He leaned in nearer to the camera, as though to impart a closely guarded family secret.

"But what our contestants weren't given," he said, in a hushed tone, "was the information that they would be baking their pie in ovens whose thermostats had been turned down by fifty degrees!"

Tate glanced over at Gina, who stood motionless in her kitchen, her hands tightly folded on the countertop. "Told ya," he said.

Gina forced herself to look pleasant when she felt murderous.

"We wanted to see how our chefs would react to this kind of real-world challenge—how they would change or adapt their game plan," Barry confided. "And as you saw, our contestants had two very different responses. Regina Foxton's bourbon pecan pie parfait was an innovative way to deal with a not-quite-set pie by first chilling it, then chopping it up and layering it with sweetened whipped cream for a pecan pie parfait. Her rival, Tate Moody, was not quite as successful. The judges just didn't love his Cajun blackened pecan pie. And so . . ."

The cameras cut to Gina, beaming.

And to Tate, who had placed Moonpie on his kitchen counter and was busily feeding him the remnants of the pecan pie. Not an astute judge of southern cooking, the dog was happily lapping it up.

And then the camera came back to Barry, his arm around Gina's shoulder.

"Regina Foxton—you're our very first Food Fight winner, and our newest Cooking Channel network star!"

While the Food Fight theme music swelled, the judges swept onto the set, to shake hands and congratulate Gina. Toni Bailey and Beau Stapleton even offered polite, if somewhat chilly greetings to Tate.

"Dude," Beau Stapleton said, slapping Tate on the back. "I don't get it. You had her beat, hands down. I watched your pie crust technique. It was flawless. And not everybody can make a pie crust. What happened up here tonight?"

"Dunno," Tate said, leaning in close enough to allow Beau to smell the bourbon fumes.

"I do," Stapleton said, stepping backward.

"Hey, Tate." D'John brandished his ever-present video camera. "I'm doing interviews for my documentary on the making of Food Fight. How would you sum up your experience here on Eutaw Island? Was it everything you thought it would be? What was it like to be stranded on an island with Gina Foxton?"

"S'great," Tate said boozily. "All of it was just great."

An hour later, with the wrap party still going, Val finally managed to slip away. She knocked on Tate's door, but wasn't surprised when he didn't answer, or to find the door unlocked and the room empty, except for his neatly packed duffel bag.

Commandeering a golf cart, she drove herself down the oyster-shell path to the ferry dock. Silhouetted in the light at the end of the dock, Tate was sitting on the edge, his bare feet dangling in the water. He had an arm around Moonpie, who seemed captivated by something in the water below.

He must have heard her footsteps approaching, but he didn't turn around.

She sat down beside him and lit a cigarette.

"Nice night," he said.

"If you happen to like temperatures in the nineties and one hundred percent humidity," she said.

"I thought you'd still be at the party."

"It's winding down. Everybody still has to pack yet. Anyway, I wasn't really in the mood to celebrate."

"Yeah." He sighed deeply, and finally turned to look at her. "Look, Val. About what happened tonight . . ."

She held up a hand to stop him. "I just want to know one thing."

"What's that?"

"Was she worth it?"

"Yeah," he said. "She's worth all of it. And more."

Chapter 66

The sound of a police siren shattered the thick morning air. She'd been in a deep sleep, so deep that awakening felt like trying to swim to the surface of a lake with her ankles chained to a pair of bowling balls. Gina threw off the covers and looked wildly around the room, uncertain of her whereabouts.

Sunshine streamed through a window covered with sheer organza curtains. A fan hummed from the top of a table, and from somewhere outside, birds called. The siren kept going. It seemed to be getting louder. Her sleep-smeared eyes focused on the nightstand by the bed. Lisa's cell phone vibrated against the wooden tabletop. Wanting only to stop the siren, she picked up the phone and instantly regretted it.

"Good morning, my television star!" Birdelle's voice trilled.

"Mama?"

"Well, who else? I guess you've been too busy with all the media interviews and that type of thing to think of calling anybody as unimportant as your mama and daddy."

"Huh? Mama, I just woke up. I haven't talked to anybody."

"Well, I have," Birdelle announced. "I've talked to the *Jesup Press-Sentinel*, the *Jacksonville Times-Union*, the *Savannah Morning News*, the *Atlanta Journal-Constitution*, WGUP, and I don't even know who all else, just since six this morning."

"About what?" Gina yawned and looked at the clock on her nightstand. It was eight o'clock.

"You, of course! About how I taught you to cook, and how you were always such a bright, adorable little girl. I'm waiting for one of those courier service folks right now, to come pick up the pictures."

"Pictures of what?"

"Why, you, silly," Birdelle said. "I'm giving them copies of you with your 4-H project when you were eight, and then, of course, that precious picture of you with your trophy and tiara when you were runner-up Miss Teen Vidalia Onion—"

"Oh, Mama, not the Vidalia Onion picture! I look like a total rube in that homemade dress and that bad perm—"

"You were just as lovely as you could be," Birdelle said serenely. "Your daddy still carries a copy of that picture around in his billfold."

She looked at the clock again. Eight o'clock! The ferry was leaving in exactly an hour—and she still had to shower and dress and pack.

"Mama, I can't talk right now," Gina said. "I've got a million things to do before the ferry leaves."

"Not even famous for twelve hours, and already she's too busy to speak to her loved ones," Birdelle said mournfully. "All right. Put your sister on."

"Sister?"

For the first time it registered in her foggy brain that she was alone in the room. Lisa's bed was still made up. Gina checked the bathroom. Empty. And there was no telltale pile of her sister's clothes on the floor to indicate that she had ever been there.

"Put Lisa on the phone," Birdelle repeated.

"Uh, Lisa's in the shower right now," Gina fibbed. "But I'll have her call you as soon as she can." And before her mother could protest, Gina disconnected. And then she turned the phone off.

Where on earth was Lisa? Barry had been adamant that the ferry would leave the dock at nine o'clock sharp. And since she and Lisa had to drive to Savannah to catch a noon flight back to Atlanta, they were on an uncomfortably tight schedule.

She tried to think back. Last night's party had gotten kind of wild. Her last memory, before begging off to go to bed, was seeing D'John trying to teach Zeke and Barry Adelman how to do the Electric Slide. The memory of the black-clad New Yorkers attempting to boogie-oogie-oogie with a bald black man in a white caftan was surreal.

In fact, the whole day seemed surreal.

As she stood under the shower, she replayed the taping in her mind. Even with the disaster with the oven, everything had gone so much better than she could ever have anticipated. The pecan pie parfaits had been a huge hit. Everybody had seemed genuinely glad that she'd won the Food Fight.

The only thing that could have made her victory sweeter was sharing it with the one man she couldn't seem to please.

Tate. She'd looked all over for him, but he'd disappeared as soon as the taping was over. Even Val said she didn't know where he'd gone. Obviously, he'd slunk off to lick his wounds by himself. That hurt. If he truly cared for her, couldn't he have been happy for her?

As she rinsed the conditioner out of her hair, she slung her head from side to side, willing him out of her mind—and heart—for good.

She was toweling off when she heard the bedroom door open and close. "Lisa?" she called anxiously.

"Yeah?"

"Where have you been? We have to be down at the ferry in thirty minutes." Gina wrapped a towel around her chest and stepped into the room, ready to give her truant sister a piece of her mind.

Lisa sat on her bed, holding out a mug of coffee. "I went downstairs to get you a cup of coffee. Is that okay?"

"Mama called," Gina said. "She was asking about you, and naturally, I couldn't tell her you never came home last night."

"Yes, I did," Lisa said. "I got in right after midnight. You were snoring your head off. Still snoring when I got up at seven. I showered, dressed, packed, and you never moved a muscle. Just how much of that Eutaw Yeehaw punch did you drink last night?"

"None," Gina said. "Wait. Seriously? You're packed and ready to go?"

"Yup," Lisa said. "You're packed too, except for your overnight bag. Everything's been taken down to the dock. You'll just have time to grab some breakfast if you'll hurry up. Iris and Inez are both downstairs. They want to congratulate you and tell you good-bye."

People!" Zeke stood in the lobby of the lodge, checking off items on his clipboard, as the crew members darted in and out with luggage and equipment. "We need everybody out on the porch, loading up in the golf carts immediately."

"Hey, you," Lisa said, kissing him lightly on the cheek. "Just let Gina grab a bite, all right?"

"All right," Zeke said, blushing. "But we really have to hurry, okay?"

Lisa led Gina into the dining room, where a plate of ham biscuits was set out on the sideboard alongside glass carafes of juice and coffee. She was helping herself to a biscuit when the two old ladies came bustling out of the kitchen.

"There she is!" Inez said, beaming wildly, and digging her elbow in her twin's side. "I done tol' my sister the first time I saw you that you was a winner. Come here and hug an old lady's neck."

Gina wrapped her arms around Inez's shrunken shoulders. "I could never have done it without your help. Thank you so much for everything."

"That's all right, honey," Inez said, patting her hand. "You sure enough did me proud this week. I never seen a chile from off-island take to a place like you did. Fishin' and swimpin' and crabbin'."

"Look like she mighta had a lot more help than Mr. Tate," Iris grumped.

"Listen at her!" Inez crowed. "She just mad 'cuz she been tellin' everybody Mister Tate gonna put her on his TV show after he won this Food Fight. Now that old fool gonna have to eat crow while I'm eatin' fried chicken made with mashed-up Frosted Flakes."

Gina laughed. "How about if I put both of you on my new show? Would that be all right, Iris?"

"Don't know," the old lady said. "How much you reckon bus fare might be from Darien to New York City?"

"No buses," Gina promised. "We'll either come down here and film a show with you right here on Eutaw, or we'll fly you up to New York."

"New York'd be good," Iris allowed. "You reckon we could ride in a taxicab? I always did want to ride in one of them yella cabs."

"Cabs, limos, whatever you like," Gina said.

"Gina, Lisa," Zeke poked his head into the dining room. "Last call, girls."

"Here!" Inez said suddenly. She thrust something into Gina's hand, turned, and ran back into the kitchen.

"What is it?" Lisa asked.

Gina smiled as she unfolded the rumpled sheet of notebook paper and read the tiny, cramped handwriting. "It's the secret shrimp salad recipe," she said. "Now that's what I call a real prize."

Scott found her up on the top deck, her arms on the stern rail, watching the island slowly recede into the horizon.

"There you are!" he said, tipping up his sunglasses and crowding in beside her, much closer than was necessary.

"Here I am." She inched sideways.

"Great party last night," he said. "Of course, we totally earned it. Did I tell you how proud I am of you?"

"Several times." He'd gotten amazingly drunk in an amazingly short period of time, and had spent most of the evening slobbering on her shoulder.

"Sorry to interrupt your reverie," he said now, pulling a sheaf of papers out of the back pocket of his slacks. "But I've been looking over this contract from Adel-Weis, and frankly, I can't believe the kind of penny-ante crap Barry's trying to get away with." He slapped the papers on his thigh and sighed dramatically. "I've already told him we can't accept this thing."

Gina blinked. "You . . . did what?"

"This contract is a piece of garbage," Scott said angrily. "For one thing, they're only offering us six shows! With no guarantees that the network will order a full season. It's an insult, and I told Barry so in no uncertain terms. And don't even get me started on what they're offering us for syndication."

Gina felt her ears buzzing. She felt a slow burn working its way up from her chest, to her cheeks, to her ears, and then she knew, definitely, that her head was on fire.

"Give me that!" She snatched the contract out of Scott's hands and shoved it in the pocket of her capris.

"But—"

"But nothing." Gina bit the words out. "I've tried repeatedly to tell you this, but your selective hearing keeps tuning me out."

She grabbed one of his ears in each hand. His designer sunglasses went flying off and into the brine.

"Are you listening?" she asked.

"Gina, for God's sake." His face was pale. Although his ears were getting pretty red, clutched as they were between her thumb and forefinger.

"Listening?" She pinched tighter.

"I'm listening." It came out as a squeak.

"You don't represent me, Scott. I fired you back there in Atlanta, after you slept with Danitra Bickerstaff and got my show canceled. I shouldn't have let you come to Eutaw. That was a mistake on my part. So I want to be very clear with you now. There is no *we*. My contract with TCC has nothing to do with you. You are not my producer. You are not my agent. You are not my friend. You are not my boyfriend. Do you hear me, Scott?"

"You don't mean that. You're overtired, overexcited. You don't know anything about these kinds of negotiations. You're a naive small-town girl; these Yankees will eat you alive."

She rotated the right ear clockwise and the left ear counterclockwise, as though tuning a faulty radio.

"Aaaiii-eeee," he screeched. "Stop, for Christ's sake."

Reluctantly, she returned his ears to their normal upright position.

"Gina," he whimpered, clawing at her hands.

"Scott." She whispered it. "Are you listening?"

"Yes." He had real tears in his eyes. She really should stop. She was starting to enjoy this much more than was seemly for a nice Christian girl.

"Good," she said. "I'm going to count to three, and then I'm going to let you go. At that point, I want you to go to the farthest end of this boat. I don't want to talk to you again, or see you again, or hear your weaselly voice ever again. Do I make myself very clear?"

"Yes." A thin trail of snot worked its way down his handsome, tanned face.

"Excellent. Because, Scott? You are dead to me. Now. One. Two. Three."

She released her hold. He tore away from her, slid on a slick spot on the deck, fell hard on his butt, scrambled to his feet, and scurried away. She noted, with satisfaction, a large streak of grease on the seat of his formerly immaculate linen slacks.

Gina leafed through the contract, but in the harsh sunlight, and without her reading glasses, the small print swam before her eyes. But that was all right. The last time she'd gone to a University of Georgia football game she'd run into one of her classmates at halftime. Sharon Douglas had laughingly confessed to being a failure at journalism, which was why she'd ended up going to law school. These days, she was an entertainment lawyer in Los Angeles. Gina had her business card tucked away at home.

Home. For the first time it occurred to her that the town house wouldn't be home for much longer. Funny. She'd been panicky about keeping it after *Fresh Start* had gotten canceled. Now she'd gotten her heart's desire—and she'd still have to move.

She turned and rested her back on the rail, leaving Eutaw Island behind. She closed her eyes and willed herself to be still. She wanted to be in the moment, in the sunlight, with the wind whipping her hair, and just for now, just until this ferry docked in Darien, she didn't want to think about the future or the past. Just the now.

Chapter 67

G ina needed to pack. She needed to pack, she needed to look at the schematics for the kitchen set for her new show, she needed to read the TCC contracts Sharon Douglas had faxed over—two days ago— and she had a list of phone calls to return.

Instead, she lay on the floor of her living room and stared up at the ceiling fan, which whirred away effortlessly. She had the telephone on one side of her, and her list, neatly typed by Lisa, on the other. But she had neither the energy, nor the will, to do much more than wonder at that ceiling fan. She'd lived in the town house two whole years, and never even cleaned its blades, which were caked with dust. What would Birdelle say about such a state of affairs?

The curtains at her windows fluttered slightly, and she could see and hear the gray rain beating down on the balcony. Pop-up thunderstorms, the weatherman called this kind of summer rain. The front would move through soon, and more of the usual stifling humidity would blanket Atlanta. In a way, the thought comforted her. It matched her mood.

She glanced at her to-do list. It was actually a list of lists, with numbers and bullets, even an index of color-coded Post-its. When had her party-child sister suddenly become such a model of anal-retentiveness?

Gina heard the lock turn in the door, but didn't bother to get up.

Lisa and D'John came bustling in, their arms full of boxes and bags, the rain glistening on their faces.

"Geen," Lisa called, but she stopped short when she saw her sister, lying prone on the floor.

"What's wrong?" Lisa asked, dropping an armful of shopping bags from Neiman-Marcus, Bloomingdale's, and Saks, and kneeling beside her sister. "Oh, my God, tell me you didn't fall and break something."

"I'm fine," Gina said, fanning her arms and legs to demonstrate how fine she was.

"Then why are you just lying there like a beached jellyfish when we have about a bajillion things to do?" Lisa demanded. She picked up the list. "Did you check anything off this while we were gone?"

"I'm feeling overwhelmed," Gina said.

"*You're* feeling overwhelmed? I'm the one who's been running all over town, trying to get everything ready for New York," Lisa said. She yanked at her sister's arm. "Come on, get up. D'John and I brought back all these yummy clothes for you to try on. That'll cheer you up."

"What's wrong with her?" D'John asked, opening up a row of shoe boxes and propping a shoe on each lid. He gave Gina's outfit—faded black yoga pants, baggy white T-shirt, and bare feet—a withering appraisal. "I mean—besides those rags she's wearing."

"She's been like this since we got back from Eutaw," Lisa said, removing the protective plastic from the thick bundle of hanging clothes. "She hardly eats, sleeps most of the day, won't leave the house. And you can see for yourself, she's decided to dress like a bag lady. You'd think she'd lost the damned Food Fight instead of Tate Moody."

"There's nothing wrong with me," Gina said, standing up slowly. "I'm fine. Gimme the danged clothes." She took an armful of dresses and retreated to the bedroom.

"Come out and show us when you've got the first thing on," Lisa instructed. "And for God's sake, do something with your hair."

"Ooh," D'John said, reaching into the black leather Prada messenger bag hanging from his shoulder. "I've got a surprise for you girls. Wait till you see."

He handed Lisa a diskette. "Here. Put that in the DVD player. It's my masterpiece."

"How's this?" Gina asked, emerging from the bedroom. She wore a brilliant lime green, scoop-neck silk tank over a short pink, yellow, and lime flowered skirt. She'd combed her hair, but it still hung limp around her face.

"Stand up straight." Lisa poked her between the shoulder blades.

"Turn around."

Gina did a desultory twirl.

"I don't get it." Lisa's face puckered in concentration. "This outfit looked adorable on the mannequin."

"I'm not a mannequin," Gina said.

"Right," Lisa said. "A mannequin has a spine."

"Girls, girls, girls," D'John said, brandishing the remote control. "Play nice. Now let's sit down together and watch the show."

Lisa sat on the sofa, and Gina flopped down onto the love seat. "What's this supposed to be?" Gina asked, fiddling with the sash of the skirt.

"It's my documentary of the Food Fight," D'John said. "I only just finished editing it this morning. And it's fabulous, if I do say so myself. I call it 'A Star Is Born.' "

"That's original," Gina said.

"Shhh." D'John and Lisa both glared at her.

The television screen flickered on, and Gina and Lisa appeared on camera, standing arm in arm in front of the ferry at Darien, before their departure for Eutaw Island.

"Nooo," Lisa wailed, covering her face with her hands. "I am soooo hungover. My face is pea green. Gina, how could you let me go out in public looking like that?"

From off camera, D'John's voice asked, "Are you girls excited about the Food Fight?"

Gina's face glowed. "We're gonna kick butt! Girls rule. Boys drool." The girls turned toward each other and slapped a giddy high five.

Now Tate Moody was strolling toward the ferry, his back to the camera, with Moonpie trotting along right beside him.

Lisa leaned toward the television to get a closer look, and sighed. "He does have the cutest ass."

"Why do you think I shot him from this angle?" D'John giggled.

"Tate, hey, Tate," D'John's voice called from the television.

Tate turned and frowned briefly when he saw he was on camera.

"Oh. Hey, D'John."

"All of America wants to know. Do you think you can outcook Gina Foxton and win this Food Fight?"

Tate stuck his hands in his pockets. "I'm gonna give it my best shot. The lady's good, no doubt about that. I feel like I've gotta dig deep and stay focused. But I'm feeling great. Moonpie and I are bringing our A game. We came to play."

"Could he stick in one more tired sports cliché?" Gina muttered.

"It'll be a fight to the finish," Tate concluded.

Gina settled back into the sofa cushions, her gaze riveted to the screen.

For the next hour, D'John's documentary had the two women groaning, cheering, and catcalling as the moviemaker caught the cast and crew at work and at play on Eutaw Island.

"Booo!" Gina called, the first time Beau Stapleton strolled onto the set. "Do you believe that pompous twit with his greasy ponytail? Who does he think he is, Steven Seagal?"

"Look at Zeke," Lisa cooed. "Y'all, I know he's kind of a geek, but seriously, don't you think he's so geeky he's adorable? And now that I've gotten him out of all that dreary black, and into some decent clothes and eyeglasses made in this century, doesn't he look kind of like a young George Clooney?"

"He's transformed," Gina said dryly.

"By the love of a good woman," D'John added.

They watched each of the first two challenges, and cheered and jeered at the judge's comments, and made catty comments about everybody who appeared on screen.

"It's a good thing you filmed all this," Gina told D'John. "By the time we got to that third challenge, I was so tired, I could barely hold my head up. I honestly don't know how I managed to be coherent on camera."

The documentary showed Barry giving both Tate and Gina their recipes, and unveiling the ingredients, and then skipped ahead to the first break in the television shoot.

"Speaking of coherency, or the lack of," Lisa said, pointing with a can of Natty Lite to the screen, where D'John's camera focused on Tate, taking a healthy belt from the pint bottle of Jack Daniel's.

"I still can't believe Tate did that," she went on. "He didn't even bother to try to hide the fact that he was drinking. Zeke was really upset about it. He even warned Tate during the break, but he said Tate just blew him off."

"So, Tate, how do you think it's going?" D'John's disembodied voice asked.

The camera showed Tate leaning against the kitchen counter, sipping from a bottle of water. "It's all right."

He frowned a little. "I'm a little concerned about the oven. It doesn't seem to be hot enough. Plus, these idiots gave us butter to make a pie crust. But what do you expect? They probably think lard is something straight out of *Deliverance*."

D'John laughed off camera, and the two men chatted for a moment more, until Zeke's voice could be heard. "People, people?"

The camera panned over the counter, showing Tate's mixing bowl and rolling pin, the opened sack of flour, and the Jack Daniel's bottle.

"Hey," Lisa said, pointing again with her beer can. "Does that bottle look pretty full to y'all?"

"Can you back this thing up?" Gina asked.

Lisa took the remote control and reversed, until she came to the still life of the counter again.

"It's totally full," Gina said, leaning forward to stare. "And when Tate was talking to you, D'John, did it seem like he was totally sober?"

"Sure," D'John said.

"Hmmm." Gina sat back against the cushions again, watching the rest of the movie with renewed interest, especially any part that showed Tate Moody.

"He's fine when he's not on camera, when he thinks nobody's watching," she said as the movie wound down. "But as soon as that green light flashes on, he's slurring his words and stumbling around and acting like a total butthead."

"A total drunk butthead," Lisa added.

"Did you take another shot of Tate's kitchen?" Gina asked.

"Can't remember," D'John said. "I had hours and hours of tape. It took me all night just to boil it down to a little under two hours."

He picked up the remote control and punched the play button again.

Gina leaned forward, all her concentration focused on the television.

"There," she said, pointing at the screen, where Tate busily cleaned up his kitchen. His movements were quick and efficient.

"He's not drunk at all," Gina said, her eyes widening.

"But why would he act drunk?" Lisa asked. "That makes no sense."

"He's faking the whole thing," Gina said angrily. "He deliberately threw the last challenge so that I could win."

"But why?" D'John asked.

"Because he didn't think I was good enough to win on my own," she said, choking on the words. "Damn him."

Chapter 68

Gina blew into the *Vittles* production office without bothering to knock. She found Val Foster hunched over her laptop, her long fingertips racing over the keyboard as a lit cigarette spiraled smoke ceilingward.

"Where is he?" Gina demanded.

"Hello, nice to see you too," Val drawled. "I'm fine, thanks for asking."

"He deliberately threw the Food Fight," Gina said. "He lost on purpose."

Val propped her chin on her fist. "Ya think?"

Without waiting for an invitation, Gina unloaded a teetering pile of mail, tapes, and scripts and collapsed into the only other chair in the room.

"You knew?"

Val took a long drag on her cigarette. "Yes."

It was not the answer she was expecting. Gina sat back in the chair. "And that was okay with you—that he blew your chances at a network show?"

"No," Val said. "It wasn't okay. I wanted to wring his neck. But he didn't ask for my permission. So, excuse me for asking, but what's your complaint? And why are you even here? Aren't you supposed to be in New York for production meetings?"

"We leave in the morning," Gina said. "And my complaint is—I don't need Tate Moody patronizing me. I'm a danged fine cook all on my own. Winning it this way—that's not what I wanted. It changes everything. Cheapens it."

Val stubbed out the cigarette and lit another one. "Oh, no. You're not gonna give me a load of ethics crap, are you? This is show business, sweetie. There's no room for ethics in our line of work. The bottom line is, you won. That's all that counts."

"Not with me," Gina said, crossing her arms over her chest. "I don't want to win this way. I won't. So just tell me where he is."

"He's gone."

"Where to?"

"Somewhere up in the mountains. He's supposed to be scouting a location for the fall shoot. He doesn't check in with me on a regular basis when we're not in production. All I know is, when he came by here a couple of days ago, he had the Vagabond hooked up to his truck."

"All right." Gina stood, hesitated, then stuck out her hand. "Thanks, Val. I appreciate your honesty. And don't worry. I'm going to straighten this whole thing out."

Val ignored the peace offering. "Good luck trying. I should tell you, once he makes up his mind about something, Tate Moody gets what you southerners call downright mulish. And he's got his mind made up about you, Regina Foxton."

"I'm pretty mulish myself," Gina said.

"Suit yourself."

"I will."

Gina was halfway down the hall, standing in front of the elevator, when Val stuck her head out the office door.

"Hey, Reggie," she called.

Gina turned around and frowned. "Nobody calls me that."

"Excuse the hell out of me," Val said. "I just remembered. Tate said something about a caddis fly hatch on the Soque."

"What's a caddis fly? And what's the Soque?"

"I'm not sure about the caddis fly part, but the Soque is a river. Or more like a stream, if you ask me. Up in the mountains. We did a show up there last summer. I remember we bought groceries in Clarkesville. Whole damn county is dry. I had to drive all the way to Gainesville just to buy a bottle of Dewar's."

"Okay. That's a start. Thanks."

"Just don't tell him I told you where to look," Val cautioned. "He made it pretty clear when he was here that he didn't want any company."

Even though it was midweek, traffic on I-85 was especially brutal. It was only when she sailed past the exit for Lake Lanier that Gina allowed herself a brief, grim smile of satisfaction. She and Scott had spent several weekends at the lake earlier in the year. He'd made noises then about the two of them moving in together, but by then her mother had already shipped Lisa to Atlanta to live with her. Thank the Lord for Lisa, Gina thought, and not for the first time that week.

Gina headed north on U.S. 441, and before long she saw the deep green of the mountains ahead. The highway dipped and rose, and she sped past signs for towns like Homer, Lula, and Cornelia, intent on trying to make it to Clarkesville before five.

She slowed as she reached the courthouse square in Clarkesville, realizing for the first time that she had no idea where to start looking for Tate Moody. The map she'd consulted before leaving Atlanta showed the Soque River as a thin blue squiggle, meandering all over Habersham County.

When she saw a gas station with a sign advertising "Soda, Cigs, Milk, Red Wigglers, Ice, Bread," she pulled in.

Gina got a Diet Coke out of the walk-in drink cooler, and, after making sure no one else was in the store, a large bag of fried pork rinds.

The elderly woman behind the cashier's counter added up her purchases, and Gina handed over her money.

"Excuse me," Gina said, offering what she hoped was a winning smile. "I'm trying to track down an old friend of mine who's up here fishing this week. And I'm wondering if you could suggest where would be a good place to start looking?"

The woman, who wore a flowered cotton scarf over a headful of pink sponge rollers, looked doubtful. "Honey, I ain't much for fishin'. Farris, my husband, he liked to fish some, but he passed back in October."

"Oh, I'm so sorry," Gina said, impulsively reaching out and clasping the old woman's hand. "I think my friend was going to fish on the Soque. And he might have stopped in here, for groceries or something. He drives a red pickup truck, and he's got this big silver travel trailer that looks kind of like an old toaster hooked up to it. And a dog. He's got an adorable English setter, named Moonpie. Maybe you've seen them?"

"You talking about Tate Moody?"

"Yes!" Gina cried. "Do you know where he is?"

"He come in here yesterday, bought some potted meat, soda crackers, and bananas," the old woman said. "He didn't tell me his name, but me and Farris, we used to watch *Vittles* all the time. I knowed him right off the bat. He's shorter in real life, you know."

"Yes, I know," Gina said.

"But he's real easy to look at," the woman went on. "I wouldn't kick him out of my bed, if you know what I mean."

"Did he say where he'd be staying?"

"Didn't ask," the old woman said. "But last summer, him and that whole gang of show folk stayed over at Glen-Ella Springs."

"That's a motel?"

"More like an inn. I reckon I could call Barrie, see if he's there."

"Oh, would you? I'd be so grateful."

The old woman plucked a cell phone from a holder on her hip and punched in the number. "Barrie? It's Annette from the Gas 'n' Go. Listen, there's a pretty young lady here huntin' Tate Moody. He come in the store yesterday, and I thought maybe he's stayin' with you."

She listened and nodded. "That so? I'll tell her. You too."

"Is he there?" Gina asked.

"Well, he comes in there in the morning and gets breakfast with Barrie and Bobby, and she lets him use her shower, but she says she thinks he's got the camper set up on Don Pate's property on Twin Branch Gap. You know where that's at?"

"I don't know where anything's at up here. Could you draw me a map?"

The woman sketched a drawing on the back of a brown paper sack and handed it over. "It ain't easy to find," she warned. "And once you leave the county road, it's all gravel back up in there. Gets pretty dusty this time of year."

"I'll be all right," Gina said. "Thank you again for all your help."

The old lady studied her face for a minute. "I keep thinking you favor somebody famous. You ever been on television your ownself?"

Gina dimpled. "Well, as a matter of fact—"

"I knew it," the old lady said, slapping her palm on the counter. "You're Peggy Jane Shannon from QVC—right? I just love those Capodimonte statues you sell on there." She grabbed her pen and another paper sack. "Would you autograph that for me? Wait till I tell my sister who come in here today. Peggy Jane Shannon. Lookin' for Tate Moody. Boy howdy."

"Boy howdy is right," Gina said, scribbling the QVC host's name on the sack.

An hour later, as the Honda wheezed up the steep grade of Twin Branch Gap Road in a cloud of dust, Gina was having serious doubts about the Gas 'n' Go lady's talents as a cartographer. Thick greenery crowded in from both sides of the narrow road, and occasionally, off to her left, she could see the glint of the sun on rocks and water, down a dramatic incline.

"He better be here," Gina fumed, scanning the horizon for any sign of a bright red truck or a big silver canned ham on wheels. She'd crunched her way through the whole cellophane bag of pork rinds as she rehearsed her lines. Now if she could just find the rat . . .

It was close to seven o'clock when she spotted a flash of silver through the tree line. She turned the Honda into a short, rutted dirt path that cut through a blooming meadow of daylilies, Queen Anne's lace, and purple clover. At the end of the path, the Vagabond was set up in the shade of a huge sycamore tree, with Tate's truck parked beside it. A bright blue awning extended from the Vagabond's side, and beneath it were a charcoal grill, a folding picnic table, and a beach chair.

Gina pulled the Honda alongside the truck and got out. The air was cool and sweet and smelled of honeysuckle.

"Tate?" She strode over to the Vagabond, intent on treeing her quarry.

Moonpie, who'd been sprawled on his side in the open doorway of the trailer, sprang to his feet, his bark surprisingly fierce. But when he saw who the visitor was, he leaped up, placing his front paws on her chest.

"Hey, spotty." Gina scratched the dog's ears. "You glad to see me?"

The dog slurped her face lovingly.

"Where's the boss?" she asked, stepping inside the trailer.

Gone fishing was the obvious answer. The Vagabond's interior was tidy. A coffee mug sat in the dish drainer, a faded blue work shirt hung from a hook by the bunk area, and a laptop computer was stowed on the dinette table, beside a flat plastic box that held an assortment of tiny fishing flies stuck to a strip of Styrofoam.

"Dang it," she said, clomping back down the steps. She followed a worn path through the meadow and came to a steep bluff looking down at the rock-bound Soque River.

She cupped her hands over her mouth to make a megaphone. "Tate Moody! Where are you?"

When no answer came, she considered climbing down to the river. But her shoes, flat-soled canvas espadrilles, would be no match for the rocky incline. And anyway, she had no idea of which direction to take.

"Tate Moody," she called again. "I want to talk to you."

Gina stood on the bluff, staring down at the deepening shadows on the riverbank. It would be dark soon, she knew. He'd have to come back. And when he did, she would be right here, waiting to rip him a new one.

She didn't have long to wait.

Ten minutes later, she heard footsteps in the underbrush, and Moonpie went shooting past, scrambling with ease down the slope to meet his master.

"Hey, buddy. What's happening?"

He had a fly rod slung over one shoulder, and a canvas fishing creel slung over the other. His face was tanned even deeper than usual, and he climbed the bluff slowly in hip-high rubber waders.

"About durned time," she called down.

"Reggie!" His face creased into a wide smile. "I knew you couldn't stay away from me for long."

"I need to talk to you," she said, steely-eyed.

"So I gathered." He walked past her, to the camp-site. He put his fishing equipment on the picnic table and sat down on the bench beside it, slipping off the suspenders that held up the waders.

"I get the feeling this isn't strictly a pleasure visit," he said quietly, stepping out of the boots and hanging them from a clothesline he'd strung between the tree and the Vagabond. "So what's up?"

"I know what you did," she said, glaring at him. "It took me a while. But then I saw D'John's movie, and it became very clear."

"You're not very clear," Tate said, leaning back on his elbows. "Or else I'm pretty dense. Exactly what are we talking about here?"

"You rat! You threw the Food Fight! You weren't drunk. It was all a big fake-out. You deliberately lost."

He got up and opened the door to the Vagabond. "You want a beer or something? Or dinner? I've got a couple of steaks in the cooler."

"Hey!" Gina yelled. "I'm talking to you. Don't just walk away like you can't hear me. At least give me that much respect."

Tate ducked inside the Vagabond and emerged a minute later with two bottles of beer. "I hear you," he said, extending a beer toward her. "Hell, the whole county probably hears you. I just thought we could discuss this quietly like a couple of mature adults, over a cold beverage and a hot steak. How do you like yours, by the way? Me and Moonpie generally go rare."

"I . . . don't . . . want . . . a . . . steak," Gina said, her fists clenched. "That's not why I came here."

He dumped some charcoal in the grill, squeezed some lighter fluid onto it, and flipped in a match. Flames shot up, and he nodded his approval. He dropped the grate back onto the grill and took a seat at the picnic table.

"So why are you here?"

All the sentences she'd so carefully rehearsed on that dusty mountain road were gone. The logic, the chilly demeanor she'd imagined, had fled. Anger, rage, resentment—these simmered in her chest, and to her dismay, boiled over in a well of hot tears.

"How could you?" she cried. "I thought you cared about me. How could you deliberately humiliate me like that?"

"Humiliate?" He seemed dumbstruck. "What are we talking about here? I mean, yeah, I admit it, I deliberately screwed up. But it's no big deal. You probably woulda won anyway."

"No big deal? Are you serious? This is my career we're talking about. My life. I had everything on the line. And you took it upon yourself to throw it all away.

And by the way—just so you know? I would have won without your help." She stuck her chin out. "I don't need to cheat to win. And I don't need you to cheat for me. I told you that even before we got to Eutaw. I thought you understood. I can't stand a cheater. But then, you're a man. That's how you play. You make up your own rules, and the hell with everybody else."

"That's what you think?" Tate grabbed her by the shoulders. "That I don't care about you? That I did this lightly? Woman, you don't get it, do you? Damn it, Reggie, I love you. But every time I get close, you back away. You were so all-fired intent on winning this stupid Food Fight; that's all you could talk about. Then, out there on Rattlesnake Key, in one moment of weakness, one crazy, amazing moment, you let your guard down. You actually let me in. And then a minute later, you shut me out."

Tears stung her eyes. "I told you, that was a mistake."

"And I told you, you're a liar. And now I'm telling you, you're a damned fool too. I thought I was giving you what you wanted. I gave you a gift when I threw the Food Fight. A gift of love. Okay, it was the wrong thing to do. But I did it for all the right reasons."

She wrenched away from him. "You want to give me a gift? How about believing in me? That's the only gift

I want from you, Tate Moody. Everything else, you can keep."

Somehow, she made it back to the Honda. She slammed the car into reverse and sped out of the meadow. In the waning light of dusk, she saw him, in her rearview mirror, turn and go back to his fire, to his dog, to his life. Without her.

Chapter 69

Thanks to Lisa's ruthless efficiency, most of the furniture in the town house was already packed or crated. But some of the bedroom furniture was still intact: her bed, and the dresser holding her television set. Arriving home at ten o'clock, Gina flung herself facedown onto the bed.

Eventually, hunger pangs reminded her that she'd had no food for most of the day. She padded out to the kitchen and found that Lisa's annoying efficiency extended to the refrigerator too. It was bare, except for a plastic takeout container of fried chicken wings and Lisa's cache of Natty Lite.

She helped herself to the chicken and a can of beer and went back to bed. Eventually she would have to decide what to do about the mess she called her life.

But for now, she decided, it was much easier to dwell on the recent past.

Gina popped D'John's documentary in the DVD player. Propping herself up on her pillow, she gnawed on a drummette, then washed it down with a dainty swig of beer. She'd watched D'John's documentary all the way through once, and was halfway through a second viewing when she heard the front door open. She heard her sister's footsteps in the hall, and then Lisa was standing in the doorway. Gina was miserable, heartbroken, and depressed. Lisa, on the other hand, was runway-ready, with new blond highlights in her hair and full makeup. She wore a chic short black chiffon cocktail dress and stiletto-heeled bronze sandals.

Gina put down the chicken wing and wiped her fingertips on the edge of her sheet. 'Hey," she said dully. "Is that my dress?"

"Yeah, sorry," Lisa said. "The girls wanted to take me clubbing one last time for old time's sake. All my stuff's already packed. I'll have it cleaned when we get to New York."

"Keep it," Gina said. "It never looked that good on me."

"For real? Thanks!" Lisa sat down on the bed beside her sister. "Wait." She picked up the empty chicken container. "You ate this whole thing?"

"Yup."

Lisa held up an empty beer can. "How many of these did you drink?"

"How many were in the fridge?"

Lisa pursed her lips in disapproval. "You drank five cans of Natty Lite? You don't even like beer."

"True," Gina said. "But it's not so bad with the fried chicken. Could you move over to the other side of the bed? You're kinda blocking my view."

Lisa turned to look at the television. "Oh. D'John's masterpiece."

She went into the other room, and when she padded barefoot back into the room, she was dressed for bed in an oversize Hi-Beams football jersey.

"Scoot over," she told Gina, climbing into the bed. "The movers took all my stuff already, so I'm bunking in here with you tonight, if that's okay."

"S'okay," Gina said with a sigh. She picked up the remote, pointed it at the television, and punched the play button. The DVD started again.

"How many times have you watched this tonight?" Lisa asked.

"This makes three," Gina said. "Shh." She fast-forwarded the DVD until it came to a segment showing Gina and Tate horsing around on their kitchen set, in between shoots for Food Fight.

Gina was listening to something Zeke was saying off camera, and Tate was pelting her with what looked like Ritz crackers. For a while, she ignored the rain of crackers, but then, suddenly, she turned and without warning dumped a pan of thick white stuff on his head. The goo dripped onto his face, and Gina could be heard giggling hysterically off camera.

"Oh, my God." Lisa laughed. "What was in that pan?"

"Cold grits," Gina said mournfully. She pointed the remote and fast-forwarded again, this time to a scene where she and Tate sat rocking and talking on the front porch of the lodge at Rebeccaville. Perched on a porch rail in the background, Scott glowered at them, unnoticed.

"This is my favorite part," Gina said, fast-forwarding again. In this scene, Tate and Gina stood at the end of the ferry dock at sunset. Tate had a long bamboo fly-casting rod and reel in his hand, and he was patiently trying to demonstrate its use to Gina, who repeatedly ended up snagging the line on pilings, the dock, and even the ferry itself. On the film, D'John could be heard laughing, saying to Gina, "You suck!"

The sisters watched the rest of the movie in companionable silence. When it was over, Lisa gently pried the remote from her sister's hand before she could hit the play button again.

"Can I say something here?" Lisa asked, lying back on her pillow and turning out the lamp on the bedside table.

"Only if it's not 'I told you so.' "

"Okay. We'll skip that part. Even if it's true."

Gina sighed deeply and turned on her side, her back to her little sister. "I'm listening."

"Geen, this is just so stupid. You're making yourself sick over Tate Moody. You want him, but you don't want to want him—have I got that right?"

"It's slightly more complicated than that."

"You only want to make it complicated," Lisa said. "You're furious with him because he let you win—right?"

"It's more than that."

"He let you win because he loves you. Is that such a crime?"

Gina sat up in bed and pounded the mattress. "I could have won without him! I know I could. But now everybody who knows will always wonder—what if? What if he hadn't thrown that last challenge?"

"Why can't you both win?" Lisa asked.

"Don't be silly," Gina said. "What—TCC is going to give us both our own shows? Two southern cooking shows? Never happen."

"Not two shows," Lisa said. "One show. Starring Gina Foxton and Tate Moody. Together."

Silence. Lisa could hear her sister thinking it over. "Keep talking."

"You saw the DVD," Lisa said. "The two of you are great together. Don't get mad at me, but I think you're better together than separate. You know—like the sum equals more than the parts? Zeke talks all the time about chemistry, about how that emotional connection can't be faked, not even for television. You and Tate have chemistry. The way you laugh and tease and look at each other—Geen, it gives me goose bumps. It's the real deal."

The light snapped on again. Gina turned and put her arms around her baby sister's neck, resting her forehead on Lisa's. "When did you get so dadgummed smart?"

Chapter 70

Gina kicked the Honda into a low gear and gritted her teeth at the slow, dusty ride down Twin Branch Gap. She'd gotten a late start leaving Atlanta. It was nearly ten o'clock. Would he be out on the river still? And after her performance just a day earlier, would he even be willing to listen to what she had to say?

She saw the turn-in for the meadow and pulled up, but knew immediately it was too late. The Vagabond was gone. She got out of the car and walked over to the spot where it had been less than twenty-four hours ago. The only sign that he'd even been here were the ruts in the grass and meadow flowers.

"Damn," she cried. She ran over to the bluff and looked down. The river flowed below, but no fisherman stood on its banks, flicking a fly back and forth over the water.

She pulled into the parking lot at the Gas 'n' Go and ran inside. Annette, her informant from the previous day, stood at the cash register, unloading bags of potato chips and clipping them to a metal rack.

"You find your friend yesterday?" the old lady asked.

"Unfortunately." Gina winced. "I kind of made a mess of things. I came up here this morning to apologize, but his trailer's gone. I know it's not your job to keep track of Tate Moody, but I was wondering—"

"He's at the Bargain Mart on 441," Annette said promptly. "Which is where I'd be too, if I didn't have this durned store to run. Every woman in this county is headed over there right now, to watch him and that dog of his demonstrate some kinda mini deep-fat fryer. They're givin' away hot dogs and Cokes too, but I'd settle for a front row seat if I just had somebody to mind this place."

"Maybe your boss wouldn't mind if you took an early lunch?" Gina suggested, looking down at her watch. "It's nearly noon."

Annette clipped the last of the potato chip bags to the rack. She went to the door and flipped the OPEN sign over so that it read CLOSED. "Now you're talking, sister," she said, holding the door for Gina. "It's my durned store, and if I want to take lunch early, it's nobody's business but my own."

Multicolored plastic flags waved gaily in the wind, and a uniformed sheriff's deputy stood in the middle of the highway, directing a logjam of cars and trucks into the Bargain Mart parking lot.

Gina circled the lot three times before finding a parking space, at the farthest end of the lot.

As she entered the store with a knot of women—on walkers and wheelchairs, pushing strollers or tugging on the arms of husbands—a smiling senior citizen in a blue vest offered her a bag of popcorn.

She took the bag and absentmindedly ate a handful as she followed the women toward the back of the store, where a portable stage had been set up in the housewares department.

Abandoning every vestige of good manners Birdelle had ever taught her, Gina elbowed her way through the throng until she stood at the far right edge of the stage.

A makeshift kitchen counter held a mountain of boxed mini deep-fat fryers, and standing in the middle of the counter was Tate Moody, in the flesh.

He wore a bright blue golf shirt with the Bargain Mart logo embroidered on the sleeve, and khaki cargo shorts. There was a cordless mike clipped to the collar of the shirt, and Moonpie sat quietly at the edge of the stage, looking expectantly out at the audience.

"Now, folks," Tate was saying, holding up a big green mixing bowl. "There's about a hundred different recipes for fish breading and hush puppies. But as far as I'm concerned, there's only one that's worth making—and that's the one my mama taught me when I was no bigger than a tadpole."

The crowd laughed on cue. Tate held up a bag of stone-ground cornmeal and dropped two handfuls into the bowl. He poured in some buttermilk and, with a fork, quickly mixed up the batter.

"Now," he said, looking up and flashing an intimate smile, "we'll wait a minute for the oil to heat up in our Fry-Baby. We're using peanut oil here today, but you could use whatever oil you happen to have on hand. While we wait, does anybody have any questions they'd like to ask?"

"What's the biggest fish you've ever caught up here in the mountains, and what'd you catch him on?" a man in a green-and-yellow John Deere hat called out.

"Caught a brownie that weighed seven pounds on a woolly bugger last summer," Tate said. "I've been over on the Soque for the past couple days, but didn't do much good."

"What's your favorite thing to cook?" a hefty woman in a flowered blouse asked.

"Hmm," Tate said. "I guess it'd have to be bluefish. Hard to beat fresh-caught bluefish with just a squeeze of lemon and fresh herbs cooked on a grill over a wood fire."

Gina's hand shot up. "Hey, Tate," she called. "I thought you liked to bake pies. Especially pecan."

"Who said that?" He stepped out from behind the counter and peered into the audience.

"Right here," Gina called, stepping forward.

Moonpie gave a short, happy yip of recognition and wagged his tail wildly.

"You," Tate said, frowning down at her. "Why aren't you in New York?"

"Hey, Tate," a woman to Gina's right called. "I read in *People* magazine about that Food Fight you did this summer. How did it turn out? Who won?"

"She did."

"He did," Gina said loudly.

"Ignore her," Tate said. "She's unstable."

"I'm not going to New York," Gina said, looking up into his face. "Not without you, anyway."

"Hey, Tate," hollered a stringy old man at the back of the crowd. "Your Fry-Baby's smokin'."

"So's he." A trio of teenage girls standing beside Gina dissolved in a fit of giggles.

Tate walked right up to the edge of the stage and looked down at her. "What are you talking about?"

"Come down here, and I'll tell you," Gina said quietly. "I've got a proposition I'd like to discuss."

"Nope. You come up here. The last time you propositioned me, you took it back. I want witnesses this time."

Gina's face turned bright crimson. "No. Really. Look, this can wait till your demonstration is over."

Tate held out his hand. "Now or never." He looked out at the audience. "Right, folks?"

"Yeah!" the crowd yelled. "Do it!"

"Booooo," the girls called.

"I'll take him if you don't want him," yelled their ringleader, a petite blonde in an orange tube top and booty shorts.

Tate's hand stayed right where it was. "You coming or not? I need to get those hush puppies going before this bunch turns on me."

"Do it. Do it. Do it," the crowd chanted. Moonpie ran around the stage in circles, barking wildly.

Reluctantly, Gina took his hand and allowed him to lead her up to the stage. Her pulse was racing like a gerbil on steroids.

"Now. What was it that you wanted to ask me?" Tate said. He lowered the mesh cooking basket into the vat, took a spoonful of the cornmeal batter, and carefully dropped it into the boiling oil. He rapidly added half a dozen more blobs of batter.

"See, folks?" he said cheerfully. "The Fry-Baby has a built-in thermostat, so you don't have to worry about making sure the oil's hot enough."

"I don't want to win," Gina said, under her breath. "Not if it means losing you."

Tate cupped his hand to his ear. "Come again? I don't think the folks heard that." He tapped the microphone clipped to his shirt collar. "Speak right in here, Reggie, so everybody can hear."

She could feel herself blushing all the way to the roots of her hair. She edged as close to him as she could get. He smelled like soap and fried foods. He pulled her closer, his hand resting lightly on the curve of her spine.

Gina took a deep breath. "I said I love you, Tate Moody. I don't want to move to New York I don't want to win if it means losing you I think we should do a cooking show together." She looked up into his hazel eyes and felt herself melting, madly, deeply, crazily.

The audience erupted in a wild chorus of cheers and applause.

She took another deep breath and spoke again into the mike. "Also, you forgot to say they should definitely use stone-ground white cornmeal, not yellow, and beat the egg whites separately to make the lightest possible hush puppy."

"Quit while you're ahead," he ordered, and then he kissed her quiet.

Epilogue

S he knew she should be nervous, but for the first time in her adult life, Gina Foxton felt totally fearless. They had two hours to go until their first taping before a live Atlanta audience, but already she felt alive with excitement and anticipation. Their show would be a hit. And the best part was—they were doing it right here, at home, in front of a hometown audience.

Val and Lisa had been disappointed at Tate's insistence on keeping the production in Atlanta, but they'd both been somewhat mollified with the promise that at least four shows a year would be taped in the TCC studios in New York. Things were working out beautifully.

Now, if only her costar would concentrate on dressing himself instead of undressing her.

"Stop," she said, slapping Tate's hand away from the zipper on her bright cotton sundress. "Put your shirt on. I can't concentrate on what I'm supposed to be doing."

Tate nuzzled her neck. "Then concentrate on me. I'm what you're supposed to be doing."

"Absolutely not." Gina giggled. But she caught his hand in hers and kissed it.

"Just get yourself dressed, and let me get dressed, and get this show done, and I'll do whatever you want. Deal?"

"Whatever I want?" He turned her around and circled her waist with her hands. "Can I get that in writing?"

Gina fumbled around on the floor for her shoes. "Did anybody ever mention that you have a one-track mind?"

"It's what makes me great," Tate agreed. "Did anybody ever tell you what a great little butt you have? I've been admiring it since that day the UPS driver ran over your phony pumpkin, and you had to crawl under my car to get your canned goods."

"Speaking of goods," Gina said. "Did I ever tell *you* that Lisa and all her college girlfriends invented a drinking game they played while they watched *Vittles*? Every time the camera showed your backside, they'd chug a Natty Lite. They were all totally obsessed with your butt. And your abs. And your pecs."

Smirking, Tate flexed his muscles and did a slow-motion pelvic grind. "And they haven't even seen my best feature."

Gina reached out and caught him by the belt. "And they better not. Ever."

"Never," Tate agreed. "I'm like Moonpie. A one-woman dog."

"Hey," Gina said, looking around. "Where is Moonpie?"

"D'John took him for a walk," Tate said casually. "And then he said he's going to give him a comb-out. Whatever that is."

He took her by the hand and pulled her toward the Vagabond's bunk. "So . . ."

"Tate Moody," Gina said, pretending to be shocked. "You bribed D'John to take the dog so we could be alone. You conniving, calculating—"

"Horny bastard," Tate said. "I'm the victim here. You've been so busy with all this tour and publicity, you've been neglecting your wifely duties."

"I am not your wife. Yet," she reminded him primly.

"Two more weeks," he said. "As soon as we get the first six shows in the can. It's practically a done deal."

"Not as far as my mama's concerned, it's not," she said.

He stretched out on the bunk and pulled her down beside him "Your mama's not here. But I am. And I'm tense as all get-out. You know what would relax me?"

"A cold beer?"

"Afterward," he agreed, working on her zipper again.

"We can't," she murmured, even as her lips found his. "You'll mess up my hair."

"And D'John will comb you out too," Tate said. "I bribed him double."

Val Foster paced back and forth in the parking lot of Morningstar Studios, chewing her Nicorette at a machine-gun pace as she listened to Barry Adelman on her cell phone.

"Barry, I swear, everything is under control," she said. "The crew is great. We've got the best guys from *Fresh Start* and *Vittles*, and the prep girls have worked their asses off getting everything ready. Did I tell you? They're doing Brunswick stew—whatever that is—sounds gruesome to me, but what do I know? And Gina's going to demonstrate her mother's recipe for pickled squash. They both swear it's a southern thing. The set looks terrific, better even than the plans. Gina and Tate did another round of press interviews this morning. The *TV Guide* guy was practically drooling over Gina, and the local CBS and NBC affiliates taped cooking segments with them on their morning shows."

She nodded as Barry rattled off yet another set of unnecessary instructions.

"Got it," she said, rolling her eyes. "Yes. I did. I wrote it all down on yellow Post-it notes. Not that Lisa needs it. The girl is a genius of organization. Better than Zeke, even, if that's possible. I'm gonna hate to lose her when film school starts in January."

She listened and nodded. "All right. Yes. I've gotta go. We've got the studio audience starting to trickle in, and I want to make sure the VIPs get seated up front. Yes. Absolutely. I'll call you the minute we're done."

"Christ." She clicked the cell phone's end button, spit out the Nicorette, took the cigarette from behind her ear, and lit up, sucking her cheeks hollow with the first drag.

Lisa stood at the studio door, clipboard in hand, checking off the guests who'd been invited to be in the audience for their first taping.

"Hi!" she said warmly, recognizing the television critic from the Atlanta paper. She checked her list and told her where to sit. More guests streamed in. The bleacher seats in the audience would hold ninety people, and Lisa nervously tried to keep count as more and more people appeared.

"Everything going okay?" Zeke stood close behind her, his hand on her shoulder.

"So far, so good," she whispered. "Have you seen Gina and Tate yet? We've only got thirty minutes."

"They were out in the Vagabond last time I checked," Zeke assured her.

"Alone?"

"Yeah. Why not?"

"Alone's no good," Lisa said nervously. "They can't keep their hands off each other. They're like a couple teenagers. I don't like it."

"Relax," Zeke said, rubbing her shoulders. "They're not going to miss their own first show."

"I guess," she said dubiously. "I'm just a little keyed up, what with everything going on. Tell me what time we have to leave for the airport again?"

"Not until six o'clock," he told her, for the tenth time that day. "We'll have plenty of time."

"I hope traffic's not . . ." She was looking out at a cluster of senior citzens who'd just arrived at the studio door. They looked somehow familiar, especially the trim redhead in the black pantsuit and pearls.

"Mama?" Lisa shrieked.

"My baby!" The redhead threw her arms around Lisa and kissed her on both cheeks.

"Look, girls," the redhead called to the chattering women. "This is my baby girl Lisa. Isn't she all grown up and gorgeous? And Lisa, you remember the Keen-Agers from home, don't you?"

The Keen-Agers surrounded Lisa, patting her head, grasping her hand, pinching her cheek, cooing and billing in their sorghum-thick South Georgia accents.

"Mama," Lisa said, pulling her mother aside. "What have you done to yourself? You look amazing."

Her mother had been transformed. Gone was the shapeless flowered housedress, gray permed hair, and sensible shoes. Gone too, Lisa calculated, was at least thirty pounds.

Birdelle patted her hair and preened a little. "Do you really like my new look? Your daddy is a little worried about my new hair color. He says the boys down at the drugstore are calling me his trophy wife."

Lisa leaned in to get a closer look at her mother. "Mama! Are you wearing lip liner?"

"And an underwire bra," Birdelle whispered. "And Spanx! Why, Spanx are my new best friend. Especially the Power Panty. You should try them, Lisa."

"I have. I know," Lisa stuttered. "But, Mama. You must have dropped three or four dress sizes since the last time I was home. How did you do it?"

"Your daddy and I have a new business concern," Birdelle said. "We opened a Curves gym in the old

Family Dollar store out on the bypass. Which you would have known if you ever returned my phone calls, young lady."

"I'm sorry," Lisa moaned. "It's just with all the wedding stuff, and my new job . . ."

Birdelle nodded at Zeke, who was standing by the doorway, listening amusedly to the whole conversation.

"And this must be Zeke?" she asked. "Your young man?"

"Oh, sorry," Lisa said, drawing Zeke closer. "Zeke, this is my mama. Birdelle Foxton."

"Your mother?" Zeke exclaimed. "Mrs. Foxton!" Zeke said, grasping both Birdelle's hands in hers. "Now I know where Lisa and Gina get their looks. Although I have to say you look more like their sister than their mama."

"Oh, stop," Birdelle said. "Charmer! I guess that's how all you Hollywood boys talk. Not that I'm complaining."

"Not Hollywood at all," Zeke said. "Not yet, anyway."

"He's just being modest," Lisa said proudly. "I'm taking him to the airport as soon as we're done shooting tonight. He's flying out to L.A. and taking a meeting with Spielberg's people day after tomorrow. They've bought his screenplay."

"Optioned," Zeke corrected her. "It's only an option."

Val rushed up. "Lisa, have you seen Gina? We've only got twenty minutes. I need everybody seated right away so we can get started on time."

"Yes, Lisa," Birdelle said. "Where is your sister? I want to see her before the show." She patted the thick pocketbook on her wrist. "I've got pictures of the altar flowers from the florist, and samples of the fabric for the tablecloths at the reception, and a tape of the soloist, and there's just so much we need to get done. You just lead me right to her."

Lisa's face paled. "Oh, well, no, Mama, that's not a good idea. Gina, uh, likes to, uh, meditate before the show. Has to be totally alone. Why don't you go sit down with the Keen-Agers, and I'll take you backstage just as soon as the show is over?"

"Well," Birdelle said tentatively. "I guess that would be all right. As long as we don't stay too late afterward. I promised the girls we'd stop at the Varsity on our way out of town, and then we've got to get the church bus back before morning."

Dusk had fallen, and the September night air was unseasonably cool. Lisa approached the Vagabond with trepidation. It didn't seem to be rocking, but on the other hand, all the lights were out. And Moonpie, who was now perfectly coiffed, was tethered to the awning outside, whining and pawing at the door.

She stopped a few yards away. "Hey, you two," she called. "It's show time. Are you decent?"

"Go away." Tate's voice, muffled.

"I can't," Lisa said plaintively. "Val sent me. And she says if you're not on set in five minutes, you're both fired."

"As if," Tate said. "Tell her we're busy."

Lisa looked down at her watch, and decided it was time to play her ace card.

"Mama's here," she said casually.

Five seconds passed. Gina's tousled head popped out of the door. "Whose mama?"

"Your mama. As in Birdelle Foxton. Right here at the Morningstar Studios."

"Holy crap," Gina said. "Be out in a jiffy."

"You better," Lisa said. "And one more thing. Val wants to know how you want to be announced. She says you guys still haven't settled on the billing."

Gina stood at the tiny mirror over the Vagabond's sink and ran her fingers through her still-damp hair. The brassy blond highlights were but a faint memory, and D'John had cut her now honey-colored hair in a short, feathery bob that fell softly around her heart-shaped face. "No time for a comb-out now," she said wryly, turning to Tate, who was standing right behind her, combing his own damp hair. "Thanks to you."

"You're welcome," he said, patting her rear. He held the Vagabond's door open for her. "Hey, what are we going to do about the billing? Is it Tate and Gina, or Gina and Tate?"

"The show *was* my idea," Gina pointed out, following him down the steps. She stopped to untie Moonpie. "So I think I get to be on top."

He took his dog's leash in one hand, and his partner's in the other. "Seems to me you've already been on top tonight."

"Don't be crude," Gina said. "We'll take turns. All right?"

D'John feathered concealer under his eyes, gave his nose and cheeks a final dusting of powder, and after a moment's careful consideration, applied a second coat of mascara to his already luxuriant eyelashes.

He stepped back from the mirror to evaluate his handiwork. "Not bad," he mused. As a final touch, he flicked the powder brush over his forehead. "Don't want to blind 'em with my patina the first time out," he reasoned.

"You look fabulous," Lisa said, standing in the doorway to the dressing room. "Now let's go. It's time."

Val was waiting for them, speaking into her headset. "Go get 'em, killer," she said, slapping him on the butt.

D'John coughed and cleared his throat. He adjusted his shirt collar and coughed again. Then he bounded out from the wings and onto the kitchen set.

"Good evening, everybody," he said in a cheery voice he hardly recognized. "My name is D'John, and I want to welcome you to the premiere of an exciting new Cooking Channel production."

He pointed to the red light hanging over the set. "Now, when that light flashes green, I want you all to cheer and clap like crazy, and make our hosts feel right at home. All right?"

He looked offstage. Gina and Tate stood in the wings, toe to toe, smiling into each other's eyes. Lisa, who was standing beside them, nodded.

"Okay!" D'John boomed. "Give it up, please, for *Eat, Drink and Be Married*—with Gina Foxton and Tate Moody!"

Reggie's Simply Sinful Tomato Soup Chocolate Cake

½ cup butter

1 ⅓ cups sugar

2 eggs

2 cups all-purpose flour

½ cup powdered cocoa

1 tablespoon baking powder

1 teaspoon baking soda

¼ cup warm tap water

1 can (10 ¾ oz.) condensed tomato soup

Preheat oven to 350°F.

Grease and flour a 9×13-inch baking pan.

In a large mixing bowl cream together butter and sugar; add eggs, beating until fluffy. In a small bowl mix together dry ingredients, including cocoa.

Mix tomato soup and water together.

Add dry and wet ingredients alternately to the butter/sugar bowl. Bake 30 minutes and let cool before frosting.

CREAM CHEESE FROSTING

8 oz. pkg. cream cheese, softened to room temperature
1 stick butter, softened
4 cups powdered sugar
1 teaspoon vanilla
1 tablespoon milk or cream

Cream butter and cream cheese together, then beat in powdered sugar. Add vanilla, and thin frosting out with milk as needed.

Tate's Grilled Ginger Peachy

Four peaches, unpeeled, halved, and pitted
Lemon juice
4 tablespoons melted unsalted butter
2 tablespoons sorghum syrup (or real maple syrup
  if sorghum is unavailable)
½ teaspoon peeled and grated fresh ginger

Brush lemon juice on cut surface of peach halves.

In bowl, combine melted butter, syrup, and ginger.
Gently toss peach halves in the mixture to coat evenly.

Grill over medium-high heat until slightly charred—
one to two minutes. Turn.

Can be served over ice cream, or topped with real
whipped cream and caramel sauce.

Tate and Gina's Brunswick Stew

This recipe is designed to serve 6 to 8 people, but Tate and Gina mostly fix it for a big crowd, so multiply ingredients proportionately if that's what you want to do too. Because Tate hunts birds, he might also throw in some quail or dove breasts, or some venison. Perfect for a crisp fall day or a chilly football Sunday.

1 whole chicken, cut up
1 onion, chopped
2 stalks celery, chopped
1 bay leaf
1 teaspoon salt
½ teaspoon cracked black pepper
1 lb. cooked pork (this can be any kind of pork roast, chops, etc.)

2 cups frozen or fresh corn, cut off the cob
1 lb. cubed small red potatoes, unpeeled
1 small bag baby peeled carrots
1 lb. fresh or frozen green beans
2 cans Ro-Tel original recipe tomatoes
1 cup barbecue sauce
1–2 cups chicken broth

Place chicken, celery, and onions in large pot. Add enough water to cover well. Add salt and pepper, then cover and simmer until the meat falls off the bones. Remove the chicken pieces and let cool. Add vegetables and cooked pork to broth in pot and cook for approximately 2 hours or until tender, stirring frequently because the tomatoes may burn.

Remove the chicken from the bones and add it to the stew, along with barbecue sauce, and more chicken broth if necessary to make a soupier consistency. Serve with corn bread and tangy coleslaw.